The Garland Library
of Medieval Literature

General Editors
James J. Wilhelm, Rutgers University
Lowry Nelson, Jr., Yale University

Literary Advisors
Ingeborg Glier, Yale University
Frede Jensen, University of Colorado
Sidney M. Johnson, Indiana University
William W. Kibler, University of Texas
Norris J. Lacy, Washington University
Fred C. Robinson, Yale University
Aldo Scaglione, New York University

Art Advisor
Elizabeth Parker McLachlan, Rutgers University

Music Advisor
Hendrik van der Werf, Eastman School of Music

Renaut de Bâgé
Le Bel Inconnu
(Li Biaus Descouneüs; The Fair Unknown)

edited, with an introduction, by
KAREN FRESCO

translated by
COLLEEN P. DONAGHER

music edited by
MARGARET P. HASSELMAN

Volume 77
Series A
GARLAND LIBRARY OF MEDIEVAL LITERATURE

Garland Publishing, Inc.
New York & London
1992

Library of Congress Cataloging-in-Publication Data

Renaud, de Beaujeu, 12th/13th cent.
   [Guinglain. English & French (Old French)]
   Le bel inconnu : (li biaus descouneüs, the fair unknown) /
Renaut de Bâgé ; edited by Karen Fresco ; translated by Colleen
P. Donagher ; music edited by Margaret P. Hasselman.
      p.   cm. — (Garland library of medieval literature ; v.
77. Series A)
   Includes bibliographical references.
   ISBN 0-8240-0698-4
   1. Guinglain (Legendary character)—Romances. 2. Arthurian
romances. I. Fresco, Karen Louise, 1947–   . II. Hasselman,
Margaret P. III. Title. IV. Series: Garland library of medieval
literature : v. 77.
PQ1512.R813   1992
016.841'1—dc20   92–8114
                                                          CIP

Printed on acid-free, 250-year-life paper
Manufactured in the United States of America

To
Alain Fresco
and
Miles Cox

Preface of the General Editors

The Garland Library of Medieval Literature was established to make available to the general reader modern translations of texts in editions that conform to the highest academic standards. All of the translations are originals, and were created especially for this series. The translations attempt to render the foreign works in a natural idiom that remains faithful to the originals.

The Library is divided into two sections: Series A, texts and translations; and Series B, translations alone. Those volumes containing texts have been prepared after consultation of the major previous editions and manuscripts. The aim in the edition has been to offer a reliable text with a minimum of editorial intervention. Significant variants accompany the original, and important problems are discussed in the Textual Notes. Volumes without texts contain translations based on the most scholarly texts available, which have been updated in terms of recent scholarship.

Most volumes contain Introductions with the following features: (1) a biography of the author or a discussion of the problem of authorship, with any pertinent historical or legendary information; (2) an objective discussion of the literary style of the original, emphasizing any individual features; (3) a consideration of sources for the work and its influence; and (4) a statement of the editorial policy for each edition and translation. There is also a Select Bibliography, which emphasizes recent criticism on the works. Critical writings are often accompanied by brief descriptions of their importance. Selective glossaries, indices, and footnotes are included where appropriate.

The Library covers a broad range of linguistic areas, including all of the major European languages. All of the important literary forms and genres are considered, sometimes in anthologies or selections.

The General Editors hope that these volumes will bring the general reader a closer awareness of a richly diversified area that has for too long been closed to everyone except those with precise academic training, an area that is well worth study and reflection.

James J. Wilhelm
Rutgers University

Lowry Nelson, Jr.
Yale University

Contents

Introduction

Life of the Author

The Renals de Biauju who names himself at the end of *Le Bel Inconnu* or *Li Biaus Descouneüs* remains a shadowy figure whose identity can only be guessed at based on a very few clues.[1] There are two mentions of his name, in line 6249 of this romance and in lines 1451-2 of *Le Roman de la Rose, ou de Guillaume de Dole*, where Jean Renart attributes a chanson from which he quotes to "Renaut de Baujieu De Rencien le bon chevalier." In addition, *Li Biaus Descouneüs* contains two references to the heraldic device on Guinglain's shield, an ermine lion on an azure field (73-4 and 5921-2).

The forms Biauju and Baujieu have led scholars to assume that Renaut must have belonged to the house of Beaujeu, a powerful clan in the Mâcon region. However, the name Renaut does not appear in its genealogical records and the blazon described above does not belong to the Beaujeu family but to the rival house of Bâgé.[2] Guerreau shows that in the Franco-Provençal linguistic region encompassing Bresse, where the Bâgé family held most of its lands, the Latin etymon of Bâgé, Balgiacum, must have developed into Baugieu by the early thirteenth century.[3]

Renaut was a favorite name in the Bâgé family; from the eleventh century on, almost each generation has its Renaut. Two fall within the period under consideration: Renaut, Seigneur de Saint-Trivier (fl. 1165-1230), and Renaut IV, Seigneur de Bâgé et de Bresse (fl. 1180-1250), the former's nephew and the chief heir in the next generation.

An additional clue to the author's identity is provided by the reference to Rencien in the *Guillaume de Dole*. As Guerreau notes, very often *n*'s and *u*'s are confused by scribes and editors. If instead of Rencien we read Rencieu (from Latin Rantiacum), this may be the town of Rancy, which lies near Saint-Trivier within the lands traditionally held by the family's younger son.[4] It is thus plausible to identify Renaut as the Seigneur de Saint-Trivier who flourished between 1165 and 1230.[5] Apparently he had no offspring since a nephew and then a grand-nephew subsequently held these lands. He may well have been a *bachelier*, the product of the genealogical strategy practiced during this period by noble families striving to consolidate their holdings rather than divide them up among numerous offspring.[6]

By the mid-twelfth century the Bâgé family was one of the half dozen most powerful in the Mâcon region. The houses of Bâgé, Berzé, Beaujeu, Brancion and those of the counts of Châlon and Mâcon were all closely related by feudal and family ties. Several of these nobles were educated. Renaut might possibly have known Hugues de Berzé, who composed lyric poetry.[7] Technically châtelains of the Count of Mâcon, that is, the representatives of the count's interests in a given region, the lords of Bâgé gradually appropriated power and land until they vied with the count himself in wealth and influence.[8] From about 1160 to 1230, a period that encompasses the life of the poet, their power and that of the other châtelains began to decline in the face of certain political and economic developments.

The conflict over the papal investiture, which pitted one pope, supported by the Capetian king Louis VII among others, against the candidate championed by the Holy Roman Emperor Frederick Barbarossa, occasioned Louis' intervention in regional disputes between the Counts of Châlon and Mâcon on the one hand, allies of the German emperor, and Cluny and the Bishop of Mâcon on the other. Thrice the clergy appealed for the king's protection and thrice he arrived with his army to reestablish order (in 1166, 1171 and 1180). In return he exacted concessions that strengthened his authority in the region at the expense of that of the local seigneurs.

The blazon of the young hero of *Li Biaus Descouneüs*, which is that of the house of Bâgé as noted above, has significance within the context of this conflict. While the eagle is associated with the Holy Roman Empire and its vassals, the lion is the emblem of their opponents.[9] Now the lands held by the Bâgé family in Bresse, to the east of the Saône, fell under the sway of the Empire so we would expect an eagle rather than a lion in their blazon. Everyone, the counts and the châtelains alike, immediately recognized the renewed political influence wielded by Louis, and Renaut III de Bâgé, the poet's father, was not alone in promptly seeking his favor. Furthermore, he was a cousin of the French king's, related through his grandmother. In a letter dated 1171, he appeals to Louis to come to his aid against the Count of Mâcon and Humbert of Beaujeu, who have put his lands to the sword and taken his eldest son, Oury (Ulrich), hostage. In another letter the same year, he promises to hold his lands in fief from Louis if only he will help him in this matter.[10] But Louis, careful not to encroach on lands traditionally associated with the Empire, never supplied this aid.[11] Bâgé's protestations of loyalty and friendship should be seen as an attempt to use the politics of the moment as leverage in an on-going local struggle with the Count over power. In the long run, as a result of this episode the lords of Bâgé found in Louis and his vassals more formidable competitors for power than the count.

During the same period inflation begins to erode their financial situation, this at a time when their status requires the considerable expense of maintaining a court.[12] The lords of Bâgé begin to break up the patrimony so carefully husbanded until now, offering to hold certain properties from others in return for a fee. The romance belongs, then, to a period when the Bâgé family's power has perhaps just passed its apogee, when its position is just beginning to slip away.[13] The pride of clan expressed in the wish to locate the founding ancestor in a mythical time, to relate it through Guinglain to the incomparable Gauvain, is best understood in this context.[14]

The date of composition of *Li Biaus Descouneüs* can be only loosely indicated.[15] Because of allusions to Chrétien de Troyes' oeuvre, it must have been composed some time after 1191, when Chrétien's patron, Philip of Alsace, died and it is thought Chrétien broke off his work. The *Guillaume de Dole*, probably composed by 1212-1213, sets the *terminus ad quem* for the chanson by Renaut from which it quotes.[16] However, this does not date the romance. We cannot even conclude that this chanson must have antedated the romance since Renaut might have composed more than the single chanson that has survived. (See the note to line 3 of the romance.) The meager evidence available does not permit one to be any more specific than to indicate a span of time, from 1191 into the first quarter of the thirteenth century, during which the romance could have been composed.

Two other narrative works, each mentioning an unspecified Renaut as its author, have been attributed to Renaut de Beaujeu (Bâgé). One is the *Lai d'Ignaure ou lai du prisonnier*, a 664-line narrative poem in octosyllabic rhymed couplets. Lejeune (1938) identifies its composer, Renaus (line 621), as the author of *Li Biaus Descouneüs* based on similarities in language, versification, tone, and narrative procedures such as interventions by the narrator and the dedication to a beloved lady. However, the mix of dialectal traits in *Li Biaus Descouneüs* and *Ignaure* is scarcely distinctive.[17] In most texts from this period Central French forms coexisted with Northern and, to a lesser extent, Eastern ones as poets freely appropriated forms from one dialect or another in order to facilitate the rhyme or meter. As regards versification, the features that Lejeune mentions are not unusual. Simple rhyme, the presence of imperfect rhymes, frequent hiatus—none of these traits are uncommon in texts from this period.[18] Lejeune discerns in both texts a tendency toward the off-color ("ce penchant vers une certaine forme de pornographie," p. 36). But surely the seductiveness of the Maiden of the White Hands when she comes to the hero's bedside (2393-2446) is a typical demeanor in such an encounter, as Lanval's tryst with the fairy, Lancelot's evening with the Amorous Maiden and Blanchefleur's visit to Perceval lead one to conclude. The breach of style in the use of a vulgar term, *foutre* (line 714), is not peculiar to *Li Biaus Descouneüs*, either; the term occurs twice in *Ipomedon*.[19] In sum, Lejeune's attribution of *Ignaure* to Renaut de Bâgé is not convincing because the characteristics which she finds in both texts are not peculiar to them.

Without giving any arguments, Guerreau raises the possibility, p. 35, that *Galeran de Bretagne* may also be ascribed to the author of *Li Biaus Descouneüs*.[20] Although scholars have dated this work to the late twelfth to early thirteenth century, partly in connection with efforts to attribute it to Jean Renart, the romance bears the stamp of a literary sensibility and taste quite different from that evident in *Li Biaus Descouneüs*. In *Galeran* there is none of the witty manipulation of literary convention or the teasing play with audience expectation that one finds in *Li Biaus Descouneüs*. Furthermore, the frequency of rich rhyme, grammatical rhyme, and rhetorical figures (various figures of repetition, alliteration, word play, metaphor) in *Galeran* distinguish it from *Li Biaus Descouneüs*.[21]

Artistic Achievement

Even though medieval romance is marked, in general, by its attention to the process of composition, *Li Biaus Descouneüs* stands out by virtue of the delight Renaut has taken in playing with romance conventions. The matter of portraits is a clear example. *Romanciers* use lengthy descriptions to signal the importance of a female character. Renaut multiplies these descriptions, applying them to one character after another: Helie (135 ff.), Margerie (1525 ff.), the fay (2217 ff.), Blonde Esmeree (3261 ff.), the fay again (3943 ff.), Blonde Esmeree again (5143 ff.). Which of these, we are left to wonder, is the prima donna?   Renaut is teasing an audience familiar with romance conventions (Colby-Hall 1984) as well as parodying the convention itself.

In romance the adventures undergone by the hero seem random and yet are destined for the hero. In this romance the adventures are repeatedly revealed to have been arranged. Helie helps the hero escape from the fay and then it turns out that it was the fay who had her sent to Arthur's court to request a champion.   Helie warns him against Lampart's evil custom but later we discover that Lampart is her mistress's steward. The plot abounds in machinations operated by the characters to manipulate each other. Robert thinks up a plan to put off Blonde Esmeree and permit his master to return to the fay. Arthur and his barons lure Guinglain back to court by having a tournament called. The serpent stays the hero's hand by cowering each time he reaches for his sword.

Two instances of ruse are particularly startling because they put the entire proceeding narrative in a new light. When the fay tells Guinglain that it is she who sent Helie to Arthur's court, thereby initiating the adventures that led him to her, she appropriates the plot up to that point (Haidu 1972). In the epilogue the poet-lover offers to reunite Guinglain and the fay if his lady will show him favor. The many instances of ruse present the plot as an illusion that we are repeatedly invited to see through. By violating the boundaries between diegetic and extradiegetic—the fay appropriates the role of plot-constructor, the poet invites his lady to determine the fate of the characters, Guinglain bears the shield of the house of Bâgé—Renaut accentuates what Perret (1988) aptly terms an "effet de fiction."[22]

The romance brings together three courtly genres. It is a lay (a knight is drawn away from the court by the love of a fay) within a romance (a knight achieves a series of exploits and is rewarded with a wife and fief) within a lyric frame (Haidu 1972, Guthrie 1984, de Looze 1986, Perret 1990). The narrative reveals Renaut's affinity for doubling; there are two heroines, two love stories, two endings. The lyric element is comprised of the parts of the text relating to the poet-lover and his lady. The opening lines develop a topic of exordium common in courtly lyric; the epilogue, which addresses the text to the poet's lady, resembles the envoy of a song. In addition the poet-lover interrupts the narrative with four lyric monologues (1967-82, 1237-71, 4198-4209, 4828-61) (Guthrie 1984, Grigsby 1968). These three generic elements do not relate harmoniously; instead they work against each other and on more than one level (see de Looze). The fay competes with Blonde Esmeree for the hero. Furthermore, she claims to have used Blonde Esmeree's plight to attract Guinglain, thus in fact subsuming the romance plot to the lay plot. In the epilogue the poet invites his lady to inspire a sequel. The envoy-like epilogue undercuts the romance's ending, invoking the state of suspended desire that distinguishes courtly love-song.

The romance narrative subverts the lyric element in turn. For if the closing lines present the text as an effort to woo the poet's lady and she is invited to view the couple in the romance as a transposition of herself and the poet, what is there in Guinglain's character that would encourage her to grant her love? He makes promises to the fay and subsequently breaks them. It is not that he is fickle like his father, Gauvain. Rather, absorbed by one project at a time, he refuses to be deflected from his goal of the moment. We are aware of him as a construct closely tied to the plot. The love affair with the fay is not an "*éducation sentimentale*" because Guinglain does not learn anything about love and is not changed by the experience (but see Perret [1990], pp. 10-12). When he leaves the fay for the tournament and realizes that he has lost her, his grief lasts one day. Thereafter he is engrossed in the tournament and then agrees to marry Blonde Esmeree without a thought for the fay or any hesitation (6191-4).

The flat, caricatural style in which Guinglain is drawn is set off by the depth given the character of the fay (Sturm 1971a and b, 1972). Renaut presents her in many lights: now transported by sensuous passion, now furious at having been slighted, now lucid about Guinglain's ignorance of love and yet loving him nonetheless.

Another aspect of the self-conscious literariness of this romance is its frequent reference to the works of Chrétien de Troyes. Scholars have long recognized the especially close relationship between *Li Biaus Descouneüs* and Chrétien's oeuvre but this has led some to dismiss Renaut as a mere epigone or even plagiarist (see, for example, Tyssens 1970). The references to Chrétien are so numerous, one might say insistent, that it is clear they are a deliberate attempt to situate the text with respect to this literary forbear, a parallel to the genealogical theme in the romance's plot.

These allusions run the gamut from blatant to subtle. The sparrowhawk joust (1579 ff.) follows the analogous episode in *Erec et Enide* closely. It is the first of a series of sustained references to the *Erec* and thus serves to alert the reader to the intertext (Bruckner 1987).[23] When Helie recognizes as her cousin the young woman whom the hero has championed—an element that Renaut has transposed from the Joie de la Cort episode in *Erec*—the effect is to underscore the kinship of Renaut's text with Chrétien's.

Various patterns of allusion can be discerned. References to a single episode in *Erec*, the Joie de la Cort, span the two sojourns at the Isle d'Or. The circle of poles topped with the armed heads of the knights defeated by Malgiers is a signal evoking this episode from Chrétien's romance. In both texts a woman with magic powers tries to retain her lover in her realm (the garden). Guinglain's role shifts during the extended comparison. The first time he comes to the Isle d'Or, he is an outsider, a stranger who penetrates an enchanted space, like Erec, to break a repressive custom by defeating a knight. When he returns, however, the part that he plays is that of Maboagrain, the lover kept by the lady in the enchanted garden. The Joie de la Cort is Erec's crowning feat; he succeeds in integrating the lovers into the world of the court. In contrast, Guinglain is drawn back under love's spell into the realm of the fay and cut off from the court. The overall effect of the extended reference to this single episode from *Erec* is to undermine the hero.[24] There is an interesting tension between Renaut's text and Chrétien's just as there is disjunction between the three generic aspects of the romance.[25]

A quite different pattern of intertextual allusion is found in the Fier Baiser adventure. Here a single episode groups references to several of Chrétien's romances, to all of them except *Erec* (and *Cligès*, to which Renaut does not refer at all). Guinglain fights two demon knights as Yvain does in Pesme Aventure. The mesmerizing polyphony of the jongleurs, a prelude to combat, may recall Calogrenant riveted by the song of the birds massed in the pine above the magic fountain. The many windows framing the jongleurs are reminiscent of the many-windowed hall in Ygerne's castle in *Perceval*. The falling battle-axes that almost kill the hero as he tries to pursue his opponent into a side room evoke the sword strokes that Lancelot dodges as he rushes to rescue his hostess from the staged rape. This clustering in a single episode of references to an array of texts serves to distinguish this adventure from the surrounding series (the first visit to Isle d'Or, Lampart, Fier Baiser, the return to Isle d'Or), where a sharply contrasting pattern of intertextual allusion prevails. It also lends dazzle to the Fier Baiser exploit, implying that it is as difficult as Pesme Aventure in *Yvain*, the Lit de la Mervoille test in *Perceval* and the staged rape in *Lancelot* all in one.

A third pattern of allusion produces a complex nested effect; Renaut rewrites a text that itself recasts a previous text. The joust with Lampart revisits Yvain's experience at Pesme Aventure, which looks back to the Joie de la Cort in *Erec* (Bruckner 1987, p. 235). In all three instances a host offers hospitality that involves a test of his guest's valor by combat. In all three texts a crowd of townspeople calls out to discourage the hero from fighting. Of course, Guinglain's situation differs from both of the others; the operation of comparison and contrast is precisely what the evocation of the intertexts calls into play. The effect is particularly complex in this instance because, due to the nested pattern of the allusions, Lampart recalls simultaneously the devious host of Pesme Aventure and magnanimous King Evrain of the Joie de la Cort; the burghers at Galigan evoke the apparently hostile crowd in *Yvain* and also the sympathetic one in *Erec*. The ambiguity is a ploy to throw the reader off.[26]

Li Biaus Descouneüs also contains verbal echoes from Chrétien's romances.[27] Some of these are easily recognizable. In bed with the fay, Guinglain remembers the hallucinations to which he was subjected: "*Quant il l'enprist a souvenir, de rire ne se puet tenir*" (4871-2), and the fay insists that he explain why he has laughed out loud. The audience will immediately think of the famous scene in which Enide remembers the criticisms she has overheard: "*Quant il l'an prist a sovenir, de plorer ne se pot tenir . . .*" (2445-6). (It is not coincidental that recollection and recapitulation are important themes in the two scenes associated here.) When Arthur urges Guinglain to marry Blonde Esmeree (6186-7), his words echo Erec's as he presents Enide to Guenevere (1553-5).

Scattered throughout the romance there are also other examples less easy to catch. Blonde Esmeree's ambassador to Guinglain appropriates lines from Guivret's speech to Erec (see the line note). The description of the castle at Isle d'Or echoes that of Brandigan in *Erec*. These allusions are interesting because they imply an audience with a detailed knowledge of Chrétien's oeuvre.

The romance contains some fifty instances of lines or line sequences repeated almost verbatim. Many are related to combat and arming scenes and thus evoke an epic style: "*Lances orent roides et fors*" (2137, 5719) and "*La lance fu et roide et fors*" (2689) or "*Molt i fu grans li capleïs!*" (5710), variants of which punctuate the account of the tournament. Other instances occur in certain portraits and can be explained by the stereotyped nature of these descriptions (see 137-8, 1527-8 and 2218; 1538 and 2241; 1536, 1876, 1932 and 2258). In this romance they also highlight what Colby-Hall calls (1984, p. 129) "the battle of the portraits" (see above, p. xiii).

In other cases we can truly speak of autocitation. Each time the three avengers of Blioblïeris appear, the narrator rehearses their names. When Robert spots them ("*Si vit venir trois chevaliers, armés sor lor corans destriers*" [965-6]), he reports to his master using almost these very words (989-990), conveying at once the urgency of the moment and his accuracy. The technique may be used to humorous effect, as when Guinglain tells his squire that he is passionately in love with the fay. Robert asks in disbelief, "*Gabés me vos?*" (3756) and his master replies emphatically "*Je ne gab [mie]*" (3759). Later, invited by the fay to stay in the castle, Guinglain asks humbly, "*Gabés me vos?*" (4447) Her ironic answer, "*O, je, sire, je ne gap mie!*" (4457) suggests that she must have overheard the earlier exchange.

The hallmark of Renaut's art is its ludic quality, its sophisticated play with literary conventions. He brings these together not in order to combine them harmoniously but to permit them to undercut each other, provoking ambiguity and disjunction. His romance grows out of the work of Chrétien, which serves as a foil; it looks forward in that it problematizes romance conventions.

Sources and Influences

In his prologue Renaut announces that he intends to extract a romance from a tale of adventure that he has heard: "*veul un roumant estraire/ d'un molt biel conte d'aventure*" (4-5). With this statement he embraces a poetic grounded in transmitting the literary heritage of the past by recasting this heritage and thus giving it new life. In these lines Renaut affirms *translatio* in a double sense, for not only does he invoke a theme traditionally developed in a prologue, he echoes the words of the great romance master, Chrétien de Troyes, in the opening of *Erec et Enide* ("*et tret d'un conte d'aventure/ une molt bele conjointure . . .*," [13-4]), signaling from the outset the intertext that will be repeatedly evoked throughout the romance, particularly in the episodes at the Isle d'Or.

Li Biaus Descouneüs is connected by shared motifs, themes, characters, episodes and even episode sequences to a whole network of texts. There are first of all three cognate romances: the Middle High German *Wigalois* by Wirnt von Gravenberg (1204-1210), the Middle English *Lybeaus Desconus* by Thomas Chestre (ca. 1350) and the Italian *Cantare di Carduino* (ca. 1375).[28] *Partonopeu de Blois* (1182-5), an Old French romance roughly twice the length of *Li Biaus Descouneüs*, presents many parallels: a fay who has acquired her magic powers through education, a hero who falls in love with her but twice leaves her, a narrator-lover who repeatedly compares his lot to that of the hero. Two later prose romances are also related, *Le Chevalier du Papegau* (fifteenth century) and *L'Hystoire de Giglan* (1530) by Claude Platin, a prose compilation that intertwines *Li Biaus Descouneüs* and the Provençal romance of *Jaufre*. Ulrich von Zatzikhoven's *Lanzelet* (1194-1203) and Chaucer's *Wife of Bath's Tale* have both been associated to the group of Fair Unknown narratives through the loathly lady motif, and Malory's *Tale of Sir Gareth* has elements in common with the adventures at the Golden Isle and Snowdon. The Welsh *Peredur* and the Perceval story as told by Chrétien have also been related to the Fair Unknown story and to *Li Biaus Descouneüs* in particular.[29]

A word should be said about the relation between *Li Biaus Descouneüs* and the *First* and *Second Continuations* since the possibility of a connection has been raised but not addressed in any detail since Wrede's discussion in his unpublished dissertation. The *Continuations* are two long verse sequels to Chrétien's unfinished *Conte du Graal* (or *Perceval*). The *First* (or *Gauvain*) *Continuation* features Gauvain's adventures and its shorter redaction is dated before 1200. The *Second* (or *Perceval*) *Continuation* follows Perceval's adventures although a short series of episodes (numbers 29-32) relate to Gauvain; it is dated 1190-1200.[30] It has been suggested that these works were "sources" for *Li Biaus Descouneüs*.[31] Surprisingly, it is the *Second* (or *Perceval*) *Continuation* rather than the *First* (*Gauvain*) *Continuation* that shares the clearest and greatest number of similarities with *Li Biaus Descouneüs*. At one point (Episode 5) Perceval borrows a brachet hound and, while he is hunting a stag with it, a maiden steals the brachet, refusing to return it despite Perceval's entreaties. There are clear echoes here with Helie's theft of the huntsman's brachet (1278 ff.). Later on (Episode 16) Perceval meets a knight riding along with his ugly *amie*. He offends the knight by smiling and after they joust the knight tells him that he considers this lady, whose name is Rosete, the most beautiful woman in the world. The parallels with Giflet's blind love for Rose Espanie (1709 ff.) are evident. Both *Continuations* relate scenes in which Gauvain and Perceval, respectively, awaken out in the open, their arms and horses at hand, the castle where they lodged the

Episode 6) Gauvain failed to meet the Grail test the previous evening. The *Second Continuation* (Episode 20), however, presents more striking resemblances to Guinglain's predicament (5397 ff.). The previous evening Perceval was entertained at the Castle of the Maidens, where he was waited on by beautiful women. When he awakens the next morning, he finds himself beneath a tree and gives vent to his bewilderment. In none of these cases are there verbal echoes between *Li Biaus Descouneüs* and the *Continuations*.

Both *Continuations* relate encounters between Perceval and Gauvain, in turn, and Biaus Descouneüs. In the *First Continuation* (Section V, Episode 8) Gauvain does battle with his son, who is defending a ford. In the *Second Continuation* (Episode 14) Perceval comes upon the Fair Unknown and they joust. When the youth learns who his opponent is, he surrenders and identifies himself as Biaus Desconeüs, Gauvain's son. Later in the narrative (Episode 32) Gauvain himself meets his son. The handsome youth asks who the stranger is and, when he learns that this is Gauvain, he announces that he is Guinglain, his son, whom Arthur had named Biaus Desconeüs.

According to Wrede, the *First Continuation* includes a series of events constituting the childhood of Gauvain's son: the circumstances of his birth, his interruption of a combat between his father and uncle, his upbringing by a fay and his meeting with his father. Gallais, p. 212, comments that all the manuscripts punctuate this narrative with allusions to other adventures that are being omitted. This raises the possibility that a fuller story of the Fair Unknown (not necessarily *Li Biaus Descouneüs*) was drawn upon for the *First Continuation*, a hypothesis at least as likely as that the *First Continuation* served as a source for *Li Biaus Descouneüs*, particularly as the two works are roughly contemporaneous. It also suggests that, since an account of the youth of Gauvain's son was known, it was a deliberate artistic choice for *Li Biaus Descouneüs* not to begin with the hero's birth and childhood but instead to allude to them later in the narrative (3235-42 and 4964-78).[32]

Fascinated by the echoes and resemblances among this great mass of Fair Unknown texts, a generation of scholars has tried to establish filiations among them.[33] The speculative nature of these constructs as well as their conflicting theses have led to skepticism regarding their conclusions. Furthermore, where many of the elements repeated in a group of romances are highly conventional in nature, it is extremely difficult to account for a similarity by positing a direct link between two works. We must be content to note similarities between *Li Biaus Descouneüs* and other works and conclude some sort of relationship among them without specifying it. Of another order is the exceptionally close relation between *Li Biaus Descouneüs* and Chrétien's romances, especially *Erec*. The allusions and echoes are so dense that they constitute an important trait of Renaut's style (see above, p. xv-xvii).

To determine a work's posterity is quite as delicate a matter as establishing its sources. *Lybeaus Desconus* refers to a "Frensshe tale" (Lambeth MS, l. 245) but was this *Li Biaus Descouneüs*? Chestre's work is different from Renaut's in important ways. The hero does not return to the fay at the Golden Isle and his experience of love is not developed. *Wigalois* is contemporaneous to *Li Biaus Descouneüs* and it is impossible to determine whether Wirnt knew Renaut's poem (or vice versa). Platin's *Hystoire de Giglan* appears to be a prose paraphrase of *Li Biaus Descouneüs* but there are some differences in detail. Are these Platin's doing or was he simply not working from the version preserved in the Chantilly codex? Did Malory know Renaut's romance or Claude Platin's version or is it more likely that he drew on another story about a young unknown knight, *La Cotte Mal Tailliee*, which he would have found in the *Prose Tristan*?[34]

Another context for *Li Biaus Descouneüs* is of interest. This is the mention of a romance, "*del Bel Desconogut*," recited by minstrels during a court festival that is described in the Provençal romance *Flamenca* (late thirteenth century). The long list of works that are sung or recited on this occasion is really a catalogue which distinguishes rough groups: stories derived from Greek and Roman legend, Biblical tales, Arthurian romances, epic songs about Charlemagne and others. The Fair Unknown story (mentioned in line 679) falls within the Arthurian category, following a list of Chrétien's romances: *Yvain*, *Lancelot*, *Perceval*, *Erec*, *Ugonet de Peride* (a lost romance), *Gouvernail and Tristan* (Chrétien's lost Tristan romance?), *Cligès*, *Le Bel Inconnu*, etc. This reference to a Fair Unknown romance indicates that it was a well known part of the Arthurian canon. Although it is impossible, of course, to determine whether the romance in question is Renaut's, the place of the reference in the list makes one wonder whether this is not in recognition of its close association to Chrétien's oeuvre.

Editorial Policy for this Text and Translation

The Manuscript

Li Biaus Descouneüs is contained in only one codex, Chantilly 472, in the collection of the Duc d'Aumale at the Musée Condé. It is dated to the end of the thirteenth century (Micha 38-39; descriptions of the manuscript may also be found in Winter's edition of *Hunbaut* and Frescoln's edition of *Fergus*). The manuscript has been bound in red calfskin with the Bourbon-Condé coat of arms on the cover; the spine bears the title *Connoiss. de Toutes Choses 1250*. When the bookbinder trimmed the codex, the title in large ornamental letters at the head of Renaut's romance was cut off but just enough of the lettering remains to suggest that it might have read "De Guinglain." The title that we use derives from the explicit.

Judging from the hand, one scribe appears to have copied the series of romances *Fergus*, *Hunbaut* and *Li Biaus Descouneüs*. (The scribal titles are symmetrical: "De Fergvs," "De Gunbaut," "De Guinglain.") Most of the works in the codex begin a new signature and the gatherings vary in size as extra pages were tipped in to accommodate the lengths of the romances. Frescoln has determined that *Fergus* originally started a new gathering. This and the fact that the scribal title for *Hunbaut* does not appear at the head of the folio but near the top of the right-most column supports the hypothesis that these three romances constitute a unit within the codex.

Chantilly 472 is an anthology made up for the most part of Arthurian romances which feature Gauvain: *Les Mervelles de Rigomer*, *L'Atre Perilleus*, *Erec et Enide*, *Fergus*, *Hunbaut*, *Guinglain* (*Li Biaus Descouneüs*), *La Vengeance Raguidel*, *Yvain*, *Le Chevalier de la Charrette*, *Perlesvaus* (a fragment relating Gauvain's quest), and several branches of the *Roman de Renart* (this final unit headed by the scribal rubric "*De Renart*").[35] *Li Biaus Descouneüs* falls squarely at the midpoint, the sixth of eleven units. It is significant that in a collection focussing on the work of Chrétien's successors, in which three of Chrétien's romances are surrounded by works by later writers so as to suggest a dialogue, the compiler has chosen Renaut's romance for this pivotal place, in recognition perhaps of the effects that it draws from recasting, rewriting and quoting Chrétien's works.

Previous editions

Li Biaus Descouneüs has been edited three times. C. Hippeau's 1860 edition is riddled with errors—misreadings of individual words, lines out of order, some ninety lines omitted. He also added ten lines of his own devising, in most cases to fill out a couplet.

The two other editions are the work of G. Perrie Williams. The first of these, published in 1915, is a conservative edition but includes quite a few misreadings. In the 1929 edition, based on a new collation of the manuscript, Williams wished to withdraw certain superfluous corrections made to the manuscript in her first edition and reproduce the text with greater accuracy. Line notes provide only rejected readings, indications of deficiencies in the manuscript (lacunae, repeated lines, mutilations), and additional corrections to the text. Emendations are not explained or justified. Some errors in reading persist but, on the whole, this is a careful edition which has been a valuable aid in the preparation of the present project.

The Present Edition

New readings distinguish this text from Williams' second edition. In a number of instances I have corrected misreadings of the manuscript text, among them 1808, 3060, 3125, 3500, and 3726. Sometimes I have retained readings changed by Williams (1981 and 4158). I have also emended where she did not (3419, 3784-5, 3923, 4381-2, 5303, 5591-2, 5699 ff.) or where she incorporated a different interpretation (3327). In several of these cases changes were either suggested (3419, 3923, 4381-2) or corroborated (1793-4, 3076) by intertexts. I discuss the changes that I have made and cite the relevant intertexts in the Textual Notes.

The transcription was done from a film copy with the entire text checked against the manuscript itself. I have been generally conservative in editing the text. The corrections that I have made were guided by two considerations. The first was to make the text clear wherever necessary. For example, now and then the scribe writes *i* for *il*; I restore the *l* in order to avoid confusion with *i* meaning 'y, there'. Where the scribe writes *dont* for *donc* I replace -*t* with -*c* for the convenience of readers familiar with modern French. Sometimes the scribe's tendency to drop the final consonant leads to confusion about the subject of a verb; in these cases I restore the final consonant: *pris*, for example, is corrected to *prist* (892; see the note to line 66). The mistake in flexion in line 4200 is of thematic significance and I call it to the attention of the reader in a note to this line.

I was also guided in correcting the text by a wish to be attentive to pronunciation, sound, voice, and music, which is so important in this text. Spellings like *tieg*, *puic*, and *besoig* are replaced by *tieng*, *puinc*, and *besoing* as better reflecting pronunciation. I have restored final consonants where liaison requires them to be pronounced. For example, I changed *le iouls* to *les iouls* (141) but I retained *l'avoien cil* (883). Now and then the scribe hesitates between *c* and *g*. Because the facing translation helps to make the meaning of the text clear for the reader, I have kept these spellings (*vicor* for *vigor*, *gongié* for *congié*; see the note to line 1534). The hesitation between *a* and *ai* is much more frequent. I have retained these spellings too, not just as an index to pronunciation but in the interest of providing a context for passages in which the confusion between the first and third person of verbs raises interesting ambiguities (for example, *a* for *ai*, *donnai* for *donna*, etc.; see the notes to lines 242 and 3238).

I have also intervened to clarify the sound of a rhyme obscured by the spelling in the manuscript. Thus *pujosse* is changed to *pujoisse:voisse* (671-2). Similarly, I restore the final consonant to a rhyme word: *jor* > *jors:lors* (4923-4). On the other hand, I retain rhymes that match -*en*- with -*an*- since these would pose no problem of pronunciation. Where the order of the elements in a description has produced an irregular rhyme (4309-10), I change the order so as to remedy this. The Textual Notes contain explanations of all emendations not immediately comprehensible, and the rejected readings immediately below the Old French text present, without exception, all the manuscript readings that I have replaced.

In punctuating the text I have been attentive to the often vivid, expressive rhythms in the Old French verse and to the scribal punctuation that underscores this aspect of the style. The scribe uses a single raised dot and two raised dots resembling a colon, apparently interchangeably, most often to mark a *rejet* following an enjambment of some force. Each instance is noted in the Textual Notes.

I have indicated two instances of possible lacunae in the text beyond the sixteen noted by Williams. In order to maintain her line numbering, I have designated these 3178.1 and 3183.1. Some of these lacunae are evident in the codex. The two longest (6066-80 and 6118-32) are due to a corner torn from folio 153. In two cases empty lines are left in the text (741 and 762-6). Sometimes incomplete syntax and an orphan rhyme indicate that material is missing (2359, 2739, 4752, 4922, 4952, 5598, 5938, and 6007). In other instances just the lack of a rhyme to complete a couplet signals the possibility of a lacuna (719, 3178.1, 33183.1, 1584, 1736, 2094, 2942, and 4736). All but two of this last group involve a series of three (once of five) lines with the same rhyme. Williams (1929), p. iv, suggests that such frequent irregularity may reflect the practice of the poet rather than the laxity of the scribe. In two instances, however, 719 and 1736, Claude Platin's prose romance contains material that might be missing. For the sake of consistency, then, and preferring to alert the reader each time that there may be a lacuna, I have made an indication in the critical text and provided comments in the Textual Notes.

Quite often Claude Platin's *mise en prose* has been useful in suggesting just what may be missing in the text presented in Chantilly 472. In these cases I cite the relevant passage in a line note. In one instance, his text provides the correction for a passage that remains problematic even in Williams' 1929 edition (see the note to lines 4381-2).

In general, I followed conventional editorial practices in preparing the text. Square brackets set off corrections. The manuscript characters *i* and *j* are distinguished from each other, as are *u* and *v*, in order to conform to modern spelling norms. Final -*x* is resolved to -*us*. Roman numerals are spelled out for the convenience of the reader. Cases of non-modern enclisis are made clear through the use of an internal period, as in *ne.s* for the contraction of *ne* and *les*. In the use of diacritical marks, I have followed the guidelines set out in Foulet-Speer, pp. 67-73.

Together with the rejected readings below the Old French text, the reader will find the following information. When a correction has been adopted from an earlier editor or commentator, this person's name appears in brackets next to the reading rejected. A plus or minus sign and a number indicates by how many syllables a line is hyper- or hypometric. Abbreviations and ligatures are written out; the letters *i, j, u, v*, and *x* are treated as in the critical text, words are separated and capitalized, and diacritics are added but punctuation is not.

The facing English translation is intended as a guide to understanding the Old French text. We have tried to strike a balance between a readable, flowing rendition and one that follows the Old French closely.

Notes

[1] I am heavily indebted to the thorough, cogent analysis of the biographical information presented by Guerreau, pp. 29-36.

[2] Guichenon (1660), 1:1161 (the family tree of the house of Beaujeu). 1:347 has an engraving of this blazon. There is a family tree of the house of Bâgé on pp. 1209-10. Williams (1929), p. viii, and Brault, p. 23, mistakenly identify the Bâgé arms as "de gueules au lion d'hermine." Bâgé-le-Chastel still exists; it is the capital of the canton of Ain in the Bresse region, about 4 miles to the east of Mâcon.

[3] See Hafner, pp. 67-8, cited by Guerreau. Among Hafner's examples of this development is Baugies (Bâgé-le-Chastel).

4 Dauzat lists the etymon Rantiaco but it is for the village of Rancé in the southernmost corner of the Ain region, 10 miles north of Lyon. There are two villages named Saint-Trivier, Saint-Trivier-sur-Moignans in the Dombes area and Saint-Trivier de Courtes, 12 miles northeast of Bâgé-le-Chastel. It is the latter that was part of the Bâgé holdings, as Guichenon indicates: ". . . vn puisné de cette glorieuse famille l'eust en partage" (1650, 2:104).

5 This Renaut is named in a legal document of 1180 in which he and his brother agree to a gift made by his father to the Chartreuse of Montmerle in Bresse: "Noscant praesentes, & posteri quod ego Raynaldus de Baugiaco, laudant uxore mea; & filiis meis Vlrico videlicet atque Raynaudo, laudantibus pro salute animae meae, & antecessorum nostrorum domui sanctae Mariae Montismerulae quidquid in Francisca continetur, quod ad ius meum pertinet, concedo, & in perpetuum dono." (Guichenon [1650], 4:8). Guerreau quotes, p. 33, n. 1, from a second document in which Renaut approves another gift made after his father's death to the Church of St. Vincent in Mâcon. Guerreau speculates that the church of St. Bénigne, where this procedure took place, might be a church of that name in Dijon and that this might link Renaut with the Burgundian court. Guichenon (1650), 1:52, indicates, however, that this is St. Bénigne in Bresse.

6 The house of Bâgé forms a thread that runs through Duby's study (1971) of the shifting patterns of power in the Mâcon region; see especially pp. 349-53. Duby describes the status of the younger sons of noble families in his influential article (1964), where he suggests that courtly romance and lyric are keyed to the point of view of *bacheliers*.

7 Guerreau, noting the many allusions to Chrétien de Troyes in the romance, suggests that Renaut may have known him personally. While it is within the realm of possibility, nothing associates Renaut with the courts of Champagne or Flanders. Guerreau also states, p. 35, that Jean Renart must have had a personal acquaintance with Renaut because of the "allusion précise" in the *Guillaume de Dole*, presumably the identification of Renaut as the chevalier from Rencieu (or Rencien). But Jean Renart introduces other characters in his romance, real people drawn from the contemporary scene, with just such details. Lejeune (1935), p. 134, links Jean with the entourage

of Renaut de Dammartin, who frequented Paris, Flanders, and London. Consequently this association must remain far from certain.

8 Although most of their holdings were concentrated by this time in Bresse between the Reyssouze to the east and the Saône to the west, between the towns of Pont-de-Vaux to the north and Pont-de-Veyle to the south, the family still retained lands to the west of the Saône.

9 Pastoureau (1976), pp. 74-5, cited by Guerreau.

10 The letters are contained in *Recueil des historiens des Gaules et de la France*, 16:155-6. *The Cambridge Medieval History* quotes from the second of these letters, 5:616: "Raynald of Bâgé, lord of La Bresse, cried urgently for his help: 'Come into this country, where your presence is as necessary to the churches as it is to me. Do not fear the expense; I will repay you all that you spend; I will do homage to you for all my castles, which are subject to no suzerain; in a word, all that I possess shall be at your disposal.'"

11 Duby (1971), p. 415. The peace arranged by Louis in 1173 did not include the house of Bâgé. A letter from Renaut III to Louis does reveal that Louis went so far as to write on Renaut's behalf (Guichenon [1650], 1:50).

12 Duby (1971), 439-40.

13 By the end of the thirteenth century, there is no male heir and the Bâgé lands pass to the house of Savoy with the marriage in 1272 of Sybille, Lady of Bâgé and Bresse, to Amédée, the future Count of Savoy.

14 Several aristocratic families sought to shed glory on their dynasties by commissioning romances that traced their origins to mythic heroes. Often a woman with magic powers, who leads a double existence as human and serpent or dragon, brings wealth and power to the family. A notable instance is that of the house of Lusignan, which commissioned Jean d'Arras to write the tale of *Mélusine*. See Le Goff (1971) and Lecouteux (1978) and (1982), especially pp. 88-90 on *Li Biaus Descouneüs*.

15 Williams (1915) first dates the romance 1185-90 based on phonological criteria and on Servois' dating of the *Guillaume de Dole*; in her 1929 edition, she implies a later possible date, noting Foulet's dating of the *Guillaume de Dole* at 1210-14; the *GRLMA* gives "ca. 1200?"; Schmolke-Hasselmann includes *Li Biaus Descouneüs* among the romances in the 1204-1220 generation.

16 Lejeune (1935); she suggests 1208-10 in her 1974 article.

17 For a detailed critique of Lejeune's characterization of the linguistic traits in *Ignaure* and her comparison of these to the language of *Li Biaus Descouneüs*, see Henry's review of her edition of the lay.

18 For the frequency of simple rhyme in poems of the twelfth and thirteenth centuries, see Lote 2:139; imperfect rhyme, 1:100; hiatus, 3:80-81.

19 Holden details the irreverent obscenities in *Ipomedon*, p. 53. Ménard (1969) discusses sexual humor in courtly romance, pp. 693-695.

20 The author is given as Renaus in line 7798 although editors have corrected this to Renars, believing the romance to be Jean Renart's.

21 Lejeune (1935) details the arguments advanced to attribute *Galeran* to Jean Renart and refutes them, pp. 25-34. In comparing this description of this romance to *Li Biaus Descouneüs*, certain traits that may be pertinent in setting *Galeran* apart from the other works ascribed to Jean Renart are too widespread to justify attributing the romance to Renaut de Bâgé. This is the case for the use of elaborate portraits and descriptions of towns, or the inclusion of lengthy monologues and dialogues. Other traits—the presence of certain dialectal forms, the use of a compound subject with a verb in the singular—are rejected by Lejeune as valid bases for determing the attribution of a text.

22 This smudging of diegetic boundaries is reflected in the confusion between third person references to the hero and the first person voice of the poet-lover; see the note to lines 4199-4203.

23 Louveau and others have found that earlier episodes in *Li Biaus Descouneüs* resemble passages in Chrétien but their observations are not convincing. A knight defends a ford against Lancelot, for instance, but no similarities in the action or wording suggest that Renaut is alluding to this episode. The adventure is a conventional one in Arthurian romance. The same can be said for the combat with two giants or the battle against the three avengers, which some have tried to show recasts Erec's confrontations with robbers. Fair Unknown's arrival at Arthur's court, his disclosure that his mother called him *Biel Fils*, are of course a plain reference to Chrétien's *Perceval*.

24 Bruckner suggests, 1987, p. 235, that the evocation of the Joie de la Cort is meant to place Guinglain at the apex of Erec's achievements.

25 Another example of this pattern is the cluster of references to the Pesme Aventure from *Yvain*, which occur in both the joust with Lampart and the following Fier Baiser adventure.

26 The same pattern of nested allusions occurs when Guinglain's tryst with the fay evokes Maboagrain and his lady in the enchanted garden, for this couple is itself a reference to Erec and Enide, self-absorbed newlyweds, at the start of their romance.

27 Schofield and Louveau detail these. Many instances that they cite must be dismissed, however, because they can be explained as set formulas pertaining to the description of combat between individuals or in a tournament, of arming, of castles or women. There are exceptions. The description of the castle at Isle d'Or can be said to echo that of Brandigan in *Erec* because two series of lines are quoted and the description is surrounded by other references to the Joie de la Cort adventure.

28 The chief similarities and differences between *Li Biaus Descouneüs* and its cognates are as follows. *Wigalois* presents clear parallels: the arrival of the maiden and dwarf seeking a champion to free their princess; the combats with a host who jousts with would-be guests; fights with two giants and with a huntsman; the joust for a bird and another with the princess's steward. Wirnt begins with the hero's childhood and includes much other material not

in the Old French romance, while omitting the fay and the spell cast over the princess. There are narratorial interventions but of a didactic nature in keeping with the focus on the story as the education of a prince. *Lybeaus Desconus* includes all the episodes up through the rescue of the lady of Synadoun. The hero does not return to the fay but marries the queen immediately. An account of the hero's childhood and upbringing opens the romance. There are no narratorial interventions or development of the love interest in a treatment that focusses on action. *Carduino* provides the shortest text (856 lines). The maiden and dwarf arrive at the court requesting a champion; they stay with a seductive enchantress who visits the hero with hallucinations; he rescues a girl from two giants; then he undergoes the kiss of the serpent, thus freeing the lady from enchantment. He marries her and returns to court. This narrative also starts with the hero's childhood. Gauvain (Calvan) is not the hero's father but his father's murderer, forgiven by Carduino at the end of the tale.

29 For detailed treatments of the relations among these works, see D. Adams 1975 and Mennung; more concise discussions may be found in Mills' edition of *Lybeaus Desconus* and Thomas' *Wigalois* 1977.

30 Because the various redactions make it problematic to refer to line numbers, I shall refer to the sections and episodes noted by Roach.

31 Wrede, 120-7; *GRLMA* IV,2:111,112; *The New Arthurian Encyclopedia*, 381.

32 Tyssens (1970), 1051, notes that translators of French romances often reveal early in the narrative details that the French *romanciers* carefully defer.

33 A summary of the principal theories will show the bewildering variety of these stemmae. Paris and Mennung hypothesize a lost source of *Carduino* and for another work, also lost, from which *Lybeaus Desconus* and *Li Biaus Descouneüs* derived. For Philipot, who was interested in the relationship between *Li Biaus Descouneüs* and Chrétien's *Erec*, Renaut's and Chestre's works were drawn from a lost source, which went back to another lost source that also influenced *Erec*. Schofield's study is the most detailed and

influential. He posited a Celtic source, on the one hand of the Perceval story (Chrétien's *Conte du Graal* and the Welsh *Peredur*), on the other, a hypothetical French source which had two branches of influence, *Carduino* and a second hypothetical French work that was the source of the other three Fair Unknown texts (*Lybeaus Desconus, Wigalois* and *Li Biaus Descouneüs*). Owen posited a lost version of a Celtic legend, the source of both the Welsh *Dream of Macsen Wledig* and a lost prototype of the Fair Unknown story, the latter the source of the four Fair Unknown cognates plus Chrétien's *Conte du Graal*. Luttrell, the most recent proponent of this approach, instead of a Celtic source posits a lost "tale of Erec," source (1) of the *conte d'aventure* mentioned by Chrétien in his prologue, (2) a lost Fair Unknown story that was the source of *Lybeaus Desconus* and *Li Biaus Descouneüs* and (3) *Carduino*.

34 It has also been suggested that *Fergus* (early thirteenth century) imitates *Li Biaus Descouneüs* but the similarities alleged between the two works may be dismissed. The stag hunt is more likely an allusion to Chrétien's *Perceval* (Schmolke-Hasselmann, p. 130). Galiene, like Guinglain, thinks of her beloved in a moment of deadly peril but it is to reproach him for being too late to save her. Arthur proposes the hero's marriage and offers him a kingdom in both texts but this is a thoroughly conventional conclusion. One element that Frescoln does not mention and that may be an echo of *Li Biaus Descouneüs*, though, is the calling of a tournament to draw the hero back to court.

35 Micha, p. 39.

Acknowledgments

Grateful acknowledgment is made to the Musée Condé and particularly to M. Frédéric Vergne, Conservateur de la Bibliothèque, and Mlle Amélie Lefébure, Conservatrice des Collections, for permission to consult Chantilly MS 472. Thanks also to the staff of the Institut de Recherche et d'Histoire des Textes in Paris for providing the microfilm copy of the manuscript and for granting access to their files on current research; to Sara Raymundo Lo, and through her, to the Library of the University of Illinois, for acquiring a film of Claude Platin's *Hystoire de Giglan*.

This work was completed in part with a grant from the Research Board of the University of Illinois at Urbana-Champaign.

Special thanks go to Samuel N. Rosenberg for encouraging us to undertake this project. Thanks also to our colleagues on the MEDTEXT-L network for their useful suggestions. Finally, we are particularly indebted to Peter F. Dembowski and James J. Wilhelm for their careful reading of the manuscript.

Select Bibliography

This bibliography contains all the works cited in the present volume, as well as others which have proven useful in the preparation of this edition and translation.

I. Editions of *Li Biaus Descouneüs*

Hippeau, Célestin. *Le Bel Inconnu, ou Giglain fils de messire Gauvain et de la fée aux Blanches Mains; poème de la Table Ronde, par Renauld de Beaujeu, publié d'après le manuscrit unique de Londres avec une introduction et un glossaire*. Collection des poètes français du Moyen Age, 3. Paris: Auguste Aubry, 1860; rpt. Genève: Slatkine, 1969. Reviews: Foerster, *Zeitschrift für romanische Philologie* 2 (1878), 78; Mussafia, *Jahrbuch für romanische und englische Literatur* 4 (1862), 411-421.

Williams, G. Perrie. *Li Biaus Descouneüs; texte publié avec introduction et glossaire*. Thèse d'Université, Faculté des Lettres de l'Université de Paris; Oxford: Fox, Jones and Co., 1915.

Williams, G. Perrie. *Le Bel Inconnu; roman d'aventures*. Classiques Français du Moyen Age, 38. Paris: Champion, 1939; rpt. 1978.

II. Translations

Mary, André. *Les Amours de Frêne et Galeran suivies du Bel Inconnu*. Paris: L'Edition française illustrée, [1920]. An adaptation in modern French, which deletes the return to the Golden Isle.

Perret, Michèle and Isabelle Weill. *Le Bel Inconnu; roman d'aventures du XIIIe siècle. Traduit en français moderne*. Traductions des Classiques Français du Moyen Age, 41. Paris: Champion, 1991. [Abbreviation: Perret 1991]

Platin, Claude. *L'Hystoire de Giglan filz de messire Gauvain qui fut roy de Galles. Et de Geoffroy de Maience son compaignom; tous deux chevaliers de la table Ronde. Lesquelz feirent plusieurs et merveilleuses entreprises; et eurent de grandes fortunes et adventures autant que chevaliers de leur temps; Desquelles par leur noble prouesse et cueur chevaleureux vindrent a bout et honnorable fin comme on pourra veoir en ce present livre; Lequel a esté nouvellement translaté de langaige Espaignol en nostre langaige Francoys.* Lyon: Claude Nourry, 1530. London, British Museum C.47.f.5

III. Bibliographies and other reference works

A. Guides to bibliography

Bulletin Bibliographique de la Société Internationale Arthurienne—Bibliographical Bulletin of the International Arthurian Society (BBSIA). Published annually since 1949.

Encomia, Bibliographical Bulletin of the International Courtly Literature Society. Published annually since 1976.

Jauss, Hans Robert, and Erich Köhler. *Grundriss der romanischen Literaturen des Mittelalters.* Vol. 4: *Le Roman jusqu'à la fin du XIIIe siècle.* Part 1: *Partie historique.* Part 2: *Partie documentaire.* Heidelberg: Carl Winter Universitätsverlag, 1978, 1984.

Last, Rex. ed. *The Arthurian Bibliography,* 3. Cambridge: Brewer, 1985.

Linker, Robert White. *A Bibliography of Old French Lyrics.* Romance Monographs, 31. University, Miss.: Romance Monographs, Inc., 1979. [Abbreviations: L, Linker]

Mölk, Ulrich and Friedrich Wolfzettel. *Répertoire métrique de la poésie lyrique française des origines à 1350.* München: Wilhelm Fink Verlag, 1972.[Abbreviations: MW, Mölk-Wolfzettel]

Reiss, Edmund, et al. *Arthurian Legend and Literature: An Annotated Bibliography.* Vol. 1: *The Middle Ages.* Garland Reference Library of the Humanities, 415. New York and London: Garland, 1984.

Spanke, Hans. G. *Raynauds Bibliographie des Altfranzösischen Liedes neu bearbeitet und ergänzt. Erster Teil.* Leiden: E. J. Brill, 1955. [Abbreviations: RS, Raynaud-Spanke]

B. Dictionaries, glossaries, grammars and general studies

Brault, Gerard J. *Early Blazon: Heraldic Terminology in the Twelfth and Thirteenth Centuries.* London: Oxford University Press, 1972.

Brial, Michel Jean Joseph. *Recueil des historiens des Gaules et de la France.* Tome seizième. Paris: Imprimerie Royale, 1814. Pages 155-6 contain letters from Raynald III to Louis VII.

Broughton, Bradford B. *Dictionary of Medieval Knighthood and Chivalry; Concepts and Terms.* New York, Westport, CT, London: Greenwood Press, 1986.

Chantilly Le Cabinet des livres. 3 vols. Paris: Plon, 1900.

Dauzat, Albert and Charles Rostaing. *Dictionnaire étymologique des noms de lieux en France.* Paris: Larousse, 1963.

Duby, Georges. "Dans la France du Nord-Ouest au XIIe siècle: les 'jeunes' dans la société aristocratique." *Annales Economies, Sociétés, Civilisations* 19 (1964), 835-846; rpt. in: *La Société chevaleresque* Hommes et structures du Moyen Age, 1. Paris: Flammarion, 1988, pp. 129-142. [Abbreviation: Duby 1964]

Duby, Georges. "Lignage, noblesse et chevalerie au XIIe siècle dans la région mâconnaise." *Annales E. S. C.* 27 (1972), 803-823; rpt. in: *La Société chevaleresque.* Hommes et structures du Moyen Age, 1. Paris: Flammarion, 1988, pp. 82-116.

Duby, Georges. *La Société aux XIe et XIIe siècles dans la région màconnaise.* Paris: S. E. V. P. E. N., 1971.

Dyggve, Holger Petersen. *Onomastique des trouvères.* Suomalaisen Tiedeakatemian Toimituksia (Annales Academiae Scientarum Fennicae), ser. B, 30. Helsinki, 1934.

Edward, Second Duke of York. *The Master of Game.* London: Chatto and Windus, 1909.

Enlart, Camille. *Manuel d'archéologie française depuis les temps mérovingiens jusqu'à la Renaissance.* Tome 3: *Le costume.* Paris: Auguste Picard, 1916.

Evans, Joan. *Dress in Medieval France.* Oxford: Clarendon Press, 1952.

Flutre, Louis-Fernand. *Table des noms propres avec toutes leurs variantes figurant dans les romans du moyen âge écrits en français ou en provençal.* Poitiers: Centre d'Etudes Supérieures de Civilisation Médiévale, 1962. Proper nouns in French and Provençal romances.

Fouché, Pierre. *Le Verbe français; étude morphologique.* Tradition de l'humanisme, 4. Paris: Klincksieck, 1967.

Gay, Victor. *Glossaire archéologique du moyen âge et de la Renaissance.* 2 vols. Paris: Librairie de la Société Bibliographique, 1887; Paris: Editions Auguste Picard, 1928.

Goddard, Eunice Rathbone. *Women's Costume in French Texts of the Eleventh and Twelfth Centuries.* The Johns Hopkins Studies in Romance Literatures and Languages, 7. Baltimore: The Johns Hopkins Press, 1927.

Godefroy, Frédéric. *Dictionnaire de l'ancienne langue française et de tous ses dialectes, du IXe au XVe siècle.* 10 vols., including supplement. Paris: Viewig (vols. 1-5); Emile Bouillon (vols. 6-10), 1881-1902.

Gossen, Charles Théodore. *Grammaire de l'ancien picard*. Bibliothèque française et romane, série A: Manuels et études linguistiques, 19. Paris: Klincksieck, 1970.

Guichenon, Samuel. *Histoire de Bresse et de Bugey, contenant ce qui s'y est passé de mémorable sous les Romains, Roys de Bourgongne & d'Arles, Empereurs, Sires de Baugé, Comtes & Ducs de Savoye, & Roys Tres Chrestiens, jusques à l'eschange du Marquisat de Saluces*. Lyon: chez Iean Antoine Huguetan, & Marc Ant. Ravaud, 1650.

Guichenon, Samuel. *Histoire généalogique de la royale maison de Savoie*. Lyon, 1660. Vol. 1, pages 1209-10 show coat of arms of Bâgé family; page 1161 shows Bâgé family tree.

Hafner, Hans. *Grundzüge einer Lautlehre des Altfranko-Provenzalischen*. Romanica Helvetica, 52. Bern: A. Francke, 1955.

Holmes, Urban Tigner, Jr. *Daily Living in the Twelfth Century, Based on the Observations of Alexander Neckam in London and Paris*. Madison: The University of Wisconsin Press, 1952.

Lacy, Norris, ed. *The Arthurian Encyclopedia*. Garland Reference Library of the Humanities, 585. New York: Garland, 1986.

Lote, Georges. *Histoire du vers français*. 3 vols. in 2. Vol. 1: *Les Origines du vers français; les éléments constitutifs du vers: la césure; la rime; le numérisme et le rythme*. Paris: Boivin, 1949. Vol. 2: *La déclamation; art et versification; les formes lyriques*. Paris: Boivin, 1951. Vol. 3: *La Poétique; le vers et la langue*. Paris: Hatier, 1955.

Ménard, Philippe. *Manuel du français du moyen âge; 1. syntaxe de l'ancien français*. Nouvelle édition entièrement refondue. Bordeaux: Sobodi, 1976.

Michel, Francisque Xavier. *Recherches sur le commerce, la fabrication et l'usage des étoffes de soie, d'or et d'argent et autres tissus précieux en occident principalement en France pendant le moyen âge.* 2 vols. Paris: Crapelet, 1852-54.

Morawski, Joseph. *Proverbes français antérieurs au XVe siècle.* Classiques Français du Moyen Age, 47. Paris: Champion, 1925.

Page, Christopher. *Voices and Instruments of the Middle Ages; Instrumental practice and songs in France 1100-1300.* London, Melbourne: J. M. Dent & Sons Ltd, 1987.

Pannier, Léopold, ed. *Les Lapidaires français du moyen âge des XIIe, XIIIe et XIVe siècles.* Bibliothèque de l'Ecole des Hautes Etudes, fasc. 52. Paris: Viewig, 1882.

Pastoureau, Michel. *Les Armoiries.* Typologie des Sources du Moyen Age Occidental, Fasc. 20. Turnhout: Editions Brepols, 1976.

Pastoureau, Michel. *Traité d'héraldique.* Bibliothèque de la Sauvegarde de l'Art Français. Paris: Picard, 1979.

Pirenne, Henri. *Les Villes du Moyen Age.* L'Histoire, 5. Paris: Presses Universitaires de France, 1971.

Pope, M. K. *From Latin to Modern French with Especial Consideration of Anglo-Norman; Phonology and Morphology.* Rev. ed. Manchester: The University Press, 1952.

Quicherat, J. *Histoire du costume en France, depuis les temps les plus reculés jsuqu'à la fin du XVIIIe siècle.* Paris: Hachette, 1875.

Schulze-Busacker, Elisabeth. *Proverbes et expressions proverbiales dans la littérature narrative du moyen âge français; recueil et analyse.* Paris: Champion, 1985.

Tanner, J. R., ed. et al. *The Cambridge Medieval History.* Vol. 5: *Contest of Empire and Papacy.* Cambridge: The University Press, 1948.

Tobler, Adolf, and Erhard Lommatzsch. *Altfranzösisches Wörterbuch.* Berlin: Weidmann-Wiesbaden: Steiner, 1925-(still publishing). The major dictionnary of Old French. [Abbreviations: T-L, Tobler-Lommatzsch]

Verdelhan, Renée. *Le Lexique courtois du Bel Inconnu.* (Typescript) Aix-en-Provence: La Pensée Universitaire, 1956.

Viollet-le-Duc, Eugène Emmanuel. *Dictionnaire raisonné de l'architecture française du XIe au XVIe siècle.* 10 vols. Paris, 1858-68. *Table analytique et synthétique.* Paris, 1889.

Viollet-le-Duc, Eugène Emmanuel. *Dictionnaire raisonné du mobilier français de l'époque carolingienne à la Renaissance.* 2e éd. 6 vols. Paris, 1868-75.

Wartburg, Walther von. *Französisches etymologisches Wörterbuch; eine Darstellung des galloromanischen Sprachschatzes.* 17 vols. and supplement. Bonn: F. Klopp, 1928- [Abbreviations: FEW, Französisches Etymologisches Wörterbuch]

West, G. D. *An Index of Proper Names in French Arthurian Verse Romances 1150-1300.* University of Toronto Romance Series, 15. Toronto: University of Toronto Press, 1969.

IV. Studies

Accarie, Maurice. "La Fonction des chansons du 'Guillaume de Dole'." *Mélanges Jean Larmat; regards sur le Moyen Age et la Renaissance (histoire, langue et littérature).* Ed. M. Accarie. Annales de la Faculté des Lettres et Sciences Humaines de Nice, 39. Paris: Les Belles-Lettres, 1982 [cover reads 1983], pp. 12-29.

Adams, Alison. "La Conception de l'unité dans le roman médiéval en vers." *Studia Neophilologica* 50 (1978), 101-112. How Renaut manipulates the quest structure to integrate episodes.

Adams, Denise A. *The Theme of Le Bel Inconnu in the Literature of England, France, Germany, and Italy in the Middle Ages and*

After. Diss. Nottingham 1975. Exhaustive review of all the literature of this subject; calls attention to the close relation between Platin's prose work and *Li Biaus Descouneüs*.

Baldwin, Dean R. "Fairy Lore and the Meaning of Sir Orfeo." *Southern Folklore Quarterly* 41 (1977), 129-142. *Li Biaus Descouneüs* one of a body of romances establishing a folklore tradition linking fairy encounters with forests, falcons.

Baumgartner, Emmanuèle. "Les citations lyriques dans le 'Roman de la Rose' de Jean Renart." *Romance Philology* 35 (1981-2), 260-266.

Beck, Jean, ed. *Le Chansonnier Cangé, Manuscrit français no. 846 de la Bibliothèque Nationale de Paris.* Vol. 1: *Reproduction phototypique du manuscrit, description et tables.* Vol. 2: *Transcription des chansons, notes et commentaires.* Corpus Cantilenarum Medii Aevi, première série. Les Chansonniers des Troubadours et des Trouvères, numéro 1. Philadelphia: University of Pennsylvania Press, 1927. Contains facsimile of Renaut's chanson in Manuscript O.

Benson, Larry D. "The Tournament in the Romances of Chrétien de Troyes and L'Histoire de Guillaume Le Maréchal." *Chivalric Literature; Essays on Relations between Literature and Life in the Later Middle Ages.* Eds. Larry D. Benson, John Leyerle. Studies in Medieval Culture, 14. Kalamazoo: Western Michigan University, 1980, pp. 1-24.

Bidder, Wilhelm Johann Kurt. *Ergebnisse von Reimuntersuchung und Silbenzählung des altfranzösischen Artusromans "Li beaus Desconus" des Renaut von Beaujeu.* Diss. Jena 1913. Study of versification based on Foerster's collation of the Chantilly manuscript.

Bloch, R. Howard. *Etymologies and Genealogies; a Literary Anthropology of the French Middle Ages.* Chicago and London: The University of Chicago Press, 1983. Especially pp. 174-197 on the courtly romance.

Boiron, Françoise and Jean-Charles Payen. "Structures et sens du *Bel Inconnu* de Renaut de Beaujeu." *Le Moyen Age* 76 (1970), 15-26. The romance incorporates two plots, that of the quest ending in marriage and that of the love story in a fairy setting, the former to appeal to bachelor knights and the latter to women in the audience.

Bozóky, Edina. "L'Utilisation de l'analyse structurale du conte dans l'étude du roman médiéval: 'Le Bel Inconnu'." *Le Conte, pourquoi? comment?* Actes des journées en littérature orale; Analyse des contes—Problèmes de méthode, Paris, 23-26 mars 1982. Eds. G. Calame-Griaule, et al. Paris: Editions du Centre National de la Recherche Scientifique, 1984, pp. 99-112.

Brakelmann, Julius. "Die altfranzösische Liederhandschrift Nro. 389 der Stadtbibliothek zu Bern." *Herrigs Archiv für die neueren Sprachen und Literaturen* 42 (1868), 241-392. Diplomatic transcription of the song attributed to Renaut on pp. 369-70.

Braet, Herman. "Le Rêve d'amour dans le roman courtois." *Voices of Conscience: Essays on Medieval and Modern French Literature in Memory of James D. Powell and Rosemary Hodgins.* Ed. Raymond J. Cormier. Philadelphia: Temple University Press, 1977, pp. 107-118. Dream of unhappy lover related to Ovidian tradition, medieval Latin poets, troubadours, Macrobian *insomnium.*

Bruckner, Matilda Tomaryn. "Intertextuality." *The Legacy of Chrétien de Troyes.* 2 vols. Amsterdam: Rodopi, 1987, 1:224-265. How Renaut reorders and amplifies or doubles material that he takes from Chrétien. [Abbreviation: Bruckner 1987]

Bruckner, Matilda Tomaryn. *Narrative Invention in Twelfth-Century French Romance; the Convention of Hospitality 1160-1200.* French Forum Monographs, 17. Lexington, Kentucky: French Forum Publishers, 1980. Especially pp. 134-138 on the dialectic between hospitality and combat reflected in the Lampart episode.

Brugger, Ernst. "Eigennamen in den Lais der Marie de France." *Zeitschrift für Französische Sprache und Literatur* 49 (1926-27), 201-252.

Brugger, Ernst. "Der Schöne Feigling in der arthurischen Literatur." *Zeitschrift der Romanischen Literatur* 61 (1941), 1-44; 63 (1943), 123-173, 275-328; 65 (1949), 121-192, 289-343; 67 (1951), 289-298.

Busby, Keith. *Gauvain in Old French Literature.* Degré second, 2. Amsterdam: Rodopi, 1980. See pp. 246-248 on *Li Biaus Descouneüs*.

Carroll, Carleton W., ed. and tr. *Chrétien de Troyes, Erec and Enide.* Garland Library of Medieval Literature, Series A, 25. New York and London: Garland, 1987.

Carter, C. H. "Ipomedon, an Illustration of Romance Origin." *Haverford Essays; Studies in Modern Literature, prepared by some former pupils of Professor Francis B. Gummere.* Haverford, Pa., 1909, pp. 237-270. Discusses similarities between *Ipomedon* and *Li Biaus Descouneüs*, pp. 255-261.

Chandès, Gérard. "Amour, mariage et transgressions dans 'Le Bel Inconnu" à la lumière de psychologie analytique." *Amour, mariage et transgressions au moyen âge.* Actes du colloque des 24, 25, 26 et 27 mars 1983. Eds. Danielle Buschinger and André Crépin. Université de Picardie, Centre d'études médiévales. Göppingen: Kümmerle, 1984, pp. 325-333. Jungian analysis; the stages of the plot represent a process of psychological individuation.

Chandès, Gérard. "Le jeu du hasard et de la nécessité: à propos du *Bel Inconnu* de Renaut de Beaujeu." *Arturus Rex.* Vol. 2: *Acta conventus Lovaniensis 1987.* Eds. G. Tournoy and W. Van Hoecke. Leuven: Peeters, 1990. [Not available for consultation]

Chênerie, Marie-Luce. *Le Chevalier errant dans les romans arthuriens en vers des XIIe et XIIIe siècles.* Publications romanes et françaises, 172. Genève: Droz, 1986.

Colby-Hall, Alice M. "Frustration and Fulfillment; the Double Ending of the 'Bel Inconnu'." *Yale French Studies* 67 (1984), 120-134. Renaut plays on structural expectations of the medieval reader.

Colby, Alice M. "The Lips of the Serpent in the *Bel Inconnu.*" *Studia Gratulatoria: Homenaje a Robert A. Hall, Jr.* Ed. David Feldman. Madrid: Playor, 1977, pp. 111-115. Relates portrait of the serpent to canons of ideal ugliness and ideal beauty.

Colby, Alice M. *The Portrait in Twelfth-Century French Romance.* Genève: Droz, 1965.

Cormeau, Cristoph. "Zur Rekonstruktion des Leserdisposition am Beispiel des deutschen Artusromans." *Poetica. Zeitschrift für Sprach- und Literaturwissenschaft* 8 (1976), 120-133. How Wirnt von Grafenberg remodelled the structure of *Li Biaus Descouneüs.* in the *Wigalois.*

Dembowski, Peter F., ed. *Jourdain de Blaye.* Cahiers Français du Moyen Age. Paris: Champion, 1991.

Donagher, Colleen P. "Socializing the Sorceress: The Fairy Mistress Theme in *Lanval, Le Bel Inconnu,* and *Partonopeu de Blois.*" *Essays in Medieval Studies;* Proceedings of the Illinois Medieval Association, vol. 4. Chicago: The Illinois Medieval Association, 1987, pp. 69-90.

Dragonetti, Roger. *Le Gai savoir dans la rhétorique courtoise.* Paris: Seuil, 1982. Comments on Renaut's chanson, p. 65.

Ferrante, Joan. "The Education of Women in the Middle Ages in Theory, Fact, and Fantasy." *Beyond Their Sex; Learned Women of the European Past.* Ed. Patricia H. Labalme. New York and London: New York University Press, 1980, pp. 9-42; discusses *Li Biaus Descouneüs,* pp. 33-34.

Fierz-Monnier, Antoinette. *Initiation und Wandlung; zur Geschichte des altfranzösischen Romans im zwölften Jahrhundert von Chrétien de Troyes zu Renaut de Beaujeu.* Bern: Francke, 1951.

Foerster, Wendelin, ed. *Les mervelles de Rigomer.* 2 vols. Gesellschaft für romanische Literatur, 19, 39. Halle, 1908; Dresden, 1915.

Foulet, Alfred, and Mary Blakely Speer. *On Editing Old French Texts.* Lawrence: The Regents Press of Kansas, 1979. Handbook for editors of Old French texts.

Fourrier, Anthime. *Le Courant réaliste dans le roman courtois en France au moyen âge.* Vol. 1: *Les débuts (XIIe siècle)* Paris: Nizet, 1960. Discusses influence of *Partonopeu de Blois* on *Li Biaus Descouneüs*, p. 440, 447-449.

Frank, Emma. *Der Schlangenkuss; die Geschichte eines Erlösungsmotifs in deutscherin Volksdichtung.* Leipzig: H. Eichblatt, 1928.

Frappier, Jean. "Le motif du 'don contraignant' dans la littérature du moyen âge." *Travaux de linguistique et de littérature publiés par le Centre de Philologie de Strasbourg* 7 (1969), 2:7-46. Describes the custom of the rash boon.

Freeman, Michelle A. "*Fergus*: Parody and the Arthurian Tradition." *French Forum* 8 (1983), 197-215. Renaut's response to the crisis in romance narrative is to experiment by introducing elements associated with other genres.

Frescoln, Wilson Lysle. *A Study on the Old French Romance of Fergus.* Diss. Pennsylvania 1961. Contains a detailed description of Chantilly 472.

Gallais, Pierre. "Formules de conteur et interventions d'auteur dans les manuscrits de la Continuation-Gauvain." *Romania* 85 (1964), 181-229.

Gravdal, Kathryn. *Originalité et tradition littéraires chez trois épigones de Chrétien de Troyes; nouvelles approches du 'Bel Inconnu' de Renault, du 'Meraugus de Portlesguez' de Raoul de Houdenc, du 'Fergus' de Guillaume Le Clerc.* Thèse 3e cycle, Université de Paris-III 1981. Pages 59-174, 243-283 on *Li Biaus Descouneüs.*

Grigsby, John L. "The Narrator in 'Partonopeu de Blois,' 'Le Bel Inconnu' and 'Joufroi de Poitiers'." *Romance Philology* 21 (1968), 536-543.

Grimbert, Joan Tasker. "Effects of Clair-Obscur in *Le Bel Inconnu.*" *Courtly Literature: Culture and Context; Selected Papers from the 5th Triennial Congress of the International Courtly Literature Society, Dalfsen, The Netherlands, 9-16 August, 1986.* Eds. Keith Busby and Erik Kooper. Utrecht Publications in General and Comparative Literature, 25. Amsterdam and Philadelphia: John Benjamins, 1990, pp. 249-260. The original use of clair-obscure for scanning and dramatic effect is a feature that distinguishes *Li Biaus Descouneüs* from the other Fair Unknown romances.

Guerin, Victoria. "Les Masques du désir et la hantise du passé dans *Le Bel Inconnu.*" *Masques et déguisements dans la littérature médiévale.* Ed. Marie-Louise Ollier. Montréal: Presses de l'Université de Montréal; Paris: J. Vrin, 1988, pp. 55-63. The unity of the romance lies in the theme of anonymity.

Guerreau, Alain. "Renaud de Bâgé: 'Le Bel Inconnu,' structure symbolique et signification sociale." *Romania* 103 (1982), 28-82. Anthropological reading; the narrative resolves the tension between the horizontal relations among the brother knights and the vertical relation of vassal to lord.

Guthrie, Jeri Schaeffer. *'Le Bel Inconnu': A Semiotic Topography.* Diss. Illinois 1983.

Guthrie, Jeri S. "The 'Je(u)' in 'Le Bel Inconnu'; Auto-Referentiality and Pseudo-Autobiography." *Romanic Review* 75 (1984), 147-161.

Haidu, Peter. "Narrativity and Language in some XIIth Century Romances." *Yale French Studies* 51 (1975), 133-146. Semiotic analysis of the narrative patterns in *Li Biaus Descouneüs, Erec, Yvain, Floire et Blancheflor.*

Haidu, Peter. "Realism, Convention, Fictionality and the Theory of Genres in 'Le Bel Inconnu'." *L'Esprit Créateur* 12 (1972), 37-60. Renaut introduces elements from other genres, the lay and the courtly lovesong.

Hanning, Robert W. *The Individual in Twelfth-Century Romance.* New Haven and London: Yale University Press, 1977.

Harf-Lancner, Laurence. *Les Fées au moyen âge; Morgane et Mélusine; la naissance des fées.* Nouvelle bibliothèque du moyen âge, 8. Paris: Champion, 1984. Pages 331-338 on *Li Biaus Descouneüs.*

Harward, Vernon J., Jr. *The Dwarfs of Arthurian Romance and Celtic Tradition.* Leiden: E. J. Brill, 1958. Chapter 11 on Teodelain.

Henry, Albert. Critical review of Lejeune (1938). *Romania* 65 (1939), 248-253.

Heuckenkamp, Ferdinand, ed. *Le Chevalier du Papegau; nach der einzigen Pariser Handschrift.* Halle a. S.: Max Niemeyer, 1896.

Holden, A. J., ed. *Ipomedon, poème de Hue de Rotelande (fin du XIIe siècle); édité avec introduction, notes et glossaire.* Bibliothèque française et romane, 17. Paris: Klincksieck, 1979.

Holmes, Urban T. "Renaut de Beaujeu." *Romanic Review* 18 (1927), 334-336.

Huet, G. "La légende de la fille d'Hippocrate à Cos." *Bibliothèque de l'Ecole des Chartes* 79 (1918), 45-59. The legend of a woman in the shape of a dragon or serpent cited in Mandeville's *Travels.*

Jauss, Hans Robert. "Chanson de geste et roman courtois; analyse comparative du 'Fierabras' et du 'Bel Inconnu'." *Chanson de geste und Höfischer Roman; Heidelberg Kolloquium, 30 jan. 1961.* Studia Romanica, 4. Heidelberg: C. Winter, 1963, pp. 61-77; rpt. as "Epos und Roman: eine vergleichende Betrachtung an Texten des XII. Jahrhunderts (*Fierabras-Bel Inconnu*)" in *Altfranzösische Epik.* Ed. Henning Krauss. Wege der Forschung, 354. Darmstadt: Wissenschaftliche Buchgesellschaft, 1978, pp. 314-337. Generic differences that distinguish *Li Biaus Descouneüs* as an Arthurian romance from *Fierabras*, an epic.

Kelly, Douglas. "Description and Narrative in Romance: The Contextual Coordinates of *Meraugis de Portlesguez* and the *Bel Inconnu*." *Continuations, BBSIA* 42 (1990), 83-93.

Kelly, Douglas. "*Matiere* and *genera dicendi* in Medieval Romance." Yale French Studies 51 (1954), 147-159.

Kibler, William W., ed. and tr. *Chrétien de Troyes, Lancelot or, The Knight of the Cart (Le Chevalier de la Charrete).* Garland Library of Medieval Literature, Series A, 1. New York and London: Garland, 1981.

Kibler, William W. "Le Bel Inconnu,' v. 2739." *Romance Notes* 13 (1971-72), 556-560.

Köhler, Erich. *L'Aventure chevaleresque; idéal et réalité dans le roman courtois.* Paris: Gallimard, 1974. Courtly romance idealizes the political, moral, and social concepts of the period.

Kölbing, Eugen. "Zur Ueberlieferung und Quelle des mittelenglischen Gedichtes: Lybeaus Disconus." *Englische Studien* 1 (1877), 121-169.

Krappe, Alexandre Haggerty. "Guinglain chez l'enchanteresse." *Romania* 58 (1932), 426-430. Celtic sources for the enchantments visited on Guinglain by the fay.

Lecouteux, Claude. *Mélusine et le Chevalier au Cygne*. Paris: Payot, 1982. Pages 88-90 on *Li Biaus Descouneüs*.

Lecoy, Félix, ed. *Chrétien de Troyes, Le Conte du Graal (Perceval), édité d'après la copie Guiot (Bibl. nat. fr. 794)*. Classiques Français du Moyen Age, 100, 103. Paris: Champion, 1972, 1975.

Lecoy, Félix, ed. *Jean Renart, Le Roman de la Rose, ou de Guillaume de Dole*. Classiques Français du Moyen Age, 91. Paris: Champion, 1962.

Lefèvre, Sylvie. "La Première aventure de Giglan: son écriture." *Le Roman de chevalerie au temps de la Renaissance*. Ed. M. T. Jones-Davies. Centre de Recherche sur la Renaissance, 12. Paris: Jean Touzot, 1987, pp. 49-66. Onomastic reasons why Platin chose to combine *Li Biaus Descouneüs* and *Jaufre*.

Le Goff, Jacques and Emmanuel Le Roy Ladurie. "Mélusine maternelle et défricheuse." *Annales E. S. C.* 26 (1971), 587-622; rpt. in *Pour un autre moyen âge; temps, travail et culture en Occident: 18 essais*. Paris: Gallimard, 1977, pp. 307-331.The link between the legend of a creature part woman, part dragon and the founding of a dynasty.

Lejeune-Dehousse, Rita. *L'Oeuvre de Jean Renart; contribution à l'étude du genre romanesque au moyen âge*. Bibliothèque de la Faculté de Philosophie et Lettres de l'Université de Liège, fasc. 61. Paris: Droz, 1935. [Lejeune 1935]

Lejeune, Rita. *Renaut de Beaujeu, Le lai d'Ignaure ou le lai du prisonnier*. Bruxelles: Palais des Académies; Liège: Vaillant Carmanne, 1938. Argues that Renaut also composed the *Lai d'Ignaure*.

Lindvall, Lars. *Jean Renart et "Galeran de Bretagne". Etude sur un problème d'attribution de textes. Stuctures syntaxiques et structures stylistiques dans quelques romans d'aventure français*. Data Linguistica, 15. Stockholm: Almqvist & Wiksell

International, 1982. A statistical study of syntactic structures to determine attribution of *Galeran*.

Lods, Jeanne. "'Le Baiser de la Reine' et 'Le Cri de la Fée'; Etude structurale du *Bel Inconnu* de Renaut de Beaujeu." *Mélanges de langue et de littérature françaises du moyen-âge offerts à Pierre Jonin*. Senefiance, 7. Publications du CUER MA, Université de Provence. Paris: Champion, 1979, pp. 413-426. The romance divides symmetrically in two around the central adventure of the Fier Baiser, each part representing a different kind of love figured by the queen and the fairy.

Loomis, Roger Sherman. "The Fier Baiser in Mandeville's Travels; Arthurian Romance and Irish Saga." *Studi Medievali (nuova serie)* 17, fasc. 1 (1951), 104-113.

Loomis, Roger Sherman. "From Segontium to Sinadon—The Legends of a *Cité Gaste*." *Speculum* 22 (1947), 520-533; rpt. with minor changes as "Segontium, Caer Seint, and Sinadon" in *Wales and the Arthurian Legend*. Cardiff: University of Wales Press, 1956, pp. 1-18.

De Looze, Laurence. "Generic Clash, Reader Response, and the Poetics of the Non-Ending in *Le Bel Inconnu*." *Courtly Literature: Culture and Context; Selected Papers from the 5th Triennial Congress of the International Courtly Literature Society, Dalfsen, The Netherlands, 9-16 August, 1986*. Ed. Keith Busby and Erik Kooper. Utrecht Publications in General and Comparative Literature, 25. Amsterdam and Philadelphia: John Benjamins, 1990, pp.113-133. The clash of elements drawn from other genres draws attention to the play of narrative codes.

Louveau, G. *Raynaud de Beaujeu, épigone de Chrétien de Troyes*. Mémoire de licence, Université de Liège 1953. Details quotations of the *Erec, Perceval, Yvain, Lancelot* in *Li Biaus Descouneüs*.

Lozachmeur, Jean-Claude. "A propos de l'origine du nom de Mabonagrain." *Etudes celtiques* 17 (1980), 257-262.

Lozachmeur, Jean-Claude. "Guinglain et Perceval." *Etudes celtiques* 16 (1979), 279-281. Proposes onomastic equivalence between Guinglain and Perceval.

Lozachmeur, Jean-Claude. "Le problème de la transmission des thèmes arthuriens à la lumière de quelques correspondences onomastiques." *Mélanges Charles Foulon* Rennes: Institut de Français, Université de Haute-Bretagne, 1980, 1:217-225. The relationship among the names Perceval and Guinglain, and Bendigat Vran and Corbenic.

Luttrell, Claude. "The Arthurian Hunt with a White Bratchet." *Arthurian Literature* 9 (1989), 57-80.

Luttrell, Claude. *The Creation of the First Arthurian Romance: A Quest.* London: Edward Arnold; Evanston: Northwestern University Press, 1974. How Chrétien derived *Erec* and the Gauvain adventures in *Perceval* from Fair Unknown tales.

Luttrell, Claude. "Folk Legend as a Source for Arthurian Romance: The Wild Hunt." An Arthurian Tapestry; Essays in Honor of Lewis Thorpe. Ed. Kenneth Varty. Glasgow: Published on behalf of the British Branch of the International Arthurian Society . . . at the French Dept. of the University of Glasgow, 1981, pp. 83-100. Studies hunt motif in *Li Biaus Descouneüs, Lybeaus Desconus,* and *Wigalois.*

Lyons, Faith. *Les éléments descriptifs dans le roman d'aventure au XIIIe siècle.* Genève: Droz, 1965.

Malaxecheverria, I. "Deux exploits de Guinglain." *Florilegium (Carleton University Annual Papers on Classicial Antiquity and the Middle Ages)* 4 (1982), 137.

Malaxecheverria, I. "L'Hydre et le crocodile médiévaux." *Romance Notes* 21 (1980-81), 376-380. Image of fecundity and strength on queen's court dress has relationship with dragon, associated with dream world.

Margeson, Robert Ward. *A Key to Medieval Fiction: Romance and Didacticism in Le Mort Arthur and Le Bel Inconnu.* Diss. University of Toronto 1971.

Méla, Charles. *La Reine et le Graal.* Paris: Seuil, 1984. Traces the ideal of Arthurian adventure in *Li Biaus Descouneüs* and *Chevalier as deus epees* in two patterns, that of the "sister's son" and that of the "demon's son."

Ménard, Philippe. *Le Rire et le sourire dans le roman courtois en France au moyen âge (1150-1250).* Publications romanes et françaises, 105. Genève: Droz, 1969. [Ménard 1969]

Ménard, Philippe. "Les vespres du tournoiement." *Miscellanea di Studi romanzi offerta a Giuliano Gasca Queirazza.* 2 vols. Ed. Anna Cornagliotti et al. Alessandria: Edizioni dell'Orso, 1988, 2:651-662. [Ménard 1988]

Meneghetti, Maria Luisa. "Duplicazione e specularità nel romanzo arturiano (dal 'Bel Inconnu' al 'Lancelot-Graal')." *Mittelalterstudien; Erich Köhler zum Gedenken.* Ed. Henning Krauss and Deitmar Rieger. Heidelberg: Winter, 1984, pp. 206-217.

Meneghetti, Maria Luisa. "Le Mythe du héros jeune entre palingénésie et restauration." *BBSIA* 31 (1979), 291-292.

Mennung, Albert. *Der Bel Inconnu des Renaut de Beaujeu in seinem Verhältnis zum Lybaus Desconus, Carduino und Wigalois; eine littérar-historische Studie.* Halle, 1890.

Meyer, Paul and Gaston Raynaud, eds. *Le Chansonnier français de Saint-Germain-des-Prés (Bibl. Nat. fr. 20050); reproduction phototypique avec transcription.* Vol. 1: *Reproduction phototypique.* (Vol. 2 never published) Société des Anciens Textes Français, 50. Paris: Firmin Didot, 1892. Contains facsimile of Renaut's chanson in Manuscript U.

Micha, Alexandre. "Miscellaneous French Romances in Verse."
Arthurian Literature in the Middle Ages. Ed. Roger S. Loomis.
Oxford: Clarendon, 1959, pp. 358-392; 370-372 on *Li Biaus Descouneüs.*

Micha, Alexandre. *La Tradition manuscrite des romans de Chrétien de Troyes.* 2e tirage. Publications romanes et françaises, 90. Genève: Droz, 1966. Detailed description of Chantilly 472.

Mills, M. "The Huntsman and the Dwarf in *Erec* and *Libeaus Desconus.*" *Romania* 87 (1966), 33-58. The English poem offers a more accurate reflection of original episodes found in Chrétien's romance than the Old French poem does.

Mills, M., ed. *Lybeaus Desconus.* Early English Text Society, 261. Oxford: Oxford University Press, 1969.

Mills, M. "A Medieval Reviser at Work." *Medium Aevum* 32 (1963), 11-23. Compares manuscript versions of the Middle English poem.

Morris, Rosemary. "The knight and the superfluous lady: a problem of disposal." *Reading Medieval Studies* 14 (1988), 111-124.

Ollier, Marie-Louise. "The Author in the Text." *Yale French Studies* 51 (1974), 26-41.

Owen, D. D. R. "The Development of the Perceval Story." *Romania* 80 (1959), 473-492.

Owen, D. D. R. *The Evolution of the Grail Legend.* St. Andrews University Publications, 58. Edinburgh and London: Oliver & Boyd, 1968. Renaut's romance and its analogues have a common point of origin in a lost Welsh legend, a version of which survives in the *Dream of Macsen Wledig.* Chapter 5 discusses *Li Biaus Descouneüs.*

Owen, D. D. R. "The Radiance in the Grail Castle." *Romania* 83 (1962), 108-117. Brightness emanates from Blonde Esmeree as it does from the Grail maiden.

Paris, Gaston. "Etudes sur les romans de la table ronde; Guinglain ou le Bel Inconnu." *Romania* 15 (1886), 1-24; rpt. of article in *Histoire littéraire de la France* 30:171-199.

Paton, Lucy Allen. *Studies in the Fairy Mythology of Arthurian Romance*. Radcliffe College Monographs, 13. Boston: Athenaeum, 1903.

Perret, Michèle. "Atemporalités et effet de fiction dans le *Bel Inconnu.*" *Le nombre du temps en hommage à Paul Zumthor.* Nouvelle Bibliothèque du Moyen Age, 12. Paris: Champion, 1988, pp. 225-235. Metaleptic quality of Renaut's narrative characterized by techniques that disrupt linear progression of plot. [Perret 1988b]

Perret, Michèle. *Le Signe et la mention; adverbes embrayeurs ci, ça, la, ilvec en moyen français (XIVe-XVe siècles).* Publications romanes et françaises, 185. Genève: Droz, 1988. [Perret 1988a]

Philipot, Emmanuel. "Un épisode d'Erec et d'Enide: La joie de la cour— Mabon l'enchanteur." *Romania* 25 (1896), 258-294. Similarities between *Erec* and *Li Biaus Descouneüs.*

Picot, Emile. "Le Duc d'Aumale et la Bibliothèque de Chantilly." *Bulletin du bibliophile et du bibliothécaire* (1897), 305-348. Traces history of the collection at Chantilly.

Pioletti, Antonio. *La Forma del racconto arturiano; 'Peredur,' 'Perceval,' 'Bel Inconnu,' 'Carduino'.* Romanica Neapolitana, 16. Napoli: Liguori, 1984. Analyzes evolution in use of Celtic myth that reflects affirmation of courtly society and crisis in feudal system.

Rayna, P., ed. "I Cantari di Carduino." *Poemetti Cavallereschi.* Bologna, 1873, pp. 1-44.

Roach, William, ed. *The Continuations of the Old French Perceval of Chrétien de Troyes.* Vol. 1: *The First Continuation, Redaction of Mss T V D.* Vol 2: *The First Continuation, Redaction of Mss E M Q U.* Vol. 3: *The First Continuation, Redaction of Mss A L P R S.* Vol. 4: *The Second Continuation.* Philadelphia: University of Pennsylvania Press, 1949; University of Pennsylvania, Dept. of Romance Languages, 1950; The American Philosophical Society, 1952, 1971.

Roussel, Claude. "Point final et points de suspension; la fin incertaine du 'Bel Inconnu'." *Le Point Final; actes du colloque international de Clermont-Ferrand.* Clermont-Ferrand: Association des Publications de la Faculté des lettres et sciences humaines de Clermont-Ferrand, 1984, pp. 19-34. Singularity of Renaut's conjointure is repeatedly to refuse to end and thus suspend the *dénouement.*

Saran, F. "Ueber Wirnt von Grafenberg und den Wigalois." *Beiträge zur Geschichte der deutschen Sprache und Literatur* 21 (1896), 253-420. Discusses the relationship between *Li Biaus Descouneüs* and *Wigalois.*

Schmolke-Hasselmann, Beate. "Der französische Artusroman in Versen nach Chrétien de Troyes." *Deutsche Vierteljahrsschrift für Literaturwissenschaft und Geistegeschichte* 57 (1983), 415-430.

Schmolke-Hasselmann, Beate. *Der arthurische Versroman von Chrestien bis Froissart; zur Geschichte einer Gattung.* Beihefte zur Zeitschrift für romanische Philologie, Band 177. Tübingen: Max Niemeyer Verlag, 1980. Various developments in Arthurian verse romance after Chrétien.

Schofield, William Henry. *Studies on 'Libeaus Desconus'.* Harvard Studies and Notes in Philology and Literature, 4. Boston, 1896. Lists similar passages in the *Erec* and *Li Biaus Descouneüs.*

Scully, Terence. "*Le Bel Inconnu*: an Anti-Tristan." Unpublished talk given at the annual convention of the Modern Language Association, 28 December, 1979, San Francisco. Deliberate parallels with the *Roman de Tristan* suggest a response to the Tristan story.

Segre, Cesare. "What Bakhtine Left Unsaid: The Case of the Medieval Romance." *Romance: Generic Transformation from Chrétien de Troyes to Cervantes.* Ed. Kevin Brownlee and Marina Scordilis Brownlee. Hanover and London: Published for Dartmouth College by University Press of New England, 1985, pp. 23-46.

Sinclair, Keith V. "Le gué périlleux dans la 'Chanson de Saisnes'." *Zeitschrift für französische Sprache und Literatur* 97 (1987), 68-72. Compares the perilous ford episode in *Saisnes, Lai de l'Epine, Li Biaus Descouneüs,* and *Didot Perceval.*

Steible, Marianne. *Strukturuntersuchungen zum altfranzösischen Versroman des 12. und 13. Jahrhunderts.* Diss. Ruprecht-Karl-Universität, Heidelberg 1968.

Stone, Louise W. "Un proverbe au moyen âge: Force paist le pré." *Zeitschrift für romanische Philologie* 73 (1957), 145-159.

Sturm, Sara. "The *Bel Inconnu's* Enchantress and the Intent of Renaut de Beaujeu." *French Review* 44 (1971), 862-869. Renaut humanizes the fairy in order to underscore the conflict between the two love-interests. [Sturm 1971a]

Sturm, Sara. "The Love Interest in *Le Bel Inconnu*: Innovation in the Roman Courtois." Forum for Modern Language Studies 7 (1971), 241-248. Renaut combines two types of narrative, the aventure of the Fier Baiser and the story of the fairy mistress. [Sturm 1971b]

Sturm, Sara. "Magic in *Le Bel Inconnu.*" *L'Esprit Créateur* 12 (1972), 19-25. Magic lends a general atmosphere of mystery and also enhances the status of the fairy as supernaturally desirable. [Sturm 1972]

Thomas, J. W., tr. *Wigalois, The Knight of Fortune's Wheel,* by Wirnt von Grafenberg. Lincoln and London: University of Nebraska Press, 1977.

Thorpe, Lewis. "L'*Yvain* de Chrétien de Troyes et le jeu des topoi." *Oeuvres et Critique* 5,2 (1982), 73-80.

Tuck, J. P. *A Study of the Structure and Spirit of Selected Thirteenth-Century French Verse Romances: 'Le Bel Inconnu,' 'Meraugis de Portlesguez,' 'La Vengeance Raguidel,' 'L'Atre Perilleux,' 'Durmart le Galois,' 'Claris et Laris'.* Diss. University of Manchester 1978.

Tyssens, Madeleine. "Les Sources de Renaut de Beaujeu." *Mélanges Jean Frappier.* 2 vols. Genève: Droz, 1970, 2:1043-1055. Challenges the validity of the notion of hypothetical prototypes in determining the relation among existing Fair Unknown texts.

Tyssens, Madeleine. "Une si granz clartez." Le Moyen Age 69 (1963), 299-313.

Vesce, Thomas E., tr. *The Marvels of Rigomer (Les Mervelles de Rigomer).* Garland Library of Medieval Literature, Series B, 60. New York and London: Garland, 1988.

Vinaver, Eugène, ed. *Malory: Works.* Oxford, New York, Toronto, Melbourne: Oxford University Press, 1971.

Weill, Isabelle. "Le jardin de la fée dans *Le Bel Inconnu* de Renaut de Beaujeu." *Sénéfiance.* Aix: CUER MA, Université de Provence, 1991. [Unavailable for consultation]

West, G. D. "The Descriptions of Towns in Old French Verse Romances." *French Studies* 11 (1957), 50-59. [West 1957]

West, G. D. "Gerbert's *Continuation de Perceval* (ll. 1528-1543) and the Sparrow-Hawk Episode." *BBSIA* 7 (1955), 79-87. Detail of defending champion's lady being ugly not necessarily taken from *Li Biaus Descouneüs.*

Westoby, Kathryn S. "A New Look at the Role of the Fée in Medieval French Arthurian Romance." *The Spirit of the Court; Selected Proceedings of the Fourth Congress of the International Courtly Literature Society, Toronto, 1983*. Eds. Glyn S. Burgess, Robert A Taylor. Cambridge: Brewer, 1985, pp. 373-385.

Whiting, B. J. "The *Hous of Fame* and Renaud de Beaujeu's *Li Biaus Descouneüs*." *Modern Philology* 31 (1933-34), 196-198. Fame's castle features niches sheltering jesters and minstrels.

Wilson, Robert H. "The Fair Unknown in Malory." *Publications of the Modern Language Association* 58 (1943), 1-21.

Woledge, Brian. *Commentaire sur Yvain (Le Chevalier au lion) de Chrétien de Troyes*. 2 vols. Publications romanes et françaises, 170, 186. Genève: Droz, 1986, 1988.

Wrede, Hilmar. *Die Fortsetzer des Gralromans Christians von Troyes*. Diss. Göttingen 1952. Relationships between Chrétien's *Perceval* and its prose and verse continuations.

Webster, Kenneth G. T., tr. *Ulrich von Zatzikhoven, Lanzelet; a Romance of Lancelot*. Revised and provided with additional notes and an introduction by Roger Sherman Loomis. Records of Civilization, Sources and Studies, 47. New York: Columbia University Press, 1951.

Winters, Margaret, ed. *The Romance of Hunbaut: An Arthurian Poem of the Thirteenth Century*. Davis Medieval Texts and Studies, 4. Leiden: Brill, 1984. Contains a detailed description of the Chantilly manuscript, pp. xi-xiv.

Zumthor, Paul. *Essai de poétique médiévale*. Paris: Seuil, 1972. Discusses resemblance between Renaut's romance and a chanson d'amour p. 343.

Zumthor, Paul. *Langue, texte, énigme*. Paris: Seuil, 1975.

Zumthor, Paul. *La Poésie et la voix. dans la civilisation médiévale*
    Collège de France, Essais et conférences. Paris: Presses
    Universitaires de France, 1984. Renaut's prologue cites voice
    itself (the chanson) as an inspiration to write, p. 34.

Li Biaus Descouneüs
(The Fair Unknown)

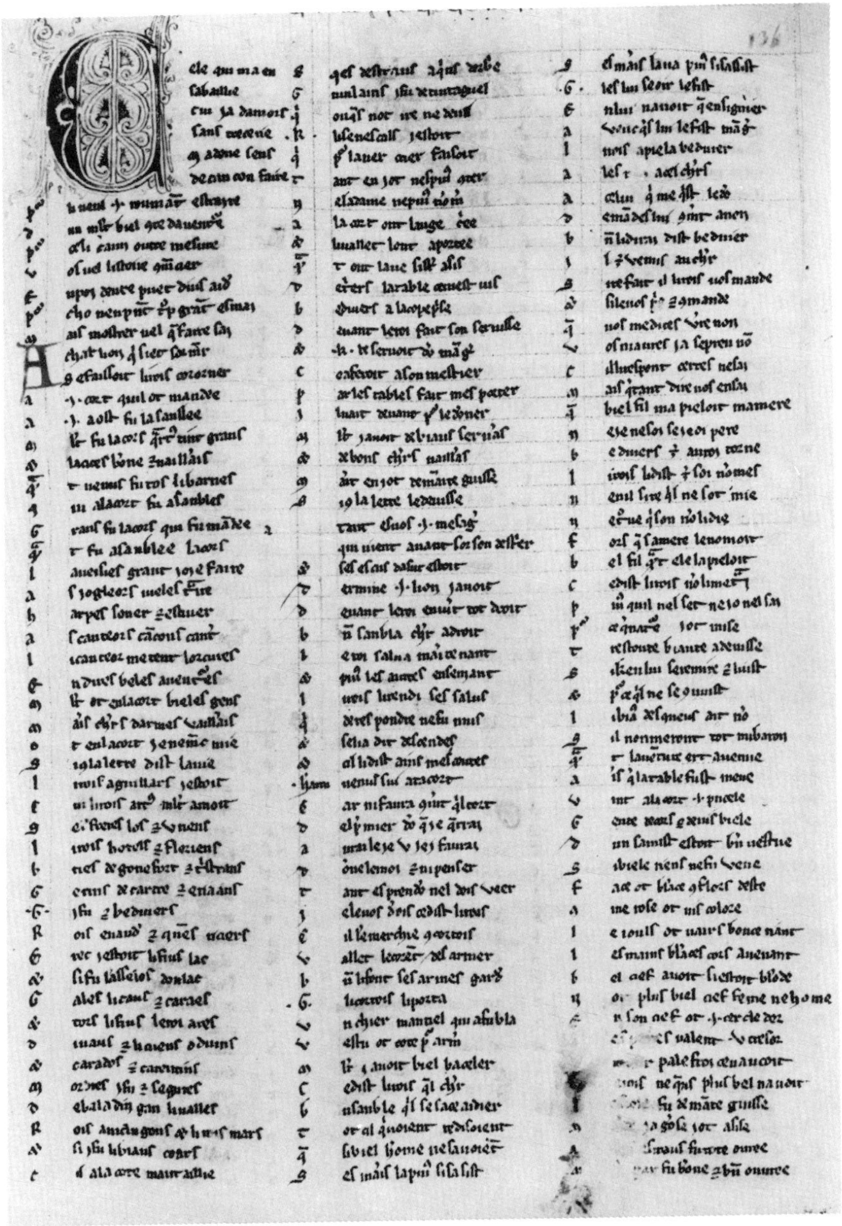

Chantilly 472, f. 136 recto
(Courtesy of the Musée Condé)

LI BIAUS DESCOUNEÜS

1   Cele qui m'a en sa baillie,   [*134 r°a*]
       cui ja d'amors sans trecerie
       m'a doné sens de cançon faire—
4   por li veul un roumant estraire
       d'un molt biel conte d'aventure.
       Por celi c'aim outre mesure
       vos vel l'istoire comencier.
8   En poi d'eure puet Dius aidier;
       por cho n'en prenc trop grant esmai,
       mais mostrer vel que faire sai.

       A Charlion, qui siet sor mer,
12   se faissait li rois coroner
       a une cort qu'il ot mandee.
       A un aost fu s'asanllee.
       Molt fu la cors qu'Artus tint grans
16   et la cités bonne et vaillains.
       Quant venus fu tos li barnés
       qui a la cort fu asanblés,
       grans fu la cors qui fu mandee.
20   Quant la cors [i] fu asanblee,
       la veïsiés grant joie faire:
       as jogleors vïeles traire,
       harpes soner et estiver,
24   as canteors cançons canter.
       Li canteor metent lor cures
       en dire beles aventures.
       Molt ot en la cort bieles gens;
28   mains chevaliers d'armes vaillains
       ot en la cort; je ne menc mie,
       si con la letre dist la vie.
       Li rois Aguillars i estoit,

12 cororner
20 Q. f. a. la c. [-*l*]
26 dires

THE FAIR UNKNOWN

For my sovereign lady I have written and sung
of a love that knows no falsehood,
according to the direction she gave.
4   Now I wish to compose a romance for her
from a beautiful tale of adventure.
And for her whom I love beyond any power to measure
I shall now begin this story for you.
8   God can swiftly lend His aid to mortals,
and so I am not greatly troubled at my task,
but wish to show you what I can do.

At Caerlion, which is by the sea,
12   King Arthur had himself crowned
at a court he held there.
The gathering was in the month of August.
Arthur's court was a very great one,
16   and the city beautiful and worthy.
When all the noble lords
had assembled at the court,
great indeed was the gathering.
20   When the court was assembled,
you could have seen great merriment there:
jongleurs playing their fiddles,
their harps and their pan-pipes,
24   and singers singing their songs.
These singers took great pains
to tell of fine adventures.
There were many fine people at the court,
28   and many knights who had proven themselves in arms
were there; I am not speaking lies,
just as the story tells the truth.
King Aguillar was there,

32   cui li rois Artus molt amoit,
        ses freres Los et Uriens,
        li rois Horels et Floriens,
        Briés de Gonefort et Tristrans,
36   Gerins de Cartre et Eriaans.
        Gavains i fu et Beduiers,
        rois Enauder et quens Riciers;
        Erec i estoit, li fius Lac,
40   et s'i fu Lansselos dou Lac,
        Gales li Caus et Caraés,
        et Tors, li fius le roi Arés,
        Dinaus et li cuens Oduïns,
44   et Carados et Carentins;
        Mordrés i fu et Segurés,
        de Baladingan li Vallés,
        rois Amangons et li rois Mars,
48   et si i fu li Biaus Coars,
        Cil a la Cote Mautaillie
        et Qes d'Estraus, Aquins d'Orbrie;   [*134 r °b*]
        Guinlains i fui de Tintaguel,
52   qui onques n'ot ire ne deull;
        Kes li senescals i estoit,
        qui por laver crier faisoit.
        Tant en i ot ne.s puis conter
56   ne l[es] dame[s] ne puis nonmer.
        A la cort ont l'auge criee
        et li vallet l'ont aportee.
        Quant ont lavé, si sont asis
60   detriers la table, ce m'est vis.
        Beduiers a la cope prise,
        devant le roi fait son servisse;
        et Kes reservoit dou mangier:
64   ço aferoit a son mestier.
        Par les tables fait mes porter:
        il vait devant por lé donner.
        Molt i avoit de biaus servans
68   et de bons chevaliers vaillans;

56 la dame [*em. Williams*]

32 a man most dear to King Arthur,
as well as his brothers Lot and Urien,
King Horel and Florien,
Briet of Gonefort and Tristan,
36 Gerin of Chartres and Eriaan.
Gawain was there, as well as Bedevere,
King Enauder and Count Richard;
Erec son of Lac was there,
40 and Lancelot of the Lake,
Galet the Bald and Caraés
and Tors, son of King Aret,
Dinal and Count Oduin
44 and Caradoc and Carentin;
Mordred was there, and so was Segures,
and the Knight of Baladingan,
as well as King Amangon and King Mark;
48 the Fair Coward was there,
along with the Knight of the Ill-fitting Tunic,
Kay of Estraut and Aquin of Orbrie;
from Tintagel had come Guinlain,
52 who never knew anger or sorrow;
Kay the Seneschal was there, who always decided
when water was to be called for before dinner.
There were so many that I cannot count them
56 or name the ladies that were there.
Water was called for at the court,
and young men brought it.
When all had washed, they sat down
60 at the table, I believe.
Bedevere took the cup, performing
his accustomed service for the king,
and Kay saw that the meal was served,
64 for such was his duty.
He had dishes brought to the tables,
and went before to serve them.
There were many handsome servants
68 and many fine and worthy knights,

maint en i ot de mainte guisse,
si con la letre le devisse.

    A tant es vos un mesagier
72   qui vient avant sor son destrier,
et ses escus d'asur estoit;
d'ermine un lion i avoit.
Devant le roi en vint tot droit.
76   Bien sanbla chevalier a droit:
le roi salua maintenant
et puis les autres ensemant.
Li rois li rendi ses salus,
80   qui de respondre ne fu mus,
et se li a dit, "Descendés."
Et cil li dist, "Ains m'escoutés.
Hartu, venus sui a ta cort
84   car n'i faura, coment qu'il tort,
del premier don que je querrai.
Avrai le je u je i faurai?
Donne le moi et n'i penser:
88   tant es preudon, ne.l dois veer!"
"Je le vos doins," ce dist li rois.
Cil l'en merchie con cortois.
Vallet le corent desarmer;
92   bien li font ses armes garder.
Gavains li cortois li porta
un chier mantiel qu'i[l] afubla;
vestu ot cote por armer:
96   molt i avoit biel baceler.
Ce dist li rois: "Quel chevalier!
B[ie]n sanble qu'il se sace aidier."
Tot cil qui.[l] voient redisoient
100   que si biel homme ne savoient.
Ses mains la[va] puis si s'assist.   *[134 r °c]*
Gavains les lui seoir le fist.

---

94 qui a.
99 qui v.
101 *line repeated at top of column c* ; s. m. la p. s'i s'a.

all manner of them and in great number,
so the written word says.

        Suddenly a messenger appeared before them,
72   riding forward on his charger,
        and his shield was azure
        with a lion of ermine blazoned on it.
        He rode right up to the king.
76   He seemed to be all that a knight should be:
        first he greeted the king
        and then all the rest of the company.
        The king returned his greetings,
80   not answering him with silence,
        and said, "Please dismount."
        The other said, "Hear me first. King Arthur,
        now that I have come to your court
84   I surely cannot fail to receive the first boon
        I ask of you, whatever may be the result.
        Shall I have my request or not?
        Grant it to me without thinking on the matter:
88   a king of your merit should not fail to do so."
        "I grant it to you," said the king.
        The other thanked him like a well-bred knight.
        Young men hastened to disarm him;
92   they saw to it that his arms were well looked after.
        The courtly Gawain then brought
        a fine cloak, which he then put on
        over the short tunic he was wearing.
96   Thus arrayed he was a handsome young man indeed.
        The king said, "What a fine knight!
        I think him a man who can give a good account of himself."
        All those who saw him readily agreed
100   that they knew of no man so fair as he.
        The knight washed his hands,
        and Gawain had him sit down beside him.

En lui n'avoit que ensignier;
104   aveucques lui le fist mangier.
Li rois apiela Beduier:
"Alés [tost] a cel chevalier,
a celui qui me quist le don;
108   demandés lui coment a non."
"Bien li dirai," dist Beduier.
Il est venus au chevalier.
"Sire," fait il, "li rois vos mande
112   et si le vos prie et comande
que vos me dites vostre non.
Vos n'i avrés ja se preu non."
Cil li respont, "Certes, ne sai
116   mais que tant dire vos en sai
que 'biel fil' m'apieloit ma mere,
ne je ne soi se je oi pere."
Beduiers est au roi torné[s].
120   Li rois li dist, "Est soi nonmés?"
"Nenil, sire, qu'il ne sot mie,
ne trove qui son non li die
fors que sa mere le nomoit
124   'bel fil' quant ele l'apieloit."
Ce dist li rois, "Non li metrai
puis qu'il ne.l set ne jo ne.l sai.
Por ce que Nature i ot mise
128   trestoute biauté a devisse
si k'en lui se remire et luist,
et por ce qu'il ne se conuist,
li Biaus Descouneüs ait non,
132   si.l nonmeront tot mi baron."
    Quant l'aventure ert avenue,
ains que la table fust meüe
vint a la cort une pucele
136   gente de cors et de vis biele.
D'un samist estoit bien vestue;
si biele riens ne fu veüe.

---

106 *word erased* [*em.Williams*], chevaliers
119 torné

There was nothing crude about the knight's behavior;

104 Gawain had him eat with him, from his own dish.

The king then summoned Bedevere,
"Go now to that knight
who requested the boon of me

108 and ask his name."

"Gladly, my lord," said Bedevere.
He went straight to the knight.
"My lord," he said, "the king has sent me

112 with the request that
you tell me your name.
You will only gain by doing so."
The other answered, "Truly, I cannot,

116 except to tell you
that my mother used to call me 'fair son';
I do not know if I have a father."
Bedevere went back to the king,

120 who said, "Did he tell you his name?"
"No, my lord, he has no idea what his name may be
nor can he find anyone who can tell him what it is.
He knows only that his mother called him

124 'fair son' when she spoke to him."
The king said, "I shall give him a name,
since neither he nor I know what his true name is.
Because Nature has bestowed on him

128 such perfect beauty
that she sees in him her own shining image,
and because he does not know who he is,
let him be named the Fair Unknown;

132 so shall all my knights call him."
Soon after this adventure,
before the tables had been removed,
there arrived at the court a maiden

136 who was lovely of form and face.
She was beautifully dressed in samite;
So lovely a creature had never been seen.

Face ot blance con flors d'esté,
140   come rose ot vis coloré;
le[s] iouls ot vairs, bouce riant,
les mains blances, cors avenant.
Bel cief avoit, si estoit blonde—
144   n'ot plus biel cief feme ne home.
En son cief ot un cercle d'or;
[l]es p[ier]es valent un tresor.
[Un] v[ai]r palefroi cevauçoit;
148   [ne] rois ne quens plus bel n'avoit.
L[a] sele fu de mainte guisse:
m[ainte] jagonse i ot asise;
a [cier]s esmaus fu tote ovree.
152   Molt par fu bonne et bien ouvree.
Coverte fu d'un drap de soie.   [*134 v°a*]
De[l] lorainn por coi vos diroie?
A fin or fu a cieres pieres,
156   et li frains et les estrivieres.
Ensanble li aloit uns nains
ki n'ert pas ne fols ne vilains,
ains ert cortois et bien apris.
160   Gent ot le cors et biel le vis;
plus male tece en lui n'avoit
fors seul tant que petis estoit.
Roube ot de vair et d'eskerlate:
164   molt ert li nains de grant barate.
Sa robe estoit a sa mesure;
molt i ot bele creature.
Li nains une corgie avoit
168   de coi le palefroi caçoit
que cevauçoit la damoissele.
Devant le roi vint la pucele,
molt le salua sinplement

---

141 le
146 *First letter and middle of second word obliterated* [em. *Williams*]
147 *First word, middle of second word obliterated* [em. *Williams*]
148-151 *Words obliterated* [em. *Williams*]
154 De l.

Her face was fair as a summer flower,
140   her cheek the color of the rose;
she had shining eyes and a smiling mouth,
fair white hands and a charming appearance.
She had beautiful fair hair —
144   no man or woman ever had lovelier.
On her head was a golden circlet,
whose stones were worth a king's ransom.
She rode a grey palfrey
148   as beautiful as that of any king or count.
The saddle was most richly worked:
it was studded with rubies and
covered with costly enamel.
152   It was a very good one, and beautifully made.
It was covered with a silken cloth.
Why should I describe the breast-strap to you?
It was adorned with fine gold and precious stones,
156   as were the reins and the stirrups.
There was a dwarf with her
who was neither a fool nor a lout,
but instead was courtly and well mannered.
160   He was fair of both form and face;
indeed, there was no flaw in him
except that he was little.
He wore a robe of scarlet lined with miniver.
164   The dwarf's appearance was elegant indeed.
His robe was tailored to his size,
and he cut a very handsome figure.
He carried a whip
168   with which he drove the horse
the maiden was riding.
She rode up to the king
and greeted him graciously,

172   et ses conpaignons ensement;
       et li rois son salu li rent,
       molt li respondi bonnement.
       Ço disoit la pucele au roi,
176   "Artus," fait ele, "entent a moi.
       La fille au roi Gringras te mande
       salus, si te prie et demande
       secors, qu'ele en a grant mestier.
180   Ne li estuet c'un chevalier;
       uns chevaliers le secorra.
       Por Diu, gentis rois, secor la!
       Molt a painne, molt a dolor,
184   molt est entree en grant tristor.
       Envoie li tel chevalier
       qui bien li puisse avoir mestier,
       trestot le millor que tu as.
188   Por Diu te prie, ne targe pas!
       Lasse! con ma dame a dolor!
       Certes, molt avroit grant honnor
       icil qui de mal l'estordroit
192   et qui le Fier Baissier feroit.
       Mais pros que il li a mestier;
       onques n'ot tel a chevalier.
       Ja mauvais hom le don ne quiere:
196   tost en giroit envers en biere."
       La pucele avoit non Helie,
       qui por sa dame quiert aïe.
       Li rois esgarde et atendoit
200   qui le don li demanderoit;
       mais n'i trove demandeor,
       car n'i ot nul qui n'ot paor
       que il aler ne li comant.
204   N'i a celui qui.n ait talent
       ne mais li Biaus Descouneüs.   [134 v°b]
       Quant il s'en est aperceüs,
       isnelement en pié leva
208   et devant le roi s'en ala.

---

188 ne *repeated*

172 as well as those with him;
   and the king returned her greeting,
   answering with great courtesy.
   The maiden then said to the king,
176 "Hear me, King Arthur.
   The daughter of King Guingras sends you
   her greetings and most heartily requests
   your aid, for she has great need of it.
180 She needs but one knight
   a single one will be able to help her.
   In God's name, noble king, send her this help!
   She is plunged in suffering and sorrow,
184 overwhelmed by sadness.
   Send her a knight
   such as she needs,
   the very best one that you have.
188 I beg you, in God's name, do not delay!
   Alas for my lady, what great sorrow is hers!
   In truth, the one who rescues her from her plight
   and accomplishes the Fearsome Kiss
192 will win great honor.
   But he must be a worthy knight.
   Indeed, no man ever had such need of valor!
   No worthless man should ask this boon,
196 for he would soon lie in his grave."
   The maiden who thus sought help for her lady
   was named Helie.
   The king watched and waited
200 to see who would ask to go with the maiden;
   but no one came forward;
   indeed, there was no knight who was not afraid
   that the king might command him to go.
204 None had any taste for it,
   save only the Fair Unknown.
   When he saw how matters stood,
   he quickly rose
208 and went before the king.

"Sire," fait il, "mon don vos quier:
je vel aler ma dame aidier.
Mon don vel ore demander:
212   au secors faire veul aler."
Ce dist li rois, "El me quesis:
trop estes jovenes, biaus amis;
trop t'i esteveroit pener.
216   Mius te vient ci en pais ester."
Cil li respont eneslespas,
"Par le covent que tu m'en as,
te quier le don que m'as proumis.
220   Raisson feras, ce m'est avis:
rois es, si ne dois pas mentir
ne couvent a nului faillir."
Ce dist li rois, "Don[c] i alés
224   puis qu'estes si entalentés.
Je vos redoins un autre don:
je vos retie[n]g a conpaignon
et met en la Table Reonde."
228   Ne pot müer que ne responde
la pucele, et dist, "Non fera!
Ja par mon cief o moi n'ira!
Jo t'avoie quis le millor
232   et tu m'as donné le pïor,
que tu ne ses se vaut nïent!
Jo n'ai cure de tel present:
trop est jovenes li chevaliers.
236   Des millors vel et des plus fiers,
que de cestui ne vel je mie;
tel qui soit de chevalerie
esprovés et de millor los,
240   si laissiés cestui a repos."
Ce dist li rois, "Suer, biele amie,
covent li ot, n'i faura mie.
Jo li a proumis vraiement,

223 dont
224 estens
226 retieg

"My lord," he said, "I now make my request of you:
I wish to go to the aid of this lady.
Now I ask that you grant me this boon:
212   I wish to go to her rescue."
The king said, "Ask for something else.
You are too young, my dear friend,
and this would exact too much from you.
216   It would be much better for you to remain here in safety."
The other answered the king at once,
"By the agreement you made with me,
I now ask for what you have promised.
220   To my mind you will be doing right to grant me this,
for you are a king, and so should never speak falsely
or fail to keep faith with anyone."
The king said, "You shall go, then,
224   since you have set your heart on it.
And I will grant you something more:
I hereby retain you as my knight
and make you a companion of the Round Table."
228   The maiden could not keep silent at this
and said, "He shall not go!
I swear that this man shall not go with me!
I asked for your best knight
232   and you have given me your worst.
You do not know if this man is worth anything at all!
I do not want such a gift as this:
this knight is too young.
236   I want only the best and the most daring,
and I will not accept this man;
I want only a proven knight
of the highest reputation;
240   as for this fellow, let him stay where he is."
The king said,"Sister, dear friend,
I have given him my word and will not break it.
Indeed I made him a promise

244 se li tenrai sans fausement.
 Rois sui, si ne doi pas mentir
 ne couve[n]t a nului faillir."
 Et la pucele en haut s'escrie,
248 "De cort m'en vois come faillie!
 Dehé ait la Table Reonde
 et cil qui sïent a l'esponde
 qui le secors ne veulent faire!
252 Ha! doce dame debonaire,
 de secors point ne vos amain.
 N'est mervelle se je me plain,
 qu'Artus ne vos secorra mie,
256 ains i sui bien de tot faillie.
 Nains, ralons ent," dist la pucele.   *[134 v°c]*
 De cort s'en part la damoisele;
 molt s'en va tost ele et li nains
260 qui avoit non Tidogolains.
 Quant de cort aler l'a veüe,
 n'a mie la parole mue
 que ses armes porter comande;
264 et si tost con il les demande,
 Gavains lor li fist aporter.
 Isnelement se fait armer:
 ses cauces lace, l'auberc vest,
268 et en son cief son el[me] trest;
 puis est montés en son destrier.
 Gavains li baille un escuier;
 son escu li porte et sa lance.
272 Dius li aït par sa puissance!
 Quant del roi a le congié pris
 et des autres, ce m'est avis,
 de la cort ist, molt tost s'en vait;
276 del don qu'il a grant joie fait.
 Li escuiers ot non Robers;
 molt estoit sages et apers.
 Poignant s'en vont par la vacele,
280 qu'ataindre veulent la pucele.

246 couvet

244   and will hold fast to it without falsehood.
        For I am a king and should never speak untruthfully
        or fail to keep faith with anyone."
        Then the maiden cried out,
248   "I am leaving this court without what I came for!
        A curse on the Round Table
        and those who sit around it,
        who do not wish to lend their aid!
252   Alas! my sweet and gentle lady,
        I bring no help to you.
        It is surely no wonder if I complain,
        for King Arthur will not help you,
256   and I have failed in all I set out to do."
        She said to the dwarf, "Let us leave this place."
        She left the court
        at all speed with her the dwarf,
260   whose name was Tidogolain.
        Even when he saw her leaving,
        the knight did not change his mind,
        but asked for his arms;
264   and no sooner had he done so
        than Gawain had them brought in.
        The knight had himself quickly armed.
        He laced his leggings and put on
268   his hauberk and his helmet,
        then mounted his charger.
        Gawain gave him a squire,
        who took his shield and lance.
272   Now may God lend him His powerful aid!
        When he had taken leave of the king
        and, I believe, the others there as well,
        he left the court, riding at a gallop
276   and rejoicing that his boon had been granted.
        The squire was named Robert,
        and he was a very bright and able fellow.
        Spurring their horses, they rode through the dale,
280   trying to catch up with the maiden.

Li Descouneüs se hasta;
tant acorut qu'atainte l'a.
Ele retorne, si le vit.
284   "U alés vos?" ce li a dit.
"Je vel aveuques vos aler.
Tant ne me deüssiés blamer
des tant que seüssiés por coi.
288 ⸱ Aiés merchi, biele, de moi."
Et la pucele li respont,
"Par celui qui forma le mont,
ja par mon gré o moi n'irés.
292   Sor mon pois venir i p[o]és
Trop vos voi jone baceler;
por ce ne vos i vel mener,
que vos ne.l poriés soufrir
296   ne tant durs estors maintenir
con vos i converroit a faire.
Vos n'en poriés a cief traire.
Mius vos en vient torner ariere.
300   Car le faites, p[a]r ma proiere!"
Et cil maintenant li respont,
"Damoissele, por rien del mont
je ne retorneroie mie
304   tant qu'ens el cors aie la vie.
Des que cest secors aie fait,
nen torneroie por nul plait."
Ce dist li nai[n]s, "Car le menés,
308   damoissele, se vos volés.
On ne doit ome blamer mie   [135 r°a]
dusc'on sace sa coardie.
Tel tient on vil que c'est folor,
312   que Dius donne puis grant honnor.
En cestui a biel chevalier.

287 D. que t. [+*1*]
292 paes
300 por
307 d. li nais l. n.
310 *Scribe corrects* corrdie *to* coardi

The Fair Unknown hurried
until he had overtaken her.
She turned and saw him.
284   "And where might you be going?" she said.
"I intend to go with you," he replied.
"You should not speak so ill of me
unless you have reason to do so.
288   Take pity on me, my fair one."
And the maiden answered,
"By Him Who made the world,
you shall not go with me if I have my way.
292   If you do so, it will be much against my will.
You look much too young to me,
and so I do not wish to take you with me,
for you could not endure this adventure
296   nor win such harsh combats
as you would be forced to undergo.
You could not accomplish what is necessary.
You would do better to turn back.
300   Please do so now, I beg you!"
The other answered her at once,
"Lady, I would not turn back
for anything in the world
304   as long as I have life left in my body.
No plea would make me turn back
until I have rendered aid to your lady."
Then the dwarf said, "Bring him,
308   my lady, if you are willing.
No man should be disparaged
until he has proven his cowardice.
One may foolishly take as worthless
312   a man to whom God later grants great honor.
This man looks like a fine knight.

Se Dius li en donne aïdier,
bien porroit estre de valor
316   au de par Diu le Creator."
Mais la pucele ançois li prie
qu'il s'en retort. Cil ne.l croit mie,
ai[n]s veut adiés avant aler:
320   coardie ne velt penser.
Or cevaucent, grant oirre vont.
Tant ont alé qu'a un gué sont
c'on claimme le Gué Perilleus:
324   li pasages est dolereus.
Sor la rive virent del gué,
de l'autre part, en mi le pré,
une biele loge galesce
328   qui fu faite de rainme fresse.
Un escu ot a l'uis devant;
li ciés fu d'or, li piés d'argent.
En la loge ot un chevalier
332   qui se faisoit esbanoier
a dous vallés a ju d'eskas.
Entr'els demainnent grans esbas.
Ensi atendoit s'aventure.
336   Maint chevalier l'ont trové dure
que il avoit ocis al gué;
molt estoit plains de cruauté.
Bli[o]blïeris avoit non.
340   Molt ot le cuer fier et felon;
millor chevalier ne vit nus.
As vallés a dit, "Levés sus!
Amenés moi tost mon destrier
344   c'or voi venir un chevalier,
et mes armes, si m'armerai.

318 retorne [+*1*, *em. Williams*]
319 Ais
325 vinrent
328 fait [-*1*]
334 esgas [*em. Williams*]
339 Bliblerieris

If God wishes to aid him,
he may indeed prove worthy
316   by the grace of God the Creator."
But the maiden still urged the knight
to turn back. He did not heed her warnings,
but rather insisted that he would ride on,
320   for he would never think of behaving like a coward.
        Then they rode on at a rapid pace
until they reached a place
that was known as the Perilous Ford.
324   Crossing this ford had brought grief to many.
On the other side
they saw, in the middle of a meadow,
a good Welsh hut
328   made of fresh branches.
A shield was leaning against the door;
the top part of it was of gold, the bottom of silver.
Inside the hut a knight
332   was amusing himself
by playing chess with two young men.
They were greatly enjoying their game.
Thus the knight awaited whatever adventure might come
        along.
336   Many knights whom he had killed
at the ford had found this adventure harsh indeed;
he was a most cruel man.
Blioblïeris was his name.
340   He was proud and wicked of heart,
but no one ever saw a better knight.
He said to the young men, "Get up!
Bring me my charger,
344   for I see a knight approaching.
And bring my weapons so I can arm myself.

Au chevalier me conbatrai
qui mainne cele damoissele.
348   Ja li ferai widier la siele!"
Li doi vallet le vont armer
a son talent sans plus parler.
Cauces de fer li ont caucies,
352   a cordieles li ont loiies.
Sainne son vis, si se leva;
isnelement et tost s'arma.
Son hauberc vest, son elme lace.
356   Molt l'arment bien en mi la place.
Sor son hauberc vest a armer
cote de soie d'Outremer.
En la place est trais ses destriers;
360   montés i est li chevaliers.
Ceval ot covert de ses armes.   [*135 r°b*]
L'escu a pris par les enarmes,
et la lance a el fautre misse.
364   Devers lui a l'eve porprisse:
nus ne pooit al gué passer
qu'a lui ne convenist joster.
Quand l'a perceü la pucele,
368   le chevalier par ire apiele:
"Vasal, esgardés que je voi!
Or ne venés plus aprés moi:
je voi la outre un chevalier
372   trestot armé sor un destrier.
Se plus volés venir sans faille,
ja vos rendra dure bataille.
Se tu plus viens, ço ert folie:
376   ja serra ta vie fenie.
Se tu vels en avant aler,
je te di bien n'en pués torner
que tu ja ne soies ocis.
380   Jo te dis bien tut a devis."

358 une c. [+2]
360 m. li [*em. Williams*]
377 Se ne v.

I shall do battle with the knight
who is escorting that maiden.
348   I shall unhorse him at once!"
The two young men began to arm him
as he wished, with no further words.
They put on his iron leggings,
352   tying them with cords.
The knight crossed himself, rose,
and was quickly armed.
He put on his hauberk and tied on his helmet.
356   They armed him most skillfully.
Over his hauberk he placed
a silk tunic from the Holy Land.
His charger was brought
360   and the knight mounted.
The horse already wore his armor.
The knight took up his shield by the straps
and placed the lance in its rest.
364   He had claimed all the water near his hut,
and would allow no one to cross the ford
without jousting with him.
When the maiden saw him,
368   she called in anger to the Fair Unknown,
"Vassal, look what I see!
Follow me no longer,
for on the other bank I see a knight
372   fully armed and mounted.
If you insist on going farther,
he will certainly give you a harsh battle.
To go on would be foolish,
376   for it would surely mean your death.
If you insist on going farther,
I tell you in all truthfulness
that you will surely be killed.
380   I am speaking honestly with you."

Li Biaus Descouneüs respont,
"Damoissele, por tot le mont
je ne retorneroie mie
384   tant con j'aie ens el cors la vie,
et s'avrai la voie furnie
car trop serroit grans couardie.
Mais passés outre, s'en irons.
388   S'il veut joster, nos josterons,
et s'il desire la bataille,
ja le porra avoir sans faille."
Puis apiele son escuier
392   qu'il li estraigne son destrier.
Quant cil ot fait, son escu prent
et aprés sa lance ensement.
L'augue passent, outre s'en vont,
396   mais molt tost aresté i sont
et li chevaliers lor escrie,
"Vos avés fait grande folie,
chevalier," fait il. "Mar passates
400   et la pucele mar guiastes!
Folie fu del gué passer;
je vos ferai cier conperer!
Je vos desfi, et gardés vos
404   car je vos ferrai a estros.
Par ci ne passerés vos mie
que bataille n'en soit furnie!"
Li Biaus Descouneüs l'entent,
408   se li respont molt docement,
"Biaus sire, laissiés nos aler.
Nos n'avons cure d'ar[est]er
trop longement en ce[le] voie.
412   Li rois Artus cha nos envoie
por secors faire a une dame,   [*135 r°c*]
et si m'i mainne ceste dame,

400 p. p mar
401 g. papasser
410 d'arer [-*1*]
411 en ce v. [-*1*]

The Fair Unknown answered,
"Lady, not for all the world
would I consider turning back
384   as long as there is life left in my body
and a clear path before me,
for that would be the act of a coward.
Go across now and we will continue our journey.
388   If the knight wishes to joust, I shall joust with him,
and if he wishes to do battle,
he shall certainly have his desire."
Then he told his squire
392   to tighten the girth of his charger.
When the man had done so, the knight took up
his shield and lance.
They crossed over to the other bank,
396   but were quickly stopped,
and Blioblïeris shouted at them,
"You have done a most foolish thing, knight!
You should never have brought
400   the maiden across the ford!
It was madness to cross,
and I shall make you pay dearly for it!
I hereby challenge you. Now have a care,
404   for I shall strike you down at once.
You will never pass by here
without a hard fight!"
When the Fair Unknown heard this,
408   he answered courteously,
"My dear lord, let us go our way.
We do not wish to delay
too long on our journey.
412   King Arthur has sent us here
to render aid to a lady,
and this maiden, who says she is her lady-in-waiting,

si dist que c'est sa damoissele.
416   Au roi Artus dist la nouviele
por coi je vois en cest afaire.
Dius le me doi[n]st a bon cief traire!"
Et cil li dist, "Sans nule faille
420   avant n'irés vos sans bataille.
Del gué passer est tels l'usages;
ensi l'a tenu mes lingnages
et je, certes, plus de set ans.
424   Maintes gens i ai fais dolens,
et maint bon chevalier de pris
i ai abatu et ocis."
Cil li respont, "C'est roberie!
428   Tant con porrai, garrai ma vie.
Quant je n'i puis merchi trover,
huimais ne.l vos quier demander."
Li uns de l'autre s'eslonga;
432   au mius que il pot s'atorna.
Quant il se sont bien atorné,
li uns a l'autre regardé.
Les cevals poingnent molt forment.
436   Or verrés ja le plus dolent!
Blioblïeris al joster
l'escu li fait del col voler;
sa lance peçoie et astele
440   si que bien le voit la pucele.
Li Biaus Descouneüs ne faut:
desous le boucle le fiert haut;
l'ecu perça, l'auberc desront,
444   le fer trençant li mist parfont.
Les arçons li a fait guerpir:
li estrier ne.l porent tenir
que ne l'abatist del destrier.
448   As paumes l'a fait apoier.
Cil se relieve vistemant:

418   doist
421   *omits* est [-*1*]
422   m. usages l.

is conducting me to her.
416 She told King Arthur about this matter,
and that is why I have set out on this quest.
May God grant me success!"
The other said, "Truly
420 you will go no further without a fight.
Such is the custom of the ford;
my ancestors maintained it,
and I myself have done so for more than seven years.
424 I have brought sorrow to many
and have unhorsed and killed
many fine knights."
The other said, "That is the wanton work of brigands!
428 I shall defend myself as best I can.
And since I find no mercy in you,
I shall not ask you for any from now on."
They moved some distance away from each other
432 and each prepared to do battle as well as he could.
When both were quite ready,
they turned to face each other.
Harshly they spurred their horses forward.
436 Now you will see who got the worst of it!
At the first encounter, Blioblïeris
made his shield fly from his opponent's neck,
shattering his lance as well,
440 all in full view of the maiden.
But the Fair Unknown did not fail to strike back:
he struck the other high on the boss,
he pierced the shield, tore through the hauberk,
444 and sank the metal tip deep into his flesh.
He knocked him from the saddle,
for the stirrups could not keep him
from falling off his horse.
448 His hands were pressed against the ground.
But he got up quickly,

de mauvaisté ne vaut noient.
Il a mis la main a l'espee.
452   Quant a s'alaine recouvree,
molt durement le vait ferir
de l'espee, par tel aïr
qu'a un cop ocist le ceval.
456   Or furent a pié par ingal.
En lor mains tiennent les espees,
dont il se donnent grans colees
sor les elmes, sor les escus.
460   Molt bien se fierent des brans nus!
De[s] elmes font le feu voler,
les esti[n]celes alumer.
Molt se rendoient grant bataille.
464   Ançois que fust la definaille,   [*135 v°a*]
va Blioblïeris lassant
por le sanc qu'il aloit perdant
de la plaie qu'il avoit prisse.
468   Ne puet mains faire en nule guisse.
Li Biaus Descouneüs le fiert
et souventes fois le requiert.
Amont sor l'[e]lme de l'espee
472   li a donnee grant colee
qu'a genillons le fait venir.
Cil ne le puet longes soufrir:
trop fu navrés. Molt li escrie
476   que por Diu laist que ne l'ocie
et il fera tot son talent.
Ja ne passera son comant.
"Se tu vels, prison m'averos
480   et de par moi pris averos."
"Ens en la cort Artus le roi,
a lui en irés de par moi."
Atant li fïance prisson
484   qu'il en ira sans okison

461 Del
462 esticeles
471 ulme

for he did not wish to be a coward.
He took hold of his sword.
452   When he had recovered his wind,
he struck the knight hard
with his sword, so furiously that
he killed the other's horse with one blow.
456   Now they were both on foot.
They grasped their swords
and gave each other great blows
on their helmets and their shields.
460   They struck well with their naked blades!
They caused sparks to fly from each other's helmets,
making the helmets flash.
Both of them fought fiercely.
464   Before the battle was over,
Blioblïeris grew weak
because of the blood he was losing
from the wound he had received.
468   This could not fail to be the case.
The Fair Unknown struck him,
attacking him again and again.
He gave him a great blow with his sword
472   high on his helmet
that brought him to his knees.
The knight could not go on for long,
for he was too gravely wounded. He cried out
476   begging him in God's name not to kill him,
and saying that he would do whatever he wished
and would not transgress the knight's commands.
"If you wish, you may take me prisoner
480   and win renown because of me."
"You must go to King Arthur's court
and say that I have sent you there."
The other then vowed, as a defeated knight,
484   that he would go at once

ens en la cort Artus le roi.
Içо li afïa par foi.
Quant fu vencue la bataille,
488   li nains en fu joians sans faille.
Ce dist li nains a la pucele,
"Grant tort aviés, ma damoissele,
qui blamïés le chevalier.
492   N'est a blamer qui'st a proissier.
Bien nos a delivré le pas.
Bele, trop l'avés tenu bas.
Il est preudon; portons l'onnor.
496   Dius li maintiene sa valor
qu'i le nos puisse longes faire!"
Molt estoit li nains debonaire.
Dist la pucele, "Il a bien fait,
500   mais ce saciés bien entresait
que se il veut o nos aler,
noiens serra del retorner.
Ocis serra, s'ert grans damages
504   que molt [est] buens li siens corages."
Mais il, tantost con il l'entent,
li a respondu maintenant
qu'il n'en torneroit por nul plait
508   jusque il ait le [se]cors fait.
Dist la pucele, "Don alons!
La nuis aproce, trop tardons."
Robers avoit pris le destrier
512   qui ert a l'autre chevalier.
A son signor tantost le mainne;
cil i monta de tere plainne.
Robers prist l'escu et [la] lance.
516   Or chevaucent sans redoutance.
Grant oirre cort et cil remaint   [135 v°b]
qui de sa plaie molt se plaint.
Li doi vallet l'en ont mené.

504 omits est [-1]
508 le cors f. [-1]
515 omits la [-1]

straight to King Arthur's court.
The Fair Unknown accepted his word.
When the knight had defeated his opponent,
488   the dwarf was delighted.
He said to the maiden,
"You were greatly in the wrong, my lady,
to speak so badly of the knight.
492   A worthy man should not be criticized.
He has opened the way for us.
Dear lady, you have esteemed him too little.
He is a valiant knight; let us therefore do him honor.
496   May God preserve his worth
so that he may long lend us his aid!"
This dwarf was very well-mannered.
The maiden said, "He has performed well so far,
500   but you may still be certain
that if he insists on going with us,
he will never return to Arthur's court.
He will be killed, and that will be a great pity
504   for he is a man of noble heart."
But when the Fair Unknown heard this,
he immediately said to her
that he would not turn back for any plea
508   until he had rendered aid to her lady.
The maiden said, "Let us go then!
Night is approaching, we are wasting time."
Robert had taken the charger
512   that belonged to the other knight.
He quickly brought him to his lord,
who mounted straight from the ground.
The squire took his shield and lance.
516   They then rode on without fear.
The knight rode at a fast pace while Blioblïeris stayed behind,
in great pain because of his wound.
The two young men led him away.

520   En sa loge l'ont desarmé
      puis l'ont coucié en un biel lit,
      mais molt i ot poi de delit.
      Blioblïeris est plaiés,
524   si dolans et si esmaiés.
      Li souvient des trois conpaignons,
      dont bien vos sai dire les nons:
      Elins li Blans, sires de Graies,
528   et li bons chevaliers de Saies,
      et Willaume de Salebrant.
      Cil sont molt preu et molt vaillant.
      Si estoient si conpaignon;
532   son comant fisent sans tençon.
      Cist trois que je vos ai conté
      querre aventure sont alé
      savoir se ja le troveroient,
536   et cele nuit venir devoient.
      Le jor vont querrant aventure;
      quant doit venir la nuis oscure,
      si tornent au Gué Perillous
540   dont li pasage est dolerous.
      Blioblïeris le[s] atent.
      Molt furent fier et conbatant.
      Ne li covient avoir esmaie
544   se aventure ne.s delaie
      que le soir ne viegne[nt] al Gué
      cil chevalier que j'ai nomé.
      Li jors faut et la nuis revient.
548   La nuis oscure lor sorvient;
      es vos venant les chevaliers,
      tos trois armés sor lor destriers.
      Si vienent lor signor devant
552   que il troverent molt dolant

527 saies
528 graies
541 B. le
545 viegne
548 s *before* r *in* oscure *expuncted*

520   They disarmed him inside the hut
       and then laid him on a very fine bed,
       although he could take little joy in it.
       Bliobl'ieris was gravely stricken
524   from his terrible wound.
       He thought of his three companions,
       whose names I can readily tell you:
       Elin the Fair, lord of Graie,
528   the strong knight of Saie,
       and William of Salebrant.
       All were good and valiant warriors.
       They were Biliobl'ieris's companions
532   and did what he asked without question.
       These three whom I have told you about
       had gone out
       looking for adventure
536   and were to return that night.
       They sought adventure by day,
       and in the dark of night
       they returned to the Perilous Ford,
540   which had brought grief to many.
       Now Bliobl'ieris awaited their coming.
       They were very fierce and warlike knights.
       He need have no fear
544   that the four knights I have mentioned
       would not come back to the ford,
       unless some adventure had delayed them.
       Day ended and night returned.
548   Dark night came upon them,
       and along came the knights
       all three armed on their chargers.
       They went before their lord
552   and found him suffering

et molt grevé d'estra[n]ge guisse
de la plaie qu'il avoit prisse.
Molt font grant dol de lor singnor
556   et il lor dist, "N'aiés dolor,
mais or pensés de moi vengier;
or m'a vostre secors mestier.
Uns chevaliers est ci passés —
560   ja millor de lui ne verrés.
A lui jostai, si m'a conquis;
ses prisons sui tot a devis.
Molt l'ai trové bon chevalier.
564   Aveuc lui mainne un escuier
et une biele damoisele;
un nain conduissoit la pucele.
Il m'abati molt malement,
568   puis s'en passa par chi devant.
Je vos dirai coment a non   [*135 v°c*]
cil a cui fïançai prison:
Bel Descouneü se nonma.
572   Certes, si grant cop me donna
qu'a painnes entendi son non.
Alés aprés, mi conpaignon,
si l'ocïés u le prendés.
576   S'a vos se rent, si l'amenés,
si m'aquitera de prison."
Molt avoit cil le cuer felon!
Cil respondent, "N'en puet aler,
580   se nos ja le poons trover,
que il ne soit u mors u pris.
Vos l'arés a vostre devis."
Atant monterent tot armé,
584   del vengier molt entalenté.
Or s'en vont li trois conpaignon,
qui de cuer sont fier et felon.
Molt volentiers le vengeroient
588   se il ja faire le pooient.

553 estrage

in great pain
because of his wound.
They were very grieved for their lord's sake,
556 but he said, "Do not be troubled,
but think instead of avenging me,
for I now have need of you.
A knight passed by here —
560 you'll never see a better one.
I jousted with him, he defeated me,
and now I am sworn to obey him.
I found him to be a valiant knight.
564 He has with him a squire
and a beautiful maiden,
who was leading a dwarf.
He gave me a grievous fall,
568 and then he rode away.
I shall tell you the name
of this knight I have pledged to obey:
he called himself the Fair Unknown.
572 In truth, he gave me such a harsh blow
that I could scarcely make out his name.
Now go after him, my companions,
and either kill or capture him.
576 If he surrenders to you, bring him here
so that he will release me from my pledge."
This man had a very treacherous heart!
They answered, "If we can find him,
580 He cannot fail to be
either killed or captured.
You shall soon have him at your disposal."
Then they mounted, fully armed
584 and thirsting for revenge.
The three companions went forth,
men fierce and treacherous of heart.
They would eagerly avenge their lord
588 if ever they could.

Or penst Dius de celui garder
car se il le püent trover,
en aventure est de sa vie!
592   Il cevauce, si ne.l set mie.
Le jor ont faite grant jornee
et quant ce vint a la vespree,
virent en la forest un pré
596   dont molt flairoit l'erbe soué.
La pucele se porpensa
et le chevalier apiela:
"Sire," fait ele, "remanons;
600   en cest bel pré nos herbergons.
Noiens serroit d'avant aler:
ne poriens vile trover
ne maisson en ceste contree
604   environs nos d'une jornee."
Et cil volentiers otria
ço que la pucele loa.
El pré descendent, si herbergent.
608   Or les gart Dius que il ne perdent!
N'ont que mangier a cel souper;
la nuit lor covint endurer.
Molt fu Robers bons escuiers.
612   Il vint a son signor premiers,
dessarmé l'a isnelement,
puis va a son ceval corent.
Entre Robert et le preu nain,
616   cui je ne tien pas a vilain,
cist doi garderent les cevals.
Molt [ert] Robers preus et loiaus;
gentius fu et molt bien apris.
620   Vait s'ent li jors, vient li seris.
De la nuit ert grant masse alee,   [*136 r°a*]
si ert ja la lune levee.
Li Descouneüs se dormoit
624   sor l'erbe fresce u il [gisoit].

618 *omits* ert [-*1*]
624 dormoit [*em. Williams*]

May God defend the Fair Unknown
for, if these men find him,
his life will be in great danger!

592   He himself was riding along, knowing nothing of all this.
       He and his companions had traveled far that day,
and when evening was drawing near,
they saw in the midst of the forest a meadow

596   filled with sweetly-smelling grass.
The maiden considered
and then said to the knight,
"Let us stay here, my lord,

600   and pass the night in this lovely meadow.
There is no reason to travel further,
for we would not find a city
or a dwelling in this land

604   within a day's journey."
And he gladly accepted
the maiden's suggestion.
They dismounted and prepared to stay for the night.

608   God grant they come to no ill by doing so!
They had nothing to eat for supper
and would have to go hungry for the night.
Robert was a very fine squire.

612   He went straight to his lord
and quickly disarmed him,
then hurried to care of his horse.
Robert and the worthy dwarf,

616   who was no lout, in my opinion,
both took care of the horses.
Robert was a worthy and loyal man,
both noble and very well bred.

620   The day came to an end, and evening fell.
The night was well advanced
and the moon had risen.
The Fair Unknown was asleep

624   on the fresh grass where he lay.

Dalés lui gist la damoissele;
deseur son braç gist la pucele.
Li uns dalés l'autre dormoit.
628   Li lousignols sor els cantoit,
quant li chevaliers s'esvilla.
Sor la fresce herbe s'acota.
En la forest oï un brait
632   lonc a quatre arcies de trait.
Molt est doce la vois qui crie.
Ce sanble mestier ait d'aïe;
molt forment crie et pleure et brait
636   come la riens qui painne trait,
et demenoit molt grant dolor;
Diu reclamoit, le Creator.
Quant cil l'oï, si l'escouta:
640   la vos adiés merchi cria.
La pucele qui dort s'esvelle
et cil del dire s'aparelle:
"Ha, pucele, oés vos crier
644   ne sai cui plaindre et souspirer?"
"Ço est fantome, al mien espoir.
Laissiés crier, ne puet caloir.
Je ne pris de rien son crier.
648   Dormés vos, si laissiés ester."
Cil respondi a la pucele,
"Iceste vois Diu molt apiele.
Ce sanble mestier ait d'aïe;
652   por ce reclaime Diu et prie.
Jo vel aler por li aidier.
Se je voi qu'ele en ait mestier,
haiderai li a mon pooir.
656   Gentius cose est, a mon espoir."
Cele li dist, "Vos n'irés mie!"
Del remanoir forment li prie
et dist, "Quiers tu donc aventures?
660   En ton cemin en a de dures.
Ja de ço ne t'estuet penser
ne fors de ton cemin aler;

Beside him lay the maiden,
her head resting on his arm.
They slept side by side.

628   The nightingale was singing above them
when the knight awoke.
He sat up on the fresh grass.
He heard a cry in the forest

632   perhaps four bowshots away.
The voice was a very sweet one.
It seemed to be in need of aid;
it wept and cried piteously

636   like a creature in pain
and complained of great suffering,
calling on God the Creator.
When the knight heard it, he listened:

640   there it was again, crying for mercy.
Then the maiden awoke,
and the knight said,
"Lady, do you hear someone,

644   I do not know who, sighing and lamenting?"
"I think it is nothing but a ghost," she said.
"Let it cry; it is of no importance.
This crying is of no concern to me.

648   Sleep now, and let the matter rest."
He said to the maiden,
"That voice is calling again and again on God.
It seems to be in need of aid;

652   that is why it cries out to Him.
I wish to go help.
If I see that it needs my aid,
I will give it as best I can.

656   It seems to me a gentle voice."
She said, "You shall certainly not go!"
She begged him to stay
and said, "Is it adventures that you want, then?

660   You will find some difficult ones on the path you are
          travelling.
You should not be concerned about this voice,
nor stray from your path;

car ains que ma dame trovois,
664   cui je que vos tant en arois
trové que vos plus n'en vauriés
ne vos plus soufrir n'en poriés.
Molt vos converra a soufrir,
668   se Dius de mort vos veut garir,
plus que chevalier qui soit nés."
Cil li a dit, "Or me soufrés,
damoissele, que jo i voisse."
672   "Jo n'en donroie une pujo[i]sse,
vasal, de quanques vos ferois.   [*136 r °b*]
Bien voi por moi rien n'en ferois;
vos ne me crés ne tant ne quant.
676   Encor vos en verrai dolant!
Tu venis ci otre mon gré;
or ne feras ma volonté!"
Et cil li dist, "Ne lairai mie
680   n'aille veoir ce qu'est qui crie."
Robert apiele l'escuier
qu'il li amainne son destrier.
Cil s'evellë isnellement,
684   se li amainne l'auferrant.
Li Descouneüs se sainna
et puis en son ceval monta.
Son escu a pris et sa lance;
688   ses corages adiés s'avance.
La pucele ne remaint mie:
pense que ce serroit folie
se seule ilucques remanoit;
692   ne set ele le troveroit.
Ele monta et puis li nains,
qui [ne] fu ne faus ne vilains.
Or en vont tuit, Robert le guie
696   devers le liu u la vois crie.

672 pujosse
680 veoior
694 *lacks first* ne [*-1*]

for, before you reach my lady,
664   I think you will have
found as many adventures as you desire,
and all that you can manage.
You will be forced to suffer a great deal,
668   more than any knight yet born,
even if God chooses to preserve your life."
He said, "Permit me
to go now, my lady."
672   "I do not care a farthing,
vassal, for anything you choose to do.
I can see that you will do nothing for my sake;
you do not believe anything I say.
676   And I shall see you suffer for it yet!
You came with me against my will,
and now you will not do as I wish!"
He said, "I shall not fail
680   to go and see who is crying out so."
He called to Robert
to bring him his charger.
The squire quickly awoke
684   and brought the horse.
The Fair Unknown crossed himself
and then mounted.
He took up his shield and lance,
688   his spirit rising.
The maiden did not stay behind:
she thought it foolish
to stay there alone,
692   and she did not know if she would find the knight again.
She mounted, as did the dwarf,
who was neither a traitor nor a lout.
So they all rode forward, while Robert led them
696   toward the place where the voice was crying.

Par le forest vont cevauçant
isnelement, Robert devant.
Venu sont vers la vois qui crie;
700   tant sont pres que bien l'ont oïe.
Un fu virent mervelles grant;
si s'aresturent maintenant.
Robers lor a le feu mostré;
704   or sevent ço qu'est qu'ot crié.
Au feu avoit dous grans gaians
lais et hisdels et mescreans.
Li uns tenoit une pucele —
708   ja nus hom ne demant plus biele
se ele n'eüst tel paor.
Mais molt demenoit grant dolor;
molt se conplai[n]t et plore et brait
712   come la riens qui painne trait,
car uns gaians molt la pressoit:
a force f[outre] le vouloit.
Mais cele ne.l pooit soufrir;
716   mius se voloit laissier morir.
De l'autre part le feu seoit
l'autre gaians qui rostissoit
. . . .
720   et aveuc son poivre faisoit.
Mangier voloient erranment
se l'autre eüst fait son talent
de la pucele qu'il tenoit.
724   Et quant li chevalier le voit,
s'apiele damoissele Helie,   [136 r°c]
qu'il menoit en sa conpaignie;
se li a mostré la pucele
728   que li gaians tenoit si biele.
Se li a dit qu'il lor taura
et qu'as gaians se conbatra.

711 conplait
714 all but f of foutre erased
725 repeated at top of column c

They sped through the forest
with Robert in the lead.
They drew near the voice,
700   until they were close enough to hear it well.
They saw a very large campfire
and stopped at once.
Robert pointed toward the fire,
704   and then they knew who it was that had cried out.
By the fire were two huge, ugly giants,
both hideous and evil.
One of them held a maiden —
708   no one could ask to see a more beautiful one
if she had not been so frightened.
But she was in great suffering;
She lamented and wept and cried out
712   like a creature suffering,
for one giant was attacking her,
intending to rape her.
She would not endure it, however;
716   She would rather have died.
On the other side of the fire
the other giant sat roasting

. . . .
720   and adding pepper to it.
They intended to eat
as soon as the other had done what he pleased
with the maiden whom he held.
724   And when the knight saw this,
he called to the lady Helie
who was with him;
he pointed out to her the beautiful maiden
728   whom the giant held in his grasp.
He said he would free her from them
and do battle with the giants.

Ce[le] li dist, "Tu vels morir?
732   Ocis serras, n'i pués faillir,
se tu te conbas as jaians,
tant les sai fels et conbatans.
Il ont tot cest païs gasté.
736   Por ce avons jeü el pré,
qu'environ nos d'une jornee
n'a maisson n'aient devoree.
Tot ont destruit, la gent ocise;
740   tote ont la terre a lor devise.
. . . .
De mort est fis cil qui.s atent.
Ne t'i conbat pas, mes fuions;
744   ja ces dÿables n'atendons!"
Mais cil ne l'en vaut croire mie.
En aventure met sa vie;
hardimens l'aloit destraignant.
748   Il point le ceval durement;
as jaians vient, si lor escrie,
"As vos n'afiert pas cele mie!"
Il laisse corre l'auferrant
752   et fiert celui premieremant
qui esforçoit la damoisele;
si l'a feru les la mamiele.
Le fer li fist el cuer serrer;
756   les ioils del cief li fist torbler.
Mort le trebuce el feu ardant.
Li autres le vint a itant,
maçue au col se.l vaut ferir.
760   Cil sot desous l'escu guencir;
point le ceval, ne l'ataint mie.
. . . .
. . . .

731 Ce li [-*1*]
737 environs *where* s *expuncted*
741 *lacuna in ms.*
762-6 lacuna in ms·

She said, "Do you wish to die then?
732   You cannot fail to be killed
      if you do battle with those giants,
      as wicked and fierce as I know they are.
      They have laid waste this entire land.
736   That is why we stopped in the meadow for the night,
      for there is no dwelling within a day's journey
      that they have not plundered.
      They have destroyed everything and killed the inhabitants;
740   all the surrounding country is now in their control.
      . . . .
      Any one who tries to fight them may be sure of death.
      Do not do battle with them, but let us flee
744   rather than go against these devils!"
      He did not heed her warning.
      Rather, he chose to place his life in danger,
      for his courage so compelled him.
748   Harshly he spurred his horse forward
      toward the giants and shouted to them,
      "You are no fit companions for this lady!"
      He let his charger run freely,
752   and struck first at the giant
      who was attacking the maiden,
      striking him in the side of the breast.
      The lance tip pierced his heart;
756   his eyes clouded.
      The knight then threw him, dead, into the fire.
      The other giant then started toward him,
      his club held high, ready to strike.
760   The knight protected himself with his shield;
      he spurred forward but did not reach the giant.
      . . . .
      . . . .

764   . . . .
        . . . .
        . . . .
        que il enporte son escu,
768   et son ceval a si feru
        que de petit l'eüst ocis
        et le chevalier tot malmis.
        Cui Dius de honte veut garder,
772   nule riens ne le puet grever.
        A cele fois a Dius gari
        le chevalier par sa merchi.
        Li jaians cort a sa maçue.
776   De son conpagnon li anuie;
        dalés le feu ocis le voit.   [*136 v°a*]
        Se vengier ne.l puet orendroit,
        il ne [se] prisoit un bouton.
780   De mellier avoit un baston,
        mais li chevaliers vint poingnant,
        le jaient fiert en ataingnant
        de la lance par les costés.
784   Li jaians est vers lui tornés:
        prendre le cuide maintenant.
        Et cil s'eslonge tot errant,
        qu'il n'a soi[n]g de sa conpaignie
788   ne de sa luite n'ainme il mie.
        Li jaians sa maçue prist.
        Navré se sent, tost en fremist;
        vengier se cuide maintenant.
792   Si est venus vers lui corant,
        se entoisse por lui ferir.
        Cil vit le cop vers lui venir,
        le ceval guencist d'autre part.
796   Ce ne fu pas fait de musart!
        Fuir vaut mius de fol atendre

778 S'en
779 *omits* se
787 soig

764 . . . .
. . . .
. . . .
so that he lost his shield
768 and struck his horse so fiercely
that he almost killed the animal,
which would have cost the knight his life as well.
But when God chooses to protect a man from shame,
772 nothing can harm him.
And so God protected
the knight through His mercy.
The giant rushed forward with his club.
776 He was angered at seeing his companion
lying dead beside the fire.
He would have considered himself quite worthless
if he could not avenge him on the spot.
780 He had a stout club of medlar,
but the knight rode forward
and struck the giant
full on the ribs with his lance.
784 The giant turned toward him,
thinking to catch hold of him.
But the other quickly moved away,
for he had no desire for the giant's company
788 or any wish to grapple with him.
The giant took up his club.
He felt himself mortally wounded, and he shook with fury;
he thought to avenge himself then and there.
792 He ran toward the knight,
and raised his weapon to strike him.
The Fair Unknown saw the blow coming,
and turned his horse aside.
796 This was no fool's move!
Discretion is the better part of valor

       puis qu'il n'i a mestier desfendre.
       Car li jaians a si feru
800   en un arbre par tel vertu
       que il fist tot l'arbre croller
       et les brances jus avaler.
       Des puins li vole la maçue;
804   ainçois que il l'ait receüe
       avra, je cuic, perte encontree.
       Car cil li cort a tot l'espee,
       si feri molt bien le jaiant.
808   Un cop li donne molt pesant
       sus en la teste, en la cervele;
       desi es dens met l'alimele,
       se li a tolue la vie.
812   A lui traist l'espee forbie;
       li jaians ciet sor l'erbe drue.
       La bataille fu si vencue.
       De son ceval a pié descent;
816   Robers i vint isnelement
       ki le desarma en la place.
       L'elme fors de cief li esrace,
       puis li a descente l'espee
820   quant ot la teste desarmee.
       L'auberc li traist de blance maille
       quant deslacie ot la ventaille.
       Li nains fu en la forest long:
824   de l'aprocier n'avoit pas soi[n]g.
       Dalés lui damoisse[le] Helie,
       qui tote fu espeürie
       de la bataille qu'ot veüe;
828   ele en estoit tote esperdue.
       Ce dist li nains a la pucele,   *[136 v°b]*
       "Grant tort aviés, ma damoissele,
       qui blamïés le chevalier.
832   Il m'est vis, bien se set aidier.

---

824 soig
825 damoisse

when you have no means to defend yourself.
For the giant struck
800   a tree with such terrible force
that he caused it to shake
and scatter its branches everywhere.
The club flew from his hands;
804   and before he could get it back,
I believe he felt its loss.
For the knight rode up, brandishing his sword,
and struck the giant hard.
808   He gave him such a mighty blow
on the head that the blade pierced his brains
right down to his teeth,
and so took his life.
812   The knight drew out his sword,
and the giant fell down on the lush grass.
Thus was the combat ended.
The knight then dismounted;
816   Robert hurried up to him
and disarmed him right there.
He removed his helmet
and, once his head was bare,
820   he ungirded his sword
after he had untied the ventail.
He took off the shining hauberk.
The dwarf had remained in the forest some distance away,
824   for he did not care to come nearer.
With him was the lady Helie,
who was filled with terror
from the combat she had witnessed.
828   She was indeed beside herself.
The dwarf said to her,
"You were very much in the wrong, my lady,
to speak badly of this knight;
832   It seems to me that he knows how to

Certes je.l cuit et bien le sai
as estors que ci veüs ai,
ausi a Blioblïeris,
836   que cis hom est de molt grant pris.
Tel cose tient on molt viument
de coi on aprés se repent.
Mais n'i puet nus metre mecine
840   que molt ne soit sa valors fine."
"Biaus amis," ce li dist Helie,
"se onques li dis vilonnie,
or l'en irai merchi rover
844   de ço que.l soloie blamer."
Cele part vint la damoissele;
del palefroi dessent a terre,
puis est au chevalier meüe
848   et molt docement le salue.
Et puis li quiert tantost merchi
de ço que si l'avoit laidi,
qu'il li pardoi[n]st a ceste fois;
852   a son plaissir prenge les drois.
Cil respondi a la pucele,
"Je.l vos pardoins, ma damoisele.
Puis que merchi m'avés rové,
856   tot vos soit ore pardonné."
La damoissele l'enclina
et bonement l'en merchia.
Merchi l'en rent, o lui sejorne,
860   et Robers les cevals atorne.
Dalés le feu herbergié sont;
quant jors serra, si s'en iront.
Dont est au chevalier venue
864   la pucele qu'il ot tolue
as dous jaiant qui le tenoient,
qui si grant painne li faisoient.
Molt i ot gente damoissele.
868   La color ot fresse et noviele;

851   pardoist

give a good account of himself.
I can see from the way I have seen him fight here
and also with Blioblïeris

836 that he is a very valiant man.
Sometimes we prize a thing very little
and afterwards see that we have erred.
No one can now deny

840 that this man is a most worthy knight."
"My dear friend," said Helie,
"If I ever spoke shamefully to him
I shall go now to ask pardon

844 for my many reproachful words."
The damsel rode up to him
and got off her palfrey.
She went to the knight

848 and greeted him most courteously,
and then she asked him to pardon her
for having so abused him;
she asked that he now forgive her

852 and said that in return she would do as he saw fit.
He said to the maiden,
"I forgive you, my lady.
Since you have asked my pardon,

856 I grant it most readily."
The maiden bowed
and thanked him courteously.
She thanked him and stayed with him,

860 while Robert got the horses ready for the night.
They settled down next to the fire,
intending to stay there until daybreak.
Then the maiden whom the knight

864 had rescued from the two giants
who had so tormented her
went up to him.
She was a very lovely maiden.

868 Her cheeks were bright and blooming,

sa color avoit recovree
de joie qu'ele ert delivree.
"Sire, tu m'as del tot garie
872   et de mon cors sauvé la vie.
Trait m'as de painne et de dolor
et de prison et de tristor
et des tormens u ere entree.
876   Tu m'as des jaians delivree:
tos jors mais serrai vostre ancele!"
As piés li cet li damoissele
et cil l'en a fait relever.
880   De joie comence a plorer.
Dalés lui l'a sor l'erbe asise,   [*136v°c*]
se li demanda en quel guisse
l'avoien cil jaiant trovee
884   qu'iluques l'orent aportee
et coment a non que li die;
qui est ne dont ne li çoilt mie.
Dist la pucele, "Je.l dira:
888   de rien nule n'en mentira.
Por voir nonmee sui Clarie
— ne vos en mentiroie mie —
et Saigremors si est mes frere.
892   Li jaians me pris[t] ciés mon pere.
En un vergier hui main entrai
et por moi deduire i alai.
Li jaians ert desous l'entree;
896   trova la porte desfremee.
Iluec me prist, si m'en porta;
ici son conpaingnon trova.
Conquisse m'avés en bataille.
900   Sire, voir vos ai dit sans faille."
Robers a trové et li nai[n]s

869 recovreee
883 avoienen [*superfluous ligature bar*]
892 pris
901 nais

for she had now recovered her color
from joy at being rescued.
"My lord, you have defended me from all danger
872 and saved my life," she said.
"You have freed me from pain and suffering,
from captivity and sorrow,
and from the great torment in which I was held.
876 You have rescued me from the giants,
and I shall forever be in your debt!"
The maiden fell at his feet,
but he quickly made her rise.
880 She began to weep for joy.
He had her sit down beside him on the grass
and asked that she tell him how
the giants who had brought her there
884 had found her
and also that she not fail to tell him her name,
who she was, and where she came from.
She said, "I shall tell you
888 without falsehood.
My name is Clarie
—I would not speak falsely to you about this —
and Sagremor is my brother.
892 The giant captured me at my father's castle.
I went into the garden there this morning
to amuse myself.
The giant was near the entrance,
896 and found the gate unlocked.
He captured me there and took me away;
here he met up with his companion.
Now you have won me in combat.
900 My lord, I have spoken truly."
Robert and the dwarf found

desos la cave trente pains
et blances napes et hanas,
904   jambes salees, oissials cras
tos roties et tos atornés.
De bon vin ont trové asés.
Andoi en sont lié et joiant:
908   or ont a mangier a talent!
Cil doi jaiant qui sont ocis,
qui gasté orent le païs,
tot ço i orent aporté
912   le mangier c'ont illuec trové;
illueques estoit lor repaires.
Mais cangiés lor est lor afaires.
Li vilains dist, "Par Saint Martin,
916   tels fait viengne, n'i cuit roissin."
Robers s'en est molt tost alés
c'a mangier a trové asés:
"Tot avrés quanques vos plaira:
920   ja blance nape n'i faura!"
Cil li respont, "Di me tu voir
qu'a mangier poommes avoir?"
Ce dist Robers, "Oïl, sans faille,
924   car trové ai la repostaile
des dous jaans qui sont ocis.
A mangier avés a devis!"
Et cil maintenant se leva,
928   les damoisseles i mena,
l'une et l'autre a par la main prise.
Robers fu molt de biel service.
L'iague donne a cascun li nains.
932   Quant il orent lavé lor mains,
les napes ont sor l'erbe mises;   [137 r°a]
si ont les puceles asises
et li Descouneüs devant,
936   qui molt lor faisoit biel sanblant.
Li nains les servoit et Robers,

915 piar

a good thirty loaves of bread in the giants' cave,
along with white tablecloths and goblets,
904 cured hams and plump birds,
roasted and all prepared.
There was also plenty of good wine.
Both were overjoyed:
908 at last they would be able to eat their fill!
The two giants, now dead,
who had laid the land waste
had stored all the food
912 that Robert and the dwarf now uncovered,
for this was where they had lived.
Now events had taken a different turn for them, however.
As the peasant says, "By Saint Martin, the one who plants
916 the vineyards doesn't always harvest the grapes."
Robert went quickly to tell his master
that he had found a great cache of food:
"You shall have everything you care to," he said,
920 "even a white tablecloth."
The Fair Unknown answered, "Is it true
that we now have food to eat?"
"Yes, indeed it is," said Robert,
924 "for I have found the cache
that belonged to the two giants you killed.
You now have as much to eat as you want!"
The knight arose at once
928 and went with the maidens,
taking each by the hand.
Robert served the meal in fine style.
The dwarf offered everyone water.
932 And when everyone had washed their hands,
Robert and the dwarf laid the tablecloths out on the grass;
they seated the maidens
opposite the Fair Unknown,
936 who smiled at them most graciously.
The dwarf served them, along with Robert,

qui molt fu sages et apers:
il estoit kels et senescaus
940 et botilliers et marissaus
et canbrelens et escuiers.
I[l] s'entremet de tos mestiers
et de cascun molt biel servoit;
944 et li nains molt biel li aidoit—
molt les savoient biel servir.
Quant ont mangié a lor plaisir,
li nains vint les napes oster
948 et celes lievent dou souper.
Et cil qui [s]avoient servir
ront mangi[é] a molt grant loissir,
si les servent les damoisseles.
952 Ne tienent pas longes novieles:
quant ont mangié tot maintenant,
s'en vont a lor cevals corant
et bien et biel les atornerent
956 et blé a plenté lor donerent
que li jaiant avoient quis
qui gasté orent le païs.
Li preus Robers pas ne s'oublie:
960 d'erbe n'avoit encore mie
que il donnast a ses cevals.
Garde, les lui vit une faux.
Quant il estoit entrés el pré
964 et de faucier fu apresté,
si vit venir trois chevaliers
armés sor lor corans destriers.
Rengié venoient et seré,
968 de totes armes bien armé.
Icil trois furent conpaignon.
Bien sai coment orent a non:
li uns estoit Elins de Graies,

942 I s'e.
949 avoient
950 mangi

who was a very bright and able man:
he acted as cook and seneschal,
940 cupbearer and marshal,
chamberlain and squire all at once.
He fulfilled all these functions
and served everyone admirably;
944 the dwarf was an excellent help to him —
between the two of them they rendered excellent service.
When the knight and the maidens had dined as they wished,
the dwarf removed the tablecloths
948 and the maidens arose from the meal.
And those who had served so well
dined in turn at their leisure,
for the ladies served them.
952 The two did not dally for long:
as soon as they had finished eating,
they hurried to the horses
and took excellent care of them,
956 giving them plenty of the grain
which the giants who had laid waste the land
had stored there.
The worthy Robert did not fail to remember
960 that he had no grass
to give to his horses.
He looked around and saw a scythe nearby.
After he had gone into the meadow
964 and was preparing to cut some grass,
he saw three knights coming,
armed on their swift chargers.
They rode in close rank
968 and were armed from head to foot.
These three were companions.
I know their names well:
one was Elin of Graie,

972   li secuns li Sires de Saies,
        et li tiers [ert] de [Sa]lebrans,
        Willaumes, qui molt ert vaillans.
        Le Biau Descouneü sivoient:
976   prendre u ocire le voloient.
        Robers les vit vers lui venir,
        si s'en comença a fuïr
        et vint tot droit a son signor,
980   qui se gisoit sor la verdor
        tres devant les dous damoiseles,
        qui molt furent gentes et bieles.
        Et cil maintenant l'esvilla
984   et a une part l'apiela.
        "Sire," fait il, "tost vos armés!   [*137 r°b*]
        De desfendre vos aprestés!
        De bien faire apensés soiés,
988   ne de rien ne vos esmaiés.
        Ci voi venir trois chevaliers,
        trestos armés sor lor destriers.
        Je pens et voir vos en cuic dire,
992   prendre vos vienent u ocire.
        Il vienent cha! Or t'en apense
        que fiere truissent ta desfensse!"
        Lors retornent [a]s damoisseles,
996   si lor conterent les novieles.
        Robers li dist, "Trop demorés!
        Par l'amor Diu, car vos hastés!
        Li demorers forment me grieve."
1000   Li sires maintenant se lieve.
        Ja vausist qu'il fust atornés!
        Mais ançois qu'il fust aprestés
        vinrent poingnant li robeor
1004   les le roce de Valcolor.
        Li premiers venoit a desroi.
        As autres dist, "Je.l voi! Je.l voi!"

973 de lebrans
995 r. les d.

972   the second was the Lord of Saie,
and the third, a most valiant knight,
was William of Salebrant.
They were pursuing the Fair Unknown,
976   intending to capture or kill him.
Robert saw them riding toward him,
and at once he ran
straight to his lord,
980   who lay asleep on the grass
not far from the two
noble and beautiful maidens.
Robert quickly woke his master
984   and called him aside.
"My lord," he said, "arm yourself at once
and prepare to defend yourself!
Set your mind on valiant deeds
988   and do not be dismayed.
I have just seen three knights riding toward us,
fully armed on their chargers.
I think, and in fact I am sure,
992   that they intend to capture or kill you.
They are coming this way! Now see to it
that they find your resistance fierce!"
Then they turned to the maidens
996   and told them what was occurring.
Robert said to the knight, "You are too slow!
For the love of God, make haste, my lord!
This long delay troubles me greatly."
1000   The knight arose at once.
He might have wished he were already armed!
Before he was quite ready for them
the brigands came galloping
1004   past the rock of Valcolor.
The first of them rushed forward.
He said to the others, "I see him! I see him!"

Il vint a lui, si dist, "Vasal,
1008 fait nos avés et honte et mal.
Mar veïstes Gué Perillous!
Ja vos ferrai tot a estros!"
Pris u ocis fust maintenant
1012 quant Helie lor vint devant.
Molt estoit preus la damoissele!
En haut le chevalier apiele,
"Signor, por Diu," ce dist Helie,
1016 "coment pensés tel vilonnie
d'asalir homme desarmé!
Molt vos serra a mal torné
se vos desarmé le tociés.
1020 Gardés, signor, ne comenciés
cose dont vos soiés honni,
c'onques si lait blame ne vi.
Or le laissiés, signor, armer.
1024 Ce ne li devés vos veer!
Il n'a pas force vers vos trois
se Dius ne li aiut manois.
Plus biel le poés armé prendre.
1028 Ne cuic qu'il se puisse desfendre,
et la u on puet sormonter,
doit on bien merchi esgarder."
Li chevalier sont aresté.
1032 Willaumes a premiers parlé:
"Signor," fait il, "ele dist voir.
Laissié le armer; ne puet caloir:
de nos ne se puet escaper."
1036 Cil respondent, "Don s'aille armer!"
Li chevaliers se traist ariere.   [*137 r° c*]
Del fu i fu grans la lumiere
et de la lune qui luissoit
1040 que de cler jor rien n'i avoit.
Li Biaus Descouneüs s'arma:
il vest l'auberc, l'elme laça,

1020 s. nel c.

	He rose up to him and said, "Vassal,
1008	you have shamed and offended us.
	Woe to you that you ever saw the Perilous Ford!
	Now I shall strike you down at once!"
	The knight would have been captured or killed on the spot
1012	had not Helie then stepped forward.
	She was indeed a worthy lady!
	She called out loudly to the attacking knight,
	"My lords, in God's name,
1016	how can you think of being so base
	as to attack an unarmed man?
	It will only do you discredit
	if you lay a hand on him thus.
1020	Take care, my lords, not to undertake
	something that will disgrace you,
	for I have never seen such base behavior.
	Let him arm himself, my lords.
1024	You must not prevent him from doing so!
	He will never prevail against the three of you
	unless God lends him His aid.
	It will be more fitting if you capture him armed.
1028	I do not believe he can defend himself;
	and whoever clearly has the advantage
	should take care to show mercy."
	The knights stopped their charge.
1032	William was the first to speak:
	"My lords," he said, "what she says is true.
	Let the man arm himself; there is no harm in that,
	for he cannot escape us."
1036	They answered, "Let him arm himself, then!"
	The knight in front withdrew.
	There was a great deal of light from the fire
	and from the moon which still shone,
1040	for it was not yet near day.
	The Fair Unknown armed himself:
	he put on his hauberk, he laced his helmet,

et Helie li çaint l'espee.
1044   "Garde," fait ele, "c'oubliee
n'i soit ma dame au ferir,
et prie Diu par son plaisir
que il vos doinst force et vigor
1048   de li secorre et de s'onor!"
Es vos son ceval c'on amainne;
il i sailli de terre plainne.
La pucele l'escu li tent
1052   et il par le guince le prent.
Au col le mist, puis prist la lance.
Diu reclama par sa puissance
que cele nuit li doi[n]st honnor
1056   et le desfende de dolor.
A genillons sont les puceles;
molt prient Deu les damoiseles
que lor chevalier doinst honnor
1060   et le maintiengne en cel estor.
Et cil qui point ne.s redouta
le ceval point, avant ala
encontre les trois chevaliers.
1064   Willaumes vint a lui premiers,
bien atornés, prés de bataille.
Tos sels i vint sans nule faille,
et a cel tans costume estoit
1068   que quant uns hom se conbatoit,
n'avait garde que de celui
qui faissoit sa bataille a lui.
Or va li tans afebloiant
1072   et cis usages decaant
que vint et cinc enprendent un.
Cis afaires est si comun
qui tuit le tienent de or mes.
1076   La force paist le pré adiés.
Tos est mués en autre guisse
mais dont estoit fois et francisse,

1055 doist

and Helie girded on his sword.
1044 She said, "Take care not to forget
my lady as you strike your blows,
and I shall pray to God that it may please Him
to give you the strength and spirit
1048 to aid her and do her honor!"
His horse was brought to him
and he mounted straight from the ground.
The maiden handed him his shield,
1052 and he took it by the straps.
He hung the shield from his neck, then took up his lance.
The knight called on God
to grant him victory that night
1056 and defend him from misfortune.
The maidens had fallen to their knees;
they prayed fervently that God
would grant their knight honor
1060 and uphold him during the combat.
Then he who had no fear of the three knights
spurred his horse forward
to meet them.
1064 William came at him first,
well equipped and ready for battle.
He came forward alone, of that you may be sure,
for at that time it was the custom
1068 that whenever a knight did battle
he need only concern himself with the one
challenging him at the moment.
But things are not as they used to be
1072 and this custom is falling out of use,
for now twenty-five may attack a single man.
This state of affairs is so common
that these days everyone holds to it.
1076 Now might makes right, or so it seems.
Everything has changed since then,
but in those days men acted with loyalty and nobility,

        pitiés, proece et cortoisie
1080   et largece sans vilonnie.
        Or fait cascuns tot son pooir;
        tot entendent au decevoir.
        Mais ce vos laisserai ester
1084   que d'autre cose veul parler.
        Del Bel Descouneü dirai;
        la bataille vos conterai
        de lui et des trois chevaliers.
1088   Willaumes vint a lui premiers
        ensi con vos contai devant.   [*137 v°a*]
        Tos sels i vint tot vraiement
        — ainc n'i ot per ne conpaignon —
1092   et sist sor un ceval gascon.
        Bien fu armés a son talent.
        Lors s'entrevinrent fierement:
        sor les escus se vont ferir,
1096   fer font brisier et fust croisir.
        Molt fu dure lor asamblee:
        l'uns en avra la destinee!
        Willaumes l'a premiers feru
1100   desor le bocle de l'escu.
        Le fer en fist par mi passer
        si que l'auberc fist desierrer.
        L'aubers fu fors, point ne faussa;
1104   la lance dusqu'es puins froissa.
        Bon chevalier furent andui.
        Li Biaus Descouneüs fiert lui:
        l'escu perce, l'auberc desront,
1108   dedens le cors le fer repont;
        mort le trebuce del ceval.
        Cil ne li fera huimais mal!
        Es vos poingnant celui de Graies;
1112   ariere remaint cil de Saies.
        Quant vit son conpaignon morir,
        vait le Descouneü ferir
        molt ruiste cop sor son escu.
1116   Trestout li a frait et fendu

with mercy, worthiness, and courtliness,
1080 and disinterested generosity.
Now each man does what he has the power to do
and all set their minds on deceit.
But I shall hold my peace on this now,
1084 for I wish to speak to you of other matters.
I shall tell you of the Fair Unknown
and of the combat he had undertaken
with the three knights.
1088 William came at him first,
just as I told you before.
He charged alone, in truth
—no friend or companion came with him —
1092 and he rode a Gascon horse.
He was as well armed as he could ever wish to be.
The two knights attacked each other fiercely:
they struck each other's shields,
1096 they broke the iron tips and split the wood of their lances.
Their encounter was indeed a violent one,
only one would emerge from it with his life!
William struck first,
1100 above the boss of his opponent's shield.
The tip came out the other side
and buried itself in the knight's hauberk.
But the hauberk was strong and did not give way;
1104 the lance split in William's hands.
Both of these men were excellent knights.
The Fair Unknown now struck William:
he pierced his shield, cut through his hauberk,
1108 plunged the iron tip into his flesh
and knocked him dead from his horse.
Never again would this man do him harm!
Now the Lord of Graie charged forward;
1112 the Lord of Saie still held back.
When he saw his companion dead,
the Lord of Graie rode rushed forward and struck the Fair
                    Unknown
a heavy blow on his shield.
1116 He split and shattered it completely

et l'auberc malmis et fausé.
A molt petit l'eüst navré
quant li fers d'autre pa[r]t glaça:
1120   ne.l navra mie ne bleça.
Et cil ra si tres bien feru
Helin de Graies par vertu
de sa lance ens el pis devant,
1124   l'auberc li ront et vait fausant.
Vausist u non au departir,
del bon ceval le fist caïr;
Si durement jus le porta
1128   que le braç destre li brissa.
De dous en a la pais sans faille;
fors qu'a un sol n'a mais bataille.
Quant vit blecié celui de Graies,
1132   es vos poingnant celui de Saies,
bon chevalier et conbatant,
des armes preu et travillant;
sor Garmadone fu armés.
1136   Por ses conpaignons fu dervés;
taint ot le vis de mautalant.
Par mi la lande vint poingnant.
Quant li Descouneüs le voit,
1140   vers lui s'adrece et vint tot droit.
Si laissent tost cevals aler: [*137 v°b*]
molt durment veulent encontrer.
Li uns a l'autre si feru
1144   c'andoi se sont entrabatu.
De la terre sont relevé;
li uns a l'autre regardé.
Les mains ont mises as espees
1148   ki bonnes sont et acerees.
Sor les elmes se vont ferir;
l'aciers faisoit l'elme tentir.
Molt se boutent et molt se fierent,
1152   sovent et menu se requierent;

1119 autrepat

and damaged the hauberk, tearing it open.
This would have dealt him a grievous wound,
but the iron lance tip went astray
1120 and did not touch him at all.
Then the Fair Unknown in turn struck
Elin of Graie such a blow
in the chest with his lance
1124 that he pierced his hauberk and tore the mail.
As he drew away, the Fair Unknown made him fall
willy-nilly from the fine horse he rode.
He knocked him down with such force
1128 that he broke the knight's right arm.
These two would clearly give him no more trouble;
now only one remained for him to fight.
When he saw Elin of Graie wounded,
1132 the Lord of Saie —
a fine and warlike knight,
worthy and practiced in arms — charged forward;
he was armed on his horse Garmadone.
1136 The fate of his companions maddened him;
his face was dark with fury.
He spurred his horse across the heath.
When the Fair Unknown saw the knight,
1140 he turned and rode straight toward him.
Both gave their horses free rein,
for they were eager for a fierce clash.
They struck each other so hard
1144 that they knocked each other down.
They got up
and looked at each other.
Each of them seized
1148 his fine, sharp-edged sword.
They struck each other's helmets,
which rang under the force of the steel blades.
Again and again they struck at each other,
1152 attacking over and over.

si s'entrefierent durement,
a genillons vienent souvent.
Lor elme sont tuit esfondré
1156   et lor escu tot decopé.
Dusqu'al jor dura la bataille
c'onques ne fu la desfinaille.
Li jors s'espant, l'aube creva.
1160   Li Descouneüs s'aïra:
celui de Saies vait ferir.
Cil se cuida molt bien covrir;
li cevals en un crues marcha
1164   si qu'a la terre trebucha.
Li Descouneüs sor lui vait
et cil s'eslonge et son pié trait
et il se cuide relever.
1168   Ja ne l'en covenist pener,
que cil le tint qui ne.l laissa
tant que prison li fiancha.
Si tres durement le tenoit
1172   que cil lever ne se pooit.
L'elme li desront et deslace,
aprés li desarme la face,
puis li a dit qu'il l'ocirra
1176   u tost prison fiancera.
Cil de Saies voit bien sans faille
qu'il est vencus de la bataille
et morir ne veut encor mie.
1180   Molt docement merchi li crie.
Cil li dist, "Se vels escaper,
fiance prison a torner
ens en la cort Artu le roi.
1184   Iluec en iras de par moi.
Se tu ne.l fais, a cest espee
avras ja la teste copee."
Cil de Saies prison fiance

1174   desarment
1184   I. e. i. apres moi d. p. m. [+3]

They exchanged fierce blows
and often fell to their knees.
Their helmets were bent out of shape
1156 and their shields hacked to bits.
The combat lasted through the night,
for no final blow was struck before daylight.
Then day spread through the land, and dawn broke.
1160 The Fair Unknown grew impatient
and moved to strike the Lord of Saie.
The other tried to protect himself,
but his horse stepped into a hole
1164 and fell to the ground.
The Fair Unknown was upon him at once
while the other pulled at his trapped leg to free it
so that he could get up.
1168 He need not have taken the trouble,
for the Fair Unknown held him and did not let go
until he surrendered.
He grasped the Lord of Saie so tightly
1172 that he could not get up.
He tore off the man's helmet,
bared his head,
and said he would kill him
1176 if he did not surrender at once.
The Lord of Saie clearly saw
that he had been defeated
and he had no wish to die.
1180 Humbly he asked for mercy.
The Fair Unknown said, "If you wish to live,
you must swear to me to go
straight to the court of King Arthur and surrender yourself.
1184 There will you go in my name.
If you do not do so,
I will cut off your head with this sword."
The Lord of Saie swore

1188 qu'il en ira sans demourance
droit a la cort Artu le roi
et cil en a prisse la foi.
Grant joie font les damoisseles.
1192 Or comandent metre les sieles.
La bataille est ensi finee;   [*137 v°c*]
li jors s'espart par la contree.
Cil de Saies monter ala,
1196 li Descouneüs l'arainna,
si li demande sa convine,
coment il va, par quel destine.
Li doi conpainnon qui estoient,
1200 qui asali l'ont, que querroient?
Cil de Saies respont atant,
"Sire," fait il, "Tot vraiement
vos en dira la verité;
1204 ja mos ne vos en ert celé.
Je sui," fait il, "sire de Saies.
Cil qui gist la sire est de Graies;
Heluins a non, molt est grevés
1208 car l'uns des bras li est copés.
Et l'autres est de Salebrans,
Willaumes, dont molt sui dolans.
Ci venimes par mon signor
1212 —par lu[i] avons ceste dolor—
Bliobliëris, que trovastes
quant le Gué Perillous passastes,
cui vos laidistes malement.
1216 Ça nos tramist il vraiement
por vos prendre u por [vos] ocire.
Males novieles li puis dire
quant revenrai a mon signor,
1220 se li acroistrai sa dolor.
Tels cuide sa honte vengier
ki porcace son enconbrier.

1217 p. lui o.
1218 puist

1188   to go without delay
       to King Arthur's court
       and the Fair Unknown accepted his word.
       The maidens rejoiced at this.
1192   They then commanded the horses to be saddled.
       Thus was the combat ended;
       bright day now filled the land.
       The Lord of Saie went to mount his horse,
1196   and the Fair Unknown spoke to him
       and asked him to tell him
       how and with what purpose he had come.
       Who were his two companions, who had attacked him
1200   and what had they been seeking?
       The other answered him at once,
       "My lord, I shall tell you
       the truth of this matter;
1204   no part of it shall be withheld from you.
       I am the Lord of Saie.
       The one lying there is from Graie;
       Elin is his name, and he is badly wounded,
1208   for one of his arms has been cut.
       And the other, for whom I mourn,
       was William of Salebrant.
       We three came for the sake of my lord —
1212   for his sake we have suffered this.
       He is Blioblïeris, whom you encountered
       when you crossed the Perilous Ford
       and whom you wounded so grievously.
1216   In truth, he sent us here
       to capture or kill you.
       Now I shall have only bad news
       to give my lord when I return,
1220   for I have deepened his sorrow.
       Sometimes a man seeks to avenge his shame
       and wins nothing but harm for himself.

Qui plus monte que il ne doit
1224   ains trebuce qu'il ne vaudroit."
Cil de Saies monter ala;
Heluin de Graies en porta.
Li Biaus Descouneüs li prie
1228   que aveuc lui en maint Clarie;
par lui a ses parens l'envoie.
La pucele en demainne joie.
D'autre part Helie et li nains
1232   et Robers, qui n'est pas vilains,
et se sire si s'atornerent
et de cevaucier s'apresterent.
Vers la Cité Gaste s'en vont;
1236   assés orés que il feront.
        Or m'escoutés: voir vos dirai,
ja, mon veul, mon mal n'i querrai.
Qui que s'oublit, je ne.l puis faire;
1240   celi dont ne me puis retraire
ne vel je mie ore oublier.
Mais Dius me gart de li fauser!
Ce dient cil qui vont treçant,
1244   li uns le va l'autre contant,
"Peciés n'est de feme traïr,"   [*138 r°a*]
mais laidement sevent mentir.
Ains [est] molt grans peciés, par m'ame!
1248   Or vos penerois d'une dame
qui n'avera talent d'amer.
Vos li irés tant sermonner
que serr[a] souprisse d'amor.
1252   Tant li prierés cascun jor,
bien li porés son cuer enbler.
De ço vos viene Dius garder!
Por vos tos [ses] amis perdra
1256   et son mari qui l'amera.

1247 *lacks* est
1251 serres [*em. Williams*]
1255 t. vos a. [*em. Williams*]

And whoever climbs higher than he should
1224   falls farther than he would care to."
The Lord of Saie turned to mount his horse;
he carried Elin of Graie away with him.
The Fair Unknown asked him
1228   to take Clarie also
and to see that she reached her family.
The maiden was overjoyed at this.
For their part, Helie and the dwarf
1232   and Robert, who was certainly no lout,
along with the Fair Unknown, prepared
to continue their journey.
They rode toward the Desolate City;
1236   soon you will hear a great deal about what they did there.
    But hear me now, for I shall tell you a truth;
never would I willingly seek my own discredit.
Whoever might take love lightly, I could never do so,
1240   and so I do not wish to forget just now
the one from whom I could never break away.
God keep me from ever proving false to her!
Those who make a habit of deceiving ladies
1244   go about saying to one another,
"It is no sin to betray a woman,"
but they are wicked liars.
On the contrary, it is a great sin, by my soul!
1248   Let us say that you concern yourself with a lady
who has no desire to love.
You regale her so often with fine speeches
that love finally catches her with her guard down.
1252   You plead your cause to her every day,
and so succeed in winning her heart.
May God keep you from doing such things!
For your sake this lady loses all her friends
1256   and the love of her husband.

Quant en arés tot vo voloir,
adont le vaurés decevoir.
Mal ait qui si acostuma
1260   et qui jamais jor le fera!
Cil qui se font sage d'amor,
cil en sont faus et traïtor.
Por ço mius vel faire folie
1264   que ne soie loiaus m'amie.
Ço qu'ele n'est l'ai apielee.
Que dirai dont? La molt amee?
S'ensi l'apiel, voir en dirai.
1268   S'amie di, lors mentirai
car moi ne fait ele sanblant.
Las, por li muir et por li cant!
Tos jors serai en sa merchi.
1272   Or vos redirai je par chi
del Descouneü qui s'en vait.
La pucele les li se trait;
une aventure va contant.
1276   Par le forest vait chevauçant;
li chevalier se regarda:
un cerf vit qui les lui passa.
Langue traite vait esfreés;
1280   de seize rains estoit armés.
Devant lui tressailli le voie—
n'i a celui qui ne le voie.
Aprés le sivent lïement
1284   bracet, viautre qui vont saillant,
qui vont aprés le cerf braiant.
Detriers vait un bracés corant.
Plus estoit blans que nule nois,
1288   orelles noires come pois,
de li qui fu au les senestre;
de l'autre part, sor le flanc destre
ot une tace tote noire.
1292   Petis estoit, ço est la voire,
graindres un poi d'un erminet.
Nus hom ne vit si biel bracet!
Devant la pucele passa,

Then, when you have had what you wish from her,
you set your mind on deceiving her.
Woe to the man who makes a habit of such things,
1260   or would ever do them at all!
Those who make themselves clever in matters of love
are false to it, they are traitors.
For myself, I would rather behave like a fool
1264   than be disloyal to my ladylove.
But I have called her something she is not.
What should I call her then? My beloved?
If I call her that, I am speaking the truth.
1268   But if I call her "ladylove," why then I shall be lying,
for she will not even look at me.
Wretch that I am, for her I am dying, and for her I sing!
I shall forever be at her mercy.
1272   Now I shall tell you more about
the Fair Unknown, who was riding away.
The maiden caught up with him
and told the story of an adventure as they went along.
1276   As he was riding through the forest,
the knight looked around
and saw a stag pass by.
He had sixteen points on his antlers
1280   and was running, terrified, with his tongue hanging out.
He shot across the knight's path
in full view of everyone.
After him in joyful pursuit
1284   came greyhounds and brachets
baying and bounding along behind.
One brachet came trailing behind the others.
He was whiter than snow
1288   with only his ears as black as pitch,
or so it appeared from his left side;
on the other side, on his right flank,
was a black spot.
1292   He was truly a very small dog,
only a little larger than an ermine.
But no one ever saw such a handsome brachet!
He crossed in front of the maiden

1296   en mi la voie s'aresta:
        el pié ot ficie une espine.   [*138 r°b*]
        La pucele vers lui se cline
        et por lui prendre a pié descent.
1300   Le bracet pris[t] isnelement
        puis est hastivement montee
        et chevauça tote l'estree.
        Le bracet dist qu'en portera
1304   et a sa dame le donra.
        Es vos poingnant un veneor
        deseur un ronci caceor.
        Ses ciens sivoit, son cor tenoit;
1308   en sa main un espiel avoit.
        Corte cote avoit d'un burel;
        le cors ot avenant et biel;
        d'unes houses estoit hosés.
1312   Estrangement estoit hastés
        quant il vit prendre le bracet
        a la pucele, qui le met
        sous son mantel et reponnoit.
1316   Et quant li veneres le voit
        si vint poignant a la pusele,
        se li a dit, "Amie biele,
        laissiés, lassiés mon cien ester!
1320   Damoissele, laissié le haler
        aprés les autres qui s'en vont!"
        La damoissele li respont
        que del bracet n'avra il mie,
1324   car biaus est, si en a envie
        et por ce si l'en velt porter,
        a sa dame le velt donner.
        Cil li respont, "Ma damoissele,
1328   ci avroit molt male novielle.
        Rendés le moi, n'i avés droit."
        Cele li dist, "N'i avrés droit.
        C'est li ciens que vos mais n'avrois

1300 pris

1296   and stopped in the middle of the path,
for he had a thorn in his paw.
The maiden bent down
and got off her horse to pick him up.

1300   She snatched the dog up,
then remounted in all haste
and galloped away.
She said she was taking the brachet

1304   to give to her lady.
Just then along came a hunter
on his horse.
He was following his dogs, his horn in one hand

1308   and holding a spear in the other.
He wore a short tunic of burel
and boots,
and was a fine-looking man.

1312   He was riding along in great haste,
for he had seen the maiden snatching up the hound
and putting him
under her cloak to hide him.

1316   When the hunter saw this,
he rode up to the maiden
and said, "Dear friend, please release my dog,
let him go!

1320   My lady, let him follow along
after the other dogs!"
The maiden answered
that he certainly could not have the brachet:

1324   he was such a beautiful dog that she wanted
to take him with her
to give to her lady.
He answered, "Lady,

1328   I should be very sorry to hear that.
Return the dog to me, for you have no right to it."
She answered, "You will certainly not have him.
You will never get this dog back

1332   por quantques vos dire saçois!"
         Li veneres se coreça
         et le chevalier apiela:
         "Sire," fait il, "estés, caele!
1336   Dites a cele damoissele
         qu'ele mon bracet n'en port pas!"
         Et cil li prie eneslespas,
         "Doce amie, c'or li rendés."
1340   Cele dist, "Ja plus n'en parlés:
         c'est li bracés que mais n'avra.
         Sive son cerf qui tost s'en va,
         que le bracet pas ne randrai."
1344   "Sire," dist li venere,"or sai
         que mon cien en faites porter.
         Faites le moi abandonner
         que mon cien la u est presisse.
1348   Certes, ja plus ne vos quesisse.
         Vostre force l'en fait porter: [*138 r°c*]
         por ce le vos doi demander.
         Del bracet n'en portera mie
1352   se vos ne li faites aïe."
         Et cil au veneor respont,
         "Por nule rien qui ssoit el mont
         ne l'abandonneroie mie,
1356   car ce serroit grans coardie.
         Mais biel me serroit se vausist
         qu'ele le bracet vos rendist.
         Car li rendés, france pucele."
1360   Lors respondi la damoisele,
         "Parler vos oi de grant folie,
         car le bracet n'ara il mie!"
         Li venere s'en vait atant
1364   sans congié prendre maintenant
         et dist entre ses dens, "Sans faille
         ne l'en menrés pas sans bataille!"
         Chevalier fu de haut parage:

1336 damamoissele

1332   no matter what you may say to me!"
At this the hunter grew angry
and called out to the knight:
"My lord," he said, "enough of this!
1336   Kindly tell this maiden
not to take away my brachet!"
And the knight said at once,
"Dear friend, please return his dog."
1340   She said, "Not one more word about it,
for he will never have the dog.
Let this fellow run along after his stag, which is getting away,
for I will not give him the brachet."
1344   "My lord," said the hunter, "now I see
that the theft of my dog is your fault.
Make her give him back to me at once;
let me take him from where he is.
1348   I certainly would not ask you for anything more.
It is being taken from me under guarantee of your protection;
therefore, it is you I am asking for its return.
The lady will certainly not manage to take my brachet
1352   unless you help her."
And the knight said to the hunter,
"Not for anything in the world
would I forsake this lady,
1356   for that would be an act of great cowardice.
But I would certainly be pleased if she
were willing to return the brachet to you.
Please give it back, my worthy lady."
1360   The maiden answered,
"You are talking nonsense,
for he will never have this brachet!"
The hunter then galloped away
1364   without taking his leave,
muttering to himself, "In truth,
you will not take the dog without a fight!"
He was a knight of noble lineage

1368   petit prisse son vaselage
       s'ensi en laist son cien porter.
       Son harnas faissoit sejorner
       a un castiel qui siens estoit.
1372   Molt pres de la u il caçoit
       le castiel i avoit fait faire.
       Quant il voloit cacer ne traire
       par le forest u il caçoit,
1376   adont el castiel sejornoit.
       Au castiel vint molt tost poingna[n]t.
       Encontre lui vont si serjant.
       "Alés," fait il, "mi escuier,
1380   amenés moi mon bon destrier
       et mes armes, si m'armerai.
       Gardés que n'i faites delai!"
       Cil les vont querre isnelement
1384   se.s aportent hastivement.
       Li uns les cauces li laça;
       vest son hauberc, l'elme ferma,
       au les senestre çainst l'espee,
1388   qui bonne estoit et aceree.
       Puis est montés sor son destrier.
       Le bracet cuide calengier.
       Son esscu prist, au col le mist,
1392   a l'arestil sa lance prist,
       del castiel ist, pongnant s'e[n] vait.
       Molt tient a honte et a grant lait
       s'ensi en laist son cien porter
1396   qu'il ne.l face cier conperer.
       Par la forest s'en vait poingnant
       si lor est venus au devant
       par une voie qu'il savoit,
1400   et quant il le chevalier voit,
       a haute vois lors li escrie,   [*138 v°a*]

1377 poingnat
1388 acerece
1393 p. se v.

1368   and would have valued his knighthood but little
if he had allowed his dog to be taken so easily.
He had left his arms
at a castle that belonged to him.
1372   He had had this castle built
near the place where he had been hunting that day.
Whenever he wished to hunt with spear or bow
in this forest,
1376   he stayed at the castle.
Now he rode toward it at a gallop.
His men-at-arms came out to meet him.
"Come, my squires," he said,
1380   "Bring me my fine charger
and my weapons, for I shall arm myself.
And be quick about it!"
The squires hurried to fetch the weapons
1384   and brought them with all speed.
One of them laced on his leg-armor,
put his hauberk on him, secured his helmet,
and girded his sword to his left side;
1388   it was a fine one, made of strong steel.
Then he mounted his charger.
He intended to make challenge for the brachet.
He took his shield and hung it at his neck,
1392   grasped his lance at its base,
then went forth from the castle, giving spur to his horse.
He would have considered it most shameful and base
to allow his dog to be taken away
1396   without making the knight pay dearly for it.
He rode through the forest, spurring his horse,
until he stood in the path of the knight and the maiden,
having followed a path he knew,
1400   and when he saw the knight,
he called out to him in a loud voice,

"Vasal, vasal, or est folie
de mon cien qu'en faites porter!
1404 Or le vos estuet conperer:
en pardon pas ne l'en menrés.
Je vos desfi: or vos gardé[s]!"
Quant cil le ve[ne]or entent,
1408 son escu prist isnelement
et puis aprés reprist sa lance.
Point le ceval qui tost li lance,
si se comande au Creator;
1412 por joster muet au veneor.
Molt orent andui bieles armes!
Les escus prendent as enarmes,
chevaus poingnent por tost aler,
1416 baissent les lances por joster.
Fendent escus, fausent haubers;
des estriers vont ploier les fers.
Des lances les esclices volent.
1420 De nule amisté ne parolent!
Des tronçons donent grans colee[s].
Aprés revienent as espees,
si s'en vont tost entreferir.
1424 Lors oïssiés elmes tentir,
l'un enforcier, l'autre pener,
vasals ferir, cevals süer!
Molt fiert bien cascuns de l'espee,
1428 molt est dure d'els la mellee;
molt sont vasal, fier caple font.
Lor elme tot enbaré sont
et lor escu tot decopé.
1432 Si furent andoi molt lassé;
tos li plus fors vait molt lassant.
Et quant ne poent en avant,

1406 garder
1407 veor
1408 insnelement
1421 colee

"Vassal, vassal, it is foolhardy of you
to allow my dog to be taken away!
1404   Now you must pay for it,
for you shall not take it freely.
I hereby challenge you: now prepare to defend yourself!"
When the knight heard the hunter,
1408   he quickly took up his shield
and then his lance.
He set spur to his horse, who charged forward,
and commended himself to the Creator;
1412   he rode forth to joust with the hunter.
What fine arms they both had!
They grasped the straps of their shields,
spurred their horses to lend them speed,
1416   and lowered their lances for the joust.
Shields were smashed, hauberks were pierced;
they bent the steel of their stirrups.
Splinters flew from their lances.
1420   No word of friendship passed between these two!
They continued to give great blows with their broken lances.
Then they both took up their swords
and rushed to strike each other.
1424   What a clang of steel on helmets,
as one knight struggled and the other strained,
as both struck blows, their horses covered with sweat!
Each struck well with his sword,
1428   and savage was the combat between them,
for they were both fine knights and fierce in battle.
Their helmets were dented
and their shields hacked to bits.
1432   But both at last grew exhausted;
even the stronger was tiring.
And finally, when they could do no more,

         as bras s'aerdent demanois
1436   et laissent les brans vïenois.
         Li uns tint l'autre durement.
         Li ceval se vont eslongnant,
         tornent sieles, ronpent poitrals.
1440   Guerpir lor estuet les chevals,
         a la terre caient andui.
         Molt prioit Diu cascuns por lui.
         Li veneres lever cuida
1444   mais cil durement le saça,
         adens l'abati mantenant.
         Ce pesa celui duremant,
         qui molt legiers et fors estoit;
1448   de relever molt s'enforçoit.
         Mais ne l[e] laisse relever:
         que que il li doie grever
         le refist jus caïr sans faille,
1452   si le sace par la ventaille,
         le cief li desarme et la face.   [*138 v°b*]
         Lors voit jesir en mi la place
         s'espee, que il bien conut;
1456   isnelement por li corut,
         mais ne laist pas le veneor
         ançois le tient par grant vigor.
         Quant s'espee avoit recouvree,
1460   ja li eust la teste copee
         se il n'otriast son voloir.
         Li veneres set bien le voir,
         que il escaper ne puet mie.
1464   Molt doucement merchi li crie:
         dist que il fera son plaissi[r],
         a son plaissir ne puet faillir.
         Cil respont, "Ne pués escaper
1468   ne fians prison a torner

1449 M. nel l.[-*1*]
1451 just
1465 plaissi

they began to grapple with each other,
1436   leaving aside their Viennese swords.
Each held fast to the other,
so that when their horses moved away from each other,
their saddles turned over and the breast-straps broke.
1440   The knights were forced from their horses,
and both fell to the ground.
Each prayed fervently that God would protect him.
The hunter tried to get up,
1444   but the other pulled him down sharply,
making him fall face down.
This greatly annoyed the hunter,
a strong and agile man,
1448   and he struggled hard to get up.
But the Fair Unknown would not let him do so:
though it angered the hunter,
the Fair Unknown made him fall down again,
1452   grabbed him by the ventail,
and bared his head and face.
The Fair Unknown spied his sword,
which he knew well, lying nearby;
1456   he quickly went to pick it up
without letting go of the hunter,
whom he held in a strong grip.
Once he had recovered his sword,
1460   he would have cut off the hunter's head
if the man had not agreed to do what he wished.
The hunter saw clearly
that there was no escape for him.
1464   He humbly asked for mercy:
he said he would do what he wished
and would not fail to do his pleasure.
The knight answered, "You must
1468   promise to go straight

ens en la cort Artus le roi.
Et se li dites de par moi,
je vos envoi en sa prison,
1472   car molt me dona rice don
quant m'envoia la dame aidier
qui bessong en a et mestier."
Li vasals dist, "Bien li dirai.
1476   Et de cui pris me clamerai?"
"Biaus dols amis, bien le sarois:
del Biel Descouneü dirois."
Del veneor a la foi prisse;
1480   une autre cose li devisse.
Li Biaus Descouneüs dist, "Sire,
mon [non] m'avés rové a dire;
or vel je vostre non savoir."
1484   Et cil li regehist le voir;
faire l'estuet ço qu'il comande:
"J'ai non l'Orguillous de la Lande.
De la prison que plevi ai
1488   ains un mois m'en aquiterai."
Li uns a l'autre congié prent;
el cevals montent errament.
Li venere s'en retorna,
1492   de son cien mie n'en porta.
Et li Descouneüs s'en vait
et Robers, qui grant joie en fait,
li nains et la dame ensement
1496   le grant cemin s'en vont anblent.
     Le jor ont faite grant jornee
et quant ce vint a l'avespree,
si issirent d'un bos foillu;
1500   un castiel de pres [ont] veü
qui molt estoit et bons et bials.
Becleus avoit non li castials.

1482 non *lacking*
1500 ont *lacking*
1501 et bons *repeated*

to the court of King Arthur.
And there you will tell the king in my name
that I have sent you to be his prisoner,

1472 for he granted me a rich boon
when he sent me to render aid to a lady
who has great need of it."
The vassal said, "I shall certainly tell him this.

1476 And who shall I say it was who defeated me?"
"My dear friend, I shall tell you:
say it was the Fair Unknown."
He accepted the hunter's word,

1480 then he asked for something else.
"My lord," he said,
"you asked me to tell me your name;
now I would like to know yours."

1488 And the hunter told him the truth,
for it was right that he do what the other required:
"I am called the Proud Knight of the Glade.
I shall fulfill the promise I made to you

1488 before a month has passed."
They took leave of each other
and straightway mounted their horses.
The hunter went home once more,

1492 still without his dog.
And the Fair Unknown, along with Robert,
who rejoiced at the way things had turned out,
and the dwarf and the lady as well

1496 set off along the main road.
They traveled a great distance that day,
and when it was early evening
they emerged from a thick forest

1500 and saw a beautiful and
well fortified castle nearby.
The castle was named Becleus.

Tot entor cort une riviere:
1504 por poissons nul millor ne quiere,
et si porte l'iaue navie;   [138 v°c]
par la i vient la marcandie
dont li pasages molt valoit.
1508 De molins plenté i avoit,
et rivieres et praeries,
et si ot grans gaaigneries.
D'autre part les viegnes estoient,
1512 qui plus de dous liues tenoient.
Li castials fu clos de fosés
grans et parfons et lons et lés.
Sur les fosés hals murs avoit
1516 dont li castials tos clos estoit.
Li Descouneüs s'aresta.
La demoissele en apiela,
se li a le castel mostré.
1520 Por l'esgarder sont aresté
et dient que bials est et gens;
millor n'en ot ne rois ne quens.
Vers le castiel s'en vont corant:
1524 li vespres va molt aproçant.
Encontré ont une pucele
en lor voie, qui molt ert biele.
D'un drap de soie estoit vestue;
1528 si biele riens ne fu veüe.
La pene d'edres fu bendee,
d'ermine, de gris geronee;
li sebelins molt bons estoit—
1532 en nul païs millor n'avoit.
Molt fu la demoissele gente,
sa crans biautés molt atalente
a cels qui virent la pucele.
1536 Onques nus hom ne vit tant biele:
le front ot large et clier le vis
et blanc con est la flor de lis;

1505 iaaue

There was a river flowing all around:
1504 no better could be found for fishing,
and many boats traveled on it,
for there was much traffic of merchandise there,
which brought great profit to the city.
1508 There were mills in great number
and rivers and meadows,
and much pasture land.
On the other side were vineyards,
1512 which covered more than two square leagues.
The castle was surrounded by deep moats
both long and wide.
High walls loomed above the moats
1516 and completely surrounded the castle.
When he saw this, the Fair Unknown stopped.
He spoke to the maiden,
and pointed to the castle.
1520 They stopped to look at it
and declared that it was a beautiful and noble one
and that, indeed, no king or count had a better.
They galloped toward the castle,
1524 for evening was fast falling.
Along the road they met
a most beautiful maiden.
She wore a silk garment,
1528 and no one ever saw such a lovely creature.
Her cloak, trimmed in swansdown,
was done in alternating bands of ermine and miniver;
its lining of sable was of the highest quality —
1532 none finer could be found in any land.
This maiden was of noble bearing,
and her great beauty delighted
all those who beheld her.
1536 No man ever saw such a lovely woman:
she had a wide forehead and glowing complexion,
and she was fair as the lily;

les sorcils peu noirs et vautis,
1540   delgiés et grailles et traitis;
le vis avoit si colouré
come le rose el tans d'esté;
bien faite boce, dens petistes—
1544   de plus biele parler n'oïstes.
Les crins ot blon et reluissans
come fin or reflanboians;
d'un fil d'arge[nt] fu galonnee,
1548   si cevançoit escevelee;
Le[s] iols ot vairs, le front bien fait;
mai[n]s ot blances, cors bien portrait—
plus bel cors n'ot nule pucele.
1552   Mais grant dol fait la damoissele:
ses puins tort, ses cevels decire,
cele qui a et dol et ire.
Del castiel vint la damoissele
1556   et li Descouneüs l'apiele
et a l'encontre tost li va.   [*139 r°a*]
Molt gentement le salua;
son salu li rent en plorant
1560   con cele qui a dol molt grant.
Cil demanda a la pucele,
"Por coi plorés, amie biele?
S'il vos plast, je le vel savoir."
1564   Cele respont, "Dol doi avoir
ne je jamais joie n'orai,
car la rien c'onques plus amai
ai je perduĕ hui cest jor.
1568   Sire," fait ele, "por ce plor,
por mon ami que perdu ai.
Ocis m'est hui, de dol morrai.
Li cuers me crieve de dolor!
1572   Lasse, coment vivrai mais jor?"

1547 darge
1449 les iols
1550 mais ot

her eyebrows were dark and arched,
1540 fine and delicate, and beautifully formed;
her face was the color
of a summer rose;
her mouth was beautifully shaped, with delicate teeth —
1544 you never heard anyone tell of a lovelier lady.
Her blonde hair shone
like fine and glimmering gold;
a silver thread had been woven into it,
1548 and she rode with her head uncovered.
Her eyes were bright, her brow well shaped;
her hands were white and her body elegant —
indeed, no maiden was more fair of form.
1552 But the maiden was weeping:
she wrung her hands and tore her hair,
for she suffered great grief and sorrow.
The maiden was coming from the castle,
1556 and the Fair Unknown called to her
and hurried to meet her.
He greeted her most graciously,
but she returned his greeting with tears,
1560 like one in the greatest distress.
The knight said to the maiden,
"Why are your weeping, dear friend?
Please tell me why; I would like to know."
1564 She answered, "I cannot help but grieve,
indeed I shall never know joy again,
for this very day I have lost
the one I loved most in the world.
1568 My lord, I am weeping
for my love, whom I have lost.
He was killed today, and I shall die of sorrow.
Alas, my heart is breaking!
1572 How unhappy I am! How shall I live another day?"

Quant cil l'oï, pitié en a.
A la pucele demanda
coment estoit mors ses amis,
1576   s'il estoit a armes ocis
u autrement, que le li die.
La pucele respont marie,
"Sire, ocis l'a uns chevaliers
1580   qui molt est orguillous et fiers,
si est sires de cest castiel.
Il a en la vile un oissiel,
esprevier bien mué et biel
1584   . . . .
En un plain, dalés un mostier,
illuec ont asis l'esprevier
sor une perce tote d'or.
1588   Li espreviers vaut un tresor.
Cele qui l'esprevier ara
et a le perce le prendra
si ara los de la plus biele.
1592   Et si couvient a la pucele
qui vaura avoir l'esprevier
que maint o soi un chevalier
por desrainnier qu'ele est plus biele
1596   que nule dame ne pucele.
Car cil qui del castiel est sire
maintenant li va contredire
et le desfent de par s'amie,
1600   et dist que si biele n'est mie
con s'amie est, ce dist, sans faille.
Issi conmence la bataille.
Sire, mes amis i ala;
1604   por l'oissel prendre m'i mena.
Quant je vauc prendre l'esprev[i]er,
li sire le vint calengier

1587 s. .j. t. dor p. *with insertion marks to correct order*
1602 la mellee b.
1605 esprever

When the knight heard this, he was filled with pity.
He asked the maiden
how it was that her love had died,
1576   whether he had been killed
in armed combat or in some other manner.
Stricken with grief, she answered,
"My lord, he was killed
1580   by a very proud and cruel knight,
who is the lord of this castle.
In the town there is a bird,
a beautiful molted sparrowhawk
1584   . . . .
In the meadow by a church
they have placed the hawk
on a perch all made of gold.
1588   This hawk is worth a king's ransom.
Any maiden who gains possession of the hawk
by taking it from its perch
will be renowned as the most beautiful of women.
1592   But the maiden who wishes
to have this hawk
must bring with her a knight
who will maintain that she is more beautiful
1596   than any other lady or maiden.
For the lord of this castle
will then dispute what the knight says
and defend the hawk on behalf of his own lady,
1600   saying that the other lady is certainly
not so lovely as she.
And so the combat will begin.
My lord, my love led me to that place
1604   so that I might take the bird.
But just as I was about to take the hawk,
the lord of the castle arrived and made challenge

que je ne le presisse mie.
1608 Li miens amis me dist, 'Amie,
prendé le tost hardïement.   [*139 r°b*]
Por demostrer sui en present
que vos estes asés plus biele
1612 ne soit la soie damoissele.'
A l'autre molt en anuia
et dist que il l'en dessdira.
Ensi enprisent la bataille.
1616 Ocis fu mes amis sans faille,
qui faire me voloit honnor,
si m'est torné a grant dolor.
Tot ont juré cil del castiel
1620 de deseur le cors Saint Marcel,
un cier cors saint qui 'st en la vile,
que vers celui ne feront gille
qui au signor se conbatra.
1624 Se il l'ocit, garde n'ara,
ne l'en covient avoir paor
ne nule dote ne cremor
ne ja nus tort ne l'en fera.
1628 Tos seürs aler s'en porra."
Cil li respont qui se li dist,
"Bon gré l'en saroies, je cuit,
qui vos rendroit cel esprevier
1632 et vostre ami porroit vengier."
Cele respont, "Sire, por voir,
bon gré l'en devroie savoir.
Grant cose i vauroie avoir mise
1636 qu'il fust vengiés a ma devise.
Qui mon ami porroit vengier,
cil me porroit bien ensgagier
en tos païs," ce dist la biele.
1640 Et cil respont a la pucele,

1609 *repeated at bottom of col. a*
1623 se *repeated*

      to keep me from taking it.
1608   My friend said to me, 'My love,
      take it at once and without fear.
      I am here to prove
      that you are much more beautiful
1612   than this knight's lady.'
      This greatly angered the other knight,
      who said he would make my friend unsay his words.
      And so they challenged each other to combat.
1616   In truth, my love, who wished
      to do me honor, was killed;
      and so this affair has turned to great sorrow for me.
      All those from the castle have sworn
1620   by the body of Saint Marcel,
      whose holy relics lie in the town,
      that they will not turn on
      any man who does combat with their lord.
1624   If the challenger should kill him,
      he need not be on his guard
      or have the slightest doubt
      that any shall do him harm.
1628   He will be allowed to leave in all safety."
      The knight said to her,
      "I believe you would not be ungrateful
      to whoever could return the hawk to you
1632   and so avenge your friend."
      The beautiful lady answered, "In truth, my lord,
      I would be most grateful to him.
      I would give a great deal
1636   for my love to be avenged as I wish.
      Whoever avenges him
      may count on my good will
      wherever he might be."
1640   Then the knight said to her,

"Venés o moi, je vos en pri.
Ne lairai pas, je vos afi,
que vostre ami n'aille vengier
1644   et ne vos rende l'esprevier."
Et la pucele li respont,
"Cil Sire qui forma le mont
vos doi[n]st qu'a cief le puissiés traire!
1648   Se vos certes le poés faire,
saciés grant honor i avrois
car molt grant proece ferois.
O vos vel aler cele part.
1652   Dius, se lui plaist, de mal vos gart!"
Ceste pucele fu montee;
Margerie estoit apielee.
Ensi vers le castiel s'en vont;
1656   passent les lices et le pont.
Vers le cort vont et Margerie
tot droit vers l'esprevier le guie.
Grant gent le vont aprés sivant,
1660   chevalier, borjois et sergant;   [*139 r°c*]
dames et puceles issoient
de lor ouvroi[r]s et demandoient
del chevalier qui il estoit
1664   qui l'esprevier querre venoit.
Pluisor respondent, "Ne savons,
mais itant dire vos poons
que ses elmes est esfondrés.
1668   Bien pert qu'il a esté portés!
Maint chevalier i ont feru.
Molt est enclé en son escu;
de cols d'espees est orlés,
1672   et ses haubers est descloés."

1641 Pris
1647 doist
1649 s. qui molt g. h. i. a. [+2]
1653 pucele *repeated*
1662 ouvrois

"Please come with me.
I promise that I will not fail
to avenge your friend
1644 and see that you gain possession of the hawk."
And the maiden said to him,
"May the Lord God who created the world
give you the strength to accomplish this!
1648 If you can, in truth, do so,
you will win great honor,
for you will be doing a most valiant deed.
I indeed wish to go to this place with you.
1652 May it please God to protect you from harm!"
The maiden, whose name was Margerie,
was already on her horse.
And so they rode toward the castle;
1656 they passed the walls and the bridge.
They rode toward the lord's seat, and Margerie
led them straight to the hawk.
A great crowd followed them,
1660 knights, burghers, and men-at-arms;
ladies and maidens left
their sewing rooms and asked
who this knight
1664 who came seeking the hawk might be.
Some of them answered, "We do not know,
but we can tell you this much:
his helmet has been dented.
1668 Anyone can see that it has been worn in combat!
Many a knight has struck it.
His shield is tattered,
slashed with sword blows;
1672 and his hauberk is torn in many places."

Ce dist cascuns sans devinaille,
"Il est bons chevaliers sans faille.
Ha, Dius! Qui sont ces damoiseles
1676   qu'il mainne o lui, qui tant sont bieles?"
Dist un borjois, "A mon sanblant
la pucele qui va devant,
ele amena le chevalier
1680   qui fu ocis por l'esprevier.
Hui main aprés messe cantant
l'ocist me sire voirement.
Molt en fu dure la bataille."
1684   Ce dist cascuns, "C'est voirs sans faille!"
Aprés le vont trestot sivant
et li chevaliers vait devant.
Si est venues a l'esprevier
1688   en la place les un vergier.
Molt fu la place biele et gente;
en mi liu ot planté une ente
qui a tos jors florie estoit.
1692   Une perce d'or i avoit
u li espreviers fu asis.
Le trait d'un arc, ce m'est avis,
estoit a conpas ordenee
1696   environ et bien delivree.
Li espreviers en mi estoit,
et tantost come cil le voit,
en haut apiele Margerie,
1700   "Venés avant, ma douce amie,
prendre a la perce l'esprevier.
P[o]r vos le vel je desrainnier:
vos le devés [molt] bien avoir,
1704   tant avés biauté et savoir,
ensement et pris et valor
et biel cors et biele color."
Et cele vint par mi la place

1702 Par
1703 v. le d. b. a. [-*l*, em. *Williams*]

Each one could say with certainty,
"Truly, he is a fine knight.
And, by heaven, who are those
1676   beautiful maidens whom he is escorting?"
One burgher said, "It seems to me
that the maiden riding in front
is the one who came with the knight
1680   who was killed because of the hawk.
In fact, my lord killed him
this morning after mass.
It was a most fierce combat."
1684   Everyone said, "Indeed, that is so!"
They followed closely behind
the knight, who rode ahead.
The Fair Unknown arrived at the meadow
1688   where the hawk was, near a walled garden.
It was a most lovely place;
in the midst of the meadow was planted a grafted tree
that was always in bloom.
1692   There sat the hawk
on a golden perch.
The meadow had been carefully cleared
on all sides, I believe,
1696   for the length of a bowshot from this tree.
The hawk was in the middle,
and, as soon as he saw it,
the Fair Unknown said to Margerie,
1700   "Come forward, sweet friend,
and take the hawk from its perch.
I intend to assert your right to it:
you should certainly have it,
1704   for you are lovely and intelligent,
full of worth and renown,
and elegant of form and face."
And so Margerie rode up

1708   a l'esprevier, si le deslace.
       Et li sires i vient poingnant,
       armés sor un ceval ferrant.
       Ses escus a argent estoit;
1712   roses vermelles i avoit;
       de sinople les roses sont.   *[139 v°a]*
       Bien fu armés sor le gascont,
       un bel ceval de molt grant pris.
1716   L'escu par les enarmes pris,
       venoit armés molt gent et biel.
       De roses avoit un capel
       en son elme, qui biaus estoit.
1720   Ses cevals tos covers estoit
       d'un samit, et si ot vermelles
       unes roses, et a mervelles
       estoit esgardés; et s'amie,
1724   qui avoit non Rose Espanie,
       en coste celui cevauçoit
       un palefroi qui bue[n]s estoit.
       Molt estoit et laide et frencie!
1728   N'i a celui cui ne dessie
       qu'il le maintient por le plus bele.
       Tot s'esmervellent cil et cele
       k'Amors li fait son sen müer.
1732   Mais nus hom ne se puet garder
       k'Amors ne.l face bestorner;
       la laide fait biele sanbler,
       tant set de guille et d'encanter.
1736   . . . .
       Li chevaliers vint a esploit
       envers le pucele tot droit.
       A molt halte vois li escrie
1740   que l'esprevier ne prenge mie,
       qu'a li n'afiert pas qu'ele l'ait.
       Li Biaus Descouneüs se trait

1722 rose; *text arranged around defect in vellum*
1726 bues

1708   to the hawk and untied it.
Then the lord of the castle came at a gallop,
armed on a steel grey charger.
He carried a silver shield,

1712   upon which was his device,
red roses.
He rode well armed on his Gascon,
a fine and valuable horse.

1716   He grasped his shield by the straps
and rode forth, quite handsome and elegant.
On his helmet he wore
a wreath of roses, a lovely sight.

1720   His horse was covered
in samite decorated
with red roses, which everyone
gazed at in wonder; and his lady,

1724   whose name was Rose in Bloom,
rode at his side
on a fine palfrey.
She was quite ugly and wrinkled!

1728   Without exception, all were displeased
that he maintained her to be the most beautiful of women.
Everyone, both men and women, wondered
how Love could so disturb his judgment.

1732   But no man can so protect himself
that Love cannot turn his mind topsy-turvy,
for Love makes the ugliest woman seem a beauty,
so skilled are her ways of deceit and enchantment.

1736   . . . .
The knight rode up
to Margerie at a gallop.
He called to her in a very loud voice

1740   not to take the hawk,
for she did not deserve to have it.
The Fair Unknown came forward

avant, se li a dit, "Biaus sire,
1744   por quel cose volés vos dire
que l'esprevier ne doie avoir?
N'a ele biauté et savoir?
Plus bele de li je ne sai
1748   et je por li desrainnerai
qu'ele doit avoir l'esprevier,
se ne li faites delaier."
Cil li respont, "N'en ara mie
1752   qu'asés est plus bele m'amie
qu'aveuc moi ai ci amenee!
Onques si biele ne fu nee,
sans mentir et sans devinaille.
1756   De mostrer sui pres par bataille
que porter n'en doit l'esprevier."
Desfient soi li chevalier.
Come homme iré les cevals poignent
1760   et por joster si s'entr'eloignent.
Tant con ceval püent aler
muet l'uns a l'autre por joster.
Si s'entrevont entreferir
1764   que les escus se font croissir.
Ronpent et çaingles et poitra[l]s ;   [*139 v° b*]
andoi s'abatent des cevals.
Ne furent navré ne blecié:
1768   isnelement sont redrecié
et traient les brans vïenois,
si s'entrefierent demanois.
Sor les elmes s'en vont ferir
1772   si que le fu en fonnt salir.
Des puins as trençans des espees
s'entredonnent molt grans colees.
En tos sanblans bien se requierent.
1776   Sor les elmes souvent se fierent;

1744 voles *repeated*
1765 portais
1768 isnelelement

and said, "My dear lord,
1744 why do you wish to claim
      that she should not have the hawk?
      Is she not lovely and intelligent?
      I know no lady more beautiful than she,
1748 and I shall assert her right
      to have the hawk,
      so kindly do not stand in her way."
      He answered, "She shall not have the hawk,
1752 for my lady, whom I have here with me,
      is much more lovely!
      No woman so lovely was ever born,
      and I say this without any falsehood or doubt.
1756 I am ready to prove in combat
      that your lady should not take the hawk."
      The two knights then challenged each other.
      They spurred their horses like men full of anger
1760 as they took their distance to prepare for the charge.
      Then they rushed toward each other
      as fast as their horses could carry them.
      They came together with such great force
1764 that it shattered their shields.
      The girths and breast-straps of their horses broke,
      and both knights fell to the ground.
      Neither was wounded,
1768 and they leapt to their feet,
      drawing their Viennese swords,
      and attacked each other straightway.
      Each struck his opponent's helmet with such force
1772 that sparks flew.
      With the sharp blades of their swords
      they gave each other great blows.
      Both fought well, it was plain to see.
1776 They struck at each other's helmets again and again

as puins souvent se vont sacier,
les las des elmes esracier.
Fiere et grans est molt la mellee.
1780 Li Biaus Descouneüs s'espee
tint, si le fiert bien a devisse
et tote sa force i a mise.
Si grant colee li donna
1784 que li chevaliers trebuça;
tos estordis ciet en la place.
Sor une piere fiert sa face
que ses vis trestos en torbla.
1788 Cil maintenant sor lui ala;
tant durement le tire et sace
que l'elme del cief li esrace.
Cil n'a pooir de relever.
1792 Que que il li doie grever,
li couvient dire et otroier,
"Conquis m'avés, ne.l puis [noier]."
Mais cil qui desous lui le tient
1796 li dist, "Sire, el i covient.
Atant n'en irés vos plus cuites:
vostre estre et vostre non me dites
et si fiancerés prison,
1800 qu[e] vos irés sans oquison
ens en la cort Artus le roi."
Li chevaliers plevi sa foi,
puis li a dit aprés son non:
1804 "Sire, Giflet m'apelë on.
Giflés, li fius Do, sui nonmés
en cest païs et apielés.
Vostre sui tos d'or en avant,
1808 car mol[t] vos sa pr[eu] et val[lant].
Atant se lievent de la place;
l'uns acole l'autre et enbrace.

1794 p. soufrir [*em. Williams*]
1800 qui
1808 c. mol v. s. dor en ava prue et val

or, grappling, each would try to break the laces
that held the other's helmet fast.
It was a fierce and mighty battle.
1780 The Fair Unknown grasped his sword
and struck his opponent hard,
putting all his strength into the blow.
He hit him with such force
1784 that the knight stumbled
and fell, completely dazed.
He struck his face on a rock,
and he grew pale.
1788 The Fair Unknown was upon him at once;
he tugged so hard at the man's helmet
that he tore it from his head.
The other did not have the strength to rise.
1792 Though it grieved him to do so,
he was forced to surrender, and so he said,
"You have defeated me, I cannot deny it."
But the Fair Unknown would not yet let him up
1796 and said, "My lord, you must do more than this.
You may not yet consider yourself free to go:
first you must tell me your name and who you are,
and then promise
1800 to go at once
to the court of King Arthur and surrender yourself."
The knight pledged his word
and then told him his name:
1804 "My lord, my name is Giflet;
Giflet, son of Do,
is what I am called in this land.
I am in your service from this time forth,
1808 for I know well your worth and courage."
Then they arose
and embraced.

Giflés, li fius Deon, l'en mainne
1812   en la soie sale demanne.
Tant debonnarement pria
c'o lui cele nuit herberga.
Molt lor fist bon ostel la nuit   *[139 v °c]*
1816   et molt i orent grant deduit.
Cele nuit traisent au castel
et furent servi bien et bel.
Bien matinet a l'ajornee
1820   que li jors pert par la contree,
li Bials Descouneüs leva,
isnelement et tost s'arma,
si se remetent a la voie.
1824   Giflés, li fius Do, les convoie,
et Margerie, la pucele,
que li Descouneüs apiele,
se li demande qu'el fera.
1828   Et dist que [ele] s'en ira
en Escoce dont fu ses pere;
rois Agolans, il est ses frere.
Sor son pui[n]g porte l'esprevier
1832   qu'ele ot conquis, si l'ot molt cier.
Quant li Descouneüs l'entent
qu'ele estoit de si haute gent
et qu'ele estoit fille de roi,
1836   Giflet a apielé a soi,
se li dist que il envoiast
un chevalier qui l'en menast
la damoissele en sa contree.
1840   Et Giflés bonnement li gree,
se li dist que bien le fera.

1812 en la s. s. len i d. [+2]
1814 herbergast
1815 *repeated at bottom of col. b*
1821 d. sarma l.
1828 Et d. q. s'en ira [-2]
1831 puig

Giflet, son of Do, led the Fair Unknown
1812   into his hall.
He asked him with great courtesy
to lodge with him that night.
Giflet received the company most hospitably,
1816   and they greatly enjoyed their stay there.
They remained at the castle that night
and were waited on handsomely.
Early in the morning, when it was light,
1820   when day had spread through the land,
the Fair Unknown arose
and speedily armed himself,
and the company resumed their journey.
1824   Giflet, son of Do, went some distance with them,
as did the maiden Margerie;
the Fair Unknown spoke to her
and asked what she intended to do.
1828   And she said she would go
to Scotland, the land of her father;
her brother was King Agolant.
On her hand she carried the hawk
1832   she had won, for it was very dear to her.
When the Fair Unknown understood
that she was of such noble birth
and a king's daughter,
1836   he asked for a word with Giflet
and told him to send
a knight to conduct
the maiden to her own country.
1840   Giflet readily agreed to this,
and said he would certainly do what he asked.

Atant a Diu le comanda.
Et quant le parole ot Helie
1844   qu'ele estoit d'Escoce norie,
si l'a molt [bien] recouneüe,
car maintes fois l'avoit veüe
et si estoit pres sa parente.
1848   Molt li est bon et atalente
que ele en porte l'esprevier.
"Cosine," fait ele, "acointier
vos deüssiés molt grant pieça,
1852   car or m'en covient aler ça
et vos en iré[s] autre voie.
Molt desire qu'encor vos revoie.
Ne sai se jamais vos venrai,
1856   mais en mon cuer vos amerai.
Or vos vel mon bracet laissier;
porterés l'en o l'esprevier.
Andoi sont conquis par bataille.
1860   N'a si bon cien en Cornouaille:
molt fu conquis par grant vigor
d'un mal chevalier veneor."
Tot li conte come ele l'a,
1864   le bracet, et puis li bailla.
Li une a l'autre pren congié;
andeus ploroient de pitié.   [140 r°a]
Li Biaus Descouneüs s'en vait.
1868   Vers Helie li nains se trait;
son palefroi aloit caçant.
        Or me vait autre riens tirant:
del Biel Descouneü dirai
1872   l'istoire si con je le sai,
qui tote jor avoit erré.
Li vespres lor fu apresté.
Ill esgarde, voit un castiel:
1876   onques nus hom ne vit si biel.

1845 Si la m. r. [-1, em. Williams]
1853 ire

He then commended the knight to God.
And when Helie heard
1844 that Margerie had grown up in Scotland,
she understood who the maiden was,
for she had seen her many times
and was a close relative of hers.
1848 Helie was delighted
that Margerie was taking the hawk.
"Cousin," she said, "I wish
you had identified yourself much earlier,
1852 for now I must take my leave,
while you follow another path.
I want so much to see you again.
I do not know if I ever shall,
1856 but I will always love you dearly.
And so I wish to give you my brachet;
you may take him along with the hawk.
Both were won in combat.
1860 There is no finer dog in all of Cornwall,
and he was taken through great prowess
from a formidable hunter knight."
She told her how she had come to have
1864 the brachet, and then presented the animal to her.
They took their leave of each other;
both were weeping for sorrow.
The Fair Unknown started along his way.
1868 The dwarf rode with Helie,
driving her palfrey along.
        Now another matter commands my attention:
I shall tell of the Fair Unknown,
1872 as the story is known to me.
He had been traveling throughout the day.
It was now nearing evening.
He looked about and saw a fortified city:
1876 no man ever saw such a fine one.

Molt fu li castials bien asis;
molt ert rices et plentevis.
Uns bras de mer entor coroit
1890   qui tote la vile açaingnoit.
D'autre part la grans mers estoit
qui au pié del castiel feroit.
Molt i avoit rice castiel:
1884   li mur en furent rice et biel
dont li castials tos clos estoit.
Nois, blances flors, ne riens qui soit
n'est pas si bel con li mur sont
1888   qui tot entor la vile vont.
De blanc mabre li mur estoient
qui le castiel entor clooient,
si hals con pooit uns ars traire.
1892   Nus hom ne pooit engien faire
qui peüst as cretials tocier.
Traire ne puet en ne lancier,
et tant estoient li mur halt
1896   qu'il ne doutoient nul asaut.
En la vile ot cent tors vermelles
qui bieles erent a mervelles,
et furent de mabre vermel
1900   qui molt reluist contre solel.
Cent conte ens en la vile estoient
ki dedens icés tors manoient
et tot sont casé del castiel.
1904   Un palais i ot bon et biel.
Cil qui le fist sot d'encanter,
que nus hom ne.l puet deviser
de coi i[l] fu, mais bials estoit.
1908   Cristal la piere resanbloit
dont li palais estoit tos fais
et a conpas trestos portrais.
A vaute fu covers d'argent
1912   et par desus a pavement.

1907 c. i f.

This city was very well situated,
opulent and richly provided.
A branch of the sea flowed around it,

1880   so that it was all surrounded by water.
On the other side the open sea
flowed right up to the walls of the city.
This town was indeed magnificent:

1884   the walls, which completely enclosed it,
were very fine and beautiful.
Nothing, neither snow nor white flowers,
was so lovely as the walls

1888   that enclosed the town.
These walls
were of white marble, and they rose
higher than a bowshot from the ground.

1892   No one could ever devise a war machine
that might reach their crenels.
They were beyond the reach of bow or catapult;
the walls were so high

1896   that they need fear no assault.
In the town were a hundred red towers
of wondrous beauty,
all made of red marble

1900   that sparkled in the sunlight.
A hundred counts
lived in these towers
and owed allegiance to the castle.

1904   There was a fine and beautiful seigneurial palace.
Its maker knew well of enchantment,
for no one could tell
what it was made of, only that it was beautiful.

1908   The rock with which the palace was made
and which adorned it all around
seemed to be of crystal.
Its roof was of silver

1912   and decorated with mosaic.

Une esclarboucle sus luissoit;
plus que solaus resplendissoit
et par nuit rent si grant clarté
1916 con se ce fust en tans d'esté.
Vint tors sostienent le palais   [*140 r°b*]
—plus bieles ne verrés jamais—
totes indes d'une color.
1920 Ainc hom ne vit nule millor.
Iluec vienent li marceant
qui d'avoir sont rice et manant;
si amainnent lor marchandie
1924 par la mer qui illuec les guie,
dont li passages molt valoit
que cele vile recevoit.
De lor avoirs qui i vient grans
1928 est la vile rice et manans.
Icis castials dont vos oiés
a l'Isle d'Or estoit nonmés.
El palais ot une pucele;
1932 onques nus hom ne vit si biele.
Les set ars sot et encanter
et sot bien estoiles garder
et bien et mal—tot ço savoit.
1936 Mervillous sens en li avoit.
Cele estoit dame del castiel:
molt ot le cors et gent et biel;
ses pere n'ot oir fors que li,
1940 encor n'avoit ele mari.
C'est la Pucele as Blances Mains
—de ço sui je molt bien certains—
et molt estoit grans sa biautés.
1944 Li chevaliers s'est arestés,
s'apiele damoissele Helie
qu'il menoit en sa conpaingnie.
Se li a le castiel mostré
1948 et del palais la grant clarté

1917 *repeated at bottom of col. a*

At the very top was a carbuncle
that shone brighter than the sun
and gave out such great light at night
1916   that it seemed to be summertime.
Twenty towers supported the palace
—you will never see any more beautiful—
all of the same deep blue.
1920   No one ever saw finer ones.
Rich and powerful
merchants came to the castle;
they brought their wares
1924   from across the sea,
and the tolls they paid brought
great wealth to the town.
Because of the many goods that were brought there
1928   the city had grown rich and powerful.
This castle of which I am telling you
was called the Golden Isle.
In the palace lived a maiden;
1932   no man ever saw one so beautiful.
She knew the seven liberal arts and she knew enchantment
and how to read the stars
and good and evil—all this she knew.
1936   She was a woman of the rarest intelligence.
This maiden was the lady of the castle:
she was lovely and noble of form,
her father's only heir,
1940   and as yet unmarried.
She was called the Maiden of the White Hands
—of that I am quite certain—
and she was a woman of wondrous beauty.
1944   The knight stopped
and spoke to Helie,
whom he was escorting.
He pointed out the castle
1948   and the great light from the palace

et un tré qu'il avoit veü
qui entr'els et le castiel fu
qui molt grant place porprendoit.
1952   Et une caucie i ravoit
del pavillon dusques au pont
por les iaugues qui defors sont.
Li pavillons au cief estoit.
1956   Devant unes lices avoit
molt bien faites de pels agus,
aguisiés desos et desus.
En cascun pel ficie avoit
1960   une teste c'armee estoit;
cascune avoit l'elme lacié
qui ens el pel estoit ficié.
De chevaliers tot li cief sont
1964   qui ens es pels erent amont.
Dedens le pavillon estoit
uns chevaliers qui ja s'armoit
et laçoit ses cauces de fer;
1968   que tot esté et tot iver
atendoit iluec s'aventure,   [*140 r°c*]
qui molt estoit grevels et dure.
Quant vit le chevalier venir,
1972   son hauberc a pris a vestir.
Quant l'ot vestu, son elme lace
et vint ester en mi la place.
Espee bonne çainte avoit.
1976   Cil chevaliers amis estoit
a la pucele del castiel.
De totes armes bien et bel
estoit armés, et ses cevals.
1980   Atant est venus li vasals
que je Biaus Descouneüs apiele;
dalés lui mainne la pucele.
Vers le tré vint, si vaut passer.
1984   Mais cil li osa bien veer,
qui dedens ert, molt fierement,
si dist en halt hastivement,
"Se vos par ci volés passer,

and also a very large tent
that he had noticed
between them and the castle.
1952 There was also a causeway
between the tent and the bridge
which crossed the waters that surrounded the town.
The tent was at the head of the causeway.
1956 In front of it was a sturdy palisade
made of pointed stakes
that had been sharpened both above and below.
An armed head had been impaled
1960 on each stake;
each of the heads
wore a laced helmet.
All of these heads
1964 were the heads of knights.
Inside the tent
a knight was arming himself
and lacing on his iron leggings;
1968 for all through the year, in summer and in winter,
he awaited the adventure that was to befall him,
and it was a very harsh and difficult one.
When the knight saw the Fair Unknown approaching,
1972 he reached for his hauberk.
When he had put it on, he laced on his helmet
and went out to the middle of the field.
He had girded on a fine sword.
1976 This knight was the suitor
of the maiden in the castle.
He was well and handsomely armed
from head to foot, and his horse was armed as well.
1980 Up rode the knight
who was called the Fair Unknown
with Helie at his side.
He came toward the tent, intending to ride by it.
1984 But the knight in the tent proudly
dared forbid him to do so
and called out to him at once,
"If you wish to pass by here

1988   molt vos estera ains lasser
        as armes encontre mon cors
        u vos remanrés la defors!"
        "Sire," dist la pucele Helie,
1992   tels est l'usages, n'en ment mie,
        et cil qui ici est conquis
        si puet estre de la mort fis.
        La teste a maintenant copee,
1996   ne ja ne li ert desarmee:
        a tot l'elme serra trencie
        et puis en un des pels ficie
        avec les autres qui la sont
2000   defors les lices de cel pont."
        Set vint testes i ot et trois,
        tot fius de contes et de rois
        que li chevaliers a conquis
2004   qui ert a la pucele amis.
        Ses amis a esté [cinc] ans.
        Onques de li n'ot ses talans
        mais s'e[n]cor puet deus ans durer,
2008   si le doit prendre et espouser.
        La pucele l'a fiancie
        que se desfent si la caucie
        set ans tos plains, que il l'aura;
2012   et s'il ne.l fait, il i faura.
        Li usages itels estoit:
        quant nus de ses amis moroit,
        quant il estoit mors en bataille,
2016   celui prend[r]oit sans nule faille
        qui son ami ocis avoit.
        De celui ami refaisoit
        por qu'il peüst set ans tenir,
2020   l'usage faire et maintenir.
        Et qui set ans i puet durer,   [*140 v°a*]

2005 set [*em. Williams*]
2007 secor
2016 prendoit

1988	you must first try yourself
	in arms against me;
	otherwise you must remain outside the castle!"
	"My lord," said Helie,
1992	"He is telling the truth, for such is indeed the custom,
	and whoever is defeated here
	may be certain of death.
	He will lose his head at once
1996	without his helmet being removed,
	for it will be cut off along with his head
	and then placed on one of the stakes
	along with the others over there
2000	by the palisade in front of the bridge."
	There were a hundred and forty-three heads there,
	all belonging to the sons of counts and kings
	whom the suitor of the maiden in the castle
2004	had defeated in combat.
	He had been her suitor for five years.
	He had never had what he desired from her,
	but if he could endure for two more years
2008	he was to take her in marriage.
	The maiden had agreed that,
	if he could defend the causeway
	for seven full years, he would have her;
2012	otherwise, he could not marry her.
	Such was the custom:
	when one of her suitors died,
	having been killed in combat,
2016	she was obliged to accept
	the one who had killed her former suitor;
	she would then take him as her new suitor,
	so that he might in turn defend the causeway for seven years,
2020	according to the custom.
	And whoever could endure for seven years

a celui se veut marïer;
de li ert sire et del manoir.
2024   En cel guisse [le] doit avoir.
Ele savoit bien sans mentir
que cil qui ce porra furnir
que tant est buens qu'avoir le doit.
2028   Por l'esprovier iço faisoit.
Mais ele dist ja ne l'ara
cestui, ains dist que ains morra
qu'ele n'a cure ne talent
2032   car il est fel a tote gent.
N'avoit a garder que deus ans,
mais trop ert plains de mautalans;
il estoit fel, cuvers et mals
2036   et trop tirans et desloiaus.
Por che la dame le haoit.
Et por ce que haïs estoit,
se il son terme fait avoit,
2040   tant durement mal li voloit
que ja a nul jor n'en iert s[i]ens.
Car en cest monde nule riens
n'est que ançois ne devenist
2044   que de li ses talens fesist.
De totes gens haïs estoit,
car en la vile homme n'avoit
qui liés n'en fust et ne vausist
2048   que cil en desus en venist.
Ço voloient grant et menor
que nus a lui n'avoit amor,
mais por doutance le servoient
2052   et nient por el ne le faissoient,
qu'il n'estoit de nului amés.
Ses cevals li fu amenés
covers d'un bon paile vermel.
2056   Ainc nus hom ne vit son parel:

2024 En c. g. d. a. [-*l, em. Williams*]
2041 suens

was the one she had agreed to marry;
he would be her lord and lord of the castle.
2024   She would then be obliged to accept him.
She knew quite truly
that whoever could do this feat was such a fine knight
that he should by rights have her.
2028   This she did in order to test her suitors.
But, as for this man, she said that
she would never marry him but would die first,
for she did not want him at all
2032   since he behaved wickedly toward everyone.
He had only two years remaining,
but he was full of evil intent;
he was cruel, base, and wicked,
2036   a faithless scoundrel.
This was why the lady hated him.
And because he was so hated,
even if he had endured for seven years,
2040   the lady disliked him so intensely
that she would never accept him.
Indeed there was nothing in this world
she would not rather have done
2044   before letting him have what he desired of her.
He was hated by everyone,
and there was in fact no one in the city
who would not be happy
2048   if the newcomer could defeat him.
Both the lords and the common folk desired this,
for none had any love for him,
but served him out of fear
2052   rather than for any other reason;
he was loved by no one.
The man's horse was brought to him,
draped with a cloth of red silk.
2056   No one ever saw its equal:

par mi ot unes blances mai[n]s;
d'un samit blanc con flors de rai[n]s
furent les mains et bien ouvrees
2060   et deseur le cendal p[o]sees.
Ses escus a sinople estoit
et mains blances par mi avoit.
Sor son elme portait uns gans.
2064   D'armes estoit preus et vaillans.
Tantost con il vint au destrier
s'i est montés par son estrier.
Uns vallés son escu li tent;
2068   il tantost a son col le pent.
Uns autres li baille la lance.
As armes avoit grant poissance;
ainc nus ne fu de son pooir
2072   n'a armes peüst tant valoir.
Il s'eslaisse par mi les pres   [*140 v°b*]
puis est au pavillon tornés
u li Descouneüs l'atent.
2076   Faire le cuide tot dolent.
Quant li Descouneüs le voit
que il as armes l'atendoit,
bien set qu'il avra la bataille.
2080   Par el n'en peut aler sanns faille:
par illuec l'en estuet aler,
car par aillors n'en puet passer.
L'escu a pris, au col le pent,
2084   isnelement la lance prent,
vers le caucie vint errant.
Li chevaliers li vint devant.
Li Biaus Descouneüs dist, "Sire,
2088   proier le vos vauroie et dire
que vos nos laissisiés aler.

2057 mais
2058 rais
2060 deseuer, pasees [*em. Williams*]
2084 i. au col le pent la l. p.

hands of white samite
had been sewn in the middle,
beautifully made
2060 and white as hawthorn flowers.
His shield was red
with white hands blazoned on it.
He wore a pair of gloves attached to his helmet.
2064 He was a valiant man and worthy in arms.
He went to his horse,
put his foot to the stirrup and mounted.
A young man gave him his shield,
2068 which he hung from his neck.
Another gave him his lance.
He was very powerful in arms;
none was ever so strong as he
2072 nor so able in combat.
He rode out into the meadow
and turned toward the tent,
where the Fair Unknown awaited him.
2076 He fully expected to lay him low.
When the Fair Unknown saw him
as he waited, armed,
he knew he must meet him in combat.
2080 In truth, no other way was open to him:
he had to pass by there,
for there was no other way to go.
He took up his shield, hung it from his neck,
2084 quickly took up his lance,
and galloped toward the causeway.
The knight pulled up to block his way.
The Fair Unknown said, "My lord,
2088 I request
that you let us pass.

Nos n'avons mestier d'arester.
Ne me delaiés de ma voie,
2092   car li rois Artus m'i envoie."
Cil li respont, "Or oi folie!
. . . .
Par ci ne passerés vos mie.
2096   Cest casement tie[n]g de m'amie."
Et cil al chevalier respont,
"Sire," fait il, "por tot le mont
ne vel avoir tel casement
2100   d'ensi ocire tote gent.
Quant je plus ne puis amender
ne vos ne me laissiés aler,
j'esgarderai vostre voloir.
2104   Desfendrai moi a mon pooir."
Lors se disfïent a itant;
eslongent soi plus d'un arpent.
Il ne remaint arme et castiel:
2108   li villart et li jovencel,
les dames et li chevalier
et li clerc et li escuier
que ne viengnent a la bataille.
2112   Del signor vaussissent sans faille
que mors i fust et desconfis,
car molt estoit de tos haïs;
molt estoit sa mors desiree.
2116   La dame n'i est pas alee;
as estres de la tor ala
et les puceles i mena.
As fenestres en vint ester
2120   por la bataille resgarder
de celui que püent haïr.
Des orre sont as cols ferir.
Andoi furent de grant valor.

2093 foloie
2096 tieg
2108 jovenencel

We have no need to stop here.
Do not keep me from my journey,
2092 for King Arthur has sent me."
The other answered, "This is out of the question!
. . . .
You will certainly not pass by here,
2096 for I am defending this causeway in my lady's name."
And the other answered the knight,
"My lord, not for all the world
would I wish to have such a charge
2100 as thus to kill everyone who passes by.
Since I can do nothing else
to persuade you to let me go by,
I shall do as you wish.
2104 I shall defend myself as best I can."
The knights then challenged each other
and moved more than an acre apart.
Not a soul remained in the castle,
2108 for there was no one, young or old,
lady or knight,
cleric or squire,
who did not come out to watch the combat.
2112 In truth, they wished that their lord
would be defeated and killed,
for he was hated by all;
his death was ardently wished for.
2116 The lady of the castle did not go to the field;
she went up to the top floor of her tower,
along with her maidens;
she went to the windows
2120 to watch the one whom they so hated
as he did combat.
The two knights quickly came to blows.
Both were valorous knights.

2124   Les cevals poingnent par vicor;
       tant con ceval püent aler
       muet l'uns vers l'autre por joster.   *[140 v°c]*
       Ansi vienent andoi fendant
2128   con esfoudres va vent caçant;
       nus vens ne puet si tost aler
       con li uns vait l'autre encontrer.
       Baissent les lances con il viennent:
2132   sor les escus grans cols se fierent;
       ronpent les ais et li fus brise.
       Les lances metent a devise;
       par les hescus duqu'as haubers
2136   fisent ansdeus passer les fers.
       Lances orent roides et fors,
       si s'entrefierent par esfors.
       Tument cheval et chevalier;
2140   desous els font tumer destriers.
       Andoi se sont entr'abatu;
       molt estoient de grant vertu.
       A la terre gisent pasmé;
2144   ne sont pas li ceval levé
       car estonné sont li destrier.
       Les els gissent li chevalier.
       Tot cil qui cele joste virent
2148   molt durement s'en esbahirent,
       car molt estoit bonne et loee;
       onques miudre ne fu jostee.
       Quant sont de pamisson venu,
2152   si se sont bien entreveü;
       des fueres traient les espee[s]
       dont il se donnent g[r]ans colees.
       Les escus tre[n]cent et esclicent,
2156   haumes esfondrent et debrissent,

2125 pueen
2153 espee
2154 gans
2155 trecent

2124	They spurred their horses sharply;
	as fast as their horses could carry them
	they rushed toward each other for the clash.
	They galloped forward, cleaving the air
2128	as lightning outstrips the wind;
	no wind blows with the speed
	at which they hurled toward each other.
	Lowering their lances as they charged,
2132	they struck great blows on each other's shields;
	shafts split and wood shattered.
	They used their lances well;
	both knights plunged the tips of their lances
2136	straight through the shields to the hauberks.
	The lances were strong and solid,
	and the opponents struck each other with force;
	horses and riders both fell to the ground,
2140	the horses fell under their riders.
	The two men knocked each other to the ground;
	both were excellent knights.
	They lay stunned on the ground;
2144	nor did the horses get up,
	for they were dazed as well.
	The knights lay beside them.
	All those who had witnessed the clash
2148	were filled with admiration,
	for it was a fine joust and widely praised;
	no better one was ever fought.
	When the two knights returned to their senses
2152	and caught sight of each other,
	they drew their swords from their sheaths
	and struck each other great blows.
	Shields were split and splintered,
2156	helmets bent and smashed;

les haubers ronpent et desmaillent.
As espees souvent s'asaillent;
sor les elmes tes cols ferroient
2160   que estinceles en voloient.
A genillons souvent se metent.
Nostre Signor del ciel proumetent
aumonnes et vels plentaïs
2164   que lor sires i fust ocis.
Li chevalier cuidoit de voir
de ses hommes sans decevoir
que il proiaissen Diu por lui,
2168   mais il prient son grant anui.
Amors de force petit vaut.
Saciés que au besoi[n]g tost faut;
por ce fait bon sa gent amer
2172   que tost puet la roe torner.
Li Descouneüs tint s'espee;
celui en donne grant colee.
Il savoit asés d'escremir:
2176   desor le col le seut ferir.
A un entrejet qu'il jeta   [*141 r°a*]
les las del elme li trencha.
Li elmes chaï en la place;
2180   desarmee remest le face.
Puis le refiert en la cervele;
li chevaliers tos en chancele.
La coiffe del hauberc trencha,
2184   desi qu'al test li fers ala;
par la cervele met l'espee,
dusques es dens li est colee.
Les gens crïent et joie ont grant.
2188   Des que Jhesus forma Adant
tel joie n'ot en une place;
n'i ot celui joie ne face.
Cil chevaliers qui fu ocis
2192   Malgiers fu apielés, li Gris.

2170 besoig

they pierced each other's hauberks, tearing the mail.
Over and over they struck with their swords;
they rained such blows on each other's helmets
2160   that sparks flew.
Repeatedly they came to their knees.
The people promised Our Lord in Heaven to give many alms
and fulfill many other vows
2164   if their lord were killed.
In truth, the knight
was certain that his men
were praying to God for his sake,
2168   but they were actually praying for his harm.
Love won by force is of little value.
You may be sure that it will fail in time of need;
that is why a lord does well to love those who serve him,
2172   for Fortune's wheel can quickly turn.
The Fair Unknown grasped his sword
and dealt the other a heavy blow.
This knight knew a great deal about swordplay:
2176   he struck him on the neck
with one quick thrust,
ripping the lacings on the man's helmet.
The helmet fell to the ground,
2180   so that his face was uncovered.
Then the Fair Unknown
struck him on the head, causing him to reel.
He tore through the hood of mail
2184   so that the blade reached his skull
and pierced his brains
straight through to the teeth.
The people cried out joyfully.
2188   Since the day that Jesus formed Adam,
there was not such joy in one place
for there was no one who did not rejoice.
The knight who had been killed
2192   was named Malgier the Gray.

Le cors en fisent aporter.
A l'autre se vont presenter:
"Sire," font il, "molt as conquis,
2196   et tere et hommes et païs.
Tot soumes tien sans decevoir.
Nus roiaumes ne puet valoir
ço que tu as hui conquesté.
2200   Molt t'a Nostres Sires amé:
mort as le millor chevalier
qui onques montast en destrier,
dont nos avés mis en la joie.
2204   Sire, metons nos a la voie:
vien ton roiaume recevoir
et le millor dame veoir
c'onques fust, que tu ameras,
2208   et se Diu plaist encor l'auras."
Un ceval li ont presenté.
Es vos celui desus monté;
or l'en mainnent vers le castel
2212   u receüs fu bien et bel
a crois et a porcession.
Grant joie en fisent li baron;
el grant palais l'en ont mené
2216   et maintenant l'ont desarmé.
Atant est la dame venue.
Si bele riens ne fu veüe;
ceste ne trove sa parelle,
2220   tant estoit biele a grant mervelle.
Sa biautés tel clarté jeta
quant ele ens el palais entra
con la lune qu'ist de la nue.
2224   Tele mervelle en a eüe
li Descouneüs quant le vit
qu'il chaï jus a bien petit.
Si l'avoit bien Nature ouvree
2228   et tel biauté li ot donnee

2222 palains

The people had his body carried away.
Then they presented themselves to the Fair Unknown.
"My lord," they said, "you have won
2196   much land and many liegemen.
We shall all bear you faithful allegiance.
No kingdom can be worth so much
as the one you have won today.
2200   Our Lord has shown His great love for you:
you have killed the greatest knight
who ever mounted a charger,
and thereby brought us joy.
2204   My lord, let us be off:
come to receive your kingdom
and see the most worthy lady
who ever lived, whom you will love,
2208   and who, if it please God, will be yours."
They gave him a horse.
He mounted it
and they led him toward the castle,
2212   where he was grandly received
with a procession, a cross at its head.
The nobles rejoiced over him;
they led him into the palace
2216   and quickly removed his arms.
Then the lady herself arrived.
Such a lovely sight was never seen:
this lady would never meet her equal,
2220   so wondrously beautiful was she.
Her beauty shed such light
that she came into the palace
as the moon comes from behind a cloud.
2224   The Fair Unknown was so filled with wonder
at the sight of her
that he very nearly fell to the ground.
Nature had so wrought her
2228   and given her such beauty

[*141 rᵇ*]

que plus bel vis ne plu bel front
n'avoit feme qui fust el mont.
Plus estoit blance d'une flor,
2232   et d'une vermelle color
estoit sa face enluminee.
Molt estoit biele et coloree.
Les oels ot vairs, boce riant,
2236   le cors bien fait et avenant.
Les levres avoit vermelletes,
les dens petites et blancetes,
boce bien faite por baissier
2240   et bras bien fais por enbracier.
Mains ot blances con flors de lis
et la gorge desous le vis.
Cors ot bien fait et le cief blont;
2244   onques si bele n'ot el mont.
Ele estoit d'un samit vestue;
onques si bele n'ot sous nue.
La pene en fu molt bien ouvree,
2248   d'ermine tote es[che]keree;
molt sont bien fait li eschekier;
li orlés fist molt a pris[ier].
Et deriere ot ses crins jetés;
2252   d'un fil d'or les ot galonnés.
De roses avoit un capiel
molt avenant et gent et biel.
D'un afremail sen col frema.
2256   Quant ele ens el palais entra,
molt i ot gente damoissele!
Onques nus hom ne vit tant biele.
La dame entre el palais riant;
2260   al Descouneüs vint devant,
se li a ses bras au col mis,
puis li a dit, "Li miens amis,

2242 gorges
2248 eskeree
2250 a pris

that no lady who ever lived
had such a lovely face or brow.
Her skin was whiter than any flower,
2232   and her cheeks were bright
with beautiful red.
She was most lovely and radiant.
Her eyes shone, her mouth smiled,
2236   she was beautiful and charming of form.
She had a delicate red mouth,
dainty white teeth,
lips made for kissing
2240   and arms for embracing.
Her hands and her bosom
were as white as the lily.
She was fair of form, with golden hair;
2244   there was never a woman so beautiful in the world.
She was dressed in a cloak of samite;
never under the sun was there any cloth so lovely.
The lining was beautifully made
2248   of ermine in a checkered pattern
of the finest workmanship;
the trim was worthy of admiration.
The lady's hair hung freely down her back;
2252   she had woven a golden thread through it.
She wore a wreath of roses
that was most charming and attractive.
Her cloak was held in place with a brooch.
2256   When she came into the hall,
she was indeed a lady of noble bearing!
No man ever saw such an exquisite woman.
She smiled as she entered the hall,
2260   went straight to the Fair Unknown,
and put her arms around his neck,
saying, "My dear friend,

conquis m'avés, vostre serrai.
2264   Jamais de vos ne partirai.
Un don vos vel orendroit faire
dont venu sont molt de contrai[r]e.
Le don orendroit vos donrai;
2268   je ne.l vel pas metre en delai.
De la caucie aval garder
l'uissage vel cuite clamer;
por vos, sire, cuites serra
2272   que jamais garde n'i ara.
Et si ferai de vos signor:
ma terre vos doins et m'amor.
A mari, sire, vos prendrai.
2276   Millor de vos certes ne sai."
Molt bonnement cil l'en merchie;
la dame par le main l'en guie.
Sor une kiute de brun pale
2280   qu'aportee fu de Tesale   [*141 r° c*]
iluec se sont andoi asis.
Molt [i ot] chevaliers de pris
en la sale de totes pars.
2284   La dame pensse engiens et ars
et molt en est en grant anguisse
coment celui retenir puisse:
ses cuers a lui s'otroie et donne.
2288   Par le palais nus mot ne sonne
fors qu'il doi, qui forment s'entr'aisent
de biaus dis qui forment lor plaissent.
La dame dist que le prendra
2292   et c'ainc la nuit en parlera
a tos les pri[n]ces de s'onor:

2266 contraie
2269 cauciel
2282 M. c. de p. [*-2, em. Williams*]
2289 sentrasaient [*+1*]
2292 c'ainc lauant en [*em. Williams*]
2293 prices

you have won me, and I shall be yours.
2264 I will never leave you.
Now I shall grant you a gift,
concerning a matter which has brought many to grief.
I shall grant you this gift at once;
2268 I would not wish to delay it.
I declare that the custom
of guarding the causeway below is ended.
For your sake, my lord, it is now at an end;
2272 never again will the causeway be guarded.
And, further, I shall make you a powerful lord:
I give you my land and my love.
I shall take you as my husband, my lord.
2276 In truth, I know of none more worthy than you."
He thanked her courteously,
and the lady led him by the hand.
On a cushion of dark silk
2280 which had been brought from Thessaly,
the two of them sat down.
There were many worthy knights
seated throughout the hall.
2284 The lady, in great distress,
pondered what wiles and arts she might use
to keep the knight with her:
she had given him her whole heart.
2288 Throughout the hall no word was spoken
except by these two, who greatly enjoyed
the delightful words they exchanged.
The lady said she would take him as her husband,
2292 and that before night fell she would send word
to all the princes that served her:

si con il veut avoir s'[amor],
al uitme jor soient ici
2296   qu'ele vaura prendre mari,
et qu'il ne facent demoree.
A tos le di[t] par la contree.
Et quant ce vint a l'avespree,
2300   por laver on l'iaue portee.
Quant ont lavé, si sont asis
et tos les sieges ont porpris.
Et la dame si est asise
2304   qui molt est sage et bien apris[e].
Li Descouneüs siet les li
et Helie tot autresi.
Molt font le valet grant honnor.
2308   Trestote s'entente et s'amor
a mis la dame en lui servir
car faire voleit son plaisir.
Par la vile font joie grant
2312   et li viellart et li enfant.
Quant mangié orent a loissir,
a Helie vint a plaissir
que de la table se levast.
2316   Le Descouneüs apielast.
Levee s'est, a lui l'apiele
a une part la damoissele,
se li a dit, "Biaus tres dous sire,
2320   une cose vos sai a dire:
que la dame a envoié querre
trestous les barons de sa terre,
qu'ele vos velt a mari prendre.
2324   Et se vos en volés desfendre,
que vos ne le veilliés avoir,
si serrés pris, je.l sai de voir.

2294 sauonjor
2298 di
2304 apris
2319 trest *with final* t *expuncted*

if they wished to retain her love,
they should come within a week,
2296 for she wished to take a husband,
and they should make no delay.
This word was sent throughout the land.
Then, when evening had come
2300 water was brought.
When all had washed,
they took their seats at the table,
and the lady, who was most
2304 well bred and courtly, sat down as well.
She had the Fair Unknown sit beside her,
with Helie on her other side.
The young men of the castle served them with great honor.
2308 The lady lavished all her love
and attention in serving the knight,
for she greatly wished to please him.
Throughout the city
2312 both young and old rejoiced greatly.
When the company had dined at their leisure,
Helie decided
to get up from the table.
2316 She beckoned to the Fair Unknown.
The maiden rose
and called him aside
and said, "My noble and honored lord,
2320 I have something to tell you:
the lady of this castle has sent for
all the lords in her land,
for she wishes to take you as her husband.
2324 And if you should refuse
to take her in marriage,
you will be taken captive, of this I am certain.

Sire, n'i pensés vilonnie
2328   ne ma dame n'oblïés mie!"
Et cil li respondi, "Amie,
ce n'ert pas, por perdre la vie!
Consilliés vos ent, damoissele,
2332   que nos ferons." Et la pucele
dist, "Bien nos en porons enbler   [*141 v°a*]
et par matin de ci torner.
La cose bien atornerai.
2336   A mon ostel gesir m'irai,
qui laiens est en cele vile.
Faire nos couvient une gille.
A Robert vel conter l'afaire,
2340   qui bien le sara a cief traire.
Le ceval main atornera;
ains que le jor veoir pora,
arons nos cevals maintenant
2344   a ceste porte ci devant
u a une biele capiele.
Et vos levés matin, kaele;
vos armes en ferai porter,
2348   issi nos en porons aler.
Et qua[nt] vos venrés au portier,
aler en volés au mostier.
Ice li porés vos bien dire.
2352   Ce ne vos porra contredire."
Et cil icel consel loa;
atant lor parlemens fina.
A la dame s'en est tornés
2356   et dalés li s'est acotés.
Elie congié demanda
et dist qu'a son ostel gira.
. . . .
2360   et aveuc li faire gesir,
mais ne puet faire nul sanblant
que ele cangast son talant.

2349 Et qua

My lord, do not think of acting unworthily
2328 by forgetting my lady!"
And he answered, "My friend,
that shall never be, even if it should cost my life!
Please advise me, my lady,
2332 what you think we should do." And the maiden
said, "We can easily slip away
from here in the morning.
I shall see to the matter.
2336 Tonight I shall stay at the lodgings arranged for me
below in the town.
We must find a stratagem.
I shall tell everything to Robert,
2340 and he will know what must be done.
He will have your horse ready
in the morning; before daylight
our horses will be
2344 in front of the gate nearby;
there is a fine chapel just beyond it.
You must take care to rise early;
I shall see that your arms are brought
2348 so that we shall be able to leave.
And when you see the porter,
tell him you wish to go to the church.
This will easily convince him.
2352 He cannot forbid you to go there."
The knight praised her advice;
and so they ended their conversation.
He returned to the lady of the castle
2356 and sat down by her side.
Helie asked leave to go
and said she would sleep at her lodgings in the town.

. . . .

2360 and would have her stay with her,
but she could say nothing
to make Helie change her mind.

Robers ses armes en porta
2364   et la pucele s'en ala.
Au Descouneü font le lit
—onques nus hom plus cier ne vit—
de kiuetes pointes et de moles.
2368   Que feroie longes paroles?
Li lis fu fais ens el palés.
Plus bel ne verrés vos jamais.
La soie et l'ors qu'el lit estoit
2372   plus de cent mars d'argent valoit,
et fu covers d'un drap de soie.
Ki l'a sor lui tos tans a joie!
Lors a la dame congié pris,
2376   se li a dit, "Mes ciers amis,
le terme desir que vos aie."
De sa parole molt l'apaie
et ne vault pas atant laissier
2380   ains le comenche a enbracier
entre ses bras molt doucement.
Atant s'en par[t] et congié prent;
en sa canbre s'en est entree.
2384   Plus biele feme ne fu nee!
Trestot s'en vont petit et grant;   [*141 v°b*]
n'i a remés keu ne sergant.
Le Biau Descouneü coucierent.
2388   A son coucier le feu tocierent;
por veoir li metent devant.
Puis dormir vont tuit li sergant.
Et li Descouneüs pensa;
2392   vers l'uis de la canbre garda,
par l'uis la dame voit venir.
Lors cuide avoir tot son plaissir.
Sans guinple estoit eschevelee
2396   et d'un mantiel fu afublee

2382 par et
2385 *Line repeated from bottom of column a.*
2390 P. d. t. li s. [*-l, em. Williams*]

Robert took the knight's arms away with him,
2364 and Helie left as well.
A bed of soft quilts
—no man ever saw a finer one—
was prepared for the Fair Unknown.
2368 Why should I speak at length about it?
The bed was set up in the hall.
You will never see a handsomer one.
The silk and gold on the bed
2372 were worth more than a hundred silver marks,
and it was covered with a silken cloth.
Happy indeed he who lay beneath it!
Then the lady asked the knight's leave to go,
2376 and said, "My dear friend,
I long for the time when you shall be mine."
Her words filled him with joy
and, not wanting to leave him yet,
2380 she took him
most tenderly in her arms.
Then she took her leave and departed,
and went into her room.
2384 A lovelier woman there never was!
Everyone left, nobles and common folk,
so that not a cook or servant remained.
First they prepared the knight for bed.
2388 They brought the torches
near the bed so that he could see.
Then all the servants went to their rest.
The Fair Unknown grew thoughtful;
2392 he looked toward the chamber door
and saw the lady come through it.
Now he expected to have all he desired.
Her hair hung loose, without a wimple,
2396 and she wore a cloak

d'un vert samit o riche hermine.
Molt estoit biele la meschine!
Les ataces de son mantiel
2400   de fin or furent li tasiel.
Desus sa teste le tenoit;
l'orlé les la face portoit:
li sebelins, qui noirs estoit,
2404   les le blanc vis molt avenoit.
N'avoit vestu fors sa chemisse,
qui plus estoit blance a devise
que n'est la nois qui ciet sor branche.
2408   Molt estoit la cemisse blance
mais encore est la cars molt plus
qui la cemisse de desus.
Les ganbes vit: blances estoient,
2412   qui un petit aparissoient.
La cemise brunete estoit
envers les janbe[s] qu'il veoit.
A l'uis la dame s'apuia.
2416   Envers le lit adiés garda,
puis demanda se il dormoit;
en cel palais nului n'avoit.
"Dort il?" fait ele qui [s]e dist.
2420   "Est il ja couciés en son lit?"
Il li respont qu'il ne dort mie.
Son cie[f] dreça quant l'a oïe
et dist, "Dame, je ne dorc pas."
2424   Vers lui se [trait] trestot le pas,
que molt ot le cors gent et biel.
Son braç jeta fors del mantiel
deseur celui qui se gisoit.
2428   L'uns l'autre molt volentiers voit.

2414 janbe
2419 q. me d.
2422 cies
2424 fait [*em. Perret*]
2426 jesta *with* s *expuncted*

of green samite lined with fine ermine.
The maiden was indeed beautiful!
The clasps of her cloak
2400 were of fine gold, as were the ties.
She wore it over her head,
with the fur trim framing her face:
the black sable next to her
2404 fair face was most becoming.
She wore nothing else but her shift,
which was even whiter
than snow as it falls on the branch.
2408 The shift was white indeed,
but whiter still
was the form it covered.
The knight could see her fair legs
2412 just a little.
The shift seemed dark
next to the legs he glimpsed.
The lady leaned against the frame of the door.
2416 She looked toward the bed
and asked if he were asleep;
there was not another soul in the hall.
"Is he asleep?" she asked, as if to herself.
2420 "Is he already in bed?"
He answered that he was indeed not asleep.
He raised his head when he heard her
and said, "My lady, I am not asleep."
2424 She quickly stepped toward him,
she who was so fair and noble of form.
She reached out from beneath her cloak
and laid her arm on the knight as he lay.
2428 They gazed at each other with pleasure.

Ses mamieles et sa poitrine
furent blances con flors d'espine,
se li ot desus son pis mis.

2432   Docement li dist, "Biaus amis,
molt desir vostre conpaignie,
se Damesdius me beneïe!"
Son pis sor le sien li tenoit

2436   nu a nu, que rien n'i avoit
entre'els non plus que sa cemisse.   *[141 vᵒc]*
En lui joïr a painne mise;
les son menton li met sa face,

2440   et cil molt doucement l'enbrace.
La dame li dist, "Bials amis,
li mals d'amors m'a por vos pris.
Iço saciés vos bien de voir,

2444   que je vos aim outre p[o]oir.
Plus ne m'en pooie soufrir
de vos veoir ne plus tenir."
Et cil de bon oel l'esgarda;

2448   un doç baissier prendre cuida
quant la dame ariere se traist,
se li a dit, "Ce ne me plaist.—
tot torneroit a lecerie.

2452   Saciés je ne.l feroie mie
des que vos m'aiés esposee.
Lors vos serrai abandonnee."
De lui se parti maintenant,

2456   se li dist, " A [Diu] vos comant!"
En ses chanbres l'ont enfre[me]e
les puceles et ramenee.
Celui a laissié esbahi

2460   qui molt se tint a escarni.

2444 paoir
2447 oiel
2448 donc
2456 Se li d. a dist v. c.
2457 enfree

Her bosom
as she leaned over him
was as white as the hawthorn.
2432   Softly she said to him, "Dear friend,
how I long for your company,
may God keep me!"
She held her breast next to his own,
2436   and there was nothing at all
between them but her shift.
She lavished caresses on him.
She touched his face with her own,
2440   and he held her gently in his arms.
The lady said, "Dear friend,
I am sick with love for you.
You may know for certain
2444   that my love is quite beyond my control.
I could no longer bear to see you
and not have you in my arms."
And he looked at her tenderly;
2448   he tried to take a sweet kiss from her,
but the lady drew back
and said, "This I will not permit,
for it would lead to unseemliness.
2452   You can be sure that I shall not do such a thing
until you have taken me in marriage.
Then I shall give myself to you completely."
At that, she left him
2456   and said, "God keep you."
Her maidens escorted her to her chambers
and closed the door.
She left the knight quite dismayed
2460   and thinking himself most cruelly mocked.

Quant la [da]me s'en fu alee,
maudist sa male destinee
que trop a fait greveusse faille.
2464 Amors le destraint et travaille,
mais lasés est, si s'endormi.
En dormant a veü celi
por cui ses cuers meurt et cancele.
2468 Entre ses bras tenoit la biele.
Tote nuit songe qu'il le voit
et qu'entre ses bras le tenoit
tros qu'al main que l'aube creva.
2472 Isnelement et tost leva,
a la porte vint maintenant;
li portiers l'euvre isnelement.
Venus s'en est a la capiele
2476 u il trove sa damoissele
et son escuier et le nain,
qui son ceval tint par le frain.
Ses armes comande a porter
2480 isnelement por lui armer.
Robers son elme li laça,
hastivement et bien l'arma
et puis se metent a la voie,
2484 si cevaucierent a grant joie.
Tot quatre grant oirre s'en vont;
li solaus resluist par le mont.
Helie s'en aloit cantant
2488 et molt grant joie demenant.
Son palefroi caçoit li nains   *[142 r°a]*
et chevaucierent bos et plains.
Vers le Gaste Cité en vont;
2492 dusques as vespres erré ont.
     Atant un biel castiel coisirent
outrë un pont et une eve virent.
Les tors estoient bien antisses,
2496 bien faites environ asisses;

2461 Q. la me s.

When the lady was gone,
he cursed the wicked fate
that had been so unjust to him.
2464 Love now caused him great pain and torment,
but he was so tired that he fell asleep.
As he slept he saw the one
for whom his heart was dying.
2468 He held the beautiful one in his arms.
All through the night he dreamed that he saw her
and held her in his embrace
until the dawn broke.
2472 He quickly arose
and made for the gate;
the porter opened it at once.
He went to the chapel
2476 where he found Helie,
his squire, and the dwarf,
who was holding the reins of his horse.
He ordered that his arms be brought
2480 quickly so that he could arm himself.
Robert laced on the knight's helmet
and armed him quickly and well,
and then they set out,
2484 riding joyfully along.
All four rode at a fast pace
and the sun shone above them.
Helie rode along singing
2488 and full of joy.
The dwarf drove her palfrey,
and they rode through woodlands and plains,
journeying toward the Desolate City.
2492 They traveled until evening.
Suddenly they spied a beautiful walled city
beyond a river spanned by a bridge.
Its ancient towers were solid
2496 and well placed on all sides;

s'ert de haus murs clos li donjons.
Molt ot en la vile maissons
et li bos molt pres i estoit.
2500   Molt rices borgois i avoit
dont la vile estoit bien pluplee.
Molt estoit biele la contree
de vingnes, de bos et de plains,
2504   et si ot molt rices vilains.
De tos biens estoit raenplie;
bien estoit la vile garnie.
Li castials ot non Galigans
2508   ki ert molt biaus et avenans.
Li chevaliers dist, "Que ferons,
damoissele? Herbergerons
en cest castiel ici devant?"
2512   Cele respondi mantenant,
"Sire," fait ele, "nenil mie!
De la aler n'aiés envie
car tant en ai oï parler
2516   que molt i fait mauvais aler.
Un usage vos en dirai
dou castiel que je molt bien sai.
Li borgois qu'en la vile sont
2520   ja homme ne herbergerunt;
tot herbergent ci[é]s le signor,
car il veut faire a tos honor.
Et Lanpas a a non li sire
2524   don je vos v[el] l'usage dire.
Il ne herberge chevalier
qui viengne armés sor son destrier
se premiers ne jostent andui
2528   tant qu'il l'abatra u il lui.
Mais se Dius velt itant aidier
celui qui i vient herbergier
que il abate le signor,

2497 donjnons
2521 h. cis [*em. Williams*]
2524 v. vle (=vl')

high walls surrounded the keep.
There were many houses in the town,
which was quite near a forest.
2500 Many wealthy burghers lived there,
so that the town was well populated.
The land around the castle was a lovely sight,
rich in vineyards, woodlands, and plains,
2504 and the peasants were quite prosperous.
The castle was stocked with all kinds of goods,
and the town well fortified.
This fine and handsome walled city
2508 was called Galigant.
The Fair Unknown said, "What shall we do,
my lady? Shall we stay the night
in the city there before us?"
2512 Helie answered at once,
"No, indeed, my lord!
Please do not think of going there,
for I have heard it said
2516 that to do so is most ill-advised.
I shall tell you of a custom
observed in this city about which I know a great deal.
The townspeople
2520 lodge no visitors among them;
all stay with the lord,
for he wishes to honor them all himself.
And this lord whose custom
2524 I wish to tell you about is named Lampart.
He will lodge no knight
who approaches him armed
unless they first do combat
2528 until one of them is knocked from his horse.
If God wishes to aid
the knight who comes to seek lodging
and he unseats Lampart,

2532   ostel ara a grant honnor.
        Et se li sires abat lui,
        si s'en retorne a grant anui
        par mi la vile sans cheval.
2536   Asés i suefre honte et mal,
        car cil qui en la vile sont
        trestout a l'encontre li vont,
        et portent torces enboe[e]s
2540   qui sont de la boe loees
        et [pos] plain de cendre et d'ordure.   [*142 r°b*]
        Trop i reçoit tres grant laidure,
        que tot li ruent vers le vis
2544   les grans ordures qu'il ont pris.
        Molt fait el castiel grief entrer;
        mius vos en vie[n]t defors aler
        en tant come li murs açaint.
2548   N'a chevalier u en a maint,
        nes uns tot sels millor de lui.
        A mains hommes ont fait anui.
        Biaus sire, por ice, " fait ele,
2552   "n'irons pas." Cil li dist, "Pucele,
        por te[l] cose ne quier laissier,
        car Dius nos puet molt bie[n] aidier.
        Ja ne m'en sarïés tant dire,
2556   mais por Dius ne.l prendés a ire
        que j'en i voise herbegier,
        et jostera au chevalier
        qui si cuide par sa manace
2560   de sa maisson tenir la place
        qu'o lui ne herberc chevalier.
        A lui me vel je asaier.
        Or i alons! Ne doutés mie."

2536 suetre *corrected to* suefre *by scribe*
2539 enboes
2541 et puis
2546 viet
2553 tes
2554 m. bie (=b')

2532   that knight will be lodged with great honor.
But if Lampart knocks him down,
that knight will return in the greatest distress
through the city without his horse.

2536   He will suffer great shame,
for the townspeople
will all come out to meet him,
bringing filthy wads of garbage

2540   packed with mud
and pots full of ashes and slops.
This knight will be treated most foully,
for the people will hurl in his face

2544   all the rubbish they have gathered.
It is indeed a dangerous thing to go to this city;
it would be better for you
to make your way around the city walls.

2548   Among the many who have fought against Lampart
not a single one has ever bested him.
The townspeople have treated many knights most shamefully.
For this reason, my dear lord,

2552   let us not go there." He replied, "My lady,
I would not be swayed by such a reason,
for God can well lend us His aid.
You could say nothing to dissuade me,

2556   and so, in God's name, do not take it ill
that I wish to lodge in this castle;
I shall do combat with this knight
who seems to think that with threats

2560   he can defend his dwelling
and avoid lodging any knight there.
I wish to try myself against him.
Let us go now! Have no fear."

2564   Dist la pucele, "Dius aïe!
        Puis qu'il vos sert, or i alons.
        Dius nos soit garde et li suens nons!"
        El castiel vienent maintenant;
2568   par mi la porte entrent errant;
        par mi la grant rue s'en vont.
        Les j[a]ns qui en la vile sont,
        quant le virent, si vont riant,
2572   li uns le va l'au[t]re mostrant.
        Tuit s'atornent: les torces font,
        lor pos de cendres enplir vont
        et drapias mollie[r] en ordures
2576   por faire au chevalier laidures.
        Tot en parolent et consellent
        et de ferir tot s'aparellent,
        car il cuident de fi savoir
2580   que vers son signor n'ait pooir.
        Robers regarde lor ator,
        si le mostra a son signor
        que si vers le casteil s'en vont.
2584   Le signor defors trové ont
        u as eschés avoit joé;
        un chevalier avoit maté.
        Lanpas le voit, si s'est levés.
2588   De blanc poil ert entremelés.
        Robe ot d'eskerlate por voir
        et de vair a un seble noir;
        sans aligos la roube estoit.
2592   Uns estivals cauciés avoit
        et d'une coroie baree   [*145 r°c*]
        fu çains a argent bien ouvree.
        Molt i avoit bon chevalier;

2564 aieu
2569 ruee
2570 jns [*em. Williams*]
2572 laure m.
2575 mollies
2592 cauciels *with* l *expuncted*

2564   The maiden said, "God lend you his aid!
        Since you wish it, let us go.
        May God and His Holy Name defend us!"
        They now entered the walled city,
2568   galloped through the gate
        and went up the main street.
        When the townspeople saw them,
        they began to laugh
2572   and point to the Fair Unknown.
        All began to make ready: they prepared their mudpies,
        filled their pots with ashes
        and soaked their rags with filth
2576   so that they might subject the knight to indignities.
        They all spoke together and made plans,
        preparing to strike,
        for they were quite certain
2580   that the knight would not prevail against their lord.
        Robert observed their preparations
        and pointed all of this out to his lord
        as they rode toward the keep.
2584   They found the lord outside,
        where he had just checkmated a knight
        in a game of chess.
        When Lampart saw the Fair Unknown, he arose.
2588   His hair was turning gray.
        He wore a robe of precious silk, in truth,
        lined with miniver and black sable;
        this garment was made without slashes.
2592   He wore boots
        and a finely worked belt
        decorated with diagonal silver stripes.
        He was indeed a fine knight:

2596   en lui n'en ot que ensingnier.
        Li Descouneüs le salue;
        de son ceval ne se remue.
        Lanpars respont come afaitiés,
2600   "Bials sire," fait il, "bien vieg[n]iés!
        Je cuic vos venés herbergier,
        par sanblant en avés mestier.
        Volontiers vos herbegerai
2604   selonc l'usage que je ai.
        A moi vos estuet ains joster,
        et se jus me poés jeter,
        par raisson vos doi herbergier.
2608   Et se j'abat vos del destrier,
        sans ostel ariere en irois.
        Vilain convoi i troverois."
        Et cil molt volentiers l'otroie,
2612   de rien nule ne s'en esfroie.
        Et Lanpas l'en main en la sale
        u tenoit la costume male.
        La sale en bas vers terre estoit,
2616   que lonc que lé molt porprendoit.
        Illuec devoit a tos joster.
        Un tapit a fait aporter;
        quant a terre fu estendus,
2620   si est tost cele part venus,
        puis est de l'une part asis
        sor l'image d'un lupart bis
        que el tapi estoit portraite.
2624   De lui armer forment s'afaite.
        Cauces de fer li font caucier
        qui molt faissoient a proissier;
        plus sont blances que flors d'espine;
2628   molt est la maille blance et fine.

2600 viegmies
2608 se je j.
2621 de lu p.
2625-28 *From after* cauces *to* son ceval *a hole in the vellum separates the
        first part of each line from the second part.*

2596	no one needed to teach him courtly behavior.
	The Fair Unknown greeted him,
	still on his horse.
	Lampart answered like a well-bred man,
2600	"Welcome, my dear lord!
	I believe you have come to seek lodgings,
	for you seem to have need of them.
	I shall be glad to receive you
2604	according to my own custom.
	First you must joust with me,
	and if you can hurl me to the ground,
	then I shall be obliged to lodge you.
2608	But if I knock you from your horse,
	you will leave without a place to stay.
	You will have a most unpleasant escort through the town."
	The Fair Unknown willingly agreed to this,
2612	for he feared nothing.
	And Lampart led him to the hall
	where he maintained his dreadful custom.
	This huge hall
2616	was on the lower level of the keep.
	There it was that Lampart jousted with everyone desiring
	lodging.
	He had a carpet brought in;
	when it had been laid out,
2620	he went over to it at once
	and seated himself on one side
	upon the image of a gray leopard
	that had been woven into the carpet.
2624	He then had himself armed.
	They laced on his iron leggings,
	which looked quite handsome,
	for they were brighter than the hawthorn:
2628	the gleaming mail was tightly woven.

Son ceval li ont amené
quant de tot en tot l'ont armé,
et li chevaliers est montés
2632   qui molt ert prous et alosés.
Quant fu armés, son escu prist
et sa fort lance aporter fist.
Quanques doi vallet porter porent,
2636   estes vos que totes les orent,
grandes et roides et quarrees.
Quant les lances sont aportees,
cascuns a tost la soie prisse
2640   tele con vaut a sa devisse.
Lor regnes tornent, si s'eslongent;
por tost aler lor cevals poingnent.
Molt aloient tost li ceval,
2644   si s'entrefierent li vasal
des lances grans cols a devisse   *[142 v°a]*
dusqu'en ses puins cascuns lé brisse.
Ensanble hurtent li destrier;
2648   bien se tinrent li chevalier
que l'uns ne l'autres ne caï.
Andoi furent preu et hardi.
Et quant cascuns ot fait son tor,
2652   n'i font demore ne sejor;
lances reprendent por joster
et laiscent tost cevals aler
et puis durement s'entrevienent.
2656   Les lances alongnies tienent,
si se fierent de tel angoisse
que l'une lance l'autre froisse.
Les esclices en font voler
2660   si haut que on poroit jeter.
De grant fin sorent bien joster!
Cascuns vait lance demander
et Robers molt bien i eslist:
2664   la millor et le plus fort prist
et vint corant a son signor,
se li tendi par grant amor

Lampart's servants brought his horse to him
after they had fully armed him,
and he then mounted,
2632   a man most valiant and esteemed.
Once armed, he took his shield
and had his strong lance fetched.
As many lances as two young men could carry
2636   were brought before the two knights,
all of them long and sturdy and solid.
As soon as the lances had been brought,
each knight chose
2640   the one he wanted.
The two knights turned their horses and moved some distance
         apart;
then they spurred their mounts to lend them speed.
The horses ran most swiftly,
2644   and the knights struck each other
with such great force
that their lances split clear down to the handles.
The chargers smashed into each other,
2648   but both knights held so firmly in their saddles
that neither fell off.
Both were worthy and valiant men.
And after this first charge,
2652   neither sought a moment's delay;
they took up new lances to joust again,
let their horses run freely,
and rushed together for a fierce clash.
2656   They levelled their lances
and struck each other with such force
that both lances shattered.
The fragments flew up in the air
2660   as high as anything could ever be thrown.
Clearly, these men well knew how to joust!
Each knight now asked for another lance,
and Robert chose one well:
2664   he took the best and strongest
and then ran up to his lord,
gave it to him with great affection,

et dist, "Sire, n'obliés mie
2668   por amor Diu, le Fil Marie,
les laides torces ne les pos!
Ne soiés pas de joster sos:
molt vos cuident tost malbaillir.
2672   Ja sont tot prest de vos laidir
et les grant gens et les menues;
plainnes en sont totes les rues."
"Amis," fait il, "ne t'esmaier:
2676   Dius nos en puet molt bien aidier."
Lors retorne sans demorance
contre le chevalier sa lance,
et li chevaliers point vers lui.
2680   Lors s'entrefierent anbedui,
mais Lanpars l'a premiers feru
molt ruiste cop en son escu;
de l'autre part fait fer paser,
2684   de l'anste fist les tros voler.
Mais cil a Lanpart ne faut mie:
desus la boucle u l'ors clarie
l'a si feru del fer trençant
2688   que l'escu li perce devant.
La lance fu et roide et fors,
et il l'enpaint par tel esfors
que les estriers li fist guerpir
2692   que il ne se pot plus tenir.
Il ne fu navrés ne bleciés;
i[s]nelement est redreciés,
al Descouneü est alés.
2696   "Sire," fait il, "ça descendés.
Par droit avés l'ostel conquis: [*142v°b*]
vos l'averés a vo devis."
Et cil isnelement descent;
2700   uns damoisials son ceval prent.

2675 afait *with first a expuncted*
2677-81 *text arranged around hole in vellum*
2682 m. r. c. lia en s. e. [+2]
2694 ilnelement

and said, "My lord, for the love of God,
2668 the Son of Mary, do not forget
the mudpies and the pots full of rubbish!
You must fight better than your opponent,
for these people are ready to give you a bad welcome.
2672 They stand nearby to humiliate you,
and the streets are full
of nobles and common folk."
"My friend," said the knight, "do not be dismayed:
2676 God can easily lend us His aid."
Then without delay he turned
his lance toward the other knight,
and Lampart spurred toward him.
2680 Both then struck each other,
but Lampart first gave the Fair Unknown
a mighty blow on his shield,
so that the iron tip passed through it,
2684 sending splinters flying into the air.
But the Fair Unknown did not fail to strike in his turn:
above the boss, with its bright gold,
he struck Lampart so hard with the steel tip of his lance
2688 that he pierced the shield.
His lance was sure and strong,
and he hit Lampart with such force
that he knocked him from his stirrups
2692 and out of his saddle.
Lampart was not wounded at all;
he quickly got up
and went over to the Fair Unknown.
2696 "My lord," he said, "please dismount.
You have won the right to be lodged here,
and you shall now be as well received as you could wish."
The Fair Unknown dismounted at once,
2700 and a boy took his horse.

Lors furent vallet apresté
qui maintenant l'ont desarmé;
aprés redesarment Lanpart.
2704 Elie se trait d'une part
et Lanpars l'enbrace et acole.
A une part a li parole;
andoi molt grant joie faisoient,
2708 que molt bon chevalier estoient.
Car senescals sa dame estoit
Lanpars: por ce molt l'onneroit.
Puis li demande qu'ele fait;
2712 cele li respont entresait:
"Le roi Artus a cort trova
a Carlion, a lui parla
a ma damoisele en aïe.
2716 Dou tot cuida estre esbahie
quant cest chevalier me carça
qui orendroit a vos josta.
Il me siet bien tot a mon gré;
2720 bien l'ai en la voie esprové
es grans estors u veü l'ai.
Certes millor de lui ne sai.
Or li portés molt grant honnor
2724 car il est molt de grant valor."
Quant L[an]pars l'ot, grant joie en a.
Vers lui maintenant s'en ala,
maintenant le va acoler.
2728 Molt bel sanblant li fait mostrer.
"Sire, molt avés enduré
et molt travillié et pené.
Molt avés fait a mon plaisir
2732 as estors que savés furnir.
Or est bien tans de reposer."
Adont s'asisent au souper.

2702 maintenanant
2720 voiee
2725 Lupars
2733 reporer *corrected to* reposer *by scribe*

Then young men hurried
to remove his arms;
after that they disarmed Lampart.

2704   Helie stepped forward,
and Lampart embraced and welcomed her.
He drew her aside and spoke to her;
both of them rejoiced

2708   that the two men had shown themselves to be such fine
            knights.
Lampart was the seneschal of Helie's lady:
that is why he showed her such honor.
Then he asked why she was there,

2712   and she responded thus:
"I went to King Arthur's court
in Carlion to ask
for help for my lady.

2716   I thought I had failed
when he lent me this knight
who jousted with you just now.
But he suits me entirely;

2720   I have measured him well along our route
by the harsh combats I have seen him undergo.
In truth, I know of none better than he.
Take care to show him great honor,

2724   for he is a knight of the greatest valor."
When Lampart heard this, he rejoiced.
He went straight to the knight
to make him welcome at once.

2728   He arranged that he be given a most gracious welcome.
"My lord," he said, "you have endured much
and been sorely tried and pressed.
You have pleased me greatly

2732   by how well you do battle.
Now it is time for you to rest."
They then seated themselves for the evening meal.

Molt sont bien servi a devise
2736 et si ont mes de mante guisse.
Aprés souper tot maintenant
font porter vin a respandant
. . . .
2740 car reposer vellent aler.
Et le matin se veulent lever,
la messe oïr et Diu prier.
Puis resont a l'ostel venu
2744 u li dingners aprestés fu.
Lanpars l'avoit fait atorner,
capons cras et oisiaus torner.
Li chevalier sist au mangier
2748 un petitet por esforcier.
Et quant sont levé de digner,
les cevals fisent ensieler.   [*142 v°c*]
Lanpars au chevalier conselle
2752 priveement ens en s'orelle
cele fois [que] ne sejornast
ne nul encontre ne doutast;
mestier avrai d'armes porter.
2756 Tot son harnas a fait torser;
des ore dist qu'il s'en ira
et ses escuiers tot torsa.
Li ceval furent apresté
2760 et il sont maintenant monté.
Ensanble [o] els Lanpars s'en vait.
Pres de la pucele se traist,
se li consele par amor
2764 au nain qui tint le misaudor.
Li nain le palefroi caçoit
que la pucele cevauçoit.
Tot trois aloient consillant.
2768 Li Descouneüs vait deva[n]t
aveuc Robert son escuier.

2753 que *lacking* [*em. Williams*]
2761 E. a e.
2768 v. devait

They were very well served
2736 with many kinds of dishes.
As soon as the meal was over,
wine was brought in abundance

. . . .

2740 for they wished to take their rest.
And in the morning it pleased them to rise
that they might hear mass and pray to God.
Then they returned to their lodgings,
2744 where dinner had been prepared.
Lampart had had
fat capons and gamebirds roasted.
The knight sat at table
2748 for only a short while so that he might gain strength.
As soon as they had arisen from dinner,
the company had the horses saddled.
Lampart privately counselled
2752 the Fair Unknown
that he should stay no longer
nor fear any encounter,
but told him that he would have need of his arms.
2756 So the Fair Unknown had all his equipment prepared;
he announced that he was leaving,
and his squire took care of everything.
The horses were made ready,
2760 and they mounted at once.
Lampart went along with them.
He rode beside Helie
and shared friendly conversation
2764 with the dwarf, who was leading the charger.
The dwarf also drove the palfrey
which the maiden rode.
The three rode along conferring.
2768 The Fair Unknown rode ahead of them
with Robert his squire.

Ariere les voit consillier;
n'est mervelle se paor a:
2772   ses aventures redouta.
Et quant ce vi[n]t a l'avesprer,
une forest ont a passer
et la Cité Gaste [ont] ve[ü]e.
2776   Onques si biele de veüe
ne vit nus con cele ert jadis;
or est gaste, ce m'est avis.
Entre deus augues molt bruians
2780   sist la cités qui molt fu gran[s].
Les tors virent et les maisons
et les clociers et les dongons,
les bon[s] palais qui [resplandoient]
2784   et les aigles qui reflanboient.
Quant ont veüe la cité,
tot maintenant sont aresté;
lors descent cascuns de la sele.
2788   Lanpars ploroit et la pucele.
Les armes font avant porter
por le De[s]couneü armer.
A bonnes coroies de cer
2792   li lacent les cauces de fer.
Le hauberc li ont el dos mis,
le hiaume aprés el cief asis.
Et quant il l'orent bien armé,
2796   si l'a Lanpars araisonné:
"Sire," fait il, "or en irois
que conpaignie n'i menrois,
car cil qu'iront ensanble vos
2800   serront ocis tot a estros.
Quant vos venrés en la cité,
les murs verés d'antiquité   [143 r°a]

2773 ce vit a
2775 de vee [em. Williams]
2780 grant
2783 bon, renflanboient [em. Williams]
2790 decouneu

When he saw them riding behind him conferring,
it was no wonder that he was afraid:
2772   he dreaded the adventure that awaited him.
And when it was almost evening,
they emerged from a forest
and saw the Desolate City.
2776   No one ever saw a city
so beautiful as this once had been;
now, I believe, it all lay in ruins.
The fortress, a very large one,
2780   was placed between two roaring rivers.
The company saw the towers and the houses,
the bell towers and the keeps,
the fine, resplendent palaces
2784   and the eagles that shone in the sun.
When they saw the fortress,
they halted at once,
and each of them dismounted.
2788   Lampart and the maiden were both weeping.
They had the Fair Unknown's arms brought forward
so that they could arm him.
With strong deerskin straps
2792   they laced up his iron leggings.
They put his hauberk on his back
and placed his helmet on his head.
And when they had fully armed him,
2796   Lampart spoke to him thus:
"My lord, you must go on alone,
taking no one else,
for anyone who went with you
2800   would certainly be killed.
When you reach the fortress,
you will see its ancient walls,

et les po[r]tals et les clociers
2804   et les maisons et les soliers,
les ars volus de[s] ouvreors,
les cretials des palais auçors.
Trestous destruis les troverois.
2808   Homme ne feme n'i verrois.
Icele rue adés alés
—gardés ja ne vos retornés—
des qu'en mi liu de la cité
2812   u vos venrés d'antiquité
un palais molt grant et marbrin.
Laie[n]s irés tot le cemin.
La sale est molt grans et molt lee
2816   et li portels gran[s] a l'entree.
Vos verrés asés bien les estres:
el front devant a mil fenestres;
en cascune a un jogleor
2820   et tot sont de molt riche ator.
Cascuns a divers estremen[t]
et devant lui un cierge ardent.
De trestotes les armo[n]ies
2824   i a molt doces melaudies.
Tantost con venir vos verront,
trestout bel vos salueront.
Vos respondés, 'Dius vos maudie!'
2828   Ceste orison n'oblïés mie
et en la sal en entrerois,
vostre aventure i atandrois.
Et tant con vos amés vo vie,
2832   si gardés que vos n'entrés mie
en la canbre que vos verrois.
Quar vos en la sale serrois;

2803 potrals
2805 v. de o.
2814 Laies
2816 grant
2821 estrumens
2823 armories

its portals and its bell towers,
2804   its houses and its upper halls,
its vaulted galleries where craftsmen worked,
the crenels of its high palaces.
All of this you will find destroyed.
2808   And you will see no one, neither man nor woman.
Now follow this road
—see that you do not turn away from it—
until you have reached
2812   a great marble palace from ancient times
in the heart of the walled city.
Follow the road all the way.
The hall is both very long and very wide,
2816   with a great door by which to enter it.
You will be able to see inside very well,
for the façade has a thousand windows;
in each window will be a jongleur,
2820   each one richly dressed.
Each will have a different instrument,
and in front of him will be a burning candle.
From the harmony of all these instruments,
2824   you will hear sweet melodies.
As soon as they see you coming,
the jongleurs will greet you courteously.
Answer them thus: 'May God curse you!'
2828   Do not forget this prayer,
and then you must enter the palace
and there await what will befall you.
But if your life is dear to you,
2832   make certain that you do not enter
the side chamber you will see there.
Once you are in the hall,

tres en mi liu vos arestés,
2836   vostre aventure i atendés.
Or montés en vostre destrier
que n'i avés que atargier."
Et cil sor son ceval monta,
2840   trestos a Diu les comanda
et il recomandent lui.
Mais molt lor torne a grant anui
que il l'en ont veü aler,
2844   si comencierent a plorer.
Jamais ne.l cuident reveoir.
Or le gard Dius par son pooir!
Lanpars ploroit et la pucele.
2848   Robers ciet pasmés a la terre.
De l'autre part ploroit li nains;
les cevals traioit a ses mains.
D'estrange guisse grant dol fait.
2852   Et li Descouneüs s'en vait
tant qu'il vint a la cité.
Sor une iaugue a un pont trové   [*143 r°b*]
qui devant la porte coroit;
2856   d'une part la cité clooit.
Cinc liues duroit la cités,
close de mur[s] et de fosés.
Li mur estoient bon et biel;
2860   de mabre sont tot li quarriel,
li un es autres entaillié
et a ciment entrelacié.
Et furent de maintes co[l]ors,
2864   taillié a bietes et a flors;
et sont li quarriel bien asis,
indes et vers, gaunes et bis.
Et a cinc toisses tot entor
2868   ot adiés une haute tor,
si que on i puet bien aler
et li uns a l'autre parler.

2858 mur
2863 m. cosors

stop there in the middle
2836 and await what will befall.
Now mount your charger,
for you have no reason to delay."
The knight mounted his horse
2840 and bade them all farewell,
as did they him.
But it tore their hearts
to see him depart,
2844 and they began to weep.
They never thought to see him again.
Now may God guard him by His power!
Lampart and the maiden were weeping.
2848 Robert fell to the ground in a swoon.
For his part, the dwarf was also weeping
and tearing his hair.
He lamented most bitterly.
2852 And so the Fair Unknown went his way
until he came to the walled city.
Spanning the river he saw a bridge
that led to the city gate;
2856 this river protected the city on one side.
The city was enclosed by
walls and moats five leagues around.
These walls were handsome and well constructed;
2860 their stones were carved out of marble,
and each was fitted solidly to the other
and held in place with mortar.
Animals and flowers
2864 of many colors had been carved into these walls,
and the stones of blue, green, yellow and gray
had been skillfully arranged.
And all around, at intervals of thirty feet,
2868 high towers had been placed,
so that those who ascended these towers
could easily make themselves heard from one to the other.

En la cité homme n'avoit;
2872   tote gaste la vile estoit.
Quant il le vit, si se saingna,
par la porte dedens entra.
Le porte a trové abatue.
2876   Il s'en vait adiés la grant rue,
regardant adiés les grans rues
dont les fenestres sont marbrues;
chaoit en sont tuit li piler.
2880   Il ne se vaut mie arester
tant qu'a la sale en est venus
u les jogleors a veüs
sor les fenestres tos asis,
2884   devant cascun un cierge espris.
Et son estrument retenoit
cascuns itel con il l'avoit.
L'un voit as fenestres harper,
2888   l'autre delés celui roter;
l'uns estive, l'autre vïele,
li autres gigle et calimele
et cante cler comme serainne;
2892   li autres la citole mainne,
li u[n]s entendoit au corner
et l'autres au bien flahuter;
li un notoient lais d'amor,
2896   sonnent tinbre, sonnent tabor,
muses, salteres et fretel
et buissines et moïnel.
Cascuns ovre de son mestier.
2900   Et quant voient le chevalier
venu sor son destrier a[r]mé,
a hautes vo[i]s sont escrié,
"Dius saut, Dius saut le chevalier
2904   qui est venus la dame aidier

2890 gigles
2893 li us
2901 d. ame
2902 h. vos s.

There was not a soul in the fortress;
2872 the entire city lay in ruins.
When the knight saw this, he crossed himself
and entered the fortress.
The gate had been knocked down.
2876 He followed the main road,
looking around him at the streets
with their windows framed in marble;
all the pillars had fallen down.
2880 The knight did not stop
until he came to the great hall of the palace,
where he saw the jongleurs
all seated in the windows,
2884 each with a candle in front of him.
And each one was holding
his instrument.
The knight saw one playing the harp,
2888 while the one next to him to played a rota;
one played the bagpipes, another a hurdy-gurdy,
another a fiddle, another a shawm,
and another singing with a clear voice like a siren's;
2892 another played a lute,
one a horn,
while another played skillfully on his flute;
some played songs of love
2896 to the sounds of the tambourines and the tabors,
the cornemuses, psalteries, and pipes,
the trumpets and the horns.
Each played his own part.
2900 And when they saw the knight
coming armed on his charger,
they cried out in a loud voice,
"May God save the knight
2904 who comes from the court of King Arthur

de la mainnie Artus le roi!"
Adont fu il en grant esfroi   *[143 r°c]*
et neporquant si lor respont,
2908   "Cil Damesdius qui fist le mont
vos doinst a tos malaventure!"
Outre s'en va grant aleüre
par mi la sale cevauçant
2912   que de rien ne se va targant.
Derier l'uis ot un gougleor
qui en sa main tin[t] un tabor;
cil li a l'uis aprés fermé.
2916   En la sale avoit grant clarté
des cierges qui laiens ardoient
que tuit li jogleor tenoient.
Li palais molt rices estoit.
2920   Une grant table en mi avoit
qui seoit desus set dormans.
Li Biaus Descouneüs laiens
en mi la sale s'aresta
2924   et a sa lance s'apuia.
Iluec atendoit s'aventure.
Atant voit d'une canbre oscure
issir un chevalier armé
2928   sor un destrier molt acesmé,
l'escu au col qui vers estoit—
autre devisse n'i avoit.
Et sist deseur un destrier ver;
2932   hanste ot molt grosse a trençant fer.
Quant il voit le Descouneü,
il point a lui de grant vertu.
Quant cil le vit vers lui venir,
2936   vers lui reguencist por ferir.
Cascuns d'esperonner ne fine,
molt s'entrevienent de ravine.
Sor les escus haut se requierent,

2914 tin
2928 s. un. d. m. bien armé a.
2939 l. escuns h.

to render aid to the lady!"
At this, the knight was filled with dread,
but he said to them,
2908   "May the Lord God, Who formed the world,
bring you all to a bad end!"
He galloped past them
and into the hall
2912   without pausing for a moment.
Behind the door to the hall stood a jongleur
with a tabor in his hand;
this man closed the door behind the Fair Unknown.
2916   The hall was brightly lit
from all the candles
that the jongleurs held.
This hall was indeed a splendid one.
2920   In the center stood a large table
that rested on seven legs.
Near it, in the middle of the hall,
the Fair Unknown stopped
2924   and leaned against his lance.
There he awaited what would befall him.
Suddenly he saw emerge from a dark chamber
an armed knight
2928   riding a charger fitted for combat
and carrying a green shield—
it bore no emblem.
The knight's charger was dappled gray;
2932   he carried a huge lance with a sharp, cutting tip.
He saw the Fair Unknown
and spurred toward him at a full gallop.
When the knight saw him coming toward him,
2936   he turned to attack the newcomer.
Each one spurred his horse vigorously
as they came toward each other with great fury.
They struck each other high on the bucklers,

2940   des lances tels cols s'entrefierent
    que des cevals s'entr'abatirent.

    . . . .
    Il se relievent maintenant.
2944   Cascuns tint l'espee trençant.
    Sor les elmes, sor les escus
    ont grans cols et pesans ferus.
    De nule rien ne s'espargnoient;
2948   sovent a genillons venoient.
    Cil voit bien que riens ne li vaut
    car li Descouneüs l'asaut,
    et tant le voit bon chevalier
2952   que plus ne li velt asaier.
    Plus tost que pot vers l'uis se trait
    et en sa canbre s'en revait.
    En la canbre cil s'en entra;
2956   cil va aprés qui l'encauça.
    Par mi l'uis ens voloit entrer
    quant vit destendre et enteser
    de haces grans por lui ferir.   [*143 v°a*]
2960   Par deseur lui les vit venir,
    ariere maintenant se trait.
    Mors fust se il n'eüst ço fait!
    En mi la sale s'aresta,
2964   une grant piece i demora
    que goute n'i pooit veoir.
    Tant i faisoit oscur et noir
    que son ceval ne pot trover.
2968   Diu comencha a reclamer
    que fors de laiens le jetast
    que mal ne honte n'encontrast.
    Entrols qu'il se demente ensi,
2972   li uns des jogleors sailli,
    a tos les cierges fu touça.
    Atant la clartés repaira
    des cierges qui alumé sont.

2948 s. v. a g. *with insertion marks correcting order*

2940   giving such blows with their lances
that both were knocked from their horses.

. . . .

They got up at once.

2944   Each grasped his sharp sword.
On their helmets and shields
they rained harsh and forceful blows.
They held nothing back;

2948   often they fell to their knees.
The newcomer could see that his effort was in vain,
for the Fair Unknown attacked without respite
and showed himself to be such a fine knight

2952   that his opponent did not wish to continue the combat.
He made for the door as fast as he could
to return to his chamber from which he had emerged.
He entered there

2956   with the Fair Unknown in pursuit.
The knight was about to follow him through the door
when he saw
huge battle axes descending to strike him.

2960   He saw these blades coming down at him
and drew back at once.
Had he not done so, he would have been killed!
He returned to the middle of the hall and stopped;

2964   he remained there for a long time,
unable to see anything at all.
It was so dark
that he could not find his horse.

2968   He began to call on God
to deliver him from that place
and protect him from harm or dishonor.
While he thus lamented,

2972   one of the jongleurs jumped up,
and lit all of the candles.
At once the hall was bright again
from the light of the candles.

2976 Li jogleor lor mestier font:
      cascuns sonnoit son estrumant
      ansi con il faisoit devant.
      Quant venue fu la clartés,
2980 de rien ne s'est espaventés.
      Cele part vint corant tot droit
      u vit que ses cevals estoit;
      par le regne tantost le prent.
2984 Sa lance voit el pavement,
      puis l'a prise, si est montés.
      En mi la sale en est alés;
      iluec estoit tot a estal.
2988 Liés fu quant il ot son ceval.
      Atant est de la canbre issus
      uns chevaliers grans et corsus.
      Bien fu armés li chevaliers
2992 et tos armés est ses destriers.
      Molt est bons et ciers ses cevals:
      si oil luissoient cum cristals,
      une corne ot el front devant,
2996 par la gole rent feu ardant.
      N'ainc hom ne vit si bien movant;
      l'alainne avoit fiere et bruiant.
      Li sire fu et grans et fiers
3000 molt fu corsus li chevalier[s].
      Il vint bruiant come tonnoires,
      ses armes furent totes noires.
      La sale fu a pavement
3004 et li cevals ne vint pas lent;
      des quatre piés si fort marçoit
      que tot le pavement brisoit
      et fu et flame en fait salir.
3008 Tot en fait le païs tonbir,
      la piere dure en esmioit
      desous ses piés si fort marçoit.
      Quant li Descouneüs le voit,   [*143 v°b*]

2976 mestier *repeated*
3000 chevalier

2976   The jongleurs now began to ply their trade:
         each played his instrument,
         just as he had before.
         Once the light had returned,
2980   the knight was no longer afraid of anything.
         He made straight
         for his horse
         and seized the reins.
2984   He saw his lance lying on the floor,
         took it up, and mounted.
         He rode again to the center of the hall,
         where he again took up his position.
2988   He was pleased to have his horse once more.
         Suddenly, from the same dark chamber
         there emerged a huge knight.
         Both the knight and his charger
2992   were fully armed.
         This horse was a most rare and excellent animal:
         his eyes shone like crystals;
         he had a horn on his forehead,
2996   and bright flames spewed from his mouth.
         No one ever saw a horse move with such speed and power;
         his fiery breath roared.
         His master was a warlike man,
3000   a huge knight.
         He rode forward with a noise like thunder,
         his arms entirely black.
         The hall was paved in stone,
3004   and the horse came quickly,
         his four hooves striking the ground so sharply
         that he broke right through it,
         sending off fiery sparks.
3008   The whole place resounded with the noise
         as he shattered the hard stones
         beneath his hooves, with such force did he pound forward.
         When the Fair Unknown saw this horse,

3012 de sa façon s'esmervilloit.
   Diu reclama, le Roi de Glore,
   que vers celui li doi[n]st victore.
   Por joster muet au chevalier;
3016 des esperons fiert le destrier
   et li chevaliers point vers lui.
   Lors s'entrevienent anbedui
   des lances de totes leur forces.
3020 Ne leur valurent deus escorces
   li escus qui as cols lor pendent:
   li [cuir] ronpent et les ais fendent,
   les mailles ronpent des haubers,
3024 par les cors se metent les fers.
   Si durement se sont feru
   que andoi se sont abatu.
   Ne furent pas a mort blecié;
3028 isne[le]ment sont redrecié.
   Cascuns a sa lance a lui traite;
   il n'i ot cele qui[.n] fust fraite.
   El pavement les ont jetees;
3032 del fuerre traient les espees.
   Grans cols se fierent des brans nus
   sor les elmes, sor les escus.
   Molt s'entrerendent grant bataille.
3036 Onques cele de Cornouaille
   del grant Morholt ne de Tristant,
   ne d'Olivier ne de Rollant,
   ne de Mainnet ne de Braimant,
3040 de chevalier ne de gaiant
   ne fu tels bataille veü[e].
   Onques si grant n'ot sos la nue.
   Tant se sont andoi conbatu

3014 doist
3022 cuer
3023 les m. valent r. des h.
3028 isnement
3030 qui f. [em. *Williams*]
3041 veu

3012	he was struck with wonder.
	He called on God, the King of Glory,
	to grant him victory against this knight.
	He positioned his horse for the joust;
3016	he spurred his horse forward
	as the other knight rushed toward him.
	The two knights then came at each other
	at full tilt with their lances.
3020	The shields that hung from their necks
	did them no good:
	leather broke and wood shattered,
	the mail of their hauberks was torn
3024	and the steel lance tips pierced through to the flesh.
	The knights clashed with such force
	that both were hurled to the ground.
	But they were not seriously wounded
3028	and quickly got to their feet.
	Each took up his lance,
	but both had been shattered to bits.
	And so they threw them to the floor
3032	and drew their swords from their sheaths.
	They gave each other great blows
	on helmet and shield with their naked blades.
	They fought a fierce battle.
3036	Not even when in Cornwall
	the giant Morholt did combat with Tristan,
	nor when Oliver fought Roland,
	nor when Mainet fought Braiment—
3040	never was such a battle seen
	between any knight and giant.
	Never under the sun was a greater one fought.
	Both knights fought so fiercely

3044   et si grans cols entreferu
        que molt furent andoi lassé.
        Molt a li uns l'autre grevé;
        molt se dolen[t] et molt sont las.
3048   Neporquant ne recroient pas.
        Li Descouneüs le requiert,
        de l'espee si bien le fiert,
        l'elme li fait del [cief] voler.
3052   Cil s'en cuide, si vaut torner
        qu'il ot la teste desarmee;
        mais cil au trençant de l'espee
        l'a si bien de son cop ataint,
3056   le test del cief li brisse et frai[n]t.
        La coife ne le pot tenir
        que le cief n'en fesist partir.
        Donné li a si grant colee
3060   que mort l'abat guele baee.
        Del cors li saut une fumiere
        qui molt estoit hideusse et fiere
        qui li issoit par mi la boce.   [*143 v°c*]
3064   Li Bials Descouneüs le toce
        por savoir s'il ert encor vis.
        Sa main li met deseur le pis:
        tos fu devenus claire pure
3068   qui molt estoit et laide et sure.
        Isi li canja sa figure:
        molt estoit de male nature.
        Quant il ço voit, si [se] segna,
3072   vers son ceval aler cuida.
        Atant s'en vont li jogleor;
        cascuns enpaint par tel vigor
        sa fenestre quant il s'en part

3047 dolen
3051 cief *lacking*
3056 briesse, frait
3071 se *lacking*

3044 and gave each other such heavy blows
that they wore each other out.
They inflicted great harm on each other;
both were wounded and deeply weary.
3048 But still neither would surrender.
The Fair Unknown struck his opponent
such a harsh blow with his sword
that he sent the helmet flying from his head.
3052 The other, when he realized that his head had been bared,
tried to move away;
but the Fair Unknown hit him so hard
with his sword
3056 that he split open his head.
The hood of mail did not prevent
the knight's head from being severed from his body.
The Fair Unknown dealt him such a great blow
3060 that he knocked him down dead, his mouth agape.
From his body there arose
a horrid and fearful plume of smoke,
which spewed out of his mouth.
3064 The Fair Unknown touched him
to see if he was still alive.
He put his hand on the man's chest:
he had turned to
3068 filthy, stinking slime.
His appearance was changed utterly,
for he was of an evil nature.
When the knight saw this, he crossed himself
3072 and turned toward his horse.
All at once the jongleurs went away;
each slammed the window shutters
so violently as he left

3076   que li palais tos en tresart.
        Si durement batent et hurtent
        que tot li uis qui laiens furent
        qu'a poi qu'il n'abatent la sale
3080   de la noise hidouse et male.
        Li cierge furent enporté,
        si i faisoit grant oscurté
        que on n'i pooit rie[n] veoir,
3084   tant i faisoit oscur et noir.
        Cil ne se puet plus soustenir;
        a tere le couvient venir.
        Vis fu que ciel et tere font,
3088   des cols que les fenestres font,
        a celui qui laiens estoit.
        De sa main souvent se sainnoit;
        Diu reclama, l'Esperitable,
3092   mal ne li facent li diable.
        Et quant il fu en piés levés,
        si s'en est mai[n]tenant alés
        tot droit a la table dormant;
3096   trestot i va a atastant
        si come aventure le mainne.
        Trovee l'a a quelque painne;
        quant il i fu, si s'apuia.
3100   La noise molt li anuia.
        Diu, son Signor, aeure et prie
        que secors li face et aïe:
        "A, Dius," fait il, "ne sai que dire,
3104   mais livrés sui a grant martire.
        Jamais iço ne me faura

3076 tos sen t.
3077 duerement
3083 rie v.
3094 maitenant

3076 that the whole hall shook.
They banged
all the doors so hard as well
that they almost made the hall collapse
3080 with the fearful din.
The jongleurs had taken all the candles with them,
so that it had become very dark,
and one could see nothing
3084 in the blackness.
The knight could no longer keep to his feet;
he fell to the ground.
All the slamming of the shutters
3088 made it seem to him there inside the hall
that heaven and earth were falling.
He crossed himself again and again;
he called on God the Holy Spirit
3092 to protect him from these devils.
And when he had gotten to his feet
he made his way toward
the table in the middle of the hall;
3096 he went there feeling his way
as chance led him.
It was with difficulty that he found it;
when he had reached it, he held to it tightly.
3100 The tumult disturbed him greatly.
He prayed to God, his Lord,
to lend him aid:
"Dear God," he said, "I know not what to say
3104 except that I am given over to great suffering.
It seems to me that this clamor will never end

ne jors, je cuic, mais ne serra.
Bien sai ne puis longes durer,
3108   car je ne sai quel part aler
ne mon destrier mie ne sai.
Et neporeuc por ce m'esmai
de rien; [n]e me doi esmaier.
3112   Ce n'afiert pas a chevalier
qu'il s'esmait por nule aventure,
por qu'est armés, tant ne l'ait dure.
Entemes cil qui a amor   *[144 r°a]*
3116   ne doit avoir nule paor.
Bien me devroie aporpenser
por celi qui tant doi amer,
la Damoissele as Blances Mains,
3120   dont je parti come vilains.
Jo l'en irai merchi rover
se de ci me puis escaper.
Se Diu plaist, encor le verrai
3124   ne jamais jor n'en partirai.
S'Amors me donne ja vigor,
de rien que je voi n'ai paor!"
Atant vit une aumaire ouvrir
3128   et une wivre fors issir
qui jetoit une tel clarté
[con] un cierge bien enbrasé.
Tot le palais enluminoit,
3132   une si grant clarté jetoit.
Hom ne vit onques sa parelle,
que la bouce ot tote vermelle,
par mi jetoit le feu ardant.
3136   Molt par estoit hidosse et grant;
par mi le pis plus grosse estoit
que un vaissaus d'un mui ne soit.

3111 r. me me
3130 quem un

and that it will never again be daylight.
I know I cannot hold out much longer,
3108 for I know not where to go
and I have lost my horse.
But I shall not therefore be afraid,
nor is it right that I should be.
3112 It is not worthy of a knight
to be afraid no matter what his fate,
or how sorely he is pressed, for he is armed.
And besides, he who has love
3116 should never be afraid.
I should cast my thoughts
on her to whom I owe so much love,
the Lady of the White Hands,
3120 whom I left so unworthily.
I shall go to beg her forgiveness
if I ever escape from this place.
If it please God, I shall see her again
3124 and never leave her.
Now love gives me strength,
and I shall fear nothing that I see!"
Suddenly he saw a cupboard open up
3128 and a serpent come forth
giving out as much light
as a brightly lit candle.
It filled the hall
3132 with the great light it gave off.
No one ever saw such a serpent:
its mouth was red,
and spewed forth flames.
3136 It was huge and hideous,
wider across the middle
than a wine-cask.

Les iols avoit gros et luissans
3140 come deus esclarbocles grans.
Contreval l'aumaire descent
et vint par mi le pavement.
Quatre toisses de lonc duroit
3144 et la keue trois neus avoit,
c'onques nus hom ne vit grinnor.
Ains Dius ne fist cele color
qu'en li ne soit entremellee;
3148 desous sanbloit estre doree.
Vers le chevalier s'en venoit;
cil se saine quant il le voit.
Apoiés estoit sor le table
3152 et quant il vit si fait dyable
vers soi aproimier et venir,
isnelement por soi garnir
a misse la main a l'espee.
3156 Ançois qu'il l'eüst fors jetee,
et la grans wivre li encline
del cief dusqu'a la poitrine:
sanblant d'umelité li fait
3160 et cil s'espee plus ne trait.
"Jo ne le doi," fait il, "tocier
puis que le voi humelïer."
La guivre adés ver lui venoit
3164 et plus et plus s'en aproimoit,
et cil adonc se porpensa
que s'espee adonques traira
por icel fier serpent ferir   [144 r °b]
3168 que il veoit vers lui venir.
Et li serpens le renclina
et sanblant d'[a]misté mostra.
Il se retint, ne le trait pas;

3144 et e la
3158 poiterine [+l]
3170 demistie

It had big shining eyes
3140 like two great carbuncles.
It slithered down the cupboard
until it reached the ground.
It was nine yards long
3144 and its tail—no one ever saw a longer one—
had three loops in it.
All the colors God created
were in this serpent's tail;
3148 its underbelly seemed to be golden.
It advanced toward the knight,
who crossed himself when he saw it.
He leaned against the table,
3152 and when he saw such a diabolical creature
coming near him,
he at once put his hand to his sword
to protect himself.
3156 But before he could draw it,
the huge serpent bowed to him
from its head down to its middle:
it made a gesture of respect to him,
3160 and he did not draw his sword.
"I should not do it harm,
since I see it bowing so humbly," he said.
The serpent then moved closer
3164 and closer to him,
and so he decided
to draw his sword
and strike the creature
3168 as he saw it drawing nearer.
But the serpent once again bowed
in sign of friendship.
The knight held back and did not draw his sword;

3172   et li serpens eneslespas
        desi es dens li est alee.
        Et [cil] trait del fuere l'espee;
        ferir le vaut par la potrine.
3176   La guivre autre fois le rencline,
        vers lui doucement s'umelie.
        Il se retint, ne le fiert mie
3178.1 . . . .
        Il l'esgarde, pas ne s'oublie
3180   ne de rie[n] nule ne fercele,
        et si a molt grant [se] mervele
        de la bouce qu'a si vermelle
3182.1 . . . .
        Tant s'enten[t] en li regarder
3184   que d'autre part ne pot garder.
        La guivre vers lui se lança
        et en la bouce le baissa.
        Quant l'ot baissié, si se retorne.
3188   Et li Descouneüs s'atorne,
        por li ferir a trait l'espee.
        Et la guivre s'est arestee,
        sanblant d'umelité li fait.
3192   Encliné l'a puis si s'en vait,
        et cil a soi son cop reti[e]nt.
        De molt grant francisse li vient
        que il ferir ne le valt mie
3196   por ce que vers lui s'umelie.
        Ensi s'en est la guivre alee;

3173 d. lie e.
3174 Et t. d. f. lespee [-*1*, *em. Williams*]
3180 rie
3181 et si a m. g. m. [-*1*]
3182 verbjelle
3183 s'enten
3189 p. li f. sest arestee a t. lespee
3193 retint
3194 mlt *for* ml't

3172   and the serpent at once
       raised itself toward his mouth.
       At this the knight drew his sword from his sheath;
       he intended to strike the creature through its middle.

3176   Once more the serpent bowed
       in humility before him.
       He held back and did not strike

3178.1 . . . .
       He looked at it, his attention fixed,

3180   without moving,
       and he marvelled greatly
       at the mouth so red

3182.1 . . . .
       He was so absorbed by looking at it

3184   that he could not turn away.
       Then the serpent darted toward him
       and kissed him on the mouth.
       And when it had kissed him, it drew back.

3188   And the Fair Unknown readied himself,
       drawing his sword to strike.
       At this the serpent stopped,
       and made him a gesture of respect.

3192   It bowed to him, then left,
       and the knight held back from striking.
       It had come to him with such nobility of manner
       that he did not wish to strike it,

3196   for it had bowed to him.
       So the serpent left;

en l'armaire s'en est rentree
et l'aumaires aprés reclot.
3200 Ainc puis tabarie n'i ot
ne nule autre malaventure,
fors que la sale fu oscure
et cil del baissier fu pensis.
3204 Delés la table s'est asis.
"Dius, Sire," fait [il], "que ferai
del Fier Baissier que fait i ai?
Molt dolerous baisier ai fait!
3208 Or sui je traïs entresait.
Li dïables m'a encanté
que j'ai baissié otre mon gré.
Or pris je molt petit ma vie."
3212 Atant a une vois oïe
qui bien li dist apertement
dont il estoit et de quel gent.
En haut crie non pas en vain:
3216 "Li fius a monsignor Gavain!   [*144 r°c*]
Tres bien le savoie de voir
que chevalier n'aroit pooir,
nus ne peüst pas delivrer,
3220 nus ne peüst tant endur[er]
ne le baisier ne l'aventure
qui tant est perilleuse et dure.
El monde n'a un chevalier
3224 tant preu ne tant fort ne tant fier
qui osast enprendre sor soi
fors ton per[e], Gavain, et toi.
Autres ne.l pooit delivrer

3201 malaaventure
3205 il *lacking* [-*1*]
3220 endur
3226 per

it went back into the cupboard
and the door closed behind it.
3200   There was no further noise
nor any other strange happening
except that the hall was dark
and the knight deeply troubled because of the kiss.
3204   He sat down beside the table.
"Lord God," he said, "what shall happen to me
because of the Fearsome Kiss which I have undergone?
That kiss was indeed a terrible thing!
3208   Surely I have been betrayed.
The devil has caught me in a spell,
for I have kissed against my will.
I now set my life at a small price."
3212   Then he heard a voice
that told him quite clearly
of his origins and his lineage.
It cried aloud, so that he could hear it well:
3216   "Son of my lord Gawain!
I knew quite well
that no other knight would have such strength,
that no other could accomplish this rescue,
3220   that no other could endure
either the kiss or any adventure
so dangerous and harsh as this one.
In the world there is no knight,
3224   however strong or worthy or warlike,
who would have dared take this upon him,
none but your father, Gawain, and you.
No one else could deliver the lady

3228   ne de son grant peril jeter.
        Estorsse as par grant vaselage
        la dame qui preus est et sage.
        Li rois Artus mal te nonma:
3232   Bel Descouneü t'apiela,
        Guinglains as non en batestire.
        Tote ta vie te sai dire.
        Mesire Gavains est tes pere,
3236   si te dirai qui est ta mere:
        fius es a Blancemal la Fee.
        Armes te donnai et espee;
        au Roi Artus puis t'envoia,
3240   qui cest afaire te donna
        de secorre la dameissele.
        Bien as conquise ta querele!"
        Atant s'en est la vois alee
3244   quant ele ot sa raisson finee
        et cil remaint. Grant joie fist
        de ço qu'il ot que la vois dist.
        Bien li a dit en sa raisson
3248   qui ses peres est et le non.
        D'ore en avant vos vel traitier
        de Guinglain, le bon chevalier,
        l'istoire qui mais ne faurra
3252   tant con li siecles duerra.
        Molt estoit Guinglains travilliés.
        Deseur la table s'est couciés,
        a son cief a son escu mis.
3256   De dormir li est talens pris,
        car lassés est et travilliés.
        Dormi a, puis est esvilliés;
        grant jors estoit quant s'esvilla,

3243 alaee
3256 pres

3228   from the great danger that held her.
By valiant knighthood you have rescued
a wise and worthy lady.
King Arthur called you by the wrong name:

3232   he called you the Fair Unknown,
but Guinglain is the name you were given at baptism.
I can tell you of your entire life.
My lord Gawain is your father,

3236   and I shall also tell you who your mother is:
you are the son of Blanchemal the Fay.
It was she who armed you and girded on your sword;
she then sent you to King Arthur,

3240   who gave you this mission
to lend aid to the maiden.
How well you have accomplished your task!"
The voice faded

3244   when its discourse was finished,
and Guinglain remained alone. He rejoiced
at what the voice had told him.
Its speaker had told him the truth

3248   about his father and his name.
Henceforth I shall tell you
of Guinglain, the worthy knight,
a story which will never be forgotten

3252   as long as this world endures.
Guinglain had been sorely pressed.
He lay down on the table,
his head resting on his shield.

3256   He longed for sleep,
so great was his exhaustion.
He fell asleep,
and when he awoke, day was well advanced

3260   en la sale grant clarté a.
        A son cief trova une dame
        tant biele c'onques nule fame
        ne fu de sa biauté formee.
3264   Tant estoit fresse et coloree
        que clers ne le saroit descrire,
        ne boce ne le poroit dire,
        ne nus ne le poroit conter.
3268   Tant le sot bien Nature ouvrer
        c'onques si bie[le] n'ot el mont
        de bouce, de iols, de vis, de front,
        de cors, de bras, de piés, de mains—   *[144 v° a]*
3272   fors sel Celi as Blances Mains,
        quar nule a li ne s'aparele.
        De sa biauté est grans mervelle,
        mais molt vos os bien aficier
3276   qu'en cesti n'ot que reprochier.
        Issi l'avoit Nature faite;
        par grant estude l'ot portraite.
        D'une vert popre estoit vestue;
3280   onques miudre ne fu veüe.
        Molt estoit riches ses mantials:
        deus sebelins ot as tasials;
        la pene fu et bone et fine
3284   et si estoit de blanc ermine.
        Les ataces qui furent mises
        furent faites de maintes guises.
        Molt par faisoient a proisier:
3288   ne.s puet on ronpre ne trencier;
        ensi les ovra une fee
        en l'Ille de la Mer Betee.
        De cel drap dont li mantials fu
3292   fu li blials qu'ele ot vestu.
        Molt estoit ciers et bien ovrés;
        d'un ermine fu tos forrés.

3269 bie
3290 Mert

3260 and the hall was filled with light.
Beside him he saw a lady
so beautiful that no other
so lovely had ever been formed.

3264 Her exquisite complexion was so fresh
that no cleric would be able to describe it
nor any tongue do it justice
or tell the truth about it.

3268 So skillfully had Nature done her work
that nowhere in the world was there any so fair
of mouth, of eyes, of face, of brow,
of form, of arms, of feet, or hands—

3272 except for the Maiden of the White Hands,
for none was that lady's equal.
Her beauty was indeed a wonder to behold,
and yet I can truly say to you

3276 that no fault could have been found in this lady.
Thus had Nature made her,
and drawn her with the greatest care.
She was dressed in green silk;

3280 no finer fabric was ever seen.
Her cloak was a very costly one:
hanging from it were two ties of sable;
its lining of white ermine

3284 was fine and beautifully made.
The clasp on the cloak
was most intricately wrought.
It was indeed worthy of admiration,

3288 for it could not be cut or broken;
a fairy on an island in the Dead Sea
had made it thus.
The tunic that she wore

3292 was cut of the same cloth as her cloak.
A garment most precious and beautifully made,
it was lined with ermine.

Plus de cinc onces d'or sans faille
3296   avoit entor le kieveçaille;
as puins en ot plus de quatre onces.
Par tot avoit asis jagonsses
et autres pieres de vertu
3300   qui furent deseur l'or batu.
Guinglains a la dame veüe,
drece son cief, si le salue.
La dame resalua lui:
3304   "Sire," fait ele, "vostre sui.
Votre doi estre par raison:
jetee m'avés de prison
de vostre part u ançois fui.
3308   Ciers sires, totes vostre sui.
Je sui fille au bon roi Guingras;
de molt grant painne jeté m'as.
Sire," fait cele, "ge fus cele
3312   por cui ala la damoisele
au roi Artu le secors querre.
Por moi estes en ceste terre.
Jetee m'avés de grant painne
3316   u j'ai esté mainte semainne.
Molt par estoit le painne fiere,
si vos dirai en quel maniere.
Quant mors fu mes pere, li rois,
3320   ne tarja pas plus de trois mois
que çaiens vint uns enchantere
et aveuc lui estoit ses frere;
il i vinrent con jogleor.   *[144 v°b]*
3324   Cil doi enchanterent le jor
tote la gent de ceste vile,
dont bien en i avoit cinc mile.
Cascuns d'els cuidoit enca[r]gier.
3328   Les tors faisoient erracier
et tos les clociers jus caoir.
Mervelles peüsiés veoir:

3327 encagier

In truth, the embroidery around the neck contained
3296 more than five ounces of gold,
and there were more than four ounces at the wrists.
Into the gold there had been set
a large number of hyacinths
3300 and other stones of magical properties.
When Guinglain saw the lady,
he raised his head and greeted her.
The lady greeted him in turn:
3304 "My lord," she said, "I am yours.
It is right that I should be,
for by your strength you have delivered me
from the captivity in which I was bound.
3308 My dear lord, I am entirely yours.
I am the daughter of the good King Guingras;
you have delivered me from great suffering.
My lord, I am the one
3312 for whose sake the maiden Helie
sought the aid of King Arthur.
For my sake you came to this land.
You have delivered me from the great suffering
3316 I endured for so many weeks.
I suffered most terribly,
as I shall describe to you.
After the death of my father the king,
3320 no more than three months had passed
before an enchanter arrived here,
along with his brother;
both claimed to be jongleurs.
3324 That same day these two worked their enchantments
on all the people of this city,
of whom there were fully five thousand.
Each person believed he was going mad.
3328 The enchanters caused the towers to be ripped up
and made all the belfries fall down.
You could have seen wondrous things:

la terre veïsiés partir
3332 et durement en haut croissir;
les pieres faisoient voler
et li une l'autre encontrer.
Sire, tot sanbloit que caïst
3336 et que cius et terre fondist.
Tant fisent grans encantemens
que tote s'en fuïst la gens;
nus n'avoit pooir d'els grever.
3340 Çaens me vinrent encanter:
quant il m'orent tocie d'un livre,
si fui sanblans a une wivre.
Issi m'ont fait lonc tans ester.
3344 Quant voloient a moi parler,
andoi me venoient devant,
s'ostoient lor encantemant.
Mabons avoit non li plus sire.
3348 Cil me venoit molt souvent dire
que jo a mari le presisse
et que s'amie devenisse
et que de cuer amaisse lui,
3352 si m'osteroit de cest anui.
Et se je amer ne.l voloie,
a tos jors mais guivre serroie.
Iço me coverroit soufrir
3356 et riens ne me porroit garir
fors que li miudres chevaliers,
li plus vaillans et li plus fiers
de la manie Artu le roi.
3360 Nesun millor n'i sai de toi
fors que tes pere, dans Gavains,
qui est de totes bontés plains.
Li gogleor que vos veïstes
3364 quant vos en la sale venistes
estoient del encantement.
Molt par i avoit fiere gent!

3353 ne le [+*1*]

the earth being split asunder
3332   with a terrible crack
and rocks flying through the air
and striking one another.
It seemed, my lord, as if everything were falling down
3336   and the earth and sky were collapsing.
These two worked such powerful enchantments
that all the people fled;
no one had any power against them.
3340   Then they entered this very hall and cast a spell on me:
as soon as they had touched me with a book,
I took on the appearance of a serpent.
They made me remain that way for a long time.
3344   Whenever they wished to speak with me
they came before me
and removed the enchantment.
The elder of the two was named Mabon.
3348   Again and again he pressed me
to take him as my husband
and to become his lady
and to love him with all my heart,
3352   saying that he would then free me from this torture.
If I refused to love him
I would forever be a serpent.
I would have to endure all this,
3356   and nothing could ever set me free
except the greatest knight,
the most worthy and the most valiant in arms
from the court of King Arthur.
3360   I know of no knight finer than you,
save for your father, my lord Gawain,
who is full of all good qualities.
The jongleurs whom you saw
3364   when you entered the hall
were part of the enchantment.
These enchanters were indeed cruel men!

Li chevaliers qui vint premiers
3368   ert apielés Evrains li Fiers,
et cil aprés Mabons estoit
qui tot l'encantement faissoit.
Quant vos l'eüstes mort jeté,
3372   dont eüstes [del] tot finé
lor evres, lor encantemens;
puis si devint trestot nïens.
Li guivre qui vos vint baissier,   *[144 v°c]*
3376   qui si vos savoit losengier,
ce fui je, sire, sans mentir.
Ne pooie autrement garir
que tot adés guivre ne fuisse
3380   de si que baissié vos eüsse.
Sire, del tot vos ai dit voir
sans mentir et sans decevoir.
Or vos vel autre cose dire:
3384   de mon regne serrés vos sire.
Gales a non ceste contree
dont je sui roïne clamee,
et ceste vile par droit non
3388   est apielee Senaudon.
Por ço que Mabons l'a gastee,
est Gaste Cités apielee.
C'est de mon roiaume li ciés.
3392   Trois roi tienent de moi lor fiés;
molt par est cil roiaumes grans,
molt est rices, molt est vaillans.
Mais prier vos vel par francisse,
3396   quant vos m'avés del tot conquisse,
que vos a feme me prendés.
Rices rois serés coronnés.
Tot sevent ja par la contree
3400   que de peril m'avés jetee."

3372 e. tot f. [-*1*]
3390 apiele
3395 fracisse

The knight who appeared first
3368 was called Evrain the Cruel,
and the one who came later was Mabon,
who had worked all the spells.
When you killed him
3372 you put an end to
all their enchantments,
which have all faded into nothingness.
As for the serpent who came to kiss you,
3376 and who showed you such reverence,
this was, I tell you truly, my lord, none other than myself.
I would have remained
a serpent forever
3380 had I not kissed you.
My lord, I have told you the truth in everything,
without falsehood or deception.
Now I wish to tell you something more:
3384 you shall be lord of all my realm.
Wales is the name of this land,
whose acknowledged queen I am,
and this city is rightfully called
3388 by the name of Snowdon.
Because Mabon laid it waste,
it has come to be called the Desolate City.
This is the seat of my realm.
3392 Three kings hold their fiefs from me;
the realm is indeed a large one,
a very powerful and wealthy land.
But I beg you, in all candor,
3396 since you have won me by right,
that you now take me as your wife.
You will be crowned a great king.
All the people in this land now know
3400 that you have rescued me from danger."

Con Guinglains l'a oï parler,
molt li sot biel sanblant mostrer
se li a dit, "Ma doce dame,
3404   volentiers vos prendrai a fame
se Artus le me velt loer,
et je irai a lui parler
car sans lui ne le ferai mie.
3408   Iço serroit grans vilonnie
se je prendoie sans son los
feme; mais je ne vel ne n'os,
mais lui irai consel rouver.
3412   Sans lui ne me vel marïer.
Et s'il le loe se.l ferai
et a feme si vos prendrai."
Issi la pucele delaie;
3416   de sa parole molt l'apaie,
qui de tot cuide estre s'amie.
Atant s'en torne et voit Elie
et avec lui [Lanpart] aler;
3420   par mi l'uis les vit dont entre[r].
Robert, son escuier, revoit
et le nain qui detriers venoit.
Tot quatre venoient riant.
3424   Saciés lors i ot joie grant
quant tot ensamble se revirent;
de molt bon cuer se conjoïrent,
l'une acole l'autre et enbrache.   [*145 r°a*]
3428   N'i a celui joie ne face:
Elie et Lanpars joie font
qua[r] lor dame recouvré ont,

3411 conles
3418 ssen *where first* s *expuncted*
3419 et avec lui len vit aler
3420 entre
3425 se virent [*-1, em. Williams*]
3429 L. et j.
3430 qua

When Guinglain had heard what she said,
he showed her a most gracious countenance
and said, "My dearest lady,

3404 I shall gladly take you as my wife
if King Arthur wishes me to do so,
and so I shall go to speak with him
for I shall never do this without his approval.

3408 It would be the basest kind of behavior
for me to take a wife against his good wishes;
I do not wish to nor shall I dare do so,
but rather will I go seek his counsel.

3412 I do not wish to marry without it.
And if he gives his consent,
then I shall take you as my wife."
Thus he held the maiden at bay,

3416 and, indeed, he greatly pleased her by what he said,
for she was certain she was the one he loved.
Then he turned and saw Helie,
and with her was Lampart;

3420 they were coming through the door.
He saw his squire Robert as well,
and the dwarf following behind him.
All four of them were smiling.

3424 You can be certain that there was great rejoicing there
when they all saw one another,
for they rejoiced with their whole hearts
as they welcomed and embraced each other.

3428 There was none there who did not rejoice:
Helie and Lampart were delighted
that their lady had been restored to them,

                 et Robers joïst son signor
3432   de cui il ot eü paor.
                 Quant entreconjoï se furent,
                 por Guinglain desarmer corurent,
                 si le desarment en la place
3436   et Robers son elme deslace.
                 Quant de tot l'orent desarmé,
                 si l'ont taint et plaié trové.
                 Tant avoit ses armes portees
3440   et receü tantes colees
                 que del sanc ot perdu asés.
                 Molt estoit bleciés et navrés.
                 Et quant ses plaies ont lavees,
3444   si les ont tantost rebendees.
                 Puis l'en mainnent en une canbre
                 u ot asés d'or d'Alixandre,
                 tires, pales et siglatons,
3448   mantials vairs et gris peliçons
                 et maint bon autre garniment.
                 Asés i ot or et argent;
                 molt ert la canbre couvenable;
3452   un lit i ot molt delitable.
                 Or vos revel conter et dire
                 que nule riens n'en ert a dire
                 s'on ne.l devoit a mal torner.
3456   D'or en avant vos vel conter
                 briément, sans trop longe raisson,
                 coment de Gales li baron
                 et li evesque et li abé
3460   et tot li prinche et li casé
                 vinrent quant sorent la noviele
                 qu'estorse fu la damoissele
                 et qu'ensi est cose avenue.
3464   Puis n'i ot nule retenue
                 que tot ne venissent a cort

3637 t. furent d. [*em. Williams*]
3459 evesques [+*1*]

and Robert because of his lord,
3432   for whose life he had feared.
When they had all made their greetings,
they hastened to disarm Guinglain,
which they did then and there,
3436   and Robert unlaced his helmet.
When they had removed all his arms,
they saw that he was bleeding and wounded.
He had born his arms for so long
3440   and taken so many blows
that he had lost a great deal of blood.
He was wounded quite severely.
And so they washed his wounds
3444   and bandaged them at once.
Then they led him into a chamber
filled with gold from Alexandria,
silks from Tyre and from the Cyclades, brocades,
3448   miniver cloaks and squirrel pelisses
and many other fine garments.
There was a great deal of gold and silver there,
and the room was quite pleasant,
3452   with a very comfortable bed.
Now I wish to tell you something,
so that nothing will be left unsaid,
and that no one should take it ill.
3456   I now wish to tell you,
briefly and without wasting words,
how the noble lords of Wales
and the bishops and abbots
3460   and the princes and liegemen
came when they had heard
that their lady had been delivered
and how this had come about.
3464   All those who served her
came at once to the court

por la grant joie qui lor sort.
Tos li pules vint cele part;
3468   petis et grans, molt lor est tart
que il aient lor dame veüe.
Molt i est grans li esmeüe.
Archevesques, vesque et abé
3472   et tot li autre clerc letré
sont venu a porcession
et cantoient a molt haut ton
et portent crois et encensiers,
3476   gonfanons de riches dras chiers
[et] casses a tot les cors sains.
A lor mostiers sonent les sains.
Aigue benoite ont jeté   [*145 r°b*]
3480   par les rues de la cité;
tote ont la cité beneï,
li saint homme, li Diu ami.
Et quant fait orent le service
3484   au mostier de la maistre glise,
vers la cité tot droit s'en vont
et le service Diu i font.
Por Mabon qui avoit esté
3488   encanteres en la cité,
iauge beneoite ont jetee,
si l'ont beneïe et sacree,
et puis revont vers le palais
3492   u n'orent esté piecha mais.
Quant beneïs fu li palais,
ainc si grans joie ne fu mais
con iluec ont, quant ont veüe
3496   lor dame qu'il orent perdüe.
Molt i fu la joie enterine
quant recouvré ont la roïne,
ki france estoit et de bon aire;
3500   a tos savoit bon sanblant faire.

3471 vesques [+*1*]
3477 a casses

filled with joy at this event.
All the people came there;
3468   whether common folk or lords, they were most eager
to see their lady.
There was quite a commotion as they arrived.
Archbishops, bishops, and abbots
3472   and all the other learned clerics
came in a procession,
singing in full voice
and carrying crosses and censers,
3476   banners made from rich cloth,
and reliquaries holding the remains of holy saints.
The bells rang out in the churches.
The clergymen sprinkled holy water
3480   through all the streets of the city;
the holy men, beloved of God,
blessed the whole city.
And when they had said mass
3484   at the principal church,
they all went at once to the citadel
and said mass there.
They sprinkled holy water
3488   throughout the citadel
because of Mabon's enchantments,
blessing and consecrating it,
and then returned to the palace,
3492   from which they had so long been absent.
After the palace had been blessed,
there was never such joy
as there was then, when the people saw
3496   their lady, whom they had lost.
The joy was indeed complete
when they had recovered their queen,
for she was a noble and gracious lady
3500   and well knew how to treat everyone graciously.

Molt fu de ses barons amee
car molt l'avoient desiree,
car molt estoit et pros et sage.
3504   Ele parole a son barnage:
"Signor," fait ele, "or m'entendés.
De cest baron que me loés
ki por moi a soufert tel painne?
3508   Tel chevalier n'a dusqu'el Mainne.
Tot li devés porter honnor
car il est molt de grant valor.
Guinglain a non; molt est vasals.
3512   Ses pere est Gavains, li loials,
li niés le roi qui tint Bretaingne
et la terre dusqu'en Espaingne.
Me loés vos que je li face
3516   tel cose dont aie sa grasse?"
Tos li barnages li escrie,
"France dame, ne.l laissiés mie
que ne le prendés a mari,
3520   car il vos a de mort gari.
Molt vos a trait de grant dolor.
Cestui volons nos a signor,
car millor ne savons el mont!"
3524   Et la roïne lor respont,
"Signor, iço se lui plaissoit,
saciés que molt biel me serroit.
Des que lui plaist, ne.l quier müer.
3528   Or en alés a lui parler.
Se il me voloit a moillier,
molt l'amerai et tenrai cier."
Tot maintenant i fait aler   [*145 r°c*]
3532   trois dus molt haus a lui parler,
et quatre contes qu'ele apiele,
et Lanpars et sa damoissele,
deus evesques et trois abés.
3536   Estes les vos ja la alés

3502 mlt [*ligature bar lacking*]

She was truly loved by her nobles,
and they had longed to have her back,
for she was a most worthy and intelligent lady.

3504 She said to her nobles,
"My lords, hear me.
What counsel do you give me
concerning this lord who has suffered so much for my sake?

3508 There is no knight such as he between here and the Maine.
It is right that you all do him honor,
for he is indeed a man of distinction.
His name is Guinglain, and he is an excellent knight.

3512 His father is the loyal Gawain,
nephew to the king who rules Britain
and all the land as far as Spain.
What would you advise me to do

3516 to gain this knight's good will?"
All the lords exclaimed,
"Noble lady, you must not fail
to take him as your husband,

3520 for he has delivered you from death.
He has saved you from a great misfortune.
We wish to have this man as our lord,
for we know of no better knight in the world!"

3524 And the queen answered,
"My lords, if this should please him,
you may be certain it would please me as well.
If he wishes to marry me, I shall not seek to change his mind.

3528 Go now and speak to him.
If he wants me for his wife,
I shall truly love and cherish him."
She at once sent

3532 three of her noblest dukes to speak to Guinglain,
and four counts whom she chose,
along with Lampart and Helie,
two bishops and three abbots.

3536 And so they came to the place

u Gainglains gist, qui fu bleciés.
Robert troverent a ses piés.
Quant en la canbre sont entré,
3540 molt docement l'ont salué
et Guinglains ausi, ce me sanble,
les resalue tos ensanble.
Encontre els est un poi drecié[s],
3544 sanblant lor fait qu'il fust haitiés.
Par le canbre se sont asis.
Un rice duc qu'il orent pris
a le parole comenchie
3548 qui lor estoit devant nonchie.
"Sire," fait il, "or m'escoutés.
Ma dame et trestous ses barnés
vos mandent par moi une rien
3552 —vostre honnors ert, ce saciés bien—
c'or le prendés sans demorance
et sans nule autre porlongance
nostre dame a beneïçon.
3556 Li duc, li prince et li baron
vos ameront en bonne foi
sans fauseté et sans belloi.
Tot serront a vostre plaisir
3560 por vos honnerer et servir;
molt serrés rices et poissans.
En ceste tere, de tos sans
n'a baron qui a vos marchoist
3564 qu'a vostre comant tos ne soit.
Or prendés ma dame a mollier:
ne le devés mie laissier
car molt i conquerrés honnor.
3568 Tot vos demandent a signor
qu'en vos serra bien mis l'enpire.
D'une grant tere serés sire;
tot avrés quanqu'il i avra.
3572 Riens nule celé n'i ara:

3543 drecié

where Guinglain lay wounded.
They found Robert sitting at the foot of his bed.
They entered the room
3540 and greeted the knight most courteously,
and I believe that Guinglain
greeted all of them as well.
He raised himself up a little to greet them,
3544 and by this they knew that he was growing stronger.
They all seated themselves in the chamber.
A powerful duke who was among their number
spoke to Guinglain,
3548 as had been arranged in advance.
"My lord," he said, "hear me.
I bring a message
from my lady and all her lords—
3552 it will be to your honor, of that you may be certain.
Please accept in holy marriage,
with no hesitation or delay whatsoever,
our lady the queen.
3556 Her dukes, her princes, and her noble lords
will love you faithfully,
without falsehood or deception.
They will all be at your command
3560 to honor and serve you;
you will be a very strong and powerful king.
There is not a noble lord
in all the lands surrounding this one
3564 who will not do entirely as you wish.
Take, then, my lady in marriage:
you should not fail to do so,
for you will win great honor by this marriage.
3568 All the people have asked for you as their lord,
for the kingdom will be safe in your keeping.
You shall be lord of a great land;
all that is in it shall be yours.
3572 Nothing will be held back from you:

vos arés cïens bos, pra[ier]es,
bonnes roubes, bieles rivieres,
hostoirs, espreviers et gerfaus,
3576   faucons gentius et bons cevals.
S'arés asés or et argent
por departir a vostre gent,
a cels qui vos devront amer.
3580   Asés lor en porés doner.
Et quant vaurés armes porter
et au tornoiement aler,
a vostre voloir les arois   [*145 v° a*]
3584   et molt aïsiés en serrois.
Et molt grant gent mener porés
par tot u vos aler vaurés.
Tot seür porés tornoier
3588   c'or vostre homme vos aront cier.
Or me dites vostre corage
si le redira au barnage
et a ma dame la roïne,
3592   qui vos ainme molt d'amor fine."
Atant a respondu Guinglains,
qui molt estoit pales et vains,
"Sire, molt grant merchis vos renc,
3596   et a tos barons ensement,
de ço que je vos en oi dire.
Je ne m'en vel pas escondire
que je volentiers ne le praigne,
3600   mais primes irai en Bretaigne
au roi demander le congié,
car autrement ne.l prendrai jé.
Car se li rois ne le voloit,
3604   jo cuit que folie serroit

3573 praeries
3579 d. ester a.
3583 v. v. e les
3584 aisises *with second* s *expuncted*

here you shall have forests and meadows,
fine garments, beautiful rivers,
sparrowhawks and goshawks and gerfalcons,
3576   purebred falcons and fine horses.
You will also have much gold and silver
to distribute to your liegemen,
who will love you as they should.
3580   You will have a great deal to give them.
And when you wish to arm yourself
and go to tournaments,
you shall have the finest arms that you wish
3584   so as to be at your very best.
You can take a large retinue with you
wherever you wish to go;
you can fight in tournaments with an easy mind,
3588   for all your liegemen will hold you dearly.
Now tell me your thoughts on this matter,
and I will convey them to the nobles
and to my lady the queen,
3592   who loves you with truest love."
Then Guinglain, weak and pale,
answered him thus,
"My lord, I heartily thank you
3596   and all your nobles as well
for what you have said.
I shall certainly not deny
that I would gladly marry your lady,
3600   but first I must go to Britain
to ask the king's leave,
for I shall not marry her without his consent.
If the king did not wish it,
3604   I would consider it most ill advised

se ensi prenc feme sans lui.
Ses niés et ses mesages sui;
sans lui tel cose ne feroie.
3608 Quant il ne savoit qui g'estoie,
si me retint soie merchi.
Bon gré l'en sa. Ma dame pri
que roi Artu aut merchi rendre
3612 de ço qu'il l'a faite desfendre.
Par lui est hors de la dolor;
au roi en doit faire l'onnor.
En sa cort se doit mercïer
3616 de ço qu'il l'a fait delivrer.
Par son comant ai je ce fait;
soie est l'onnors tot entresait,
car il me donra rice don
3620 s'il me retient a conpainnon.
Ma dame lo par bone foi
qu'ele voist a la cort le roi
por grase rendre et por offrir
3624 que des ore ert a son plaisir.
Avoir i puet preu et honnor.
Et s'ele me veut a signor,
iluques m'en conscillerai.
3628 Se li rois veut, si le prendrai.
Iço li lo par bon consel:
si face tot son aparel
d'aler a cort molt ricement
3632 a biel harnas, o bele gent.
Et s'ele veut aler a cort,
molt hastivement s'en atort."
Tot a la dame creanté   [145 v° b]
3636 quanques Guinglains a devisé,
que volentiers a cort ira
et que tot son voloir fera.
D'aler ont bien lor terme pris:
3640 al uitime jor l'ont asis.

3605 e. sui p.

to marry against his will.
I am his nephew and his envoy;
I would not take such a step without first asking him.
3608 Even before he knew who I was,
through his kindness he made me one of his knights.
I am deeply grateful to him for this. I ask that my lady
go to thank King Arthur
3612 for having sent me to defend her.
Because of him she was freed from suffering,
and so she should go to do him honor.
It is right that she swear him allegiance in his own court
3616 for having brought about her deliverance.
By his command did I lend her aid,
and the honor is entirely his,
for it will indeed be a precious boon
3620 if he numbers me among the knights he loves most dearly.
I advise my lady in good faith
to go willingly to the king's court
to thank him and offer
3624 to be henceforth at his service.
She will receive honor and benefit by doing so.
And if she wishes to have me as her lord,
I shall seek counsel there.
3628 If the king so desires, I shall marry her.
This is my best advice:
that she make ready
to go to the court richly arrayed,
3632 finely equipped and with a goodly company.
And if she intends to go there
it is best that she prepare herself quickly."
The lady agreed to everything
3636 that Guinglain had suggested,
and said she would gladly go to King Arthur's court
and do all that Guinglain wished.
They fixed the date of their departure:
3640 they were to leave after one week.

Atant est li consals finés,
si s'en parti tos li barnés
et congié prisent a Guinglain
3644   qu'il laissierent et feble et vain.
A Diu les a tos comandés.
S'a la dame mires mandés
molt b[o]ns por tost Guinglain garir.
3648   A grant honnor le fist servir;
tant con longes i demora
de lui honnerer se pena.
Ains que la dame fust meüe
3652   a cort, fu tote revenue
la gens ariere en la cité
u ele avoit ançois esté.
Cil ki vif et sain remés erent
3656   e[n]sanble aveuc els aporterent
or et argent et roubes bieles.
Que vos froie longes novieles?
Tost fu la cité restoree
3660   et de bonne gent bien publee.
La roïne pas ne s'oublie:
molt a semons grant conpaignie
que o li veut mener en Bretaingne.
3664   [En] ses canbres s'aaise et baigne
et son harnas fait atorner.
A grant honnor i veut aler
que molt avoit grant conpaignie:
3668   trente cités ot en baillie.
Ele ot a non Blonde Esmeree;
issi fu par droit non nonmee.
Guinglain a mari molt desire;
3672   ses cuers a lui s'otrie et tire.

3647 biens
3656 esanble
3660 g. retrovee b. p.
3664 Et
3671 mlt [*ligature bar lacking*]

At this, the discussion ended
and all the nobles
took their leave of Guinglain,
3644 whom they left weak and tired.
He bade them all farewell.
The lady sent for some excellent doctors
so that Guinglain would be quickly healed.
3648 She had him very well cared for;
as long as he remained there,
she expended the greatest effort to show him honor.
Before the lady left
3652 for King Arthur's court, all the people
had returned to the city
where they had lived before.
Those who were still strong and well
3656 brought with them
gold and silver and fine garments.
Why should I make a long story of it for you?
The city was quickly restored to life
3660 and filled with fine people once more.
The queen neglected nothing:
she summoned a great company
whom she intended to take with her to Britain.
3664 In her chambers she bathed and made ready
and had all her baggage prepared.
She wished to go to the court in great honor,
and so she was taking many people with her,
3668 for her realm included thirty towns.
She was called Blonde Esmeree;
this name suited her very well.
She greatly desired to have Guinglain as her husband,
3672 for she had given him her whole heart.

Tant con la roïne s'atorne
Guinglain en la cité sejorne.
Tos fu garis en la quinsainne
3676   mais entrés est en autre painn[e]:
Amors li cange son pensser,
ne puet dormir ne reposser.
Onques mais n'ot il d'amer cure
3680   mai[s] or se diut a desmesure
por la Pucele as Blances Mai[n]s;
tos en devint pales et vains.
Des l'ore que il se parti
3684   de l'Ile d'Or, puis en oubli
ne le mesist por nule rien.
Si l'enpensa durement bien
que il s'en departi de lui   [145v°c]
3688   sans congié; molt en a anui.
Quant il se departi au main,
aincque puis n'ot jor le cuer sain.
Tant l'a adés puis desiree
3692   mais or li est s'amors doublee.
La joie souvent li doubla
et li sanblans que li mostra.
Et maintes fois li est avis,
3696   quant il dort mius, si voit son vis
et que il soit el lit couciés
el palais u fu herbergiés,
et c'aveuc lui voie la fee
3700   ansi d'un mantiel afuble[e],
tot a nus piés en sa cemisse,
en tel sanblant et en tel guisse
cum il le vit quant ele vint
3704   au lit el palais u le tint.

3676 painn
3680 mai
3681 Mais
3687 il ensi s'en [+2]
3700 afuble

While the queen was making ready,
Guinglain remained in the town.
He was fully healed within two weeks,
3676 but he now had a new cause for suffering:
Love had so altered his thoughts
that he could neither sleep nor take his rest.
He had never wished to be in love,
3680 but now he grieved beyond measure
for the sake of the Maiden of the White Hands;
indeed, he had grown quite pale and weak.
Since he had left
3684 the Golden Isle, he could not forget her
no matter what he might do.
It caused him great pain
to think that he had left
3688 without asking her leave; this troubled him deeply.
From the morning he had left her behind
his heart had never been whole.
Ever since then he had longed for her,
3692 and now his love had doubled.
His joy often deepened
when he recalled the gracious countenance she had shown him.
And often, while he slept most soundly,
3696 he thought he saw her face
and that he lay once more in the bed
in the hall where he had stayed,
and he saw the fay with him
3700 wearing a cloak, as before,
her feet bare, clad only in her shift,
the very same way
as when she had come
3704 to his bed, in the hall where she had lodged him.

A li penser a mis s'entente.
Un jor el palais se demente:
"Elas!" fait il, "ne sai que dire.
3708   Quels mals ço est qui si m'enpire?
Ço est amors, mien ensient.
Ensi l'ai oï de la gent
que on doit molt dames amer.
3712   Il dient voir, ne.l puis celer.
Esprové l'ai par la pucele
por cui je muir, qui tant est biele.
Molt me fist grant honnor la fee
3716   dont je m'enblai la matinee.
Mius deüsse voloir morir
que je de ço dont tant desir
me parti si vilainnement.
3720   Ço que dont fis or m'en repenc;
or en trait mes cors grief martire.
Ha, Dius! Ne li oserai dire
que me pardoinst. Dont que ferai?
3724   Il n'i a plus, por li maurai.
N'est nus qui m'en peüst aidier,
ne je ne l'os mais asaier;
ens maurai [je] de male mort
3728   que ja n'en averai confort.
Tais! Mar le di! Va li rover
merchi et va a li parler.
Ne te lai mie [martirer]
3732   quant plus ne le pués endurer,
car trop te destraint et travalle.
Se il longes te tient, sans faille
dont te coverra il morir.
3736   A mains n'en pués tu pas partir."

3716 m'eblai
3721 g. pense m.
3727 e. m. de m. m. [-1, *em. Williams*]
3731 morteiter [*em. Williams*]

He had set his whole mind on thoughts of her.
One day in the palace he began to lament:
"Wretch that I am, how shall I name
3708   this illness that so undermines me?
I believe that it is love.
I have heard people say
that one should love ladies dearly.
3712   They speak the truth, I cannot deny it.
I know this now because of the beautiful maiden
for whose love I am dying.
The fay did me such great honor,
3716   and yet I slipped away from her the next morning.
I should rather have preferred to die
than to be so base as to ride away
from the one for whom I long so much.
3720   I now repent of what I did;
I am racked with regret because of it.
Dear God! I dare not ask her
to forgive me. What shall I do then?
3724   There is nothing else but to die for her sake.
No one else can help me,
and I dare not attempt to win her favor;
rather will I die a bitter death,
3728   for I shall find no comfort.
But no! What foolish words, Guinglain!
You must go speak with her and beg for mercy.
Do not let yourself suffer so,
3732   for you can endure this state no longer,
so much does it grieve you and oppress you.
If it holds you thus much longer,
you will surely die of it.
3736   No other escape is possible."

    Il apiele son escuier

    qu'a lui se vaurra consillier.

    Cil est venus a son signor   [*146r°a*]

3740   et il li conte sa dolor:

    "Robers," fait il, "or me consele.

    Trop sui destrois a grant mervele:

    ne puis dormir ne reposer

3744   tant me mec a celi penser

    que veïsmes en l'Ille d'Or.

    Icele me destrant si or

    que de vie ne sui certains

3748   se n'en ai Cele as Blances Mains.

    Molt le desir a grant mervelle;

    s'amors m'ocist, souvent m'esvelle.

    Ço m'a duré molt lonc termine.

3752   Moi d'angoissier Amors ne fine.

    Que ferai je, frans debonnaire?

    Onques mais mal ne prissai gaire

    mais cil m'ocist tot a estros."

3756   Ce dist Robers, "Gabés me vos?

    Quant d'amors soloie parler,

    adont me soliés vos gaber."

    "Je ne gab [mie]," ce dist Guinglains.

3760   "Se onques vers Amors me fains,

    or en prent vers moi sa vengance:

    ele m'ocist de male lance."

    Robers respont, "Cele en ait los

3764   qui l'amor a en vos enclos!

    Je ne sai rien de chevalier

    ne cil ne doit avoir mestier

    c'aucune fois ne veut amer;

3768   ne cil ne doit en pris monter

    qui vers Amors n'a son corage

    se il n'est molt de grant eage.

3737 a *after* Il *expuncted*
3759 gab ce
3761 p. veres m.

He called to his squire
to give him counsel.
Robert went at once to his lord,
3740   who told him of his sorrow:
"Robert," he said, "now give me good counsel.
I am utterly undone:
I cannot sleep or take my rest
3744   for thinking of her
whom we saw on the Golden Isle.
So great is her hold on me
that I believe I may die
3748   if she of the White Hands cannot be mine.
I am filled with longing for her;
Love of her is killing me, I often lie awake.
This has been so for a long time.
3752   Love never ceases to torment me.
What shall I do, my noble friend?
I have seldom made much of suffering,
but now this torment will be the end of me."
3756   Robert said, "Are you jesting, my lord?
Before, whenever I spoke of love,
you used to make fun of me."
"I am not jesting," said Guinglain:
3760   "If I ever lacked devotion to Love,
she is now taking her revenge,
for she is killing me with a sharp lance."
Robert answered, "She who
3764   fixed this love in your heart deserves much praise!
I am not an expert in knightly matters
but there should be no knight
who wishes never to be in love;
3768   and he who has not set his heart on Love
should not increase in honor
unless he be a very old man.

Sire, ne vos esmaiés mie
3772   s'Amors vos a en sa baillie.
Ele velt les preus en se part;
mauvais et fauls ainm ele a tart.
Por ce ne vos esmaiés pas;
3776   bien passerés d'Amors le pas
et je vos en consellerai
a tost a mius que je porai.
Et se vos m'en volïés croire,
3780   quant atorné ara son oire
la roïne d'a cort aler
et fera sé mul enseler,
ses palefrois et ses cevals,
3784   [d]e rices dras enperials
et verrés carcier les [soumiers]
et carcier or fin et deniers,
trestos les en laissier issir
3788   et si vos armés a loissir
en vostre ostel que ne le voie.
Aprés vos metés a la voie.   [*146 r°b*]
Quant atainte arés la roïne
3792   a cui tos cis regnes acline,
molt bielement a li parlés
et le congié li demandés.
Dites qu'aveuc li plus n'irois,
3796   qu'autre part aler en vaurois
u vos avés asés a faire
et que vos ne targerés gaire,
car au plus tost que vos porés
3800   aprés li a la cort irés.
Et quant le gongié arés pris
et el retor vos serés mis,
puis irons tant nostre cemin
3804   a l'avesprer et au matin
que nos a l'Ille d'Or venrons.

3784 se [*em. Perret*]
3785 destriers

Do not fear, my lord,
3772 if Love holds you in her power.
She wishes to have people of merit in her service,
and she is slow to love worthless men and scoundrels.
Therefore do not fear,
3776 for you will get through the pass Love guards,
and so I shall advise you without delay
as best I can.
Here is my advice:
3780 once the queen has made ready
to go to King Arthur's court,
once she has had her mules saddled,
her palfreys and other horses,
3784 and once you see the packhorses
loaded with costly royal cloths,
fine gold and coins,
then let the company all ride forth
3788 while you arm yourself at your leisure
in your lodgings, out of sight.
Then begin your journey.
When you have overtaken the queen,
3792 the ruler of all this realm,
speak graciously to her
and ask her leave to go.
Tell her that you will go no further with her,
3796 that you wish to to go elsewhere,
that you have much to do,
that you will on no account delay,
and that, as soon as you are able,
3800 you will join her at the court.
And when you have obtained her leave to go
and have turned back,
then we shall go our way,
3804 riding by day and night,
until we come to the Golden Isle.

Vostre amie la troverons."
"Biaus amis, qu'es ce que tu dis?
3808   Serroie je tant don[c] hardis
que retorner osaisse a li?
Vilainnement m'en departi."
Robers respont, "Oïl, bials sire.
3812   Bien li porés vostre mal dire.
Qu[i] ne porcace sa besoigne
tost li puet torner a vergoigne.
Cil qui del mal sent le martire
3816   le doit molt bien mostrer au mire.
Sans nul respit, [dist] li vilains,
querre doit pain cil [cui] tient fains.
Coment sara vostre corage
3820   se devant ne l'en faites sage?
Mostrer li devés la dolor
que vos traiés por soie amor.
Bien tost porrés merchi trover;
3824   aprés plor ai oï canter."
[Guinglains] respont, "C'est lons termine!
Des que se mueve la roïne
encore a trois jors a venir.
3828   Ançois poroie bien morir
s'autrement mes mals n'asouhage."
"Sire, covrés vostre corage.
Ne vos en esmaiés de rien,
3832   que s'amor conquerrés vos bien."
Issi a Guinglains sejorné
et le mal d'amors enduré
tant que trois jor sont aconpli.
3836   Al [quart] jor quant l'aube esclarchi,

3808 dont
3813 Que
3817 *word obliterated except for downstroke of last letter, em. Williams*
3818 *word obliterated, em. Williams*
3825 Robers
3836 quint

There we shall find your lady."
"Dear friend, what are you saying?
3808   Shall I be so bold
as to dare return to her?
I left her in a most base manner."
Robert answered, "My dear lord, indeed you shall.
3812   You can readily tell the lady of your sorrow.
Whenever a man does not look to himself
it can quickly turn to his shame.
And he who is suffering from an illness
3816   should certainly see a doctor.
As the peasant says,
a hungry man had best find himself some bread.
How can she ever know your heart
3820   if you do not first reveal it to her?
You must tell her of the suffering
you endure for love of her.
You can swiftly find mercy;
3824   after weeping I have heard men sing "
Guinglain answered, "What a long time to wait!
It will be three long days
before the queen begins her journey.
3828   I could easily die before then
if I find no way to ease my suffering."
"My lord," said Robert, "do not give in to such thoughts.
Do not fear anything that may befall,
3832   for you shall certainly win your lady's love."
Guinglain remained where he was
and endured the pangs of love,
until the three days were ended.
3836   At dawn on the fourth day

Blonde Esmeree de l'aler
s'atorna et fist aprester
le menu harnas qu'avant vait.
3840 Les damoissials monter a fait,
puis fist monter ses conpaignons;   [*146 r °c*]
et portent ostoirs et faucons
et [gerfaus] et bons espreviers.
3844 Les escrins carcent as soumiers,
rices cofres et rices males.
Molt jetent grant avoir de Gales—
hanas, copes d'or et d'argent
3848 et molt rice [autre] vaillement,
escüeles et cuilliers d'or
dont molt avoit en son tresor.
Lors est la roïne montee.
3852 Cent chevaliers de sa contree
a menés en sa conpaignie;
molt estoit sa gens bien garnie.
Si s'en issent de Sinadon
3856 la roïne et tot si baron.
Cevals fist mener aveuc soi
et palefrois de biel conroi.
De la cité s'en issent tuit
3860 et Guinglains s'arme sans grant bruit.
Quant la roïne fu venue,
ançois si s'est bien porveüe
que Guinglains encor n'i est mie.
3864 "Signor," fait ele, "Dius aiue!
U est mes amis et mé sire?"
N'i est, qui voir l'en sace dire.
Arestee s'est la roïne;
3868 de Guinglain demander ne fine.
Il regardent vers la cité,
si le voient venir armé

3843 et ostoirs [*em. Williams*]
3845 et r. c. [*+1*]
3848 et m. r. v. [*-1, em. Williams*]

Blonde Esmeree prepared to depart
and had the light baggage
made ready and sent on ahead.
3840　She bade her ladies mount,
and then her knights,
and they took with them goshawks and falcons
and gerfalcons and fine sparrowhawks.
3844　The baggage, the rich caskets and coffers,
was loaded on the packhorses.
A great deal of wealth from Wales had been packed up—
cups and goblets of silver and gold
3848　and other riches,
such as golden bowls and spoons,
of which the queen had many in her treasury.
Then the queen herself mounted.
3852　She took with her
a hundred knights from her land;
her people indeed rode richly equipped.
And so the queen and all her nobles
3856　rode forth from Snowdon.
She took along with her many horses
and palfreys with magnificent trappings.
They rode forth from the city
3860　while Guinglain quietly armed himself.
When the queen had left the city,
she saw for herself
that Guinglain was not yet with them.
3864　"My lords," she said, "God lend us aid!
Where is my friend and my lord?"
No one could tell her where he was.
The queen halted her march;
3868　she inquired again and again for Guinglain.
Then the company looked toward the town
and saw him riding toward them, armed,

       et aveuc lui son escuier.

3872   Tot se prendent a mervillier

       por quel afaire armés estoit.

       Vers la roïne vint tot droit.

       Quant l'a [v]e[ü] Blonde Esmeree,

3876   envers lui a regne tiree

       si li a demandé de long

       por quel cose et por quel besoi[n]g

       s'estoit armés, que il li die.

3880   Guinglains respont, "Ma douce amie,

       jo ne puis pas o vos aler.

       D'autre part m'en estuet aler

       u ai a faire grant besoigne.

3884   Quant l'arai faite, sans ensoigne

       aprés vos a la cort irai

       isi tost come je porai.

       Le roi Artu me salués

3888   et vostre congié me donnés."

       Dist la roïne, "Merchi, sire!

       Misse serroie en grant martire."

       "Dame, ne puet estre autremant.

3892   Je m'en vois; a Diu vos comant,   [*146 v°a*]

       et vos et tos vos conpaignons."

       Issi departi des barons,

       mais a grant painne s'en depart.

3896   Son cemin torne d'autre part.

       De son aler ont grant anui,

       mais il n'en pesa tant nului

       con il faisoit a la roïne;

3900   molt se clamoit souvent frarine,

3875 *letter after* l'a *obliterated, one space between* e *and* Blonde; *em.*
     Williams
3876 a son r. [+*1, em. Williams*]
3878 besoig
3883 f. sans as g.
3888 vre [*ligature bar lacking*]
3891 ne *inserted above line by scribe*

along with his squire.
3872 They all greatly wondered
why it was that he bore his arms.
He rode toward the queen.
When Blonde Esmeree saw Guinglain,
3876 she turned her horse toward him
and asked him to tell her
for what reason and by what need
he had armed himself.
3880 Guinglain answered, "My sweet friend,
I cannot go with you.
I must go elsewhere,
for an urgent matter so compels me.
3884 When I have done what I must do,
I shall join you at the court without fail
as soon as I am able.
Please greet King Arthur on my behalf
3888 and give me your leave to go."
The queen said, "Have pity, my lord!
I shall suffer greatly if you do this."
"My lady, it cannot be otherwise.
3892 I am leaving; I bid you farewell,
both you and all your company."
At that he left the nobles,
but it was with great difficulty that he did so.
3896 He set out in another direction.
All were downcast at his departure,
but no one so much
as the queen;
3900 again and again she gave vent to her unhappiness,

de lui ne se partist son veul.
Molt fait la roïne grant dol,
dolente estoit et esmaïe;
3904   et neporquant ne remaint mie
que ele adés a cort n'en aille,
mais molt est dolente sans faille.
Bien vos ert conté et retrait
3908   coment la roïne s'en vait,
mais ains vul de Guinglain conter
ki ne fine de tost aler.
La Biele as Blance Mains le tire;
3912   que le veïst molt le desire.
De li veïr a grant besoigne;
vis li est que sa voie alonge.
Cevaucié ont des la jornee
3916   desi que vint a la vespree
plus de trente liues galesces
tant qu'il vint devant les bretesces
de l'Ille d'Or le bon castiel
3920   dont li mur sont et fort et biel.
Molt fu li castials bons et fors;
se cil qui sont dusqu'a Limors
i fuissent a siege trente ans,
3924   n'ente[r]roient il pas dedens.
Molt estoit bials a desmesure.
Mais del devisser n'ai or cure
a ceste fois qu'allors l'ai dit.
3928   Saciés nus hom plus bel ne vit
et Guinglain, [quant] il veü l'ot,
ens en son cuer forment s'i plot.
Bien a le castiel conneü
3932   de si lonc con il l'a veü;
tot entor coroit la marine.

3906 dolelente
3907 contee
3924 n'entenroient
3929 quant *lacking*

for she would never willingly have parted from him.
The queen was deeply grieved,
filled with sorrow and despair;
3904 but yet she did not delay
to go to King Arthur's court,
despite her deep anguish.
You will hear it told
3908 how the queen journeyed to the court,
but first I wish to tell of Guinglain,
who rode at a gallop and without stopping for rest.
The fair one of the White Hands was drawing him nigh;
3912 he greatly longed to see her.
His need for her was urgent,
and his road seemed long to him.
They rode from the first light of dawn
3916 until evening,
riding more than twenty Welsh leagues
until they reached the battlements
of the Golden Isle's fine fortress
3920 whose walls were both strong and beautiful.
This castle was indeed a fine and strong one;
if all the people as far as Limors
had laid siege to it for thirty years,
3924 they would never have breached its defenses.
Its beauty was beyond measure.
I do not care to describe the castle now,
for I have done so already.
3928 But you may be certain that no one ever saw a handsomer one,
and when Guinglain saw it,
his heart leapt for joy.
He knew the castle well
3932 as soon as he caught sight of it,
for he saw the water flowing all around.

Guinglains de tost aler ne fine
vers l'Ille d'Or qui siet sor mer.
3936   Dehors ont veü ceminer
dames, chevaliers ne puceles,
et il se traient envers eles.
Espreviers portent, et faucons,
3940   ostoirs, tercels, esmerillons,
car il venoient de jebiers.
Quant il les vit molt en fu liés,
car entre eles conut s'amie
3944   qui menoit cele conpaignie   [*146 v°b*]
et sist sor un blanc palefroi.
Souef anbloit et sans desroi;
el blanc fu de noir pumelés,
3948   ses crins sanbloit estre dorés.
C'est la Pucele as Blances Mains.
Molt estoit rices ses lorains:
cent escaletes i ot d'or;
3952   par grant engien le fisent Mor
car quant li bons palefrois anble,
si sonnoient totes ensanble
plus doç que soit harpe ne rote.
3956   Ainc n'oïstes plus douce note
ne de gigle ne de vïele.
Que vos diroie de sa siele
sor coi la damoissele sist?
3960   Uns maistres d'Ilande le fist;
tant par estoit et bonne et ciere
qu'a deviser n'iert pas legiere.
De fin or fu et de cristal
3964   ouvree molt bien a esmal.
La dame ert biele et honneree
et cevauçoit eskevelee.
Son mantiel osta por le caut;

3955 n. note
3956 d. rote
3959 c. sa d.

Guinglain did not break his headlong pace
toward the Golden Isle by the sea.

3936 Outside the city walls he and Robert saw
ladies, knights, and maidens,
and so they rode toward them.
These people had with them sparrowhawks and falcons,

3940 goshawks, tercels, and merlins,
for they had just come from hunting birds.
When the knight saw this group he rejoiced,
for he recognized his lady among them

3944 leading the company
and seated on a white palfrey.
The horse ambled along gently;
it was white with black spots

3948 and its mane seemed to be of spun gold.
This was indeed the Maiden of the White Hands.
The breaststrap of her horse was richly made:
a hundred tiny golden bells hung from it;

3952 Moors had crafted it with great skill,
for as the palfrey ambled along
the bells all rang together,
making a sound more sweet than that of any harp or rote.

3956 You never heard sweeter music
from any hurdy-gurdy or fiddle.
And what shall I tell you of the saddle
on which the lady was seated?

3960 A master craftsman of Ireland had made it;
it was so fine and costly
that describing it properly would be no easy task.
It was made of fine gold and crystal

3964 and skillfully inlaid with enamel.
The lady was beautiful and of dignified bearing,
and her hair hung freely as she rode along.
She had removed her cloak because of the heat;

3968   ele avoit vestu un bliaut
        ki tos estoit a or batus.
        Plus rices dras ne fu veüs;
        ovrés estoit et bien et bel.
3972   En son cief avoit [un] capiel
        qu'ele portoit por le calor.
        Ouvrés fu de mainte color—
        d'inde, de vert, de blanc, de bis.
3976   Bien li gardoit del caut le vis.
        Portrais i avoit oisials d'or;
        li capials valoit un tresor.
        Par deriere ot jeté ses crins
3980   plus reluissants que nus ors fins.
        Sans guinple estoit; a un fil d'or
        ot galonné son cief le sor.
        Flans ot bien fais et cors et hances;
3984   molt se vestoit bien de ses mances:
        bras ot bien fais et blances main[n]s
        plus que flors d'espine sor rains.
        De sa biauté plus que diroie?
3988   Por coi plus le deviseroie
        mais que tant biele ne tant sage
        ne qui tant fust de franc corage
        ne peüst on trover el monde
3992   qui le cerkast a la reonde.
        En son puing porte en esprevier
        de trois mues; molt l'avoit cier.
        Guinglains l'avoit bien conneüe
3996   de si lonc con il l'ot veüe.   *[146 v°c]*
        Son cief et son vis desarma,
        errant vint, si le salua.
        "Dame," fait il, "je vel parler
4000   a vos, et mon consel mostrer.
        Si vos traiés a une part."
        Cele respont, "Dius i ait part."

3972 un *lacking*
3985 mais

3968   she wore a tunic
        all in gold brocade.
        No one ever saw a more exquisite fabric,
        for it was finely made and decorated.
3972   She wore a shade hat
        to protect her from the heat.
        It was of many colors—
        dark blue, green, white, and grey.
3976   It shielded her face from the sun quite well.
        On it there were birds wrought in gold;
        this hat was indeed worth a king's ransom.
        The maiden allowed her hair to hang freely down her back,
3980   and it shone brighter than any fine gold.
        She wore no wimple; she had woven a golden thread
        into the gold of her hair.
        This maiden was indeed shapely of body and waist and hip;
3984   she wore well-fitted sleeves to advantage:
        her arms were lovely, her hands whiter
        than the hawthorn on the branch.
        What more shall I say of her beauty?
3988   Why should I describe it further,
        except to say that so lovely a woman, or one so intelligent
        or so noble of spirit
        could not be found anywhere in the world
3992   no matter how far one searched.
        On her hand the lady bore a hawk
        that had moulted three times and which she greatly prized.
        Guinglain had known who she was
3996   the moment he saw her in the distance.
        He removed his helmet, baring his face,
        and swiftly rode forward to greet her.
        "My lady," he said, "I wish to speak with you
4000   and tell you my mind.
        Let us speak in private."
        She answered, "As you wish."

Cil se mist devers li a destre;
4004 des or li veut conter son estre.
"Dame," fait il, "entendés moi.
Liés sui de ce que je vos voi
quar por vos muir, ne.l puis celer.
4008 Dame, merchi vos vel crïer!
Por Diu, de moi aiés pitiés
que mes mals me soit alegiés,
et que ne soiés vers moi pire
4012 por rien que vos ci m'oiés dire,
car Amors ne me laisse mie
que tot le voir ne vos en die.
Vergoigne en ai mais ne me vaut;
4016 Amors me destreint et asaut
ki tot me mainne a son talent.
Dame, saciés vos vraiement
que se je devoie estre pris
4020 u ars u pendus u ocis,
ne me peüsse je celer.
Or est en vos del pardonner;
del tot sui en vostre ballie
4024 u de la mort u de la vie."
La dame dist, "Qui estes vos?"
"Dame, vostres sui a estros
des l'ore que primes vos vi
4028 et que je m'en parti de ci."
"U vos vic je don[c] onques mais?"
"Dame, dedens vostres palais
me herbergastes avant ier
4032 quant je alai la dame aidier
qui est fille le roi Guingras.
Doce dame, je ne menc pas.
Lors me promistes vostre honnor
4036 mais je m'en parti par folor
por le secors que je vauc faire.

4029 dont
4030 vres [*ligature bar lacking*]

He placed himself at her right hand,
4004 wishing to tell her at once how things stood with him.
"Hear me, my lady," he said;
"I am glad indeed to see you again,
for I am dying for love of you, I cannot conceal it.
4008 My lady, I have come to beg your forgiveness!
In God's name, take pity on me
so that my suffering may be eased,
and do not show yourself less kind
4012 for anything you may hear me say,
for Love compels me
to tell you the entire truth.
To do so gives me shame, but there is no help for it;
4016 Love so assails and constrains me
that I am compelled to do as she wishes.
My lady, you may be certain
that, were I to be put in prison for it,
4020 or burned, or hanged, or killed,
I could not conceal my heart from you.
It lies in your power to forgive me;
whether I live or die
4024 is entirely in your hands."
The lady answered, "And who are you?"
"My lady, the one who is yours entirely
since the moment I first saw you
4028 and since the hour that I left this place."
"But when have I ever seen you before?"
"Lady, you lodged me
in your palace some days ago
4032 when I rode forth to lend my aid
to the daughter of King Guingras.
Sweet lady, I am not speaking falsely.
You promised me great honor then,
4036 but like a madman I left
because I wished to rescue the lady.

Puis m'a fait vostre amors contraire
qui dedens mon cuer est enclos.
4040   Ainc puis ne poc avoir repos."
"Coment!" fait cele, "Estes vos cil
qui si m'eüstes enpor vil
et qui fist si tres grant outrage
4044   a moi et a tot mon lingnage
qu'ensi de moi vos en enblastes
que congié ne me demandastes?
Et je vos fis si grant honnor
4048   que moi—et ma tere et m'amor—   [147 r°a]
mis en vostre susjection?
Molt fesistes grant mesproisson
come vilains et outrageus.
4052   Ne cuidiés pas que ce soit geus.
Se je amé ne vos eüsse,
envers vos si vilainne fuisse
que je vos fesisse grant lait
4056   por le honte que m'avés fait.
Car trop fesistes mespresure;
por ce estes en aventure.
Car j'ai en cest païs asés
4060   contes et dus, princes, casés,
qui tost vos averoient mort,
u ce fust a droit u a tort,
s'il vos connissoient de voir.
4064   Molt fesistes [vos] fol espoir
c'ainc retorner ariere osastes
et que de rien a moi parlastes.
Molt vos amai, bien m'en souvient.
4068   Iceste cose me detient
que je ne vos fai[s] deshonnor.
Mais il me souvient de l'amor,
car contre vos rien n'en amaisse;

4054 et v. [em. Williams]
4064 M. f. f. e. [-1, em. Williams]
4069 fait

But since then your love, which is locked in my heart,
has caused me great suffering.
4040   Since that time I can find no rest."
"What is this?" she said, "Are you that man
who used me so vilely
and so grievously insulted
4044   both me and all my lineage
as to ride away from here
without asking my leave?
And after I had honored you
4048   by placing myself—both my land and my love—
entirely at your command?
You treated me with utter scorn
like a boor and a man without shame.
4052   Do not suppose that I am jesting.
Had I never loved you,
I might now stoop
to do you great harm
4056   in return for the insult you have done me.
Truly you have committed a grievous error,
and because of that your life is now at risk.
For in this land I have many
4060   counts and dukes, princes and liegemen
who would kill you at once,
whether justly or not,
if they knew who you really are.
4064   What folly it was
for you ever to have dared return here
and speak a single word to me.
I loved you dearly, this I remember well,
4068   and this alone restrains me
from heaping dishonor upon you.
I still remember that love,
for I never loved anyone so much as you;

4072   se ce ne fust, je m'en vengaisse.
Por seul itant ne vul je mie
que vos encor perdés la vie.
Mais itant vos en di avant,
4076   que jamais en vostre comant
ne serrai vers vos si souprise
que m'amors soit vers vos trop misse."
Quant Guinglains l'oï si parler,
4080   li vis qu'il ot bien fait et cler
li devint molt pales et tains.
Molt estoit foibles et atains.
"Dame," fait il, "or est issi?
4084   De moi n'arés nule merchi?
Si en mourai tot a delivre.
Bien sai ne puis pas longes vivre;
de moi n'i ara nul confort.
4088   Vostre amors m'a donné la mort.
Il vos en averra peciés
se vos tot ensi m'ocïés.
Mais quant escaper [je] ne puis
4092   n'endroit vos nul confort ne truis,
la vie en cest païs metrai.
Bien voi que por vos i maurai,
que tant vos desirent mi oil
4096   qu'en vostre païs morir vel.
Bele, or ne m'en caut qui m'ochie
car por vos me desplaist ma vie."
Tant ont al parler entendu   [*147 r°b*]
4100   que il sont el castiel venu.
La dame a son palais descent,
la soie mainnie ensement—
si chevalier, ses damoisseles,
4104   dont il en i avoit de bieles.

4076 vre [*ligature bar lacking*]
4091 M. q. e. ne p. [*-1, em. Williams*]
4098 *line repeated at bottom of column a but lacking* por
4102 et l. s. m. e. [*+1*]

4072   if not for that, I would have avenged myself.
For the sake of that love alone I would not wish
for you to lose your life.
But I give you fair warning:

4076   I shall never be so unguarded
nor place myself so much in your power
as to give you my love again."
When Guinglain heard her speak to him thus,

4080   his face, which was so fair and bright,
grew quite pale.
He was shaken and felt weak.
"My lady," he said, "is this how matters stand?

4084   Will you show no mercy to me?
I shall surely die of this.
I know well that I cannot live long,
for there will be no comfort for me.

4088   Your love has brought me death.
The sin will be on your head
if you kill me thus.
But since I cannot escape my fate

4092   or find any comfort from you,
I shall end my life in this land.
I see now that I shall die for your sake,
and my eyes so desire to look on you

4096   that I wish to die in your country.
Lady, I do not care who may kill me now,
for because of you my life is hateful to me."
While speaking thus

4100   they had entered the city walls.
The maiden dismounted in front of her palace,
as did all her company—
her knights and her ladies,

4104   some of whom were beautiful indeed.

Tot s'en revont li chevalier
a lor ostels por herbergier.
Mais defors la vile est Guinglains,
4108   desconsilliés, foibles et vains,
ne nus a lui mot ne parole.
Or est il en fole riole!
Ne set que dire ne que face.
4112   Arestés est en une place.
"Robers," fait il, "que poro[n]s faire?
Venus soumes a mal repaire;
de consel grant mestier avons.
4116   Va querre hostel, si herbergons."
Robers respont, "Or m'escoutés.
Laiens molt bon ostel avés
en cele rue tot aval,
4120   la u jurent nostre ceval
quant ci fumes a l'autre fois.
Cortois est l'ostes et adrois.
Tot nostre estuvoir i arons."
4124   Guinglains respont, "Or i alons."
La nuit sont a l'ostel venu,
l'iement i sont receü.
Li ostes molt biel lé reçut
4128   por ce que il Robert connut.
Molt lé herberga bien la nuit
mais Guinglains n'i ot nul deduit
k'Amors l'a si pris en ses las
4132   que ses cuers est dolans et mas.
Molt le point l'amors de la biele.
Son escuier a lui apiele:
"Robers," fait il, "que ferai, las!
4136   En poi de terme me perdras:
la mort me veut Amors donner."
Cil velt a son signor parler:

4109 mot *repeated*
4112 porors
4124 G. or i a r. *with correct order indicated by insertion marks*

All the knights then went
to their lodgings for the night.
But Guinglain remained outside the city,

4108 weak, defeated, and in despair,
and no one would speak a word to him.
What a fine state of affairs this was!
He did not know what to say or do.

4112 He stopped where he was.
"Robert," he said, "what can we do?
We have come to a sad pass;
we have great need of good counsel.

4116 Go now and seek a place for us to stay."
Robert answered, "Hear me, my lord.
You shall have very good lodgings
down at the end of that street,

4120 in the place where our horses were stabled
when we were here before.
The host is a well-mannered and clever man.
We shall have all that we need there."

4124 Guinglain answered, "Let us go there then."
That night they stayed at the inn,
where they were welcomed with pleasure.
The host received them most hospitably,

4128 for he already knew Robert.
He lodged them very well that night,
but Guinglain had no joy in his lodgings,
for Love held him so tightly in bondage

4132 that his heart was sad and downcast.
The love of his beautiful lady tormented him.
He called his squire to him:
"Robert," he said, "what shall I do, wretched man that I am?

4136 You shall lose me very soon,
for Love intends to give me over to death."
Robert was eager to speak with his lord:

"Quel cose vos a respondue
4140   vostre dame qu'avés veüe?"
"Certes n'i a el que la mort
qu'en li ne truis nul reconfort.
Ains me dist bien tot entresait
4144   que molt me fesist honte et lait
se ne fust l'amors qu[i] jadis
fust de moi en son cuer asis.
Ço a dit qu'encor l'en souvient,
4148   por sel itant si s'en reti[e]nt."
"Sire, ne vos esmaiés mie.
Bien a respondu vostre amie
quant reconnost que vos ama.   *[147r°c]*
4152   De cele amor encor i a.
Ceste responsse m'asouage
qu'el dist que vos ot en corage.
Cis respons vos mostre aucun bien;
4156   or ne vos esmaiés de rien,
qu'a mon sanblant est aviaire
nos doit cis respons joie faire.
Se je peüsse a li parler,
4160   tost peüssiés merci trover."
Et Guinglains issi longement
soufre son mal et si atent,
qu'il cuide parler a s'amie.
4164   Mais ço qu'il quide n'i a mie
car ne le puet por rien veoir.
Si i despent tot son avoir,
tant poi con il en ot o lui,
4168   qu'il ne trova onques celui
que il del sien ne li donast,

4140 qu'a. perdue v.
4143 dist bien *repeated*
4145 que
4148 retint
4149 S. fait il ne v. elmaiés m. [+2]
4162 souvre

"What answer did your lady give
4140   when you saw her?"
"Without doubt there is nothing but death for me now,
for I find no comfort from her.
Indeed, she told me
4144   that she would have done me great harm and dishonor
had it not been for the love
that she once held in her heart for me.
She told me she still remembered this love,
4148   and that is all that restrained her."
"My lord, do not be troubled.
Your lady has given you a good answer,
for she admits that she once loved you.
4152   She must love you still.
This answer brings me comfort,
for she said that she once held you in her heart.
This answer shows that she is well disposed toward you.
4156   Do not be troubled at all,
for it seems to me
that her answer should bring us joy.
If I could only speak with her
4160   you would swiftly find forgiveness."
And so for a long time Guinglain
waited there and endured his suffering,
for he thought he would be able to speak to his lady.
4164   But matters did not turn out as he had expected,
for he could not see her no matter what he did.
He gave away all that he had,
the little that he had with him,
4168   for he never met anyone
to whom he failed to give something,

se il a prendre le daingnast.
Despent, acroit, barate et donne;
4172 quanques il a tot abandonne.
Tant a illueques atendu
que son harnas a despendu
tote une quinsainne enterine.
4176 Bien l'a Amors en sa saissine,
qu'il ne mangüe ne ne dort;
trop est arivés a mal port.
Amors le destraint et justice;
4180 del tot le met a sa devise,
n'en son consel ne puet trover
coment il puist a li parler.
De ço que ensi le destraint
4184 et nuit et jor por li se plaint;
Amors ne.l laisse reposer.
Son cuer atorne a penser,
le mangier laisse et le dormir.
4188 Amors le mainne a son plaisir.
Molt par fu Guinglains angoissiés:
ens en son lit estoit couciés,
nule hore ne pot hors issir.
4192 Bien cuide qu'il doie morir:
tranble, fremist, genmist, souspire.
Molt par soufre cruels martire.
Torne et retorne et puis s'estent
4196 et adens se remet souvent.
En soi a d'Amors le maniere.
    Molt l'a trové male gerriere
en celi cui je sui amis:
4200 des que primes vi[c] son bel vis,
onques puis n'en parti [m]on cuer
ne partir n'en puet a nu[l] fuer.
De moi ocire ne reposse   [*147 v°a*]

4200 vit
4201 son
4202 nu

if the person were willing to accept it.
He spent, he bartered, he lent, and he bestowed gifts;

4172   he had soon given up all he had.
He waited a full fortnight,
and by that time he had lost
all his knightly equipment.

4176   Love held him tightly in her grip,
for he could neither eat nor sleep;
he was indeed in desperate straits.
Love goaded and tormented him;

4180   she did with him whatever she wished,
and he could think of no way
to speak with the lady.
And so he was tormented

4184   and pined for her day and night;
Love gave him no rest.
He set his whole heart to thinking of his lady,
and left off eating and sleeping.

4188   Love led him around at her good pleasure.
Guinglain was plunged into the deepest torment,
and so he took to his bed
and could no longer leave it.

4192   He believed that he must die,
so much did he tremble, shiver, moan, and sigh.
He suffered the cruelest martyrdom.
He tossed and turned and stretched himself out

4196   and then turned over again and again.
He certainly acted like a man ruled by Love.
    I myself have often found the lady whom I love
to be a most cruel warrior:

4200   since first I saw her lovely face
my heart has never ceased to be hers,
nor could it ever leave her.
She makes me suffer a thousand deaths,

4204 et je l'aim plus que nule cose.
 Onques vers li rien ne mesfis
 fors tant que sui loiaus amis.
 Mais por iço me puet mal faire,
4208 que je ne m'en quier mais retraire
 mon cuer, qui a tos jors le voit.
  Or escoutés ici endroit
 coment Guinglains moroit d'Amors
4212 qui molt li fait traire dolors.
 Robers esgarde son signor
 qui molt li fait müer color.
 Bien set qu'Amors trop le destraint,
4216 car i[l] le vit et pale et taint.
 Grant paor en a et anui.
 Tot maintenant ala vers lui.
 Molt est Guinglains de mal laidis,
4220 afebloiés et maladis.
 Et Robers va a lui parler
 se.l prie molt de conforter.
 Quand Robers l'a mis a raisson,
4224 atant entra en la maisson
 une pucele bien apprisse
 qui fu de tos biens entremisse.
 Vestu ot un vair peliçon
4228 qui fu covers d'un siglaton.
 Molt estoit gente la pucele.
 Une robe aporte molt biele
 partie de deus dras divers:
4232 de soie d'un osterin pers
 et d'un diaspe bon et biel.
 La pene qui fu el mantiel
 refu molt de rice partie,
4236 de rice vair de vers Hungrie;
 l'autre d'ermi[ne] bon et fin,
 ki estoit d'un rice osterin,

4216 c. i le
4237 *end of* ermine *obliterated*

4204	and yet I love her more than anything else.
	I never did anything to offend her
	except to be her loyal friend.
	But that is why she can cause me such suffering,
4208	for I never wish to withdraw
	my heart, which longs for always.
	Now listen as I tell you
	how Guinglain lay dying of love,
4212	which caused him the greatest suffering.
	Robert looked at his lord,
	and grew pale at what he saw.
	He could see that love tormented him cruelly,
4216	for he saw how pale and sickly his master had grown.
	The squire was filled with fear and concern.
	He went straight to his master's side.
	Guinglain had been laid low
4220	and was weak and wasted from his illness.
	And so Robert went to speak to him
	and begged him to be comforted.
	While Robert was thus speaking to him,
4224	there came into the room
	a maiden of courtly manners
	and endowed with every grace.
	She wore a silk pelisse
4228	lined with miniver.
	This maiden was of most noble bearing.
	She was carrying a beautiful cloak
	made of two different fabrics:
4232	one was a blue silk from the Orient
	and the other an exquisite brocade.
	The lining of the cloak,
	priceless as well, was made of two different furs:
4236	one was a costly miniver from Hungary,
	the other an elegant ermine;
	the latter lined the blue silk,

et li vairs el diaspe estoit.
4240 Un molt rice seble i avoit
dont li mantials estoit orlés.
Molt estoit li dras bien ouvrés
de coi estoit fais li mantials.
4244 Ja mar querrés deus dras plus bials
que cil de cele reube estoit,
molt bien andoi s'entravenoient.
Guinglains la pucele a veüe,
4248 son cief dreça, si le salue,
et cele son salu li rent:
"Le Roi del Ciel omnipotent
vos doi[n]st ço que vostres cuers veult
4252 de cele rien dont plus se deut.
Sire, ma dame vos salue,
cele que vos querrés a drue,
c'est la dame de ceste vile.   *[147 v°b]*
4256 Il n'a si biele entre cent mile.
Ceste roube vos a tramise,
si vos mande qu'en nule guisse
ne soit laissié ne la veés
4260 tantost con vos garis serés."
Quant Guinglains l'ot, molt en fu liés,
se li respont, "Tos sui haitiés.
De nule rien je ne me duel
4264 puis que verrai ço que je vel.
Jo n'ai nul mal qui me retiengne
puis qu'ele veut que a li viengne.
Dius en ait los par son plaissir
4268 de ço qu'ele me veut veïr!
Bien ait la dame et li mesages
k'or est alegiés mes malages!"
A la pucele fait grant goie.
4272 Vestue a la reube de soie
que cele li a avant traite.
Molt s'atorne bien et afaite;

4251 doist

the miniver, the brocade.
4240 The cloak was also trimmed
in precious sable.
The fabrics from which the garment had been cut
were most skillfully woven.
4244 You would be wasting your time if you sought
two fabrics more exquisite than those in this cloak,
and the two went together perfectly.
When Guinglain saw the maiden,
4248 he raised his head and greeted her,
and she returned his greeting:
"May the all-powerful King of Heaven
grant what your heart desires
4252 from the one who causes it such grief.
My lord, I bring you greetings from my lady,
whose love you seek,
the sovereign of this city.
4256 Among a hundred thousand there is none so fair as she.
She sends you this cloak
and commands that on no account
must you fail to go and see her
4260 as soon as you are cured of your illness."
When Guinglain heard this, his heart leaped for joy,
and he answered, "I am entirely cured.
I no longer feel pain
4264 since I shall now see her whom I so long to see.
No illness could hold me back,
since she wishes me to come to her.
May God be praised for having willed
4268 that she should wish to see me!
May good come to the lady and to her messenger as well,
for now my suffering is relieved."
Thus he showed his great joy to the maiden.
4272 He put on the silken cloak
that she had brought him.
He dressed himself well and handsomely,

la robe molt bien li avint.
4276   Mais la dolors qu'al cuer li tint
li avoit enpali le vis;
et nequedenc ce m'est avis
que on peüst asés cerkier
4280   ains c'on trovast un chevalier
tant preu, tant sage ne tant biel.
La pucele par le mantiel
le prist, puis li a dit, "Alons
4284   a ma dame car trop tardons."
Guinglains respont, "Iço me plaist."
Envers la pucele se traist
et par le rue andoi s'en vont
4288   tot droit vers le palais amont.
Et quant sont el palais venu,
si se sont d'autre part issu
par mi un huis en un vergier.
4292   Et molt se faissoit a proissier.
Tos estoit clos de mur mabrin
qui bien fu ovrés de grant fin,
c'onques Dius ne fist cele [c]ose
4296   qui fust en tot le mont enclose
que ne fust bien el mur ouvree,
molt [bien] tallie et devisee.
Fenestres avoit tot entor
4300   par [u] i venoit la calor,
trestoutes ouvrees d'argent.
Ainc nus ne vit vergier si gent,
tant bon, tant rice ne tant biel.
4304   Ainc Dius ne fist cel abrissel
que on el vergié ne trouvast,
qui le lé et le lonc cercast.
Grant masse i avoit de loriers,   [*147v°c*]

4293 d *before* mur *expuncted*
4295 sose
4298 m. t. et d. [*-1, em Williams*]
4300 p. une i [*em. Williams*]

for the gown became him well.
4276 The suffering that had touched his heart
had made his face grow pale;
and yet I truly believe
that you might search for a very long time
4280 before finding a knight who was
so valiant, so intelligent, or so handsome.
The maiden took hold of his cloak
and said, "Let us go now
4284 to my lady, for we are delaying too long."
Guinglain answered, "That pleases me well."
He followed the maiden,
and they made their way through the streets
4288 and up toward the palace.
When they arrived there,
they went straight through to the other side
and through the gate into a garden.
4292 This garden was indeed worthy of admiration.
It was all enclosed by marble walls
made with the greatest skill and art,
for God never created anything
4296 that could be found in the world
that was not represented
in the magnificent carvings on these walls.
There were windows all around,
4300 which allowed warmth to enter the garden,
with shutters made of silver.
No one ever saw such a pleasant garden,
nor one so fine, so rare, or so lovely.
4304 Every tree in God's creation
could be found in this garden
if one searched carefully.
There were many laurels there,

4308   de figiers et d'alemandiers,
        de saigremors et de [paumiers],
        [sapins] molt et asés melliers,
        pumiers grenas, loriers ramés.
4312   D'autres arbres i ot asés,
        et s'i croissoit li reculisses
        et li encens et molt espisses.
        Dius ne fist herbe de bonté
4316   que el vergié n'eüst planté.
        Encens, gerofle et citoual
        et le caniele et garingal,
        espic, petre, poivre, comin—
4320   de ce ot asés el gardin.
        Rosiers [i ot] d'itel nature
        que en tos tans la flors i dure.
        Molt fu li vergiers gens et bials.
4324   Tos jors i avoit cans d'osials:
        de calendres et d'orïals,
        de merles et de lonsingnals
        et d'autres dont i ot asés,
4328   ne ja leur cans ne fust lassés.
        Laiens avoit itels odors
        et des espeses et des flors
        qu[e] cil qui s'estoit laiens mis
4332   quidoit qu'il fust en paradis.
        Guinglains et la pucele cointe,
        qui molt pres de lui s'estoit jointe,
        s'en vont par le vergier adiés.
4336   Tant ont alé qu'il furent pres
        de la dame qui el vergier
        s'onbrioit les un olivier,
        entor li dames et puceles;
4340   et il s'en vont adiés vers eles.

4309 sapins
4310 paumiers
4321 R. d'i. [*emendation Bidder*]
4331 qui c.

4308 along with fig trees and almond trees,
sycamores and palms,
pines and apple trees,
medlars and oleander.

4312 There were many other kinds of trees,
and licorice grew there,
along with incense and many other spice trees.
God never made any fragrant herb

4316 that did not flourish in that garden.
Frankincense, cloves, and zedoary,
along with cinnamon and galingale,
spikenard, feverfew, pepper, and cumin—

4320 all these grew there in abundance.
There were rosebushes that
bloomed throughout the year.
This garden was indeed a rare and lovely place.

4324 Every day birds sang there:
orioles and larks,
merlins and nightingales,
and many more besides,

4328 so that the sounds of birdsong never ceased.
And there was such a fragrance
of flowers and spices in the garden
that anyone inside its walls

4332 would have believed himself in Paradise.
Guinglain and the lovely maiden,
who walked close beside him,
made their way through the garden.

4336 They walked up to where
the Maiden of the White Hands was seated
in the shade of an olive tree
with her ladies and maidens all around her;

4340 Guinglain and the maiden approached these ladies.

Or voit Guinglains ço qu'il voloit.
Quant la dame venir le voit,
si ss'est encontre li levee.
4344   Ainc Elanne qui fu enblee,
que por biauté ravi Paris,
n'Iseus la Blonde, ne Bliblis,
ne Laivine de Lonbardie,
4348   qui Enee estoit amie,
ne Morge la Fee meïssme
n'orent pas de biauté la dime.
A li ne s'en prendroit nesune
4352   ne qu'[a]l solelc se prent la lune.
En tot le mont n'ot sa parelle,
tant estoit biele a grant mervelle;
molt estoit la dame honneree.
4356   Guinglains l'a premiers saluee
quant il fu devant li venus.
La dame li rent s[es] salus,
aprés la puce[le] salue.   *[148 r°a]*
4360   Et la dame par sa main nue
le prent, et puis se sont asis
sor le kiute de pale bis
et les puceles d'autre part.
4364   N'i a celi qui ne le gart,
tant estoit biaus et bien apris.
La dame l'a a raisson mis,
se li dit, "Coment vos estait?"
4368   "Madame, bien et mal me vait.
Por vos a soufert molt grant painne.
Or me doi[n]st Dius millor quinsainne

4341 1 *of* il *squeezed in later*
4342 *Scribe begins* v *after* venir, *then corrects himself.*
4343 levevee
4352 el
4358 son
4359 puce s.
4370 doist

At last Guinglain could see the one for whom he longed.
When the lady saw him
she rose to greet him.
4344 Never did Helen,
whom Paris stole away for her beauty's sake,
nor Yseut the Blonde, nor Bliblis,
nor Lavinia of Lombardy,
4348 whom Aeneas loved,
nor Morgan la Fay herself
have even a tenth of her beauty.
She outshone all others
4352 as the sun outshines the moon.
She had no equal in all the world,
so wondrously beautiful was she
and of such dignified bearing.
4356 Guinglain greeted her
as soon as he came into her presence.
The lady returned his greeting
and then greeted the maiden as well.
4360 She took Guinglain by the hand
and they sat down
on a couch covered with dark gray silk,
while the maidens sat some distance away.
4364 None of them could keep herself from looking at Guinglain,
so handsome and courtly was he.
The lady began the conversation,
saying, "How are you, my lord?"
4368 "My lady, well and ill.
For your sake I have suffered greatly.
May God grant me a more pleasant fortnight

que ce[l]e que jo ai passee,
4372   car molt i ai painne enduree.
Tant le me convenrra soufrir
con il vos venra a plaissir."
"Avoi!" fait la dame, "Biaus sire,
4376   ja poríés vos bien mius dire!
De coi vos poés vos doloir?
Par moi n'est pas, je.l sai de voir.
Mais vos me volés regingnier
4380   con vos fesisses avant ier.
Et se je [mon] amor [donnoie],
la vostre molt par tans perdroie,
car vos en iríés ausi."
4384   Quant Guinglains l'oï, si rogi;
la face li devint vermelle,
s'en fu plus biaus a grant mervelle.
Tant estoit biaus a desmesure
4388   qu'en tot le mont tant con il dure
ne trovait on un chevalier
ne qui tant fesist a proissier.
Sages et pros et cortois fu,
4392   s'a a la dame respondu
molt bonement, au mius qu'il pot,
"Dame," fait il, "tant con vos plot
le m'avés fait cier conperer
4396   que ne vauc congié demander
qua[nt] je alai le secors faire.
Ma doce dame debonnaire,
car vos prenge pitié de moi
4400   car onques rien faire ne soi
s'il vos pleüst que ne fesisse
et que merchi ne vos que[si]sse.

4371 q. cece q.
4381 et se je vostre a. perdroie
4388 monst
4397 qua [*ligature incomplete*]
4402 quesse

than the one I have just endured,
4372 for I have known great pain.
And I will be forced to suffer
as long as you so wish it."
"Come come, my dear lord!" said the lady.
4376 "You might speak more truthfully!
From what can you be suffering?
I know, in truth, that you do not suffer for my sake.
You mean rather to deceive me
4380 as you did not long ago.
And if I should give you my love,
I would soon lose yours,
for you would leave me as you did before."
4384 Guinglain blushed when he heard these words.
As his face flushed with color,
his beauty was wondrous to see.
He was so fair, beyond power to measure,
4388 that nowhere in the world, as long as it endures,
could so handsome a knight
ever be found.
He was brave and intelligent and courtly,
4392 and he answered the lady
in all sincerity, as well as he could.
"Lady," he said, "as long as it pleased you to do so,
you made me pay dearly
4396 for not having asked your leave
when I left to lend my aid to the queen of Wales.
My sweet and gentle lady,
have pity on me,
4400 for there is nothing
that I would not do if you so desired
in order to obtain your forgiveness.

Mon cuer avés, ço est voire,
4404 et se vos m'en volïés croire,
Amor m'en fera gara[n]tie.
Car je muir por vos, dame amie,
s'enfin de moi merchi n'avés.
4408 Enfin sui a le mort livrés
se vos n'atenprés ma dolor
de la vostre doce savor."
La dame li fait un regart   [*148r ʾb*]
4412 et Guinglains li de l'autre part;
a[s] iols s'enblent les cuers andui.
Car la dame ramoit tant lui
qu'ele ne.l pooit plus amer,
4416 mais son cuer li voloit celer.
De bon cuer la dame l'amoit,
mais son corage li celoit.
Andoi s'entr'amoient forment:
4420 un cuer orent et un talent,
car l'uns por l'autre [plus] se deut
que ne fist Tristrans por Yseut.
Que vos iroie je contant?
4424 Molt furent biel et avenant.
La dame esgarde son biel vis,
pui[s] li a dit, "Li miens amis,
molt mar i fu vostre proece,
4428 vostre sens et vostre largece,
qu'en vos n'a rien a amender
fors tant que ne savés amer.
Mar fustes quant ne le savés!
4432 Totes autres bontés avés,
et je vos di en voir gehir,
issi me puisse Dius merir
quanque me laist faire por lui,

4405 garatie
4413 ae
4421 c. li u. p. l'a. se d. [*em. Williams*]
4426 pui

You hold my heart, I tell you quite truly,
4404 and if you are willing to believe what I say,
Love will act as my guarantor.
For I shall die for love of you, my lady and my love,
if you do not at last have pity on me.
4408 I shall soon be given over to death
if you do not temper my suffering
with your gentle sweetness."
The lady gazed at him,
4412 and he at her,
and with that gaze, each stole the other's heart.
For the lady loved him so much
that she could not have loved him more,
4416 but what she held in her heart she wished to conceal.
She loved him with her whole heart,
but she kept from him what she felt.
They loved each other dearly:
4420 they had but one heart and one desire,
and each yearned for the other
more than Tristan for Yseut.
What more shall I tell you?
4424 Both were indeed attractive and engaging.
The lady looked at his fair face
and said, "My friend,
alas for your prowess,
4428 your judgment, and your generosity,
for there is no fault to be found in you
except that you do not know how to love.
Alas for you that you do not!
4432 You are endowed with all other virtues,
and I swear to you,
so may God reward me
for all He may permit me to do for His sake,

4436   plus vos amaisse que nului
        se vos iço faire saviés.
        Mais or vos pri que vos soiés
        çaiens en cest palais o moi,
4440   car debonnaire et franc vos voi.
        Et je vel que soiés ça sus
        car trop avés esté la jus.
        Si fait ça sus plus bel manoir
4444   et mius vos en verra, espor."
        Atant a respondu Guinglains,
        ki ne fu ne fals ne vilains,
        "Dame," fait il, "gabés me vos?
4448   Se je ço savoie a estros
        que de bon cuer l'eüssiés dit,
        onques Dius cele rien ne fist
        dont je serroie si [joians]
4452   con serroie d'estre çaens.
        En tos les lius u je serroie
        saciés molt volentiers iroie,
        k'aillors ne puisse joie avoir.
4456   Dame, dites me vos don[c] voir?"
        "O, je, sire, je ne gap mie!"
        Quant cil l'oï, si l'en merchie.
        Cele parole molt li plot;
4460   dedens son cuer grant joie en ot.
        Lors se sont d'ilueques torné;
        ens el palais s'en sont alé,
        qui molt ert biaus et delitable[s].   [*148r°c*]
4464   Ja faisoit on metre les tables,
        quar il estoit tans de souper.
        Por laver font l'iaugue crïer,
        si se sont au mangier asis.
4468   Pain et vin ont as tables mis;

4442 e. lasus l.
4451 dolans [*em. Williams*]
4456 dont
4463 delitable

4436   that I would have loved you more than all others,
         if you only knew how to love.
         But now I ask that you remain
         here with me in the palace,
4440   for I find you a noble and courtly man.
         And I would like for you to be here,
         for you have too long remained below in the town.
         This is a more pleasant dwelling place,
4444   and will, perhaps, be more to your liking."
         Then Guinglain answered,
         he who was neither false nor loutish,
         "My lady, are you jesting with me?
4448   If I knew for certain
         that you had spoken this from your heart,
         then God never made anything
         that could make me so happy
4452   as being here with you.
         No matter where else in the world I might be,
         you may be certain that I would fly to this place,
         for nowhere else could I know true joy.
4456   My lady, are you speaking truly?"
         "Indeed, my lord, I am not at all jesting!"
         When he heard this, he gave her thanks.
         These words of hers delighted him deeply,
4460   and he rejoiced with all his heart.
         At that they left the garden
         and went into the palace,
         which was a most beautiful and pleasant place.
4464   The tables were already being set,
         for it was time for the evening meal.
         Water for washing was called for,
         and the household sat down to dine.
4468   Bread and wine were placed on the tables;

de tot quanques mestiers lor fu
ont tot a lor voloir eü.
Quant mangié orent a lossir,
4472   a grant aisse et a lor plaissir,
si sont des tables levé tuit.
Grans piece estoit ja de la nuit
et tans estoit ja de coucier.
4476   As ostels vont li chevalier
aval en la vile gesir.
Or fu Guinglains a son plaisir,
ki dejoste s'amie fu
4480   qui el palais l'ot retenu!
Li uns a l'autre gabe et rit.
Li canb[re]lenc ont fait un lit
a [l'ues] Guinglain ens el palais.
4484   Li lis ne fu mie mauvais;
tant i ot pales gregoi[s]
qu'a honnor i geüst un rois.
Quant li sergant ont fait un lit,
4488   si a la dame a Guinglain dit,
"Amis, en cest lit vos girois,
qu'a honnor i giroit uns rois.
N'en alés or pas sor mon pois
4492   con vos fesistes autre fois.
Et [j]e en ma canbre girai
et l'uis trestuit ouvert lairai;
il ne serra mie anuit clos.
4496   Gardés que ne soiés tant os
que vos laiens anuit alés.
Sor mon desfens pas n'i entrés.
De l'uis est vostre lis si pres,
4500   gardés ne soiés tant engrés
que en ma cambre entrés anuit.

4482 re *in* canbrelenc *obliterated*
4483 a eols G. [*em. Williams*]
4485 gregoit
4493 Et e en

everything they might have wished
they had in abundance.
When they had dined
4472   at their leisure and with great enjoyment,
everyone rose from the tables.
By then the evening was well advanced
and it was time to go to sleep.
4476   The other knights went down
to their lodgings in the city.
But Guinglain now had what he most desired,
for he was staying
4480   in the palace with his lady!
The two of them laughed and jested with each other.
The chamberlains prepared a bed
for Guinglain in the hall.
4484   This was no pauper's bed, of that you may be certain;
it was covered with so many fine Byzantine silks
that a king could have slept there with honor.
When the servants had prepared the bed,
4488   the lady said to Guinglain,
"My friend, you shall sleep here in this bed,
which is worthy of a king.
Do not leave it as you did before,
4492   or I shall be most displeased.
And I shall lie in my chamber
with the door wide open;
it shall not be closed at all tonight.
4496   Take care that you be not so bold
as to come into my chamber during the night.
You must not enter against my prohibition.
Your bed is very near the door,
4500   but take care not to be so rash
as to enter my chamber tonight.

Paor me feriés, je cuic!
Ne le faites sans mon comant.
4504 Je m'en vois; a Dius vos comanc."
Guinglain respont, "Dame, et je vos."
Ensi departirent andols.
La dame est en sa canbre entree
4508 et cil l'a adés regardee
de tant come veïr le puet;
onques de li ses iols ne muet.
Aprés s'est ens el lit couciés.
4512 Molt fu dolens et esmaiés;
ne puet dormir ne reposer:
villier l'estuet et retorner.
Vers l'uis [regarde] molt souvent   *[148v°a]*
4516 savoir s'il venroit essement
la dame de sa canbre issir
et a son lit a lui venir
si con ele fist l'autre fois.
4520 Quant ne le vit, si fu destrois.
Molt fu Guinglains en grant ferfel;
onques la nuit ne pris[t] soumel
mais a l'uis tot dis esgardoit
4524 qui tos ouvers adés estoit.
Souvent se levoit en seant
et de l'entrer li prent talant,
puis se comence a porpenser
4528 et a lui meïsme estiver:
"Dius," fait il, "Sire, que ferai?
Irai je u [je] remanrai?
Ma dame le m'a desfendu
4532 et par sanblant ai je veü
qu'ele veut bien que je i aille.

4515 recorde
4519 frois *with* r *expuncted*
4521 G. *rather than* GG *for* Guinglains
4522 pris
4530 *second* je *lacking*

I believe it would frighten me if you did that!
Do not do this unless I so command.
4504 I shall leave you now; I bid you a good night."
"And I you, my lady," Guinglain replied.
Thus they parted from each other.
The lady entered her chamber
4508 and Guinglain watched her go
as long as he could still see her;
his eyes never left her.
Then he lay down.
4512 He was very distressed and perturbed,
and could neither sleep nor take his rest:
he could do nothing but lie awake and toss and turn.
He kept looking toward the door
4516 to see if the lady
might leave her chamber
and come to him in his bed
as she had done before.
4520 When he did not see her, he was plunged in despair.
Guinglain was now in a tumult;
he could not sleep at all that night,
but kept looking toward the door,
4524 which still lay wide open.
He often sat up,
seized with the desire to go through the door,
but then would begin to consider
4528 and debate with himself:
"Dear God," he said, "what shall I do?
Shall I go in or stay here?
My lady has forbidden me to go,
4532 and yet her face seemed to tell me
that she was quite willing for me to do so.

Se je remai[n]g, je crim sans faille
que ne me tiegne a recreant.
4536 Dius, que ne sace son talent!"
Souvent se levoit por aler
et puis si se laissoit ester.
Veut et ne veut, si se remaint.
4540 Ens en son lit souvent se plaint,
souvent dissoit, "Or i irai.
Non ferai, voir. Voir si ferai!"
Ensi le destraint et justice
4544 Amors, qui le mainne et justice.
Mais or ne laira qu'il n'i aut;
Amors le destraint et asaut.
Atant s'est de son lit levés
4548 et d'un mantiel est afublés.
Vers la canbre s'en vait san bruit;
ja estoit pres de mie nuit.
Quant il quide en la canbre entrer,
4552 a l'uis ne pooit asener.
Sor une plance est vis qu'il soit;
une grant iaugue sos avoit,
rade et bruiant plus que tenpeste.
4556 Guinglains a le place s'areste
quant il ne pot avant aler
n'ariere ne put retorner,
tant par estoit la plance estroite.
4560 Molt [bien] desire et [molt] convoite
qu'il eüst la plance passee.
Aval a l'iaue regardee
qui si fait la plance croler
4564 qu'il ne se puet sor piés ester.
Ço li est vis qu'il quaie jus:
il se tient as mains de desus

4534 remaig
4558 retornier
4559 conv *struck out after* tant
4560 Ml d. et c. [-2, *em.Williams*]

I fear that, if I stay,
she will indeed think me faint-hearted.

4536 Dear God, if I only knew her wishes!"
Again and again he rose to go
and then lay back down.
He both wanted and did not want to go, and so he remained.

4540 He lamented over and over in his bed,
saying, "I shall go now.
No, truly I shall not. Yes, indeed I shall!"
Thus Love, his mistress,

4544 continued to goad and torment him.
But in the end he could not fail to go,
so harshly did Love pursue and assail him.
He arose from his bed

4548 and dressed himself in a cloak.
Silently he moved toward the lady's chamber;
it was now nearly midnight.
Just when he believed he was about to enter the chamber,

4552 he could not reach the door.
He thought he found himself standing on a wooden plank
that had been laid as a bridge over a great rushing river,
which raged more furiously than a tempest.

4556 Guinglain stopped where he was,
for he could go no further
nor could he turn back,
so narrow was the plank on which he stood.

4560 He greatly wished
to be across this footbridge.
He looked down at the torrent,
which was causing the plank to tremble so violently

4564 that he lost his footing.
He felt himself falling
and grabbed hold of the bridge

et l'autre cors aval pendelle. [*148v°b*]

4568 S'il a paor ne m'en mervelle!
Desous lui voit l'iaue bruiant;
li bra[s] li vont afebloiant:
perdre cuide tantost la vie.

4572 Au plus haut que il puet s'escrie,
"Signor," fait il, "aidiés! Aidiés!
Por Diu, car ja serai noiés!
Secorés moi, bonne gens france,

4576 car je penc ci a une plance
ne je ne me puis mais tenir!
Singnor, ne m'i laissiés morir!"
Par le palais se lievent tuit.

4580 Li sergant qui oent le bruit
candoiles, cierges ont espris.
Trovent Guinglain qui si fu pris
a le perce d'un esprevier,

4584 si avoit paor de noier.
A le perce as mains se tenoit;
li autres cors aval pendoit.
Lués qu'il ot veüs ses sergans,

4588 s'en f[u] alés l'encantemans.
Guinglains s'est d'iluesques partis
tos vergondés et esbahis.
En son lit si est retornés,

4592 si s'est couciés trestos lassés.
Molt en ot grant honte et grant ire;
les sergans voit jüer et rire
de ço que il orent veü.

4596 Bien sot que il enfaumentés fu;
de vergoigne mot ne lor dist.
En son lit vient, en pais se gist;
li sergant se vont recoucier.

4600 Guinglains si a pris a villier
qui d'amors fu en grant torment;

4570 brar
4588 fa

so that the rest of him hung in midair.

4568 I do not wonder if Guinglain was afraid!
Below him flowed the raging river,
and his arms were growing weak:
he believed he was about to lose his life.

4572 He cried out as loud as he could:
"My lords, help me! Help me!
In God's name, I am drowning!
Help me, good people!

4576 For I am clinging to a plank,
and I cannot do so much longer!
Do not let me die, my lords!"
This woke up everyone in the hall.

4580 The servants who had heard the noise
lit candles and tapers.
They found Guinglain clinging
to a hawk's perch,

4584 fearing he was about to drown.
He held to the perch with both hands
while the rest of him hung in midair.
As soon as Guinglain saw the servants,

4588 the spell was broken.
He climbed down from the hawk's perch,
deeply ashamed and bewildered.
He went back to his bed at once,

4592 and climbed into it, exhausted.
He was greatly troubled and embarrassed,
for he saw the servants joking and laughing
at what they had seen.

4596 Guinglain knew he had been tricked by a spell,
but was so embarrassed he did not say a word to them.
He got into bed and lay quietly,
and the servants went back to bed.

4600 But Guinglain lay awake,
for he was tormented by love.

il ne se repose nïent.
Saciés que molt est esmaiés
4604 de ce que tant est travilliés.
De l'amor la dame li manbre
et puis regar[de] vers le canbre.
"Ha, Dius!" fait il, "qu'ai je veü?
4608 Quels cose est ce que j'ai eü?
Je cuic que c'est fantomerie.
Bien sai que laiens est m'amie
qui cest mal me fait endurer.
4612 Ke ne vois je a li parler?
Se devoie perdre la vie
ne.l deveroi je laissier mie
a l'angousse que je en ai
4616 que la ne voisse u je le sai.
Que n'i vois je don[c], las caitis?
Voire, car molt m'en est bien pris
de ço c'orendroit i alai: [*148v°c*]
4620 tos vergondés m'en retornai!
Molt sui or fals quant iço di,
que ço fu songes que je vi.
Por ço ne doi je pas laissie[r]
4624 qu'encore n'i voisse asaier
se je poroie a li parler.
Ausi ne puis je ci durer."
De l'aler a molt grant talant;
4628 molt va la canbre regardant.
Amors tel corage li donne
que il d'aler s'en abandonne.
Quant les sergans endormis vit,
4632 molt tost se lieve de son lit;
vers la canbre s'en vint tot droit.
Tot li est vis qu'il soustenoit

4606 regar
4617 dont
4623 laissie
4633 drooit

He could take no rest at all.
You may be certain that he was deeply troubled
4604   by the suffering he had to endure.
He remembered his love for the lady
and looked toward her chamber.
"Dear God," he said, "what did I see?
4608   What can have happened to me?
I believe it was all an illusion.
I know that my lady is there in the room,
and that she is making me endure these troubles.
4612   Why should I not go speak with her?
Even though it should cost my life,
I must not fail to go
to the place where I know she is,
4616   so great is the anguish I suffer because of her.
Wretched man, why not go to her?
Why, because things have turned out so well for me
when I tried to go just now:
4620   I have come back covered with shame!
But no, I am wrong to say this,
for what I saw was only a dream.
And so I should not fail
4624   to go once more and see
if I may speak with her.
I cannot in any case bear to remain here."
He greatly desired to go;
4628   he looked long at the chamber.
Love so guided his thinking
that he at last resolved to go.
When he saw that the servants were asleep,
4632   he quickly rose from his bed
and went straight toward the lady's chamber.
And all at once it seemed to him that

totes les vautes de la sale.
4636 Molt li est ceste amie male,
tel mal li fait et tel angoisse!
Ce li est vis les os li froisse
li grans fais qui sor lui estoit:
4640 a poi li cuers ne li partoit.
Ensi haut con il pot hucier
cria c'on li venist aidier:
"Signor!" fait il, "Aiue! Aiue!
4644 Bone gens, qu'estes devenue?
Sor le col me gist cis palais:
ne puis plus soustenir cest fais!
A mort je cuit serrai grevés
4648 se de venir ne vos hastés!"
Lors se relievent maintenant,
cierges ont espris li sergant.
Guinglain ont trové come fol
4652 son orillier deseur son col,
et si n'avoit autre besongne.
Quant il les vit, si ot vergoingne.
Jus le jete plus tost qu'il pot
4656 l'orillier, si ne sonna mot
ne les sergant pas n'araissone;
de nule rien mot ne lor sonne.
Son cief a enbrucié en bas,
4660 puis s'est couciés eneslespas
ens en son lit, tos esmaris
et de honte tos esbahis.
Amors le destrai[n]t et tormente.
4664 A lui meïsme se demente,
"Halas!" fait il, "Con fiere cose!
Bien voi la canbre n'est pas closse
et si n'en puis entrer dedens.
4668 Je cuic ço est encantemens
qui çaens est en cest palais.
Vergondés sui a tos jors mais;

4663 destrait

all the arches in the hall were pressing down upon him.
4636 His lady was indeed being unkind to him
to cause him such trouble and anguish!
He felt his very bones being crushed
from the great weight that was pressing him down,
4640 and he very nearly lost consciousness.
And so he cried out for help
as loud as he could:
"My lords, help me! Help me!
4644 Good people, where are you?
The weight of this hall is resting on my shoulders:
I can no longer hold it up!
I believe that I shall die
4648 if you do not make haste to help me!"
At once the servants in the hall got up again
and lit candles.
They found Guinglain like a madman
4652 with his head under his pillow,
the only weight that bore him down.
When he saw them, he was filled with shame;
he threw down the pillow at once
4656 without saying a word
or speaking to the servants;
he would not tell them anything about what had happened.
He hung his head
4660 and at once lay down
in the bed, quite bewildered,
dismayed, and filled with shame.
Love still pursued and tormented him.
4664 He lamented to himself:
"Alas, what an unkind turn of events!
I can see quite well that the lady's chamber is open,
and yet I cannot go in.
4668 I believe there is enchantment
at work in this hall.
I have been forever dishonored by this;

molt par sui laidement traïs.
4672   Dius! Por coi sui je si hardis?
       Ja m'avoit desfendu m'amie
       que je por rien n'entraisse mie.
       Sor son defois le cuidai faire,
4676   mais torné m'est a grant contraire.
       Tels cuide bien faire qui faut.
       Or sai que penssers petit vaut.
       Ç'a fait mes fals cuers envious,
4680   qui tant par est contrarios.
       Li penser qui dedens est clos
       ne puet avoir bien ne repos.
       Deus hontes m'a ja fait reçoivre;
4684   encor se l'en voloie croire,
       me feroit la tierce sentir.
       Mais mius me lairoie morir
       que mais anuit por rien i aille:
4688   bien sai que je feroie faille.
       Deus hontes me vient mius avoir
       que trois ne quatre recevoir."
       Bien dist que ja plus n'i ira.
4692   Vers l'uis de la canbre garda
       et vit venir une pucele,
       gente de cors et de vis biele.
       Ele portoit une cierge espris,
4696   e[n] son puign destre l'avoit mis.
       Fors de la canbre estoit issue,
       si ert au lit Guinglain venue.
       Le covertor un petit tire,
4700   puis li a dit, "Dormés vos, sire?"
       Guinglains respont quant l'ot veüe,
       "Pucele, bien soiés venue.
       Jo ne dorc mie. Que vos plaist?"
4704   "Bien sai que grans joie vos nast:
       ma dame ici a vos m'envoie

4696 e s.
4702 Pucelele *with last* le *expuncted*

I have been most shamefully used.

4672   Dear God! Why was I so rash?
My lady strictly
forbad me to enter her chamber.
I tried to do so against her prohibition,

4676   but this has certainly turned out badly.
Sometimes a man may try his best but fail.
I can see that intention alone is worth little indeed.
My false and all too eager heart is to blame for this,

4680   for it has brought all this upon me.
The thoughts that are locked inside it
can bring me no comfort or rest.
These thoughts have twice brought me shame.

4684   And if I wished to heed them again,
they could do so yet a third time.
But I would rather let myself die
than try again to enter that chamber tonight,

4688   for I know that I could never succeed.
It is better to be shamed twice
than three or four times."
He said he would certainly not try to go in again.

4692   Then he looked toward the chamber door
and saw coming toward him a maiden
fair of both form and face.
She carried a lighted candle

4696   in her right hand.
She came forth from the lady's chamber
and went to Guinglain's bed.
She tugged on the bedcovers gently

4700   and said, "My lord, are you asleep?"
When he had seen her, Guinglain answered,
"I bid you welcome, my lady!
No, I am not asleep. What is your wish?"

4704   "I know that great joy will soon be yours:
my lady has sent me,

qui talent a qu'ele vos voie.
Par moi vos mande parlement
4708   dedens sa canbre u vos atent.
Biaus sire, alés parler a li,
k'ele vos tient a son ami."
"Pucele," fait il, "est ce songes?
4712   Or me ser[vés] vos de mençoignes."
"Ahi, sire!" fait la pucele,
"Ja vos metrai es bras la biele
que vos tenés por vostre amie,
4716   si sarés que je ne menc mie.
Cest songe ferai avere[r].
Venés a ma dame parler!"
Quant Guinglains l'ot, molt li fu biel.
4720   Il afubla un gris mantiel;
del lit sali a molt grant joie,
qu'il cuide que s'amie voie.
"Bele," fait il, "alons, alons!"   [*149 r°b*]
4724   Doce suer, trop i delaions.
France cose, ne demorés:
cest petit pas pris que doublé[s]!"
Et la pucele aprés s'en rist
4728   et adonc par le main le prist.
Atant par le canbre s'en vont,
tres par mi l'uis entré i sont.
Quant en la canbre sont entré,
4732   tot maintenant [i ont trové]
une si tress douce flairor
dont asés mius valoit l'odor
k'encens ne petre ne canele.
4736   . . . .
Tant [i] avoit bone odor

4712 ser v.
4717 avere
4726 double
4732 t. m. entré i sont [*em. Williams*]
4737 i *lacking*

for she wishes to see you.
She bid me ask you to come speak with her
4708 in her chamber, where she now awaits you.
My dear lord, go speak with her,
for she holds you to be her true friend."
"My lady, is this a dream?
4712 Could these be falsehoods you are telling me?"
"Indeed not, my lord!" said the maiden.
"I shall lead you to the arms
of the fair one whom you hold as your lady,
4716 and you shall know I am not speaking falsely.
I shall make this dream of yours come true.
Come now and speak with my lady!"
Guinglain rejoiced to hear this.
4720 He put on a gray cloak
and joyfully leapt from his bed,
for he now expected to see his love.
"Let us go, dear lady!
4724 Sweet maiden, we are delaying too long.
Noble lady, do not dally:
please double that dainty pace of yours!"
And the maiden laughed
4728 and took him by the hand.
They went toward the chamber,
and straight through the door.
As soon as they had entered
4732 they were made aware of
an exquisite fragrance
much rarer than frankincense
or feverfew or cinnamon.
4736 . . . .
So wondrous was this fragrance

que qui eüst mal ne dolor
s'un petit i peüst ester,
4740   lués se peüst tot sain trover.
Laiens avoit cierges espris;
la canbre sanbloit paradis.
Asés i ot argent et or;
4744   de tos biens i ot grant tressor.
Paree fu de dras de soie
de molt cier pris. C'aconteroie?
Mais molt en i ot de divers:
4748   bofus roiés, osterins pers,
tires, pales et siglatons
i ot de molt maintes [façons],
dyapes et bons bogerans
4752   . . . .
Molt par estoit la canbre noble.
D'un pale de Costantinoble
estoit desus encortinee
4756   et desous ert tote pavee
de cieres presiousses pieres
dont i ot de maintes manieres:
esmeraudes, safirs eslis
4760   et cal[ce]donies et rubis;
il i ot de maintes colors.
Li pavemens fu fais a flors,
a images et a oisials.
4764   Tant fu bien fais et tant fu bials
qu'en tout le mont ne en la mer
n'a bieste c'on sace nonmer
—poisson, [dra]gon n'oissel volant—
4768   ne fust ouvrés el pavement.
La dame se geist en son lit.
Onques nus hom plus cier ne vit;
bien vos diroie le façon

4750 colors [*em. Williams*]
4760 caldonies
4768 pavemt [*ligature bar missing*]

           that anyone who was ill
           had only to be in that room for a short while
4740   and he would soon be well again.
           There were candles burning;
           the room seemed a paradise.
           It was filled with silver and gold
4744   and all kinds of riches, worth a king's ransom.
           Costly silk cloths had been hung everywhere.
           Why should I name them all?
           But, truly, there were all kinds of fabrics:
4748   heavy striped silks and deep blue silks,
           silks from the Tyre, cloth of gold and rich brocades
           of the most diverse kinds,
           figured silks and light silks from Boukhara
4752   . . . .
           The chamber was royally decorated.
           The ceiling had been draped
           with a silken cloth from Constantinople
4756   and the floor was covered
           with a mosaic made from
           all manner of precious stones:
           there were emeralds and finest sapphires
4760   calcedones and rubies
           of many different colors.
           This mosaic had been arranged in the form of flowers,
           birds, and many other things.
4764   The floor was so fine and so well made
           that you could name no animal
           that dwells on land or in the sea
           —whether fish, dragon, or bird—
4768   that had not been portrayed in it.
           The Lady of the White Hands was lying in her bed.
           No one ever saw a more beautiful bed than this;
           I could easily describe it in all its details

4772   sans mentir et sans mesproisson,
        mais por sa grant joie coitier,
        que molt en avoit grant mestier,
        ne le vuel entendre a descrire
4776   que trop me costeroit a dire.   *[149 r°c]*
        La pucele tint par le main
        et mainne dusqu'al lit Guinglain
        tant que il i sont parvenu.
4780   La pucele cortoisse fu,
        s'a misse sa dame a raisson:
        " . . . .
        que je vos ai ci amené.
4784   Un petit de sa volenté
        l[i] faites por l'amor de moi.
        Gardé le bien a bone foi."
        La dame respont maintenant,
4788   "Damoissele, vostre comant
        ferai por l'amor c'ai a vos.
        Alés vos ent, laissiés le nos."
        "Or tenés don[c]: je le vos renc."
4792   La dame par le main le prent
        et cil s'est dalés lui cociés.
        Ainc mais ne fu nus hom si liés,
        et Guinglains, quant il fu el lit,
4796   des or ara de son delit.
        Ensanble li amant se jurent.
        Quant il furent ensanble et jurent,
        molt docement andoi s'enbracent;
4800   les levres des bouces s'enlacent,
        li uns a l'autre son droit rent.
        Fors de baissier n'orent content
        et cascuns en voloit plus faire
4804   de baissier dont son cuer esclaire.
        As baissier qu'il firent d'amors

4785 1 f.
4791 dont
4800 s'enlancent

4772   without telling lies or leaving anything out,
        but that would delay Guinglain's joy,
        of which he has great need right now,
        and so I shall not describe the bed,
4776   for that would simply take too long.
        The maiden led Guinglain by the hand
        toward the bed
        and right up to it.
4780   She was a courtly maiden,
        and she spoke thus to her lady:
        ". . . . .
        whom I have brought here to you.
4784   I ask that, for my sake, you grant him
        a little of what he desires.
        I pray you, treat him loyally."
        The lady then answered,
4788   "I shall do as you command, my lady,
        for the sake of my love for you.
        I bid you go and leave him in my care."
        "I hereby entrust him to you," said the maiden.
4792   The lady took Guinglain by the hand
        and he lay down beside her.
        No man was ever so happy as he,
        for very soon
4796   he would take his delight.
        The two lovers lay together.
        Side by side
        they embraced tenderly;
4800   their lips met,
        and both thus received what was theirs by right.
        Their sole joy was to kiss each other,
        and each vied thereby
4804   to gladden the other's heart.
        The loving kisses which they exchanged

del cuer se traient les dolors
et si les aboivrent de joie.
4808   Amors les mainne bone voie.
Les ioels tornent a esgarder,
les bras metent a acoler,
lé cue[r]s s'atornent al voloir.
4812   L'uns velt de l'autre pres manoir.
Por l'amor qu'entr'els deus avoit
vaut l'uns ço que l'autres voloit.
Je ne sai s'il le fist s'amie
4816   car n'i fui pas ne n'en vi mie,
mais non de pucele perdi
la dame dalés son ami.
Cele nuit restoré se sont
4820   de quanques il demorré ont.
Or a Guinglains ço que il volt,
qu'il tient ço dont doloir se s[o]lt,
n'ele ne s'esmaie de rien,
4824   car a gré prent tos ses jus bien.
De tos les mals et le contraire
c'Amors a fait a Guinglains traire
iluec le gueredon li rent.
4828   Por ço d'amors ne m'en repenc,
que desloiauté n'i falt mie
envers Amors n'envers m'amie.   *[149 v°a]*
En un jor me puet bien merir
4832   plus que ne puis ja deservir.
Molt doit on cele rien amer
qui si tost puet joie donner.
Cil ki les dames servir veut,
4836   s'il tot un termine se deut,
por ce ne s'en retraie mie;

4809 ioiels
4811 cues
4822 selt
4823 s'esmaient
4825 contraires

drew all sadness from their hearts,
and flooded them with joy.

4808 Love acted as their guide.
They gazed at each other,
reached out their arms to embrace,
and set their hearts on their desire.

4812 Each wanted to be close to the other.
Because of the love they shared,
each desired what the other wanted.
I do not know whether he made her his true love,

4816 for I was not there, and I saw nothing of it,
but I know that the lady lost the name of maiden
there at her love's side.
That night these two were well consoled

4820 for the long delay they had suffered.
At last Guinglain had what he desired,
for he held the one for whom he had long suffered,
and she was not at all afraid

4824 but gladly received his caresses.
Love gave Guinglain his due reward
for all the griefs and setbacks
with which she had troubled him.

4828   That is why I do not repent of having loved
or of having always been loyal
to Love and to my lady.
In a single day she could easily grant me

4832 more than I could ever deserve.
We should truly love the one
who can so swiftly bring us joy.
The man who wishes to serve ladies

4836 should never renounce his service
though he suffer a long time for it;

que dames ont tel signorie
que quant veulent guerredonner,
4840 si font le travail oublïer
que il avra lonc tans eü.
Dius lé fist de si grant vertu,
de tos bien les forma et fist
4844 et biautés a eles eslist!
Et Dius nos vaut, je cuic, former
por eles toutes honnerer
et por lor comandement [faire].
4848 Por ce est fauls qui s'en veut retraire
que des dames tos li biens muet.
Fols est qui amer ne les veut.
Dius qui Sire est lor amaint joie!
4852 Doucement li prie qu'il m'oie.
Et cels qui sont maldisseor
des dames [et] de fine amor
maudie Dius et sa vertus
4856 et de parler les face mus.
Car a cele ouvre que il font
demonstrent bien de coi [il] sont,
qui tant se painnent de mentir.
4860 Ha, Dius! arai ja mon plaissir
de celi que je ainme tant?
          D[e] Guinglain vos dirai avant.
Il avoit joie en sa baillie:
4864 entre ses bras tenoit s'amie
que il souvent ac[ole] et baisse.
Molt estoient a[ndo]i a aisse.

4839 que q. dames v. g. [+2]
4847 faire *lacking*
4854 *word after* dames *obliterated*
4858 d. b. de c. s. [-1, *em. Williams*]
4862 D G.
4865 *second part of* acole *obliterated*
4866 andoi *partially obliterated*

for the sovereignty of ladies is such that,
when they wish to grant rewards,
4840   they cause a man to forget
whatever torments he has suffered for so long.
God gave ladies such excellence,
so many wonderful qualities,
4844   and bestowed such beauty on them!
And I believe that God made us men
to honor all ladies
and do as they command.
4848   And so the man who turns away from them is false,
for all that is good comes from ladies.
He who refuses to love them is a fool.
May the Lord God bring them all joy!
4852   I humbly pray that He will hear me.
And may God curse
all those who speak ill
of ladies and true love,
4856   and may He strike them dumb!
For by their deeds
they clearly show what they are made of,
those who take such pains in telling lies.
4860   Dear God! shall I ever receive what I wish
from the one I love so much?
        Now I shall tell you more about Guinglain.
He now had true joy at his command:
4864   in his arms he held his love,
whom he embraced again and again.
These two were happy indeed!

        Guinglains souvient de l'o[ri]llier
4868   et de la perce a l'esprevier
        u tel paor eü a[voi]t.
        Mervelle soi que ço estoit.
        Quant il l'enprist a souvenir,
4872   de rire ne se puet tenir.
        Quant la dame rire le vit,
        se li a tot man[te]nant dit,
        "Di[t]es le moi," fait ele, "amis,
4876   por quel cose vos avés ris?
        Ris avés, je ne sai por coi.
        Biaus ciers amis, dites le moi:
        moi ne.l devés vos celer mie."
4880   Cil li respont, "Ma douce amie,
        certes j'ai ris de le mervelle,
        onques nus hom n'ot sa parelle.   *[149 v°b]*
        En cest pailais m'avint anuit
4884   quant endormi se furent tuit
        et je en mon lit me gisoie;
        si angoissés . . . .
        que je ne pooie dormir,
4888   si me fist vostre amors frenmir
        et tant torner et retorner,
        si me fist de mon li[t] ver[ser],
        por ci venir a vos me mui
4892   mais jo si enfaumentés fui,
        (ne sai se fu encantemens)
        mais quant je vauc entrer saens,
        si me trova sor une [p]lance.

4867 orillier *partially obliterated*
4869 avoit *partially obliterated*
4874 mantenant *partially obliterated*
4875 Dides
4883 avint m'anuit *with insertion marks to correct order*
4886-87 *written as one line with second hemistiche of line 4886 lacking*
4890 li ver
4895 blance

Then Guinglain thought of the pillow
4868 and the hawk's perch
which had caused him such fright.
He wondered what could have happened to him.
When he brought all of this to mind,
4872 he could not help but laugh.
When the lady saw this,
she said to him,
"Tell me, my love,
4876 what has caused you to laugh?
You laughed, but I do not know why.
My dear love, tell me the reason,
for you should not conceal it from me."
4880 He answered, "My sweet love,
in truth, I was laughing in wonder at an adventure
of whose like no one has ever heard.
It happened to me this evening in the hall
4884 when everyone else was asleep
and I was lying in my bed;
so filled with anguish. . . . .
that I could not sleep.
4888 I was thrashing about for love of you
and tossing and turning so much
that I finally fell out of bed.
And so I arose to come to you,
4892 but I was overcome by an illusion
(perhaps it was some enchantment)
for, when I was about to enter your chamber,
I found myself on a footbridge.

4896   Des[o]s coroit une iaigue blance
           qui molt bruians et corans er[e].
           Je chaï jus en tel maniere
           qu'a le [p]lance me pris as mains:
4900   de chaïr fui trestos certains.
           Grant paor [oi] de chaïr jus!
           Tos les sergans fis lever sus
           por et secorre et aidier.
4904   A la perce d'un esprevier
           me troverent, s'i me tenoie.
           Autre besoigne n'i avoie!
           Puis me vint une autre aventure
4908   ki plus me fu pesans et dure.
           Molt grant angoisse i endura,
           la verité vos en dirai,
           que painnes ai asés eü.
4912   Dame, savés vos que ce fu?
           Dites le moi se vos savés,
           car molt f[u a]nuit encantés."
           "Amis," fait ele, "bien le sai.
4916   La verité vos en dirai.
           Ceste painne vos ai je faite
           que vos avés issi grant traite
           por la hon[te] que [me] fes[s]istes
4920   que vos issi de moi partistes.
           Et por ce vos ai ice fait:
           . . . .
           que vos engardés a tos jor[s]
4924   que ne soiés tant fals ne lors

4896 Desus
4897 ert
4899 blance
4901 *word obliterated, em. Williams*
4914 *end of third word and beginning of fourth obliterated,*
4919 te *of* honte *and* me *obliterated;* festistes
4923 jor

4896 Below me flowed a noisy
   and rushing torrent.
   I slipped and fell, but in such a way
   that I managed to grab hold of the bridge,
4900 but I was certain I would fall into the river.
   Truly, I was terrified that I would do so!
   And so I awoke all the servants,
   calling for them to rescue me.
4904 They found me
   holding fast to a hawk's perch.
   This was the only danger I faced!
   Then another adventure befell me,
4908 even harsher to undergo.
   It caused me the greatest anguish,
   I tell you in truth,
   for I suffered greatly from it.
4912 My lady, do you know what happened to me?
   If you do, please tell me,
   for tonight I was subject to much enchantment."
   "My love," she said, "I know all about it.
4916 I shall tell you the truth of the matter.
   I caused you the troubles
   that you have undergone here
   because of the dishonor you did me
4920 when you left me here.
   And this is why I have done these things:
   . . . .
   so that you may forever keep yourself
4924 from being so false or so foolish

que dames [vei]lliés esgarnir,
car vos n'en poés pas joïr.
Car cil qui dames traïra
4928   hontes et mals l'en avenra.
Por ce des or vos en gardés.
Or vos dirai se vos [volés]
en quele maniere et coment
4932   jo sai faire l'encantement.
Mes pere fu molt rices rois
qui molt fu sages et cortois.
Onques n'ot oir ne mais que moi,
4936   si m'ama tant en bonne foi   *[149 v°c]*
que les set [ars] me fist apre[ndre]
tant que totes les soc entendre.
Arismetiche, dyomotrie,
4940   ingremance et astrenomie
et des autres asés apris.
Tant i fu mes cuers ententis
que bien soc prendre mon consel
4944   et a la lune et au solelc,
si sai tos encantemens fare,
deviner et conoistre en l'ar[e]
quanques dou mois puet avenir.
4948   De vos seu je bien sans faillir,
quant vos ci venistes l'autre ier,
que n'i vaurïés delaier;
bien soc que vos vos en iriés.
4952   . . . .
mais je ne.l vaussise por rien
por che [que] je savoie bien
que vos parferïés l'afaire.

4925 *beginning of third word obliterated;* esgarnier
4930 volés *lacking*
4935 n'ot roi n. *with* oir *written above* roi
4937 ars *lacking;* f. savoir apre *with* savoir *crossed out*
4946 l'ar
4954 que *lacking*

as to behave lightly toward ladies,
for no good will come to you for doing so.
He who ill uses a lady
4928   will gain only shame and evil thereby.
You must always keep yourself from such things.
Now, if you wish, I shall tell you
how I came to learn
4932   to work magic.
My father was a very powerful king,
a most intelligent and courtly man.
I was his only heir,
4936   and he loved me so dearly
that he had me study the Seven Liberal Arts
until I had mastered them all.
I learned a great deal about arithmetic and geometry,
4940   necromancy and astronomy,
and all the other arts as well.
I studied with such diligence
that I well learned how to consult
4944   both the moon and the sun,
and how to work all kinds of enchantment,
to tell the future so that I know at once
what will happen a month in advance.
4948   When you were here before,
I knew beyond all doubt
that you would not choose to remain;
I knew that you would go away.
4952   . . . .
but I would on no account have wished it,
for I knew that you would accomplish
all you had set out to do.

4956   Bien s[o]i que le poriés faire,
        si c'onors vos en averroit.
        Et mes corages bien savoit
        que au plus [tost] que vos poriés
4960   par moi ariere revenriés.
        Trestout ço [s]o je par mon sens.
        Et saciés que molt a lonc tens
        qu'amer vos començai premiers.
4964   Ains que vos fuissiés chevaliers
        vos amai je, car bien le soi
        qu'en la mainnie Artus le roi
        n'en avoit un millor vasal
4968   fors vostre pere le loial.
        Por ce vos amai je forment.
        Ciés vostre mere molt sovent
        aloie je por vos veïr,
4972   mais nus ne m'en fesist issir.
        Vostre mere vos adoba,
        au roi Artus vos envoia;
        et si vos comanda tres bien
4976   q'au roi demandissiés del sien
        le don, coment que il fust ciers,
        que vos li queriés premiers.
        Ce so ge tot premierement
4980   l'aventure certainnement
        que vos avés ici trovee,
        et tote vostre destinee.
        Je resavoie par mon sens
4984   qu'a la cort venriés par tens.
        Biaus amis, certes, je suis cele
        qui fis savoir a la pucele
        qui estoit apielee Helie
4988   qu'a la cort alast querre aïe
        por sa dame a Artus le roi,   [*150 r°a*]

4956 sai
4959 tost *lacking*
4961 ço o je

4956   I knew that you could fulfill this task,
      and that you would win honor thereby.
      And in my heart I knew
      that as soon as you could
4960   you would come back to me.
      All this I knew through my learning.
      And you may be certain it was long ago
      when I first began to love you.
4964   Before you became a knight
      I loved you, for I knew
      that in all King Arthur's court
      there was no finer knight than you,
4968   save for your father, the loyal Gawain.
      And that is why I loved you so dearly.
      I often went to the house
      of your mother to see you,
4972   and no one could ever have made me leave it.
      It was your mother who gave you your arms
      and sent you to King Arthur;
      it was she as well who advised you
4976   to ask the king to grant
      the first boon you asked of him,
      whatever the cost might be.
      And I was the very first to know
4980   the truth about the adventure
      that you encountered
      and all that was to befall you.
      I also knew through my learning
4984   that you would soon arrive at King Arthur's court.
      In truth, my dear love, I am the one
      who said to the maiden
      who is called Helie
4988   that she should go to King Arthur
      to seek help for her lady,

que certainne fui en droit moi
que vos i querrïés le don
4992   d'oster la dame de prisson.
De tot mon pooir i aidai
por ce que je molt vos amai.
Et si sui cele, biaus amis,
4996   quant eüstes Mabon ocis
et quant le Fier Baissier fesistes,
la vois que vos aprés oïstes
qui vostre non vos fis savoir.
5000   Ço fui je, biaus amis, por voir
por vos faire souef ester,
dormir et la nuit reposer.
Puis fis savoir par la contree
5004   que lor dame estoit delivree.
Sacié molt me sui entremisse
en tos sanblans, en tos servisse,
coment avoir je vos peüsse
5008   ne coment vostre amie fuisse.
Or vos ai je, Dius en ait los!
Des or mais serrons a repos,
entre moi et vos, sans grant plait.
5012   Et saciés bien, tot entresait,
que tant que croire me vaurois
ne vaurés rien que vos n'aiois.
Et quant [mon] consel ne croirés,
5016   ce saciés bien, lors me perdrés."
"Taisiés vos, dame," cil respont.
"Por tot l'avoir qui est el mont
ne por del cors perdre la vie
5020   ne feroie si grant folie
que de vo comandement isse,
ne ja mais anui vos fesisse."
Atant ont lor raisson finee.
5024   Au main quant l'aube fu crevee,
li saint sonnent au grant mostier.

5015 men [= m *with ligature bar above it*]

for I was quite certain
that you would ask for the privilege
4992   of rescuing the lady from her captivity.
With all my strength I lent my aid to this,
because I loved you so dearly.
Indeed, my dear love, the voice you heard,
4996   and which told you your name
after you had killed Mabon
and accomplished the Fearsome Kiss
was none other than my own.
5000   In truth, dear love, I did that
to calm you
so that you might sleep and take your rest that night.
I then made it known throughout the land
5004   that the queen had been set free.
You may know that I have taken great care,
in many ways and with all kinds of services,
to win you
5008   and become your true love.
Now I have won you and may God be thanked for it!
Henceforth we shall know peaceful days together,
with no trouble between us.
5012·   And you may know beyond any doubt
that, as long as you heed what I say,
you shall have all you desire.
But when you cease to listen to me,
5016   you may be certain that you will lose me."
"Have done with such talk, my lady!" he answered;
"Not for all the wealth in the world
nor even to preserve my life
5020   would I commit such folly
as to stray from your commands
or do anything that might displease you."
Thus they ended their conversation.
5024   When dawn had broken the next morning,
the bells sounded in the great church.

Tuit sont levé li chevalier;
Guinglains s'est levés et s'amie.
5028   Au mostier de Sainte Marie
s'en alerent andoi orer;
la dame fist messe canter.
Quant la messe cantee fu,
5032   si s'en sont el palais venu
et la dame a par tot tramis
as dus, as contes, as marcis
que il viegnent a la cort tuit
5036   a lor leece, a lor deduit,
car son ami a recovré
que ele avoit tant desiré.
Quant ve[nu] furent li baron,
5040   la dame lor dist sa raisson:
"Signor," fait ele, "or escoutés.   *[150 r°b]*
Cil chevalier que vos veés,
c'est cil cui tant ai desiré.
5044   Qui molt m'avra servi a gré
si soit engrés de lui servir
et de faire tuit son plaissir,
car c'est li chevaliers el monde
5048   en cui graindre proece abonde.
Je vel que faciés son comant."
Cil respondent comunaument
que il li feront grant honor
5052   et que le tenront a signor.
Or fu Guinglains de joie sire;
tot ot quanques ses cuers desire.
        Or dirons de Blonde Esmere[e],
5056   qui mut de Gales, sa contree,
et va s'ent vers le cort Artus.
Quatre jornees, voire plus,
avoit chevauchié la roïne
5060   quant a l'issir d'une gaudine

5039 Q. ve f.
5055 Esmere

All the knights arose;
and Guinglain and his lady did so as well.

5028 They went together to pray
at St. Mary's church,
and the lady had mass sung.
When the service had ended,

5032 they returned to the palace
and the lady sent out a message
to all her dukes, her counts, and marquis
that they should come to the court

5036 to rejoice and make merry,
because she had once more found her friend,
whose company she had long desired.
When her nobles had arrived

5040 the lady spoke to them thus:
"Hear me, my lords.
This knight, whom you behold,
is the one whose company I have so long desired.

5044 Whoever has willingly served me
should eagerly serve him as well
and do all that he wishes,
for in all the world there is no knight

5048 more valiant than he.
It is my desire that you do his command."
The noble lords answered as one
that they would honor Guinglain

5052 and hold him as their lord.
Guinglain's joy was now complete,
for he had all his heart desired.
Now I shall speak of Blonde Esmeree,

5056 who had left her land of Wales
and was traveling toward the court of King Arthur.
The queen had been riding
for more than four days

5060 when she emerged from a wood

a trové quatre chevaliers
sor lor palefrois, sans destriers;
escus ne armes ne portoient.
5064   Tot quatre vers le cort aloient.
Espreviers portoient müés
que ja plus biaus ne demandés.
Quant la roïne atains les a,
5068   tos ensanble les salua,
et cil son salu li rendirent
et a tos cels qu'i[l] aveuc virent.
Ele les a araisonnés:
5072   "Signor," fait ele, "dont venés?
Qui et dont estes savoir wel,
si ne demant por nul orguel."
Cil ont la dame respondu,
5076   "Dame, nos soumes ci venu
qu'a la cort Artus en irons
car ens[i] fiancié l'avons.
Por prisons nos i covient rendre;
5080   fiancié l'avons a atendre.
Cascuns de nos fiancié l'a
a un chevalier qui ala
por delivrer une pucele;
5084   li Biaus Descouneüs s'apiele.
En bataille nos a conquis.
Nos ne soumes pas d'un païs;
trové nos soumes el chemin,
5088   trestot quatre tres ier matin,
et nos vos avo[n]s ci trovee.
Dont estes vos, de quel contree?"
"Par Diu del ciel! Signor," fait ele,   [*150 r°c*]
5092   "Sachiés por voir que je sui cele

5068 t. ens e.
5070 qu'i, vinrent
5078 c. ens f.
5084 D. l'a.
5089 avos

and saw four knights
mounted on palfreys instead of chargers;
they bore neither shields nor arms.
5064 All of them were traveling toward the court.
They carried moulted hawks,
as fine as you might ask for.
When the queen had caught up with the knights,
5068 she greeted them all,
and they in turn greeted her
along with all her company.
She said to them,
5072 "My lords, from whence have you come?
I should like to know your names and from what lands you
come,
if I may ask this without giving offense."
They answered her,
5076 "My lady, we are on our way
to the court of King Arthur,
for we have sworn to go there.
We must surrender to him
5080 in fulfillment of our word.
Each of us made this pledge
to a knight who was on his way
to lend his aid to a maiden;
5084 this knight is called the Fair Unknown.
He defeated us all in combat.
We are not all from the same country;
the four of us met along the road
5088 early yesterday morning,
just as we have now met you.
And from what land do you come?"
"By Heaven's King!" she said. "My lords,
5092 you may know for certain that I am the maiden

que cil aloit por delivrer,
qui en prison vos fait aler!
Estorsse m'a par grant vigor
5096   et par prohece et par valor.
Bons chevalier est et seürs,
et en bataille fors et durs.
Mais il n'est pas a droit nonmés
5100   par cel non que vos l'apielés.
En batesme a a non Guinglain;
ses peres est li bons Gavains.
A la cort me comande aler
5104   por le roi Artus merchïer
de ço que il rescosse m'a;
li rois, ce dist, l'i envoia.
Por ce l'en weut faire l'onnor,
5108   que il le tient a son signor.
Il doit a le cort repairier
se Dius le garde d'enconbrier.
Il est ne sai quel part tornés.
5112   Lie sui quant vos ai trovés;
or irons a la cort ensanble.
Preudomme estes si con moi sanble."
Cil respondent, "Vostre voloir
5116   ferons, dame, a nostre pooir."
Des or se metent a la voie.
La roïne fait molt grant joie
de ce qu'a trovés les prisons.
5120   Bien vos dirai de tos les nons:
li uns ert Blioblïeris,
qui preus estoit et bien apris;
li autres fu de Saies sire;
5124   del tierc vos sai bien le non dire:
l'Orguillous de la Lande fu,
qui maint chevalier a vencu;
li quars fu Giflés, li fils Deu.
5128   Molt estoient tot quatre preu.
Or chevaucent tot une plaigne
tot le droit chemin vers Bretaingne.
Tant ont le droit chemin erré

whom the knight that defeated you
was on his way to rescue!
He won my freedom through his great strength,
5096   his prowess, and his worth.
He is a fine and valorous knight,
strong and sure in battle.
But the name by which you called him
5100   is not his proper name.
He was given the name Guinglain at baptism;
his father is the noble Gawain.
He bade me go
5104   to render my thanks to King Arthur
for having delivered me,
for he said the king had sent him to me.
Guinglain now wishes me to swear allegiance to Arthur,
5108   who is his sovereign lord.
Guinglain is to go to the court himself
if God protects him from hindrance.
But I do not know where he has gone.
5112   I am happy to have found you.
Let us go to the court together;
you seem to me to be worthy men."
They answered, "My lady, we shall do
5116   as you wish, as well as we are able."
And so they set out along the road.
The queen was truly delighted
to have found the knights whom Guinglain had defeated.
5120   I can readily tell you all their names:
the first was Blioblïeris,
a worthy knight and well mannered;
the second was the lord of Saie;
5124   I know well the name of the third:
he was the Proud Knight of the Glade,
who had defeated many a knight;
and the fourth was Giflet, son of Do.
5128   All four of these men were excellent knights.
The company journeyed through a plain
along the shortest road to Britain.
They followed this route

5132   qu'a Londres ont le roi trové.
        Iluques ensengniés lor fu.
        Ançois qu'il i fuissent venu,
        la roïne a avant tramis
5136   ses sergans, qui ont otels pris
        molt rices et bien atornés.
        Uns sergans est encontre alés.
        Es vos la dame qui descent,
5140   et li chevalier et sa gent.
        En une canbre encortinee
        s'en est don[c] la roïne entre[e].
        Ilueques se fait atorner   [*150 v°a*]
5144   de chiere reube d'Outremer
        qui tant estoit et biele et riche
        qu'en tot le mont n'ot cele bisse—
        caucatri, lupart ne lion,
5148   ne serpent volant ne dragon,
        n'alerion ne escramor,
        ne papejai ne espapemor,
        ne nesune bieste sauvage
5152   qui soit en mer ne en bocage—
        que ne fust a fin or portraite.
        Molt estoit la roube bien faite!
        El mantiel ot pene de sable
5156   qui molt fu bone et avenable.
        Li orles estoit de pantine.
        (Ço est une beste mairine;
        plus souef flaire que canele.
5160   Ainc ne fist [Dius] beste si biele.
        Dalés le mer paist la rachine
        et porte si grant medechine,
        qui sor lui l'a ne crient venin

5142 dont, entre
5144 chieres reubes
5149 n'alerieon
5160 Dius *lacking*

5132 until they found King Arthur in London.
They had been told that he was there.
Before they arrived at the court,
the queen sent her servants
5136 on ahead, and they procured
some very fine and well-furnished lodgings.
A servant came out to meet them when they arrived.
The lady dismounted,
5140 as did the four knights and her followers.
The queen then entered a room
that was all draped with tapestries.
There she had herself arrayed
5144 in a costly robe from the Holy Land,
so beautiful and rare
that in all the world there was no wild creature—
whether crocodile, leopard, or lion,
5148 or winged serpent or dragon,
or eagle or escramor
or popinjay or espapemor
or any other wild beast
5152 that lives in the sea or the forests—
that was not embroidered there in fine gold.
Truly, this robe was exquisitely made!
The cloak was lined with sable
5156 soft to the touch and of excellent quality.
It was trimmed in pantine fur.
(The pantine is a sea creature
that gives off a fragrance finer than cinnamon.
5160 God never made a creature more lovely.
It feeds on herbs beside the sea,
and its fur has such medicinal powers
that whoever wears it need fear no poison

5164   tant le boive soir ne matin.
        Mius vaut que conter ne porroie.)
        Et d'une çainture de soie
        a or broudee tot entor
5168   si s'en estoit çainte a un tor
        molt cointement la damoissele.
        Or fu tant avenans et biele
        que nus hom son per ne trovast
5172   en tout le mont, tant le cerkast.
        De parler ne fu mie fole;
        cortoisse fu de sa parole.
        D'amor estoient si regar[t].
5176   Onques n'ot de biauté le quart
        nule dame qui don[c] fu nee.
        Quant ele fu bien atornee
        et si baron tuit atorné,
5180   si se sont vers la cort torné.
        [E]n son pailais trova le roi
        et maint bon chevalier o soi,
        maint roi [et maint duc] et maint conte;
5184   tant en i ot n'en sai le conte.
        Quant la dame el palais entra,
        li rois encontre li leva,
        et quant l'a veü la roïne,
5188   si le salue et si l'engline.
        Tuit li baron se releverent,
        li uns les autres salüerent.
        Et li rois l'a par le main prisse,
5192   si la dejoste lui asisse.
        Et quant asis se furent tuit
        que nus n'i fist noisse ne bruit,

5164 ne *repeated*
5175 regar
5177 dont
5181 *space for capital but guide letter cut off*
5183 m. r. et m. c. [*-3, em. Williams*]
5193 furenent [*redundant ligature bar over* n]

5164 that he may swallow by night or day.
I could not possibly tell you its worth.)
The lady had taken a silken girdle
richly embroidered with golden thread

5168 and tied it about her waist
to elegant effect.
She was now so lovely and full of grace
that no one could have found her equal

5172 in all the world, no matter how he searched.
Nor was she foolish when she spoke;
rather her speech was courtly indeed.
Her very glances inspired love.

5176 No lady who had ever been born
had even a fourth of her beauty.
When she had thus arrayed herself,
and her nobles had also made themselves ready,

5180 they all set off for the court.
They found the king in his palace
along with many fine knights
and kings and dukes and counts;

5184 I could not tell you how many there were.
When Blonde Esmeree came into the palace
the king arose to meet her,
and when the queen had seen him,

5188 she bowed and extended him greetings.
All the king's nobles arose as well
and exchanged greetings with the queen's party.
Then the king took the lady by the hand

5192 and had her sit down beside him.
When all had taken their seats
and everyone grown quiet,

la dame araisonne le roi: [*150 v°b*]
5196   "Sire," dist ele, "entent a moi.
Je sui fille le roi Guingras,
cui le chevalier envoias
ki Biaus Descouneüs ot non.
5200   Mal l'apielerent li Breton:
par droit non l'apielent Guinglain,
si est fius monsignor Gavain;
si l'ot de Blancemal, la fee.
5204   Tu l'envoias en ma contree
por moi a rescoure et aidier.
Molt par i a bon chevalier;
jetee m'a de grant torment.
5208   Sire, grant merchis vos en renc
de ço que vos le m'envoiastes,
et ma pucele le cargastes.
A tos jors m'en avés conquisse,
5212   ne jamais n'iert en nule guisse
que treü n'aiés en ma tere,
des que vos l'envoierés quere
de Gales, dont je sui roïne.
5216   Or vos pris, rois de france orine,
que vos a mari me donnés
Guinglain, si ert rois coronnés.
Je le vos quiert et mi baron.
5220   Sire, ne me veés cest don.
En Gales de moi se parti;
onques puis, sire, ne le vi.
Il doit venir ne sai quele eure.
5224   Grant paor ai que tant demeure
ne remaigne en autre païs
et qu'il autre co[n]sel n'ait pris.
Remés est en aucune guerre,
5228   car molt entent a pris conquerre."
Quant li rois entent la parole,

5226 cosel

the lady spoke thus to the king:

5196 "Hear me, my lord," she said.
"I am the daughter of King Guingras,
she to whom you sent the knight
who was called the Fair Unknown.

5200 The Britons called him by the wrong name,
for his true name is Guinglain,
and he is the son of my lord Gawain
and of Blanchemal the Fay.

5204 You sent him to my land
to aid and deliver me.
He is truly an excellent knight,
who rescued me from great suffering.

5208 My lord, I heartily thank you
for having sent him to me
in the company of my lady-in-waiting.
You have won my allegiance forever

5212 and you shall never fail
to receive tribute
as soon as you ask it
from the land of Wales, whose queen I am.

5216 I now request, o king of noble lineage,
that you give me in marriage Guinglain;
he will then be crowned a king.
Both I and my nobles request this of you.

5220 My lord, do not refuse me this boon.
He parted from me in Wales, my lord,
and I have not seen him since that day.
He is to come here, but I do not know when.

5224 I fear from his long delaying
that he may have remained in another land
and taken another decision.
He may well be fighting in some war,

5228 for his heart is set on winning renown."
The king was delighted to hear this,

molt en fu liés, la dame acole.
Gavain et ses hommes apiele,
5232   si lor reconte la nouviele
que la dame li ot contee.
Gavains grant joie en a menee
et bien sot que ses fius estoit
5236   et que la fee amee avoit.
Grant joie en font tuit li baron.
Atant revienent li prisson
qui a la dame s'asanblerent
5240   el cemin u il le troverent.
Au roi se rendirent por pris
si con [Guinglains] lor ot apris.
Saciés lors fu la joie graindre.
5244   Tuit comencent Guinglain a plaindre
de ço qu'i[l] n'estoit pas venus.
Grant dol en fait li rois Artus,
Gavains et tuit cil de la cort: [*150 v°c*]
5248   grant paor ont qu'i[l] ne retort.
Li rois s'est d'iluques levés;
de ses barons a apielés,
a consel d'une part les trait.
5252   Trestous premiers Gavains i vait,
ensanble lui rois Goalans,
et aprés lui i vait Tristrans;
Kes i revient, li senescals,
5256   rois Ama[n]gons, Gales li Caus
et des autres barons asés.
Li rois les [a] araissonnés:
"Signor," fait il, "et qu'en loés

5230 d. apiele a.
5242 c. li rois l.
5245 qu'i
5248 qu'i
5252 p. li rois G. *with* li rois *struck out*
5256 Amagons
5258 a *lacking*

and gave the lady good welcome.
He called Gawain and his other knights
5232 and told them the news
the lady had brought him.
Gawain rejoiced to hear this,
for he knew at once that Guinglain was his son
5236 and that he had loved the fay.
The other nobles rejoiced as well.
Then the knights whom Guinglain had defeated arrived,
the ones who had joined the queen's party
5240 when they met her along the road.
They surrendered themselves to the king,
as Guinglain had told them to do.
You may be sure this increased the joy at the court.
5244 But then they all grew sad
because Guinglain had not arrived.
King Arthur was deeply troubled,
and so was Gawain and the rest of the court:
5248 they greatly feared he would not return.
The king arose;
he called to some of his nobles
and took them aside for counsel.
5252 Gawain was the first to follow him,
and with him went King Goalan,
and afterwards Tristan;
Kay the Seneschal went as well,
5256 King Amangon and Gales the Bald
and many others of the noble lords.
The king addressed them, saying,
"My lords, what advice do you give me

5260 de cel Gui[n]glain dont vos oés?
   Coment recouvrer le porons?
   Grant damage ert se le perdons!
   Por nule rien ne le vau[roie];
5264 jamais mes cuers n'en aroit joie
   tant que nos l'arons recovré."
   Amangons a premiers parlé:
   "Sire," fait il, "vos avrés droit,
5268 car qui tel chevalier perdroit
   molt i averoit grant damage.
   Or vos en dirai mon corage,
   tel consel con je sai donner.
5272 Il ainme molt armes porter:
   faites prendre un tornoiement,
   et ce soit fait proçainnement.
   Et quant cil en ora parler,
5276 saciés qu'il i vaura aler.
   Por nule rien ne.l laissera
   quant la nouviele en apenra
   que il don[c] ne viegne au tornoi.
5280 Iço vos lo en bonne foi.
   Et si vos lo bien de la dame
   que vos lor li donnés a fa[me],
   car molt est ses roiaumes grans,
5284 molt par pora estre poissans.
   Car j'ai esté en cel païs
   a un tornoi u je fui pris.
   Guingras m'acuita sans avoir.
5288 Faites la dame remanoir
   tant qu'aions le tornoi eü
   qui par les marces ert seü.
   Les quatre prisons retenés;
5292 de no mainie les tenés."

5260 Guiglain
5263 ne le vau
5279 dont
5282 fa

5260	concerning Guinglain, of whom you have heard?
	How may we bring him back?
	What a misfortune if we should lose him!
	For nothing in the world would I trade his company;
5264	my heart will never again be glad
	until we have brought him back."
	Amangon was the first to speak:
	"My lord," he said, "you speak rightly,
5268	for whoever lost such a knight as he
	would suffer a great misfortune.
	I shall now tell you my mind,
	the best advice I can give you.
5272	Guinglain so loves to bear arms;
	I suggest, therefore, that you hold a tournament
	sometime not long hence.
	And when he hears the proclamation
5276	you may be sure he will wish to go.
	He will not fail,
	when he hears the news,
	to come to the tournament.
5280	I give you this counsel as your true adviser.
	Regarding the lady, I further advise
	that you give her to him in marriage at that time,
	for she rules a great domain
5284	and Guinglain would then be a powerful king.
	For I myself have been in that land
	at a tourney, where I was defeated.
	King Guingras freed me without any ransom.
5288	Let the lady remain here
	until we have held the tourney,
	and let it be announced in all corners of the realm.
	I suggest that you also retain the four prisoners
5292	among your household knights."

Li rois a le consel loé
et tuit li autre creanté;
tuit sont a cel consel tenu.
5296   Atant sont ariere venu
la u erent li chevalier,
et li rois a fait fiancier
le tornoiement a sa cort,   [*151 r°a*]
5300   et dist que cascuns s'en atort.
La u les plaingnes furent bieles
entre le Castiel as Puceles
e[t] Valedon fu fianciés.
5304   Premiers s'est Tristrans avanciés,
devers Valedon le fianche;
li rois de Montescler s'avanche
qui le fiance d'autre part.
5308   Puis ont del terme pris esgart,
si fu a un mois establis.
Et li rois s'est d'iluec partis,
si a ses mesages tramis
5312   tot maintenant par le païs,
par les marces et par l'enpire
por le tornoi crïer et dire.
La dame dist que remansist
5316   et cele tot son voloir fist.
Les quatre chevaliers prisons
a retenu a conpaignons.
        Guinglains fu ensanble s'amie,
5320   qui dou tot vers lui s'umelie.
Tot avoit ce que il voloit
a l'Ille d'Or u il estoit.
Quant il voloit, s'aloit chacier
5324   et es forés esbanoier
por traire as bestes et berser,
quant lui anuioit sejorner,
u en gibier u en riviere.

5303 en V.
5313 l'epire

The king then praised this counsel
and the others did so as well;
all approved this advice.

5296   The king and his knights then returned
to where the others awaited,
and the king commanded his court
to organize a tourney

5300   and told them all to make preparations.
Upon the beautiful plains
between Valendon and the Castle of the Maidens
the tournament was to take place.

5304   Tristan came forward first
and pledged himself to lead the Valendon side
and then the King of Montescler
pledged himself for the other side.

5308   They fixed the date of the tournament
at one month from that day.
And then the king departed
and told his messengers

5312   to go at once throughout the realm,
through all the empire and outlying lands,
and proclaim the tournament.
He asked Blonde Esmeree to stay,

5316   and she gladly did as he wished.
And the four defeated knights
he retained among his companions.
    Meanwhile Guinglain was with his lady,

5320   who was attentive to his every wish.
He had everything he desired
there on the Golden Isle.
Whenever he wished, he could go out

5324   to amuse himself
hunting wild beasts or birds in the forest
or fish in the river
when he wearied of being in the palace.

5328   Tot avoit quanque bon li ere
de s'amie, tot son voloir.
Tot çou que il voloit avoir
si estoit trestout apresté
5332   ançois que il l'eüst pensé.
En son palais estoit un jor.
Atant es vos un jogleor
qui del tornoi dist les noveles,
5336   qu'al Castiel serroit as Puceles
et ço que molt par serra grant.
Quant Guinglains l'ot, s'en fu joiant:
en son corage se pensa
5340   qu'a cel tornoiement ira.
A s'amie en ala parler
qu'a cel tornoi le laist aler.
Quant cele l'ot, molt [fu] marie,
5344   si dist, "Amis, vos n'irés mie!
Par mon los et par mon otroi
n'irés vos pas a cel tornoi.
Bien ai coneü par mon art
5348   et des estoiles au regart
que se vos au tornoi alés,
que del tot perdue m'avés,
car la vos atent une dame   *[151 r°b]*
5352   qu'Artus vos veut donner a feme."
"Estés, dame," Guinglain respont.
"Par tos les sains qui sont el mont
nesune feme ne prendroie
5356   fors vos, pas ne vos mentiroie.
Dame, volés que je i aille:
je revenrai molt tost, sans faille.
Et se vos plaissoit, bien matin
5360   me coverroit metre au cemin,
qu'autrement venir n'i poroie
se je bien matin ne movoie."
Cele respont, "Mes ciers amis,

5343 fu *lacking*

5328 He had everything that he liked
and all that he wished from his lady.
All he desired
was at once made ready for him,
5332 before his wish had been formed in his mind.
One day Guinglain was in his hall.
Suddenly a jongleur came in
and told of the tournament
5336 at the Castle of the Maidens
and what a great gathering it was to be.
When Guinglain heard this, he rejoiced,
and he fixed in his heart the intention
5340 to go to that tourney.
He went to ask his lady
to give him her leave to go.
When she heard of this, she grew deeply distressed
5344 and said, "My love, you shall not go!
Not by my counsel or with my permission
will you go to that tournament.
For I have seen through my arts
5348 and by consulting the stars
that if you go to that tournament
you will lose me forever,
for there a lady awaits you
5352 whom King Arthur wishes to give you in marriage."
"My lady," he answered, "you need have no fear.
By all the saints in the world I swear
never to take any wife
5356 but you, nor would I ever speak falsely to you.
My lady, give me your leave to go:
I will quickly return, of that there is no doubt.
And if you consent, I must set out
5360 quite early tomorrow morning,
for I could not otherwise
arrive in time."
She answered him, "My dear love,

5364 bien sai qu'ensi l'avés enpris
d'aler a cel tornoiement,
mais ce n'ert pas a mon talent.
Bien sai vos ne m'avés tant chiere
5368 que le laissiés por ma proiere.
Je n'en puis mais, ce poisse moi.
Or puet on veïr vostre foi."
Riens ne puet Guinglain retenir
5372 car molt cuide tost revenir.
De l'aler grant talent avoit
et molt couvoitous en estoit,
car grant piece avoit ja esté
5376 que il n'avoit armes porté.
Guinglains cuit del tot son corage;
ainc om ne fist si grant folage.
Son escuier apiele et dist
5380 que son hauber li blancesist
et que son harnois aprestast,
et demain lever s'aprestast
et si ait tos mises ses sieles.
5384 Robers fu liés de ces novieles;
tot le harnois a atorné
si con Guinglains l'ot comandé.
Li jors faut, la nuis est venue.
5388 Guinglains se couce les sa drue;
dalés li se jut tote nuit,
si orent molt de lor deduit.
Por ce que main devoit lever
5392 et puis sor son ceval monter
s'est endormis dalés s'amie,
car ses corages le desfie.
Qui le bien voit et le mal prent,
5396 saciés que aprés s'en repent.
Quant Guinglains au matin s'esvelle,
de ce qu'il vit ot grant mervele
car il se trova en un bois.
5400 Dalés lui trova son harnois;
son cief tenoit sor son escu
et devant lui si ra veü

5364   I know you have set your heart
on going to that tournament,
but it will be against my will.
I see that you do not love me enough

5368   to renounce this because I ask you to do so.
I can do nothing more, and this grieves me sorely.
Now it is clear what your pledge to me is worth."
Nothing could keep Guinglain from going,

5372   for he truly believed he would quickly return.
His desire to go was great
and he deeply longed to do so,
for it had been a long time

5376   since he had borne his arms.
Guinglain put his faith in his heart's desire;
no man ever committed such folly.
He called to Robert his squire and told him

5380   to polish his hauberk,
prepare his equipment,
and plan to rise early
to saddle the horses.

5384   Robert was happy to hear this;
he readied all the equipment
as Guinglain had commanded.
Day came to an end and so night fell.

5388   Guinglain lay down beside his love;
he lay by her side all night
and they took love's greatest delights.
Since he had to rise early

5392   and ride away,
he fell asleep at his lady's side,
for his heart's desire was working against him.
Who sees the good and chooses the bad

5396   will soon regret it, of that you may be certain.
When Guinglain awoke the next morning,
he was amazed
to find himself in a forest.

5400   Beside him was his equipment;
his head was resting on his shield,
and before him he saw

son ceval qui fu atachiés.   [*151 r°c*]
5404   Robert ra veü a ses piés;
        par le frain son renchi tenoit,
        desous son cief un fust avoit.
        Or lor a mestier garisson!
5408   De tel penser, tel gueredon.
        Quant li uns a l'autre veü,
        molt en sont andoi esperdu.
        Bien voit Guinglains mal a esté.
5412   Li uns a l'autre resgardé.
        "Robert," dist Guinglains, "que dis tu:
        avons nos ci anuit jeü?
        Ersoir me couçai je ailloirs
5416   dalés m'amie a grans honnors.
        Or me sui en un bois trovés,
        tos esbahis et esgarés.
        Et tu, venis te ci ersoir?"
5420   Ce dist Robers, "Naie, por voir!
        Ersoir en mon lit me dormi.
        Or me resui trovés ichi."
        "Robert, con male destinee!
5424   Molt ai m'amie mal gardee.
        Bien me dist ier soir je.l perdroie
        se je au tornoi m'en aloie.
        Perdue l'ai par mon folage.
5428   Halas!" fait il, "con grant damage!
        Or ai je tos jors mais dolor."
        Et Robert dist a son signo[r],
        "Sire, nos n'en poons el faire,
5432   mais alons ent en nostre afaire.
        Grans bien nos puet aventurer;
        on ne se doit desconforter."
        Guinglains res[pont], "Donques alons."

5410 andoi *repeated*
5428 con *repeated*
5430 signon
5435 G. res D

his horse, which had been tied up.
5404 At his feet lay Robert,
his head resting on a tree trunk
and holding the reins of a packhorse.
Now they were truly in need of aid!
5408 As a man sows, so shall he reap.
When the knight and the squire beheld each other,
they were both quite bewildered.
Guinglain could see that some misfortune had occurred.
5412 They looked at each other.
"Robert," said Guinglain, "what do you say to this:
did we sleep here during the night?
But last night I went to a different bed,
5416 beside my lady, who showed me all honor.
Now I find myself in a wood,
quite bewildered and at a loss.
And you, did you come to this place last night?"
5420 Robert said, "Indeed, I did not!
I fell asleep in my bed last night.
And now, like you, I find myself here."
"Robert, what a cruel fate!
5424 How foolishly I have lost my lady.
Last night she said I would lose her
if I left her to go to the tourney.
I have lost her now through my folly.
5428 Alas, what a terrible loss!
Now I must grieve for the rest of my days."
And Robert said to his lord,
"My lord, there is nothing we can do about this;
5432 let us therefore pursue our business.
Great good may thereby come to us;
a man should never give in to his sorrow."
Guinglain answered, "Let us go then."

5436 Atant cauce ses esperons;
     li escuiers l'aubert torsa
     et cil sor son ceval monta,
     si se sont mis en un sentier.
5440 Des or pensent de chevaucier
     tant qu'il trovent un pelerin
     qui lor ensaigne le cemin
     le plus droit au tornoiement.
5444 Molt fu Guinglains en grant torment.
     Cel jor cevaucha tos iriés
     et tos dolans et coreciés
     de ce que s'amie ot perdue;
5448 ne set que ele est devenue.
              Or cevaucent plains et boscages
     et landes et vals et rivages.
     Tant ont erré par les contrees
5452 et tant erré par lor jornees
     et tant lor droite voie tinrent
     qu'al Castiel des Puceles vinrent.
     Quant il sont au Castiel venu,   [*151 v°a*]
5456 tot s'en estoient ja issu
     li chevalier por tornoier.
     Guinglains ne se vaut plus targier
     ains s'en est aprés els alés,
5460 si a les chevaliers trovés
     qui lor cauces de fer cauçoient
     et a coroies les laçoient.
     Molt i ot grant chevalerie.
5464 Yvains, li rois de Lindezie,
     i fu bien a set vins escus,
     hiaumes laciés, haubers vestus.
     D'Escoce i fu rois A[n]guizans,
5468 qui s'armoit [sos] deus arbres grans;

5450 b *unexpuncted before* rivages
5464 Lindezeie
5467 Aguizans
5468 sor

5436	He put on his spurs;
	Robert folded his master's hauberk,
	Guinglain mounted his horse,
	and they set off along their way.
5440	They journeyed until
	they met a pilgrim
	who showed them the shortest
	road to the tournament.
5444	Guinglain was plunged in the deepest anguish.
	All that day he rode along greatly troubled,
	filled with grief and dismay
	because he had lost his lady;
5448	he did not know what had become of her.
	They rode through fields and woodlands,
	though glades and valleys and along rivers.
	They rode through many lands
5452	and for many long days
	and kept to their path
	until they came to the Castle of the Maidens.
	When they arrived there,
5456	all the knights had left
	to go to the tournament.
	Guinglain did not wish to delay any further,
	and so he followed after the knights
5460	and found them
	putting on their iron leggings,
	lacing them up with thongs.
	A very fine company of knights had assembled there.
5464	Yvain, the king of Lindezie,
	was there with a hundred and forty strong,
	their helmets all laced and wearing their hauberks.
	King Aguizan, who had come from Scotland,
5468	stood arming himself beneath two tall trees;

```
        set vins chevaliers ot o soi
        qui tot furent a son conroi.
        De Gohenet li rois Hoël,
5472    issus sor un ceval isnel;
        o soi avoit cent chevaliers,
        molt bien armés, sor les destriers.
        Et li rois de Baradigan
5476    que o[n] apiele Canaan,
        il fu armés en la canpaigne;
        quatre vins ot en sa conpaigne.
        Rois Ban de Gom[or]et i fu;
5480    nuef vins en sont o soi issu.
        Li rois de la Roge Cité
        cent chevaliers ot amené;
        et Guivrés i refu, li rois,
5484    qui ot amenés les Irois.
        Geldras, li rois de Dunelie,
        cil vint ot grant chevalerie,
        quatre cens chevaliers amainne
5488    que il tenoit o soi demainne.
        Li Lais Hardis de Cornouaille
        est venus au tornoi, sans faille;
        cent chevaliers amainne o soi,
5492    n'i a celui n'ait bon conroi.
        Kahadinst i estoit venus
        qui de Lanprebois estoit dus.
        Li Sors i fu de Montescler,
5496    son elme lace, bel et cler;
        deseure ot une conissance.
        Acuitier i vint sa fiance:
        set cens chevaliers amena
5500    por ce que il le fiancha.
        S'i fu Percevals li Galois,
        uns chevaliers preus et cortois.
```

5476 o
5479 Li r. B. de Gomet i fu
5485 Duneline

he had a hundred and forty knights with him,
whom he had equipped himself.
King Hoël of Gohenet
5472 had ridden forth on a swift horse;
with him he had a hundred knights,
very well armed on their chargers.
And the king of Baradigan,
5476 who was known as Canaan,
stood already armed in the field of combat;
there were eighty in his company.
King Ban of Gomoret was there,
5480 and with him a hundred and eighty men.
The King of the Red City
had brought a hundred knights;
And King Guivret was there as well,
5484 along with his Irishmen;
Geldras, the king of Dunelie,
had come with a great company of knights:
he led four hundred,
5488 all of them his own vassals.
The Ugly Hero of Cornwall
had come to the tournament, of that you may be certain;
he had brought with him a hundred knights,
5492 and not a one of them badly equipped.
Kahadinst, the Duke of Lanprebois,
had also come.
The Red-Haired Knight of Montescler
5496 was lacing on his glittering helmet;
on it he had fixed his emblem.
He was there to fulfill his pledge:
he had brought seven hundred knights with him,
5500 for he had vowed to do so.
Perceval the Welshman was there as well,
a knight both valiant and courtly.

Li Vallés de [B]aladingant
5504 i fu armés molt richemant
et voloit aler asanbler
contre le Sor de Mon[t]escler.
Et Lansselos dou Lac se rarme   [*151v°b*]
5508 en un onbrier dalés un carme.
Li dus Elias i refu,
ki le poi[l] ot entrekenu,
mais molt i ot bon chevalier
5512 et bien savoit un droit jugier.
Et cil de la Haute Montaingne
i refu a molt grant conpaingne.
De Truerem li quens i fu,
5516 armés sor un ceval krenu;
miudres ne fu onques a dire;
de l'Ille Noires estoit sire.
Grahelens de Fine Posterne
5520 se rarmoit dalés une ierne,
les lui ses freres Guingam[u]er,
ki s'entramerent de bon cuer.
Et Raidurains i fu armés,
5524 en cui avoit molt de bontés.
Tos armés i refu Yder
sor un ceval covert de fer.
Gandelus fu ensanble lui;
5528 bon chevalier furent andui.
De Gorhout i refu Gormans
et de Lis i fu Melians.
D'uns et d'autres tant i avoit
5532 que nus le nonbre n'en savoit.
Molt bel estoit cele c[o]npaingne.
De l'autre part, devers Bretaingne,

5503 Paladingant
5506 Monescler
5510 poit
5521 Guingamier
5533 canpaingne

	The Knight of Baladingant
5504	was also there, splendidly armed
	and eager to do combat
	with the Red-Haired Knight of Montescler.
	And Lancelot of the Lake was arming himself
5508	in the shade of a hornbeam tree.
	Duke Elias was there as well,
	a very fine knight
	despite his gray hairs
5512	and a man of the most excellent judgment.
	And the Knight of the High Mountain
	was there as well with a fine company.
	The Count of Truerem was there,
5516	already armed on a horse with flowing mane;
	no one could tell you of a finer knight
	than this man, who was lord of the Black Isle.
	Grahelens of Fine Posterne
5520	was arming himself beside a bush
	not far from his brother Guingamuer;
	these two loved each other dearly.
	And Radurans, a man of many fine qualities,
5524	was being armed there as well.
	Yder was already fully armed
	on a horse well armored in mail.
	with him was Gandelus;
5528	both of these men were fine knights.
	Gornemant of Gorhout was also there,
	along with Meliant of Lis.
	These two had so many knights with them
5532	that no one could tell their number.
	This was indeed a splendid company.
	On the other side, fighting for Britain,

estoit Artus et si baron
5536   qui estoit devers Valendon.
        Molt ravoit devers lui grans gens;
        a ensaigne en ot bien vint cens.
        De la refu Gaudins li rois
5540   d'Illande, qui molt fu cortois,
        et avoit en sa conpaignie
        cinc cens chevaliers de mainnie.
        S'i fu rois Mars de Cornouaille,
5544   et avoit bien en sa bataille
        set cens chevaliers desfensables,
        molt biaus de cors et honnerables.
        Li rois Amangons i estoit
5548   qui aveuc lui mile en avoit,
        et des Illes li rois Bruians
        seur destriers sors, bais et bauçans,
        o cinc cens chevaliers armés
5552   qui ja millors ne demandés.
        Hardis estoit come lupars
        mais molt ert de donner escars.
        Et si refu li rois Ydés
5556   qui donnoit a trestols adés;
        il fu de pouvre acointement,
        mais large fu a tote gent.
        Uit vins en ot a sa baniere;   [151v°c]
5560   n'i a celui qui bien ne fiere.
        La roïne Blonde Esmere[e]
        en i ot cent de sa contree
        qu'ele ot amenés el païs,
5564   se.s ot a cel tornoi tramis;
        a Lanpart les avoit carciés,
        se.s ot de bien faire proiés.
        Gavains i fu, li niés Artu;
5568   miudres de lui ne fu veü.
        Et s'i estoit le rois Mordrés

5547 r. avoi A.
5561 Esmere

were Arthur and his noble lords,
5536 who had assembled near Valenden.
Arthur had a great number of knights
under his banner, two thousand or more.
Gaudin, the king of Ireland,
5540 a most courtly man, was among them,
and in his company
five hundred of his household knights.
King Mark of Cornwall was there as well,
5544 with a good seven hundred to fight alongside him,
men able to give a good account of themselves,
men of honor and handsome in arms.
King Amangon was there
5548 with a thousand knights
and King Bruians of the Isles
with five hundred armed knights
on sorrel, bay, and piebald horses,
5552 such fine men you could ask for none better.
This Bruians was bold as a leopard,
but a stingy man with his goods.
And King Yder was there as well,
5556 a man free and easy in giving;
although not splendidly equipped,
he was generous to all.
A hundred and sixty rode under his banner,
5560 all of them able in combat.
And the queen, Blonde Esmeree,
had a hundred knights from her country,
whom she had brought with her
5564 and now led to the tourney;
she had given Lampart command of these knights
and urged them on to fine deeds.
Gawain was there, King Arthur's nephew;
5568 no one ever saw a knight finer than he.
And King Mordred was there

et uns suens freres Segurés.
Et Gunes, nés d'Oïrecestre
5572   estoit dalés Gavain a destre.
Et li riches dus de Norgales
i fu, et Erec d'Estregales
et Bedüer de Normendie
5576   i fu o biele conpaignie.
Flores i ravoit, des François,
uns rices dus, soisante et trois.
De Nantes i refu Hoël
5580   qui s'armoit dejoste un ruissel.
Armés se restoit Careheuls
et Tors, li fius le rois Arels.
Tristrans se restoit ja armés
5584   et de bien faire ert aprestés.
Le tornoi avoit fianchie
et portoit le mance s'amie;
Yseuls la biele l'ot tramisse;
5588   deseur son hauberc l'avoit misse.
Por asanbler el ceval monte
et li autre dont ne sai conte.
De la Ronde Table li [pl]us
5592   estoi[en]t [o] le roi Artus.
Quant armé furent li baron
en la plaingne sous Valenton,
la veïssiés tant elme cler
5596   et tante ensaingne venteler
et tant destriers bauchant et bai
. . . .
et tans escus reflanboier
5600   et tante guinple desploier
sor elmes tantes conissances,
tant blanc hauber et tantes lances

5571 niés d.
5583 Tristraans
5591 libnus
5592 estoit aveuc le

with a brother of his, named Segures.
And Gunes of Worcester
5572 rode at Gawain's right hand.
And the powerful Duke of North Wales
was there, along with Erec of East Wales;
and Bedevere of Normandy
5576 was there with a splendid company.
Flores, a powerful duke,
led sixty-three French knights.
From Nantes there was Hoel,
5580 who was arming himself by a stream.
And Caraés was arming himself as well
along with Tors, the son of King Arel.
Tristan stood already armed
5584 and ready for valorous deeds.
He had pledged to fight in this tournament
and he bore the sleeve of his lady;
the fair Yseut had sent him this sleeve,
5588 and he had fixed it to his hauberk.
He mounted for the combat
along with all the others, whose number I could not tell you.
Most of the knights of the Round Table
5592 were there on King Arthur's side.
When all these knights had armed themselves
in the plain below Valenton,
there were so many bright helmets
5596 and so many fluttering banners,
so many chargers, both spotted and bay,
. . . .
and bright shields flashing
5600 and pennants unfurling,
so many emblems on helmets,
so many bright hauberks and lances

             paintes a or et a ason,
5604   fremir tant vermel siglaton
             et tant pingnon et tante mance,
             et çainte tante espee blance
             et tant bon chevalier de pris,
5608   tant roi, tant conte, tant marcis—
             jamais tels jens n'iert asanblee!
             Li jors fu bials par la contree
             et la place fu grans et lee.
5612   Atant e vos par la valee   [*152 r°a*]
             venir le Sor de Montescler;
             a Tristran venoit asanbler.
             O lui avoit vint chevaliers;
5616   por joster venoit tos premiers.
             Atant es vos Tristran u vint;
             l'escu au co[l], la lance tint;
             sa route grans aprés venoit.
5620   Quant li uns l'autre venir voit,
             si traient avant les escus
             qu'il avoient au col pendus
             et poingnent les chevals andui.
5624   Tristrans le fiert et il sor lui
             de la lance par tel ang[oi]sse
             que sor Tristran sa lance froisse;
             et Tristans le ra si feru
5628   deseur la boucle de l'escu
             que tant con la hanste li dure,
             l'abati a la terre dure;
             le ceval prent delés se jent.
5632   Atant la route au Soir [se prent]
             trestout ensanble a le rescosse;
             sor lui cascuns sa lance estrousse.

5617 vient
5618 cos
5625 angausse
5626 la lance *after* sor *struck out*
5632 A. la r. au S. [-2, *em. Williams*]

painted in gold and blue,
5604 and red silk streamers and sleeves
flying in the breeze,
so many bright swords girded on for combat,
and so many valiant knights,
5608 marquis and counts and kings—
never was such a company assembled!
The day was fair,
the field of battle was splendid and wide.
5612 The Red-Haired Knight of Montescler
came riding down the valley;
he sought to joust with Tristan.
With him rode twenty knights;
5616 he was the first to ride forward for combat.
And then Tristan rode forth,
his shield at his neck and grasping his lance,
his own large company following after.
5620 When the knights saw each other,
they positioned the shields
that hung from their necks
and spurred their horses forward.
5624 They struck each other
with such great force
that the Red-Haired knight broke his lance;
and Tristan struck him
5628 such a blow on the boss of his shield
with the strong shaft of his lance
that he hurled him to the ground.
He took the man's horse to entrust to his men.
5632 At once the Red-Haired Knight's company
rushed as one man to the rescue,
their lances at the ready;

Cil se tient bien qu'il ne caï,
5636   mais le destrier lor a gerpi.
Por Tristran rescorre et aidier
repoingnent tuit li chevalier
sor cels au Sor de Montescler.
5640   La veïssiés maint cop donner,
ferir de lances et d'espees,
quant les routes sont asanblees.
Molt le fist b[ie]n et belement
5644   li Vallés de Baladi[n]gant.
Le Sor rescoust par sa poissance:
tant i feri cols de sa lance
que molt en abati le jor.
5648   Molt le faissoit bien en l'estor
quant sor lui vint li rois Idés
et si conpaingnon a eslais.
Li Valés se va desfendant,
5652   et cil li viegnent atangnant
encontreval une praiele.
La ot widié mainte sele
et maint chevalier abatu.
5656   Por poi que n'orent reten[u]
le Vallet de Baladingant
quant le reçut Brus de Bralant.
Set vins chevaliers ot o soi;
5660   il point as gens Yder le roi.
Cil relaissent cevaus aler,
durement les vont encontrer.
La ot tant gonfanon brissié
5664   et tant chevalier trebuchié   [*152 r°b*]
et tant cheval i ot perdu.
Atant es vos Guinglain venu
qui ariere s'estoit armés.
5668   Quant il ot les rens regardés,

5643 bn [*ligature bar lacking*]
5644 Baladigant
5656 retene

Tristan held fast in his saddle,
5636 but had to give back the horse he had taken.
Then all of Tristan's knights
spurred forward to aid him
against the men of the Red-Haired Knight.
5640 Many a blow was given there
with lances and swords
when these two companies came together.
The Knight of Baladingant
5644 fought skillfully and well.
By his strength he rescued the Red-Haired Knight:
he struck so many blows with his lance
that he unhorsed many a knight that day.
5648 He was fighting quite superbly
when King Yder bore down upon him
along with his companions.
The young knight defended himself well as he rode,
5652 but Yder's men caught up with him
at the edge of a meadow.
There many were unhorsed
and many hurled to the ground.
5656 Yder's men would have captured
the Knight of Baladingant
had Brun of Bralant not protected him.
Brun had a hundred and forty knights with him,
5660 and he spurred toward King Yder's company.
These in turn gave their horses free rein
and rushed to meet them head on.
Many standards were broken there,
5664 many knights thrown from their horses,
and many horses lost to their riders.
But suddenly Guinglain appeared;
he had armed himself in the rear.
5668 When he had observed the assembled ranks,

si laisse corre le ceval
et fiert si Kels le senescal,
qui venus estoit asanbler.
5672   L'escu li fist au braç hurter
et les estriers li fist laissier
si qu'envers l'abat del destrier.
Ver le roi Ider point avant,
5676   si le fert sor l'escu devant
de la lance par tel devisse,
l'escu perce, la lance brisse.
En sa main retint le tronçon
5680   et vait ferir tot a bandon
del tros de lance qu'il tenoit
la u la grinnor presse avoit
sor cel elme par tel aïr
5684   si que le renc fait tot fremir.
Sovent gue[n]cist, point et desroie;
quel part qu'il voist faissoit bien voie.
Molt par estoit grans li tornois
5688   de dus, de contes et de rois.
Li rois Mars point et sa bataille,
qui sire estoit de Cornouaille;
contre lui point li rois Hoël
5692   et cent chevalier a isnel.
Li un vont les autre ferir,
la presse fissent departir.
Escus fendent, h[ia]umes esclicent,
5696   escus esfondrent et deslicent.
Li rois Bruians vint au tornoi
et fist apoindre son conroi;
et li bons rois [Gaudins] d'Illande
5700   ses chevaliers poindre comande.
Bruians point desous devers destre

5685 guecist
5695 haiumes
5696 deslicencent
5699 Condrins

he galloped forward
and struck Kay the Seneschal,
who had come to join the fighting.
5672   He hit him on the arm with his shield,
which caused him to lose his stirrups
and fall from his horse.
Then he spurred forward toward King Yder
5676   and struck him squarely on his shield
with such great skill
that he pierced Yder's shield and shattered his own lance.
Holding fast to his broken lance,
5680   Guinglain struck again and again
with the stump
so forcefully on whatever helmets he saw
there where the fighting was thickest
5684   that he broke the ranks of the assembled knights.
Again and again he attacked, then wheeled and slipped away.
Wherever he went he cleared a path before him.
Great indeed was this tournament,
5688   with so many dukes and counts and kings.
King Mark, the lord of Cornwall,
along with his knights, spurred his horse to a gallop ;
against him charged King Hoël
5692   with his own hundred knights.
These two groups engaged one another,
causing the crowds around them to flee.
They split shields, shattered helmets,
5696   smashed shields into splinters.
King Bruians rushed into the fighting
and ordered his knights to the gallop;
and noble King Gaudin of Ireland
5700   commanded his knights to set spurs to their horses.
Bruians rode toward the right

et li rois [Gaudins] vers senestre.
Le tornoi ont andui forclos;
5704   le roi Hoël i ont enclos
et abatu de son destrier.
Illuec ot pris maint chevalier,
maint cop receü et donné.
5708   Par mi les plains et par le pré
les encaucent tos desconfis.
Molt i fu grans li capleïs!
Quant Guinglains torna et guencist,
5712   le cheval poi[n]t, l'anste brandist.
Fiert le roi Gaudi[n] en l'escu,
trestout li a frait et fendu.
Atant li rois Bruians dessere;
5716   li cevals met les piés a terre   [*152 r°c*]
vers Guinglain et Guinglains vers lui,
si s'entreviennent anbedui.
Lances orent roides et fors
5720   si se fierent par tels esfors
desor les boucles des escus,
desque sor les haubers menus
en fist cascuns passer le fer;
5724   mais molt sont rice li hauber,
que maille n'en fausse ne ront.
Des lances volent contre mont
les esclices et li tronçon.
5728   Molt bien se tien[nent] li baron,
qu'il ne s'entr'abatirent mie.
Guinglains tint l'espee forbie,
des esperons fiert le ceval.
5732   En son pui[n]c tint le branc roial
et fiert Mordet sor l'elme cler

5702 Baudrins
5712 poit
5713 Gaudi
5728 tient
5732 puic

and Gaudin toward the left.
Between them they scattered the fighting men
5704 and trapped King Hoël,
hurling him from his horse.
There many a knight was captured,
many a blow received and given.
5708 Across the fields and meadows
they drove their opponents in disarray.
What a great battle this was!
But Guinglain turned and veered away,
5712 spurring his horse and brandishing his lance.
He struck King Gaudin's shield,
smashing and shattering it.
Then King Bruians galloped up;
5716 his horse charged forward
toward Guinglain and Guinglain toward Bruians,
and so they hurled together.
Their lances were strong and stout,
5720 and they struck each other with such force
on the bosses of their shields
that the tips of both lances
pierced right through to the fine mesh of the hauberks;
5724 but the hauberks were good ones,
and they did not tear or break a single link.
Bits of their lances
flew up in the air.
5728 Both knights held fast in their saddles
and neither unhorsed the other.
His gleaming sword in his hand,
Guinglain spurred his horse forward.
5732 He grasped his excellent sword
and struck Mordred on his shining helmet,

si que tot le fist estonner;
sor le col del destrier le plaisse.
5736   Autre refiert et celui laisse
de l'espee par sous l'escu
que tot li a frait et fendu.
Molt durement se desfendoit
5740   de l'espee que il tenoit.
En la presse se met souvent;
si bien le fait, si se desfent
et tant i fiert cols demanois
5744   que tos recovre li tornois.
Tuit recouvrent cil devers lui
en un biau plain au pié d'un pui.
La ot feru de grans colees
5748   de roides lances et d'espees.
Molt par estoit li caples grans!
Bien le faisoit li rois Bruians
qui devers les Bretons estoit.
5752   Le roi Hoël tot pris avoit
quant point li rois Cadoalens,
o lui de chevaliers trois cens;
les lui li rois de Lindesie
5756   qui molt ravoit grant conpaignie.
Andoi sont au tornoi venu;
par mi les rens se sont feru.
La ot maint escu estroué
5760   et maint chevalier aterré,
tant gaïgnié et tant perdu,
tant cop donné, tant receü
et tante lance peçoïe
5764   et tant de siele i ot widie,
tant fierent d'antes et de tros
que le roi Hoël ont rescos.
Les un rocier en un biaus pres
5768   estoit li tornois arestés.   [152 v°a]
Iluec ot mainte joste faite,

5735 l *before* col *expuncted*

leaving him dazed
and slumped down on the neck of his charger.

5736 Guinglain left Mordred and struck another
on his shield with his sword,
completely smashing and shattering it.
He defended himself fiercely

5740 with the sword that he grasped.
Again and again he plunged into the fighting;
he fought with such skill, he defended himself so well,
and struck such forceful blows

5744 that he turned the tide of the tournament.
The knights on his side all rallied around him
in a fair plain at the foot of a hill.
There many great blows were struck

5748 with stout lances and swords.
This was a great battle indeed!
King Bruians, on the side of the Britons,
was fighting most ably.

5752 He had only just captured King Hoël
when King Cadoalens came riding up
with three hundred knights;
beside him rode the king of Lindezie,

5756 who had a large company with him as well.
Both joined in the combat,
tearing into the rows of fighting men.
Many a shield was pierced

5760 and many a knight was knocked to the ground,
Much was won and much was lost,
and many blows were given and taken,
lances were shattered

5764 and saddles were emptied
and many blows struck with sheared-off lances
before these two companies rescued King Hoël.
There by a rock in a beautiful meadow

5768 the tournament gathered.
Many a joust was fought there,

maint cop feru d'espee traite.
    Entre deus rens Guinglains estoit;
5772   l'escu au col, l'anste tenoit
et sist deseur un vair destrier
qu'ot gaïgnié d'un chevalier;
a joste l'avoit abatu.
5776   Vers le cief dou rent a veü
Erec, un molt bon chevalier
sor un cheval fort et legier;
por joster avoit l'escu pris
5780   et le lance sor fautre mis.
Guinglains encontre lui s'adrece,
l'ante brandist, l'escu enbrece,
des esperons au cheval donne.
5784   Li uns envers l'autre esperonne,
molt tres durement se requierent;
par si grant vertu s'entrefierent
que li escu percent et croissent
5788   et les lances brissent et froissent.
Ensanble hurtent li ceval;
molt bien se tinrent li vasal
que l'uns ne l'autres ne balance.
5792   Atant Guinglains prist une lance
que Robers li ot aportee.
Sa regne a autre part tornee
quant le roi Cadoi[c] poindre voit
5796   qui devers les Bretons estoit.
Set vins chevaliers ot o soi
qui tot poingnent a son conroi;
au renc venoient por ferir.
5800   Et quant Guinglains les vit venir,
si lor laisse cevals aler;
tos les vait ensanble encontrer,

5773 deseuer
5781 G. *rather than* GG. *for* Guinglains
5785 durerement
5795 Cadoit

many a blow was struck with drawn sword.
As for Guinglain, he rode between two companies,
5772 his shield at his neck and his lance in his hand,
astride a dappled charger
he had won from a knight
whom he had unseated.
5776 At the head of one company he saw
Erec, an excellent knight,
astride a strong, swift horse;
he had taken up his shield to joust
5780 and set his lance in its rest.
Guinglain turned toward Erec,
brandishing his lance and holding tight to his shield,
and spurred his horse forward.
5784 They galloped toward each other
and hurled together with a fearful clash;
they struck each other with such great force
that they pierced and smashed each other's shields
5788 and shattered their lances.
The horses struck each other hard,
but the knights held fast in their saddles
and neither unhorsed the other.
5792 Then Guinglain took up a fresh lance,
which Robert had brought to him.
He turned his horse in another direction
when he saw King Cadoc,
5796 who was fighting for the Britons, come galloping forward.
Cadoc had a hundred and forty knights,
all charging along with him;
they rode forward to strike the assembled knights.
5800 And when Guinglain saw them coming,
he gave his horse free rein;
he charged them all,

si a Cadoc premiers feru
5804   qu'a devant les autres veü.
Feru l'a par si grant puissance
droit en mi le pis de la lance
que nule riens ne.l pot tenir
5808   qu'a terre ne.l fesist venir.
Mais les gens Cadoc poingnent lors
tot sor Guinglain a grant esfors.
Molt durement le vont ferir
5812   et ains qu'il se peüst guencir,
l'orent de maintes pars feru,
qui sor elme, qui sor escu
u sor hauberc u sor destrier.
5816   Guinglains traist l'espee d'acier,
si se desfent come lupars.
Cil li furent de totes pars
qui molt se painnent de lui prendre.
5820   Lors veïssiés home desfendre   *[152 v°b]*
et ferir grans cols de l'espee!
Qui il consiut fiert tel colee
que puis n'ot talent de retor
5824   ariere en cel liu en estor.
Guinglains fu forclos en la presse.
Atant li rois Geldras s'eslesse
et la route qu'avuec lui erre;
5828   uit vins furent a sa baniere.
Les lui repoi[n]t uns rices rois,
Guivrés, li sires des Irois;
cent chevaliers ot de gra[n]t los.
5832   La u Guinglains estoit forclos
poingnent ensanble li doi roi
et lor chevalier a desroi.
Durement vienent por ferir.
5836   Rois Ama[n]gons les vit venir

5829 repoit
5831 grart
5836 Amagons

striking first Cadoc,
5804 whom he saw in the lead.
He struck him with such force
full in the chest with his lance
that nothing could have prevented the king
5808 from being hurled to the ground.
But then Cadoc's men charged forward
at full speed toward Guinglain.
They meant to strike him hard,
5812 and before he could turn aside,
they had attacked him from many sides—
some struck his helmet, some his shield,
some his hauberk, and some his charger.
5816 Guinglain drew his steel sword
and fought like a leopard.
The knights bore down on him from all sides,
doing their best to take him captive.
5820 Here was a man defending himself well
and striking great blows with his sword!
All those he pursued he struck so hard
that they soon had no wish
5824 to return to the fighting.
Guinglain was trapped in the thick of the combat.
Now came King Geldras
and the company that rode with him;
5828 a hundred and forty followed his banner.
Beside him galloped a powerful king,
Guivret, the lord of the Irish,
and with him a hundred knights of renown.
5832 These two kings
and their knights rushed forward
to the place where Guinglain had been surrounded.
They charged with great force to attack.
5836 King Amangon, who was fighting for the Britons,

qui fu devers cels de Bretaingne,
cent chevaliers en sa conpaingne;
rois Bans de Gomorret ausi,
5840   il et tuit si home autresi—
cent chevaliers avoit et plus.
Cascuns s'est en l'estor ferus.
Cil doi roi pongnent contre cels.
5844   Molt [fu] cil encontres cruels;
de fors lances se vont ferir.
La oïssiés escus croissir
et seur chevals gens enforcier
5848   et tant chevalier trebucier!
La fu abatus Amangons
et asés de ses conpaignons.
Geldras li rois abatus ere
5852   tos envers en une jonciere.
Illueques p[o]ingnent tuit ensanble;
tos li tornois sor eils asanble.
Molt s'esforçoient de tos sens.
5856   Iluecques fu li caples grans!
Fierent de tronçons et d'espees.
La veïssiés tantes mellees
por le gaai[n]g, por les prissons
5860   et por les bons destriers gascons!
Guinglans point souvent par le plag[ne]
et sist sor un ceval d'Espaingne.
Souvent le point des esperons
5864   et souvent guencist as Bretons.
Chevaliers prent, cevals gaaigne
mais molt petit mener les daig[ne].
Quant il trove qui li requiere,
5868   si lé donne sans grant proiere.

5844 fu *lacking*
5853 paingnent
5859 gaaig
5861 plag
5866 daig

saw them coming;
he had a hundred knights in his company;
King Ban of Gomoret rode forward as well,
5840 along with all his men—
he had a hundred knights and more.
Each plunged into the fighting.
These two kings charged the other knights.
5844 This was a mighty clash indeed,
for they attacked with strong lances.
What a din as shields were smashed
and knights were captured on their horses
5848 and many others hurled to the ground!
There Amangon was unhorsed,
along with many of his companions.
King Geldras was knocked
5852 from his horse into a marsh.
All the combatants rushed to the scene,
and the whole tournament drew in about them.
Both sides grew in numbers from every direction.
5856 What a great combat this was!
Knights struck blows with swords and broken lances.
What struggles there were
for prizes, for prisoners,
5860 and fine Gascon horses!
Again and again Guinglain raced over the field,
astride a Spanish horse.
He spurred him again and again
5864 to charge at the Britons.
He captured knights and took chargers,
but took no care to hold them.
He readily gave them over
5868 to anyone who asked him.

Quanques il gaaigne as Bretons
donne as croisiés et as prisons.
Plus le criement li chevalier
5872   qu'estornel ne font esprevier.   [152 v°c]
Erec molt bien le refaisoit.
Et Guinglains lors venus estoit;
entre deus rens point et desroie,
5876   s'a encontré en mi sa voie
le rice conte Galoain.
A son ceval lasque le frain,
si le fiert si de grant ravine
5880   en l'escu deseur la poitrine
que tot l'escu li perce et brisse
si que del bon ceval de Frisse
le trebucha en[s] e[l] sablon.
5884   Puis point vers un autre a bandon,
si le fiert si sor le mamiele,
ne.l pot tenir potrals ne siele
que ne l'abatist del destrier.
5888   De l'anste volent li quartier.
Puis a mis le main a l'espee;
le ceval point par mi la pree,
les rens cerçoit de totes pars.
5892   Molt bien le refaisoit Lanpars;
souvent poignoit par le tornoi.
A cent chevaliers qu'ot o soi
des chevaliers Blonde Esmeree;
5896   li biens faires molt lor agree.
Lanpars bien les caele et guie;
bien fust mis en lui grans baillie.
Sa roite molt bien le faissoit
5900   et il adiés primes feroit
et au retort venoit deriere.
Molt le font bien de grant maniere.

5874 G. *rather than* GG. *for* Guinglains
5883 en ens s.

Whatever he won from the Britons he freely gave to knights
who had taken the cross or been made prisoner.
The knights feared Guinglain more
5872 than the sparrow fears the hawk.
As for Erec, he also was fighting superbly.
And then Guinglain rode up;
he galloped along between two battle lines
5876 and there in the middle of his path
he met Galoain, a powerful count.
He gave his horse free rein
and struck the count with such great force
5880 on the shield he held to his chest
that he pierced and shattered the shield to bits,
knocking Galoain down from his fine Frisian horse
onto the sandy soil.
5884 Then he spurred with great force toward another knight
and struck him on the chest;
no harness or saddle could keep the man
from being hurled from his charger.
5888 Bits of the lance shaft flew up in the air.
Guinglain then put his hand to his sword;
he spurred his horse across the meadow,
crying out a challenge in every direction.
5892 Lampart as well was fighting superbly;
again and again he galloped through the lines.
He had a hundred knights with him,
from among the knights of Blonde Esmeree;
5896 fighting well greatly pleased these men.
Lampart led them ably;
the troops had been well entrusted to him.
His men fought splendidly,
5900 and he was often the first to strike
and the last to ride off when his men veered away.
Truly, they fought in great style.

                    Encor n'estoit Artus venus
5904   ne au tornoiement veüs.
        Ariere estoit li riches rois
        trestos armés et ses conrois.
        Tos les soufri a asanbler
5908   ançois qu'il i vausist aler.
        Quatre cens chevaliers armés,
        que ja millors ne demandés,
        avoit Artus a sa baniere;
5912   li plus mauvais molt vaillans ere.
        A lui vint un vallés poingnant
        qui venoit del tornoiement.
        Icil li a dit et conté
5916   que tot estoient asanblé
        fors que sol A[n]guissans li rois,
        qui molt ert sages et cortois,
        mais tot li autre sont venu.
5920   "Un chevalier i ai veü
        quë i porte un escu d'azon
        u d'ermine a un blanc lionn.
        Icil le fait si durement
5924   que tot vaint le tornoiement.   [153 r°a]
        Nus ne veut poindre cele part
        ne le crime plus c'un lupart."
        Li rois pense que Guinglains soit
5928   por ce que tels armes avoit
        quant il vint a la cort premiers
        et por ce qu'ert bons chevaliers.
        Il pense voir: ço estoit il
5932   qui ot esté en maint peril.
        Artus n'i vaut plus demorer;
        des or veut au tornoi aler.
        Lors veïssiés çaingler cevals,
5936   elmes lacier, fermer poitrals,
        çaindre espees et lances prendre,

5917 Aguissans
5936 p. f.

King Arthur had not yet come forward
5904 nor been seen at the tournament.
The powerful king was still in the rear
with his knights, all of them fully armed.
He intended to wait until all others had joined the battle
5908 before going in himself.
Four hundred armed knights
—you could never have asked for better—
did King Arthur have under his banner;
5912 the worst of these men was an excellent knight.
A young man came riding up;
he had come from the tournament.
He told the king
5916 that all had now entered the fighting
except King Aguissans,
a most wise and courtly man,
but all the others were there.
5920 "I saw a knight," he said,
"who carried a shield with an ermine lion
upon a field of azure.
This knight is fighting so fiercely
5924 that he is winning the tourney.
All those who choose to fight him
fear him more than they would a leopard."
The king thought that this was Guinglain,
5928 for the young man had carried such arms as these
when first he came to the court
and because Guinglain was an excellent knight.
The king thought rightly, for this was the man
5932 who had undergone many dangers.
Arthur wished to delay no longer;
he meant to ride at once to the tourney.
Imagine the scene then as horses were harnessed,
5936 helmets laced on and breaststraps tightened,
swords girded on and lances seized,

. . . .
Quant il furent bien acesmé,
5940   es cevals montent tuit armé,
        puis s'en vont seré et rengié
        tant que les rens ont aprocié.
        Lors point li rois par grant vertu
5944   la u li graindres estors fu
        et ensanble lui vait li route.
        Dis corneors ot en sa rote;
        buissine[s] portent et grans cors
5948   que il sonnent par grans esfors.
        Quant li rois vint, cho fu avis
        que tos en tra[n]blast li païs.
        Li rois point, si a encontré
5952   le roi de le Roge Cité;
        si le fiert si en l'escu haut
        qu'estriers ne sele ne li vaut
        que del destrier ne l'abatist;
5956   sa lance fraist, outre se mist.
        Si rencontrent si conpaignon,
        cent en abatent el sablon.
        La veïssiés hardis Bretons
5960   et gaïngnier destriers gascons,
        de tant chevaliers les fois prendre,
        lances baissier et escus fendre
        et tant poindrë et tant guencir,
5964   d'espees si grans [cols] ferir!
        Les gens Artu si bien le font
        que cels de la desconfis ont.
        Tos fu desconfis li tornois;
5968   Artus les chace, li bons rois.
        Pris estoit qui voloit torner;

5947 buissinent
5950 trablast
5957 rencontrenent [*superfluous ligature bar*]
5964 cols *lacking*

. . . .
When all were fully equipped,
5940   the armed knights mounted their chargers
and rode forth in close formation
toward the assembled ranks of the tourney.
The king made a mighty charge
5944   there where the fighting was thickest,
and his knights all charged along with him.
He had ten trumpeters among his men;
they carried great horns and trumpets,
5948   and they sounded them vigorously.
As the king galloped forward, it seemed
that all the land around him trembled.
The king spurred his horse to attack
5952   the King of the Red City;
he struck him high on his shield with such force
that neither stirrups nor saddle could keep him
from being hurled from his horse.
5956   King Arthur shattered his lance, then rode on;
his companions attacked as well
and hurled a hundred knights to the sandy ground.
What a sight were these bold Britons,
5960   winning Gascon chargers,
defeating so many knights,
lowering their lances and smashing shields,
charging and wheeling
5964   and striking great blows with their swords!
The knights of King Arthur fought so well
that they quite overmatched their opponents.
The tournament was routed,
5968   and good King Arthur put them all to flight.
All who chose to turn and fight were captured:

n'i avoit riens de recouvrer
quant li rois A[n]guissans d'Escoce
5972   point a l'issue d'une broche
a set vins chevaliers molt pros;
les regnes prendent par lé nous.
A[n]guissans point, baisse la lance
5976   et fiert Floire, le duc de France,
en mi le pis par tel aïr   *[153 r°b]*
que del dest[r]ier le fist partir.
Si conpaignon ront tuit feru,
5980   qui mai[n]t en iront abatu.
A[n]guissans ne fine ne cesse;
todis fiert e[n] la grinor pr[e]sse.
Il et li suen si bien le font
5984   que le tornoi recouvré ont;
par anguisse recouvrent tuit.
Sos cels qui kaient a grant bruit
sonnent flahutes et buissines.
5988   Chevalier fierent sor poitrines
et sor escus et sor haubers;
de cevals kaent tos envers;
lances brissent et escus fendent
5992   et li fers des estriers estendent;
hauberc faussent et escu fendent;
escu percent et escantelent;
arçon vuident, chevalier tument
5996   et li destrier süent et f[u]ment;

5970 recouvrier
5971 Aguissans
5975 Aguissans
5978 destier
5980 mait
5981 Aguissans
5982 f. e la g. prisse
5984 sont *after* recouvré *expuncted*
5993 fendendent
5996 fment

no chance for them to regain their ground;
but then Aguissans, the King of Scotland,
5972   charged forth from the edge of a wood
with a hundred and forty valiant knights
grasping the knots of their reins.
Aguissans spurred forward, he lowered his lance
5976   and struck Flores, the Duke of France,
square on the chest and with such force
that he knocked him from his charger.
All his companions attacked as well,
5980   felling many opponents.
Aguissans never paused for rest
but always attacked where the fighting was thickest.
He and his men fought so well
5984   that they turned the tide of the tourney.
With his leadership his men regained the advantage.
Loud was the sound of the flutes and the trumpets
as men were hurled to the ground.
5988   Knights struck each other blows on the chest,
on shields and on hauberks;
knights fell from horses;
lances were shattered, shields were split,
5992   and iron stirrups gave way;
hauberks were rent and shields split
and pierced and broken to pieces;
saddles were emptied, knights fell from their saddles,
5996   chargers sweated and steamed,

ceval trebucent, seles brissent.
Li un vers les autres s'aïrent;
regnes ronpent, espees fraingnent;
6000   un perdent et autre gaaignent;
li un keurent por les fois prendre,
li autre keurent por desfendre;
tant cop reçoivre et tant ferir,
6004   li un les autres envaïr.
Molt estoit grans li capleïs
et des lances li froisseïs,
. . . .
6008   et d'espees et de bastons!
De toutes pars fremist li rans.
Molt par i est la noisse grans,
des cols et des lances li frois;
6012   de totes pars sont a d[es]rois.
En grant presse et en tel mellee
cascuns fiert grans cols de l'espee
que n'i oïssiés Diu tonnant.
6016   Es vos entre deus rens poignant
Guinglain qui fiert le Saigremort
amont sor son escu a or
de la lance par tel desroi
6020   qu'il l'abati en un erboi.
Celui laisse et autre rabat
a tere del cheval tot plat.
Molt bien le refaisoit Gavains;
6024   maint chevalier prist a ses mains.
Giflés et B[l]ioblïeris,
qui au Gué Perillous fu pris,
et l'Orguillos et cil de Saies
6028   ne poignoient pas en manaies,
ains le parfaisoient si bien
que nus n'i puet amender rien.   [*153 r°c*]
Mais nus prendre ne se pooit

6012 a drois [*-1, em. Williams*]
6025 Bioblieris

horses stumbled, saddles were smashed.
Knights rose up in anger against one another;
reins were snapped and swords were shattered.
6000 Some knights lost and others won;
some rushed to take oaths of submission
and others hastened to defend their companions.
Many a blow was received and given
6004 as each side attacked the other.
What a great battle was this,
and what a din of shattering lances,

. . . .
6008 of swords and broken lances!
Everywhere lines of battle were broken.
What a deafening noise
as sword blows were struck and lances were shattered;
6012 everywhere lines were in disarray.
So great was this crowd, this huge mêlée
as each knight struck great blows with his sword
that you would never have heard God's thundering.
6016 Then at a gallop between two ranks
came Guinglain, and he struck Sagremore
high on his golden shield
so forcefully with his lance
6020 that he laid him down on the grassy field.
He left Sagremore and hurled another
from his horse and flat on the ground.
Gawain, for his part, was fighting superbly;
6024 by himself he captured many a knight.
And Giflet as well as Blioblïeris,
whom Guinglain had captured at the Perilous Ford,
the Proud Knight of the Glade and the Lord of Saies
6028 did not spare themselves as they galloped forth
but rather distinguished themselves so well
they could not have fought any better.
But no one could compare

6032   a Guinglain, qui tos les venquoit;
ço que il ataint tot destruit.
De totes pars l'esgardent tuit
por che que tos les autres vaint.

6036   L'esgardoient chevalier maint:
tant fiert de l'espee forbie
que tuit li porten garantie
qu'il avoit vencu le tornoi

6040   et que le pris en porte o soi.
Solaus cacha et vint li vespres;
si faillirent atant les vespres.
Et Anguissans li rois guencist

6044   et Guinglain par lé regnes prist,
se li a dit qu'aveuc lui soit
et qu'aveuc lui herbergeroit.
Tant le losenge et tant li prie,

6048   Guinglains remaint, molt l'en merchie
et les vos au mangier tornés.
Quant il less orrent atornés,
si se sont au mangier asis.

6052   Escuier ont livrison pris;
trestot quanques lor fu mestier
orent a planté escuier.
La nuit jurent a grant deduit.

6056   Bien main au jor se lievent tuit
que li ssaint sonent au mostier;
a messe vont li chevalier.
Escuier estrillent et ferent,

6060   haubers rollent, lances enferent;
siles metent, ferment potraus,
torssent et çainglent ces cevaus;
atornent ces cauces de fer,

6064   metent i coroies de cer,
les elmes afaitent et terdent,
regnes noent et escus f. . . . ;
dedens vont, regardent les . . ,

6068   afaitent les, metent . . . . . . ;
referment les bar. . . . . ;
as ostes se vu. . . . . ,

6032   with Guinglain, who defeated all comers;
        all that he touched he laid low.
        All eyes were on him from every side,
        for he vanquished all his opponents.
6036   Many a knight was watching Guinglain:
        he struck so well with his gleaming sword
        that all could bear witness
        that he had won the tournament
6040   and that he should have the prize.
        The sun went down, the evening came,
        and thus the first day of the tournament ended.
        King Anguissans rode up to Guinglain,
6044   took the reins of his horse,
        and asked him to come along
        and take his lodgings with him that night.
        He urged this so graciously
6048   that Guinglain agreed with many thanks,
        and so they went to dinner.
        When everything was prepared,
        they sat down to the meal.
6052   The squires had obtained provisions;
        anything that they needed
        the squires had in abundance.
        That night they rested in great comfort.
6056   Early next morning they all arose
        when the bells rang out in the church;
        the knights then went to mass.
        The squires curried and shod the horses,
6060   polished the hauberks and put tips on the lances;
        they saddled the horses and fastened the breaststraps,
        put on the harnesses and tightened the girths;
        they readied the metal leggings,
6064   threading in deerhide laces;
        they readied the helmets and wiped them clean,
        tied the reins and reinforced the shields,
        went into the tents to look at the . .
6068   readied them, put. . . . .
        closed the . . . .
        they wished to . . . the hosts

```
        et li canteor . . . . . . . . . . . . .
6072    et vont . . . . . . . . . . . . . . . . .
        Garço . . . . . . . . . . . . . . . . .
        bien . . . . . . . . . . . . . . . . . .
        q . . . . . . . . . . . . . . . . . . . . .
6076    . . . . . . . . . . . . . . . . . . . . . . .
        . . . . . . . . . . . . . . . . . . . . . .
        . . . . . . . . . . . . . . . . . . . . . .
        . . . . . . . . . . . . . . . . . . . . . .
6080    . . . . . . . . . . . . . . . . . . . . . .
        ne ve[ï]st tant cop feru,                           [*153 v°a*]
        ne tant gaïgnié ne perdu.
        Que vos iroie je contant?
6084    Bien l'avoit fait Guinglains devant,
        mais or le fist il asés mius,
        car ainc on ne vit a ses iueus
        chevalier qui mius le fesist:
6088    tot le pris dou tornoi conquist.
        Par verité, dire vos os
        que tot l'en donerent le los.
        [L]i rois Bruians bien le refist.
6092    Au vespre li tornois falist.
        Artus tramist de l'autre par[t]
        Giflet, le fil Due, et Lanpart
        por demander que cil estoit
6096    qui le tornoi vencu avoit
        et savoir se Guinglains i ere.
        Et cil font del roi la proiere;
        quant il se furent desarmé,
6100    isnelement i sont alé.
        Ensanble a Anguisel le roi
        trouvent Guinglain, qui el tornoi
        avoit vencu. Quant il se virent,
6104    saciés que grant joie se fisent.
```

6081 veust
6091 *space for capital but guide letter cut off*
6093 par

and the singers . . . .
6072 and they went . . . .
Boys . . . .
well . . . .
. . . .
6076 . . . .
. . . .
. . . .
. . . .
6080 . . . .
had never seen so many blows struck,
so much won or so much lost.
Why should I tell you all the details?
6084 If Guinglain had fought well the day before,
he now fought even better,
for never had anyone seen
a knight fight better than he:
6088 he won the prize of the tournament.
I can tell you quite truthfully
that everyone gave him the glory.
King Bruians also fought very well.
6092 When evening came, the tournament ended.
From the other side King Arthur sent
Giflet, son of Do, and Lampart
to ask the name of the knight
6096 who had won the tournament
and whether Guinglain had fought there.
These knights did as King Arthur had asked them;
when they had removed their armor,
6100 they went there with all speed.
They found Guinglain, who had won
the tournament, with King Anguissans.
When these knights saw one another,
6104 you may be sure that they rejoiced.

Quant entreconjoï se furent,
por aler a la cort se murent
Lanpars et Giflés et Guinglains.
6108 Tant ont chevaucié par les plains
et tant ont lor cemin tenu
qu'il sont a Valedon venu.
A son ostel trovent Artus.
6112 Quant il les vit, si lieve sus;
Guinglain conuit, va le baissier
et de ses deus bras enbracier.
[L]ors veïssiés grant joie faire,
6116 les chevaliers vers Guinglain traire,
[le] salüer et conjoïr;
. . p cosentir de lui servir;
. . . le baissent et acolent
6120 . . . . a lui parolent
. . . . nor joie fesissent
. . . . oels veïssent
. . . . oie fol et sage
6124 . . . . e
. . . . t
. . . .
. . . .
6128 . . . .
. . . .
. . . .
. . . .
6132 . . . .
as uns hermines engolés,   [*153 v°b*]
as autres deniers moneés,
et maintials vairs et siglatons
6136 et cotes et vairs peliçons,
bons palefrois, roubes de soie.
Molt fisent cele nuit grant joie.
L'uns portoit vairs, li autres gris;

6115 *space for capital but guide letter cut off*
6117 *first word missing due to loss of corner of folio*

After they had happily greeted each other,
Lampart, Giflet, and Guinglain
then left to go to the court.
6108 They rode across the plain
and kept to their path
until they came to Valendon.
They found the king in his lodgings.
6112 When he saw them, he arose;
he knew Guinglain and went to embrace him,
clasping him in his arms.
What great rejoicing there was then
6116 as the knights went up to Guinglain
to greet him and make him welcome,
... to pledge themselves to his service;
..... they hugged and embraced him,
6120 .... spoke to him,
.... .had greater joy
.... eyes had seen
.... .wise and foolish
6124 ....
....
....
....
6128 ....
....
....
....
6132 ....
collars trimmed in ermine to some,
coins and money to others,
and cloaks of silk and miniver
6136 and tunics and miniver pelisses,
fine palfreys and silken garments.
That night there was a great celebration.
Some wore miniver, others squirrel;

6140 foire sanblast, ce v[o]s fust vis;
   cotes a armer ont garçon.
   La nuit jurent a Valendon,
   et quant ce vint au bien matin,
6144 si se mist Artus an cemin.
     A Londres s'en vont trestot droit
   la u Blonde Esmeree estoit;
   ensanble o lui Guinglains s'en vait.
6148 Li rois [Artus] grant joie en fait,
   qu'il a son cosin recovré.
   Tant ont cevauchié et erré
   que il sont a Londres venu
6152 u furent volentiers veü.
   Quant Blonde Esmeree le vit,
   saciés que grant joie li fist;
   Guinglain enbracha et salue.
6156 Li rois le prist par le main nue
   et par le main ra Guinglain pris,
   si s'est entre ces deus asis.
   S'i apiela de ses barons.
6160 Premiers i vint rois Amangons
   et Gavains et li rois Bruians,
   Yvains l'aoutres et Tristrans,
   Lanpars et Kes li senescals,
6164 Saigremors et Gales li Cals
   et des autres i vint asés.
   Li rois lor dist, "Or escoutés."
   Lors a Guiglain a raisson mis,
6168 "Biaus niés," fait il, "biaus ciers amis,
   molt par sui liés en mon coraje
   quant vos voi tant preu et tant saje
   et que je vos ai recovré.
6172 Molt vos avoie desiré;
   des or mais vos vel ensaucier.
   Or vos vel d'une rien proier:

6140 ce us f. [*em. Williams*]
6148 Artus *lacking*

6140   you would have thought it a feast day.
The young boys were given surcoats.
That night they slept at Valendon,
and when morning came,

6144   King Arthur set out on his journey.
They traveled straight to London,
where Blonde Esmeree awaited;
Guinglain went with the king.

6148   The King made much of his nephew
and rejoiced at having found him again.
They rode along the way
until they came to London,

6152   where the people were happy to see them.
When Blonde Esmeree saw Guinglain,
you may be sure she welcomed him joyfully;
she greeted him and embraced him.

6156   The king took her hand
and the hand of Guinglain as well,
and then sat down between them.
He called to some of his vassals.

6160   The first to come was King Amangon,
then came Gawain and King Bruians,
Yvain the Bastard and then Tristan,
Lampart and Kay the Seneschal,

6164   then Sagremore and Gales the Bald,
and a number of others as well.
The king then said to them, "Hear me."
He spoke to Guinglain as follows:

6168   "Dear nephew and friend," he said,
"it brings great joy to my heart
to see you so worthy and wise
and to have found you again.

6172   I have deeply desired your company;
henceforth I wish to show you great honor.
And so I have something to ask of you:

que vos prendés ceste roïne
6176   a cui molt grans regnes acline.
A feme, biaus niés, le prendés
si en serrés rois corounés,
molt poiss[a]ns et de grant pooir.
6180   Et vos le devés bien avoir
que par armes l'avés conquisse
et de molt grant peril fors mise.
Por li vos estes molt penés.
6184   Plus bele avoir vos ne poés   [*153 v°c*]
et si est de molt grant parage.
Ne por biauté ne por lingnage
ne le devés vos laissier mie,
6188   que molt est de grant signorie
et qui molt vos ainme et desire.
Si veut que vos soiés se sire."
Li rois et tuit l'ont tant proié
6192   que Guinglains lor a otroié.
Il vit la dame et biele et saje,
se li plot molt en son corage.
Li rois dist ses noces fera
6196   et son neveu coronnera;
mais ne le veut Blonde Esmeree
tant qu'ele soit en sa contree,
que de la coronne son pere
6200   et de celi qui fu sa mere
i soient andoi coronné.
Guinglains a cest consel loé.
Le roi prient que il i aille,
6204   si fera il, ce dist, sans faille
qu'andeus lé veut molt onerer.
Lor oire font tost atorner.
Cele nuit a grant joie furent
6208   a Londre la cité u jurent.

6179 poissons
6205 onenerer

that you take in marriage this queen,
6176 the ruler of a great realm.
Take her as your wife, dear nephew,
and you will be a king
both powerful and strong.
6180 It is right that she should be yours,
for you have won her through force of arms
and delivered her from great danger.
For her sake you have suffered greatly.
6184 You could have no wife more beautiful
or more nobly born than she.
Neither her beauty nor her lineage
should cause you to disdain her,
6188 for she is a powerful queen
and she loves you dearly as well.
She wants you to be her lord."
The king and the others so pleaded with him
6192 that Guinglain agreed to do as they asked.
He saw that the lady was wise and fair,
and she pleased him deep in his heart.
The king said he would hold the wedding himself
6196 and crown his nephew king;
but Blonde Esmeree
wanted the wedding to be in her own land,
so that Guinglain might wear the crown
6200 of her father
and she the crown of her mother.
Guinglain advised that it be as she wished.
They both asked the king to go to Wales,
6204 and he said he would certainly do so,
for he greatly desired to honor them both.
They hastily made their plans to travel.
That night they stayed in London
6208 amid the greatest rejoicing.

Au main quant li aube est crevee,
si se lieve Blonde Esmeree
et Guinglains et Artus li rois.
6212   Escuier torsent le harnois.
Que feroie longes novieles?
Es cevals ont mises les sieles;
puis n'i ont sis ent[r]e Bretaingne.
6216   Molt mainne Artus biele conpaingne.
Or cevaucent a grans jornees;
tant passent marces et contrees
que il sont en Gales venu.
6220   La sont a joie receü
et a molt grant porcession
en la cité de Sinaudon.
Par Gales va la renonmee
6224   que lor dame estoit retornee
et que celui prendre voloit
qui de l'angoisse osté l'avoit.
Ceste noviele molt lor plot.
6228   Et la dame mandé les ot,
si s'en vont tuit vers Senaudon
del roiaume tuit li baron.
Or vos puis bien dire por voir,
6232   puis que Dius fist et main et soir
ne fu nus hom plus bien venus
n'a plus grant joie receüs
con Guinglains fu en cele tere.
6236   Quascuns voloit s'amor conquerre;
tot le veulent a lor signor   *[Begin bound-*
Artu reporter grant honor.   *in leaf]*
Que vos iroie je contant
6240   ne autres choses devisant?
Iluec fu Guinglains coronnés,
de cui devant oï avés,
et la dame ra esposee
6244   et aveuc lui fu coronnee.

6215 sis ente B. [*em. Williams*]

When dawn broke the next morning,
Blonde Esmeree arose
as did Guinglain and King Arthur.
6212   The squires prepared the baggage.
Why should I tell you all the details?
They saddled the horses
and departed from Britain.
6216   Arthur took with him a very fine company.
They rode from morning till night;
they passed many lands and countries
until they arrived in Wales.
6220   There they were received with joy
and with a great procession
in the city of Snowdon.
The news went out through all of Wales
6224   that the queen had now returned
and intended to take as her husband
the knight who had freed her from suffering.
This pleased her people greatly.
6228   And the queen commanded
that all the noble lords of the realm
come to Snowdon.
I can tell you with all certainty
6232   that, since God first made morning and evening,
no man was welcomed more warmly
or received with greater joy
than Guinglain was in that land.
6236   Everyone wanted to win his good will;
all wished to do great honor
to Arthur their liegelord.
Why should I make a long tale of this
6240   or tell you all that happened there?
Guinglain was crowned in Snowdon,
this knight of whom you have heard so much,
and he took the queen in marriage,
6244   and she was crowned along with him.

Puis fu rois de molt grant mi[m]ore
si con raconte li istore.

Ci faut li roumans et define.
6248   Bele vers cui mes cuers s'acline,
Renals de Biauju molt vos prie
por Diu que ne l'oblïés mie;
de cuer vos veut tos jors amer.
6252   Ce ne li poés vos veer.
Quant vos plaira, dira avant
u il se taira ore a tant.
Mais por un biau sanblant mostrer
6256   vos feroit Guinglain retrover
s'amie que il a perdue,
qu'entre ses bras le tenroit nue.
Se de çou li faites delai,
6260   si ert Guinglains en tel esmai
que ja mais n'avera s'amie;
d'autre vengance n'a il mie.
Mais por la soie grant grevance
6264   ert sor Guinglain ceste vengance,
que jamais jor n'en parlerai
tant que le bel sanblant avrai.

Explicit del Bel Descouneü.

6245 Pius, minore
6263 grevantce

Guinglain was a long remembered king,
as the story tells.

Here ends the romance.

6248   Fair lady, my heart's sovereign,
Renaut de Bâgé most humbly prays
you not to forget him, in God's name,
for he wishes to love you always and with his whole heart.

6252   You cannot forbid him this.
And if you wish it, he will speak further,
or else be silent forever.
If you show him a gracious countenance,

6256   then Guinglain will once more find
his lady, whom he has lost,
and hold her naked in his arms.
But if you delay in granting him this,

6260   Guinglain must bear the sorrow
of never finding her again;
no other revenge will Renaut take.
But because his grief is so great,

6264   this vengeance will fall on Guinglain,
for until you look kindly on me,
I shall nevermore speak of him.

Textual Notes

3   Williams understands an allusion to a single song, p. 195, but more than one may be implied as A. Colby-Hall (1984) has noted, p. 123.

4   Kelly points out, p. 147, that this is "one of the first unequivocal examples of generic usage of the word *roumant*." Lines 4-5 and 10 echo the prologue of *Erec* 13-18 (Bruckner [1987], p. 232). To cite all the echoes of Chrétien's romances in *Li Biaus Descouneüs* is impractical. I will note the most important instances or ones that are of particular interest and have not been noted before. The reader may refer to Schofield and Louveau for extensive lists of Renaut's allusions to Chrétien's oeuvre.

22   *Viele* was a general term used to denote most bowed instruments before 1300 (Page, p. 145). Since it is not specified whether the *viele* is *à archet* or *à roue,* we shall follow what seems to be common usage and translate 'fiddle'.

53   The *seneschal* was a steward, one who supervised the lord's estate, audited the accounts and oversaw general husbandry arrangements.

66   *lé* for *les.* The scribe frequently leaves the final consonant off a word, be it a definite article, direct object pronoun, preposition, or verb, when it is followed by a word beginning with a consonant. This suggests that this final letter was not pronounced and in these cases I have left the reading of the manuscript. I make exception to avoid any confusion about the person of a verb (e.g., 892 and 4522, where *pris* stands for *prist*; see also 316, 2298 and 2382 for analogous instances. In 4817, *perdi* for *perdit* is required to rhyme with *ami*.) When the following word begins with a vowel, I add the final consonant to provide the liaison.

73-4   Guerreau has identified this, p. 30, as the heraldic emblem distinct to the house of Bâgé since the thirteenth century. Brault cites this as an instance of "heraldic flattery," pp. 22-3.

83-8   The custom of the rash boon, a recurrent motif in Arthurian romance especially, requires that the person petitioned to grant a request do so without knowing what it will be. Keeping this promise invariably poses a dilemma for this person. See Frappier.

95   The *cote por armer* was a knee- or calf-length tunic, sometimes of silk, worn over the hauberk. See Verdelhan, pp. 68-9.

96   *Baceler*, a knight who has been dubbed but has not yet received a fief, who is not yet *casé* hence not marriageable. For a discussion of the social status of this class, see Duby (1964).

99   *qui* for *qui.l*. The direct object pronoun is restored. The scribe has a tendency to drop final consonants; see the note to line 66.

104   It was the custom to set the table with a bowl for every two people. See Holmes, pp. 87-8.

115-7   An allusion to *Perceval* 344-5?

137   Samite was a heavy silk used for outer garments as well as in trappings for a knight's charger (see line 1721). Often it was embroidered or brocaded in silver or gold.

149   The saddle bows were of wood and could be decorated with ivory or metal inlays. Precious stones were soldered onto the pommel or even, as here, the bridle, from which sometimes metal pendants or little bells were attached, as in the case of the fay's palfrey (lines 3950-1). See Holmes, pp. 20-1.

157   This courtly, elegant dwarf stands in contrast to the ugly, malevolent ones that one typically encounters in Arthurian romance. There are, however, other instances of friendly dwarfs (Guivret le Petit in Chrétien de Troyes' *Erec et Enide*, for example, or the dwarf

herdsman in *Le Chevalier as deus espees*) who have their counterparts in Celtic tradition. See Harwood, specifically the chapter "Teodelain," pp. 88-9.

163   Although *roube* can refer to an outer garment, in this romance it appears to be a general term designating an ensemble made from one fabric. (Verdelhan, p. 77) *Vair* was a fur lining composed of the pelts of a species of squirrel whose coat turns grey in winter. A checkered pattern is achieved by alternating the grey with the white pelts from the animal's belly. (Verdelhan, p. 94) In this romance *vair* is always used to line a garment of *eskerlate*, a costly cloth of silk woven in Flanders, England, and Paris by the time the romance was composed. It was dyed in shades of red as well as in blue, green and grey. (Verdelhan, pp. 85-6).

177   The manuscript bears *Guigras* with a bar indicating nasalization over the letters *ui* at all the occurrences of this name but this one, where the first *g* has a tilde over it, a ligature that indicates *r*. West, who gives *Gringras* following Williams, notes no other romances containing this name.

235   This line has one syllable too many. It would be a shame to tamper with it to correct the meter: Helie throws Arthur's own words ("*Trop est jovenes*" line 214) back in his face.

242   The confusion of the graphies *ai* and *a* is common in Picard scripta. (See Gossen, p. 53.) Besides *faura* for *faurai*, we find *a* for *ai*, Pres. Indic. 1 of *avoir*, in lines 243 and 4369; *sa* for *sai*, Pres. Indic. 1 of *savoir*, in line 1808; *dira:mentira* for *dirai:mentirai*, Fut. 1, in lines 887-8; *jostera* for *josterai* in line 2558; *verra* for *verrai* in line 4444; *trova:parla* for *trovai:parlai*, Pret. 1, in lines 2713-4; *endura* for *endurai* in line 4909, etc. These graphies occur alongside regular Central French forms.

267   A knight's armor consisted of a hauberk, a tunic of chain-mail that came down below the knee and often had wrist-length sleeves. It extended into a hood (*coiffe*) worn beneath the helmet (*elme*), which was held in place by laces (*las*) tied under the chin. A triangular piece of mail, the *ventaille*, was laced across the throat and over the mouth.

Mail leggings (*cauces*) covered the front of the legs and were laced up the back (with *cordieles*). Over the hauberk went a loose-fitting surcoat (*cote*), belted at the waist and slit in front and behind for ease in riding. The shield (*escu*), kite-shaped, was made of boards (*ais*) covered with hide (*cuir*) and fitted with a boss (*boucle*) at the upper center to deflect blows. If one wished to keep one's hands free, one would hang the shield from a neck strap (*guince*). Alternatively, one would pass one's left arm through a series of straps (*enarmes*) in order to parry blows.

314   *Aidier* occurs here as a noun meaning 'help'.

316   Perret (1991) notes that *au de par* is a compound preposition of the type described in her work (1988a), p. 47, n. 8.

330   *Ciés* or *cief* is a heraldic term for the upper part of the shield whereas *piés* or *pié* designates the shield's base, distinguished from the field by a horizontal line and of a different color. Brault cites this line, p. 143.

351   *Cauces de fer:* see the note to line 267.

390   Picard *le* for *la*. This form occurs frequently throughout the text (e.g., lines 442 [*le boucle*], 697 [*le forest*], 713 and 865 [*le = pucele*], 1004 [*le roce*], etc.) alongside Central French *la*.

418   The scribe frequently omits the bar that indicates nasalization. Since *doinst* occurs elsewhere in the text (e.g., 1047, 1059, 2909), I have restored the *n* here and subsequently for the convenience of the reader.

431 ff. That the following combat is typical is evident from the description by Holmes, p. 172: "When going into action against each other, two knights would take position at the required distance. They spurred forward, dropped their reins on the necks of the horses, raised their shields on the left arm, and held the lance [under the arm]. If one knight was unhorsed, the other was not obliged to get down. If he did not, he was apt to have his mount killed by the adversary who was seeking for equal advantage. If both lances were broken, or if both men

were unmounted, the swords were drawn and used until the battle was over."

442   *Boucle*, see the note to line 267.

483   In return for being allowed to go free, the defeated knight promised to adhere to his captor's conditions (*fiancer prison*).

527-8   The names *Saies* and *Graies* have been switched in order to conform to subsequent mentions of these personages in the romance.

558   In this construction *vostre secors* is the subject (T-L 5:1700).

596   *soué*, an interesting form, replaces *souef* to rhyme with *pré*.

608   *Perdre* occurs here in the absolute: 'to lose one's life, to die.' Greimas cites this line.

672   The *pujoisse* or *pougeoise*, a coin in currency from the twelfth through the fifteenth century, was worth a quarter of a *denier* and thus came to express something of little value. (FEW 9:645b; Godefroy, 6:345b, is incorrect in limiting its currency to the reign of Saint Louis.)

675   *crés*, Pres. Indic. 5, for *creés* or *creez*, is a form that evolved by analogy to *vez* (for *veez*). (Fouché, p. 62 and note 1)

702   The form *s'aresturent*, an example of a refection by analogy to *estut* < **stetuit*, disappeared by the sixteenth century. (Fouché, p. 327)

714 · A small hand pointing to this line has been drawn in the margin. That the use of *foutre* constitutes a breach of style is borne out by the texts cited in T-L 3:2174-5 and Godefroy 4:106c: fabliaux, the *Roman de Renart*, a proverb, and the *Roman de la Rose*. Holden notes the use of *fotre* and various other obscene or off-color expressions in *Ipomedon*, which he characterizes as generally comic in tone. (See his edition, p. 53.)

719   Although there is no gap in the manuscript text, the lack of a rhyme for line 720 indicates a lacuna of at least one line. Claude Platin's prose adaptation, which follows *Le Bel Inconnu* very closely, indicates at this point that the giant was roasting a whole deer: "*Et l'autre geant estoit pres du feu qui rotissoit ung cerf tout entier en attendant que l'aultre eust fait de la pucelle . . .*"(1 [iv] r°) *Carduino* stresses that the giant was roasting a whole animal ("*Con tutto il cuoio e con tutte le zanpe*" 2,33). D. Adams, pp. 215-226, has called attention to the fact that Platin's text could suggest what material is missing from the Chantilly manuscript. Henceforward, the relevant passages from Platin will be quoted whenever they point to what the missing lines in *Le Bel Inconnu* might have contained. These quotations will be punctuated for the convenience of the reader.

729   *taura* is the Fut. 3 of *toldre, tolre*, used here in the absolute: 'he will take her away.'

741   The manuscript shows space for two lines left blank but the rhyme scheme suggests that only one line is missing, the one that would have rhymed with *atent*, line 742. Claude Platin's prose version gives the following at this point: ". . . *ils ont tout gasté ce pays et n'y est demouré ne homme ne femme* **que ne s'en soyent tous fouys en aultres contrees**; *pource je vous avoye fait coucher au pré . . .*" (1 [iv] r°, boldface added) Although the order is slightly different, the portion in boldface may be what was left out.

750   Williams emends this line to read *cele amie*.

762-6   The manuscript shows space here for five lines of text. In Claude Platin's prose version, the giant attacks Bel Inconnu with the roasting spit: "*Apres s'en vint a lautre geant l'espee en la main. Le geant qui estoit grant et puissant luy vint au devant a tout la broche ou il rotissoit le cerf et la lansa apres le Descongneu lequel gauchit au coup et le geant ne l'attaignit pas car s'il le eüst attaint il l'eüst tué luy ou son cheval.*"(1 [iv] r°) *Carduino* (2,33) and three ms. versions of *Lybeaus Desconeus* contain the same detail. Adams hypothesizes, p. 218, that in the missing part the giant must have lost his club (line 759), and then attacked with the spit. Subsequently, in line 775, he makes a second attack with his club, which he has retrieved.

771-2   Proverbial expression listed in Schulze-Busacker as number 440. See also Morawski 252: "*Bien est gardez qui Deus velt garder.*"

775-6   The rhyme *maçue:anuie* is typical of Northeastern and Eastern dialects which retained *ui* as a descending diphthong later than others. (Pope, p. 492, ¶ vii)

780   *mellier*, 'medlar,' a hardwood of which cudgels and sticks were often made.

797-8   Schulze-Busacker proverb number 1245 B2a: "*Mielz valt fuie que fole atente.*"

822   *ventaille*, see the note to line 267.

837-8   Proverb cited by Morawski no. 2313: *Tel(le) chose ait on en despit que puis est mout regretee.* Cf. *Erec* 2-3.

886   *Çoilt*, Pres. Subj. 3 of *celer*.

887-8   *Dira* for *dirai* and *mentira* for *mentirai*. For the occurrence of graphy *a* for *ai* in the text, see the note to line 242.

902   *la cave*: Perret (1991), p. 104, notes that the use of the definite article suggests that some lines may be missing telling of the discovery of the giants' underground cache. Platin briefly mentions this: ". . . *le bon escuyer Robert, en allant parmy le boys querant de l'herbe pour donner aux chevaulx, il trouva la loge ou les geans se tenoient . . .*" (1 [iv] r°)

915-6   This aphorism resembles one listed both by Morawski (no. 229) and Schulze-Busacker (no. 229 A2b): "*Belle vigne sans resin ne vault rien.*"

963 ff.   Compare the attack by the three robber knights in *Erec* 2757 ff.

993   The manuscript shows punctuation, a raised dot, after *cha*.

1066-82   These lines amplify a reflection the narrator makes as three robber knights descend upon Erec: "*Adonc estoit costume et us/que dui chevalier a un poindre/ne devoient a un seul joindre/et, s'il l'eüssent anvaï,/vis fust qu'il l'eussent traï.* " (*Erec* 2788-2902)

1076   Morawski, Schulze-Busacker no. 1003. In her article on the meaning of this proverb, Stone notes that it is closely associated with accounts of battles against a foe of overwhelming numbers. The saying thus echoes epic texts and underscores Helie's fear that her champion will fail. Cf. Dembowski, ed. *Jourdain de Blaye* CFMA, line 211.

1135   *Garmadone* (the ligature could also be interpreted as *Gramadone*) appears to be the name of Saie's horse. T-L cites one text, 4:175, in which it appears to be a weapon that is thrown with enough force to destroy a wall: "*Lai veïssiez un estor commancier, L'un mort sor l'autre verser et trebuchier; A garmadones et grans espiels d'archier Veulent les murs malmetre et peçoier.*" (*Enfances Guillaume* 1485)

1163-4   One may wonder about the narrative logic of these two lines since the knights are now fighting on foot.

1221-2   Morawski no. 2351; see also 2338, 1185. Schulze-Busacker 2351: "*Teus cuide venchier sa honte qui la crost.*"

1223-4   Schulze-Busacker 2091: "*Qui plus haut monte qu'il ne doit De plus haut chiet qu'il ne voldroit.*" See also Morawski 1368, 2090.

1265-9   Compare Lancelot musing about Guenevere: "*Ne sai se die amie ou non;/ne li os metre cest sornon*" (*Le Chevalier de la charrete,* 4363-4).

1266   The scribe has put a mark of punctuation, two raised dots arrayed like a colon, after *dont.*

1284   Hunting dogs fell into two general groups, those that hunted by sight and those that hunted by smell. The *brachet* is of the second type, a small scenting hound that hunted in a pack. Verdelhan finds its presence in a stag hunt unusual (p. 128) but the editors of *The Master of the Game* state that it was used to hunt both stag and wild boar during the Middle Ages. The *viautre* or *veltre*, a large greyhound, is of the first type; prized for its swiftness, it would relay the pack of scenting hounds. According to Verdelhan, p. 138, it was used chiefly to hunt wild boar.

1309   *Burel* was a coarse woolen cloth usually dyed a dark color.

1392   *arestil*: the grip of the lance.

1436   The steel forged in Vienne, south of Lyon on the Rhône, must have been famous, for it is frequently cited as an epithet denoting excellence (e.g., *Erec* 5918, *Roland* 997).

1460   This line is not hypermetric because *eust*, Imperf. Subj. 3 of *avoir*, has one syllable instead of two (contrast *eüst* 722, 4561, 4738), a reduction that took place in the late thirteenth century. See Fouché, p. 348.

1500   West (1957) cites this description of a castle, p. 54, as one of the best examples of a type that emphasizes the fertile setting.

1512   A league was a measure that varied considerably from one region to another in a period when fields were measured by how much one could plow from sunrise to sunset. It is clear that what is meant here is that the vineyards covered an impressive expanse.

1529-30 In his work on medieval clothing, Enlart (3:230) refers to the unusual feather lining of the lady's cloak. Ermine was commonly used in bands or stripes, however. (Viollet-le-Duc, *Dictionnaire raisonné du mobilier*, 3:382)

1534   *crans* for *grans*. Here and there we find *c* for *g* (*claire* for *glaire* 3067, *vicor* for *vigor* 2124) and *g* for *c* (*gongié* for *congié* 3801, *esgarnir* for *escarnir* 4925, and *engline* for *encline* 5188). These spellings occur alongside regular forms: *grans* 1881, 1927, etc.; *vigor* 1047, 1458; *congié* 273, 1364, etc.

1531   Both Viollet-le-Duc (3:382) and Verdelhan (p. 93) note that sable was most often used as a border.

1547   Women wore their hair in two long plaits which were either braided or intertwined with ribbons (Verdelhan, pp. 59-60).

1553   Williams reads *detire* for *decire*.

1583   This episode is clearly a retelling of the Sparrowhawk joust in *Erec et Enide*. Compare ll. 557-1069 in Carroll's edition. For comments on Renaut's treatment of this material, see Philipot (1896); Schofield; Schmolke-Hasselmann, pp. 162-3; and Bruckner (1987), pp. 233-4.

1584   The rhyme scheme indicates that a line is missing here although there is no break in the manuscript text.

1670   The verb in this line contains the subject, a neuter 'it'. *Enclé* = *anglé*, and adjective whose sense, 'angular,' is extended to mean 'dented, nicked.' Perret (1991) suggests *anglés* 'découpé,' p. 105.

1713   *Sinople* means 'gules' or 'red' during this period. In the second half of the fourteenth century, it came to mean 'green,' perhaps to avoid the confusion between *vert/vair*. (Brault, p. 275)

1731   *Amors*, feminine, and the lady are very close in the text. See, for example, the intentional ambiguity in lines 4828-32. Therefore, although one could use 'it,' we translate with feminine pronouns throughout.

1736   The lack of a rhyme for line 1735 indicates that a line is missing. It might have contained a transition from the reflections on love's blindness to the episode at hand as Adams notes, p. 219. Platin's text contains such a transition: "*Quant il veit que la damoiselle prenoit l'espervier, il luy escria..*" (m [iv] r°).

1743   The manuscript has punctuation, two raised dots, after *avant*.

1791-4 Compare Maboagrain ceding to Erec: "*Cil chiet adanz sor la poitrine,/ne n'a pooir de relever;/que que il doie grever,/li covint dire et otroier:/'Conquis m'avez, nel puis noier '(Erec* 5960-4)." The intertextual echo bears out Williams' correction.

1808 *Sa* for *sai, vallant* for *vaillant.* For the occurrence of the graphy *a* for *ai* in the text, see the note to line 242.

1843 ff. Compare Enide's recognition of Moboagrain's lady in *Erec* 6202 ff.

1855 *Venrai* for *verrai.* In Picard **viderat* became either *venra* or *verra* (Fouché, p. 397). This form occurs elsewhere in the text alongside Central French forms (e.g., *verrai,* line 3123).

1875 The description of the castle on the Golden Isle follows a pattern characteristic of a certain type of castle "portrait": introduction; the castle's setting; its walls; its towers; the palace. West (1957) praises the careful construction of this description, p. 55.

1886 The manuscript has punctuation, a raised dot, after *Nois* and *flors.*

1895-6 The *l* in *halt* being a graphy for vocalized *l,* the rhyme in these two lines is regular.

1903 *Casé,* 'beneficed vassals, those holding fiefs,' as opposed to household vassals, those whom the lord maintained in his court.

1907 In seven instances the scribe writes *i* for *il,* in five before words beginning with a consonant and in one before a word beginning with *l.* (See line 154 for a similar phenomenon.) I restore the *l* in each case to prevent any confusion with *i* = 'y'.

1913 In the lapidaries of the twelfth and thirteenth centuries the carbuncle is distinguished by its extraordinary luminescence, associated with a supposed etymological link with coal: *De la clarté del vif charbun A ceste piere pris son nun (Pannier,* p. 163).

1933   The Seven Liberal Arts, that is, the Trivium (grammar, rhetoric, dialectic) and the Quadrivium (arithmetic, geometry, astronomy, music). In lines 4939-40, where the Fay describes her education, magic seems to replace music in her Quadrivium.

1956 ff.   Compare the Joie de la Cort episode in *Erec* 5734 ff.

1961-2   The requirements of the rhyme are at odds with those of the syntax here; *ficie* is the Picard reduction of *ficiee*, which modifies *qui* (= *teste*). Similar rhymes occur at lines 2009-10 and 5585-6.

1979   This is a very early mention of horse armor, which is generally considered to have come into service in the thirteenth and fourteenth centuries. According to Viollet-le-Duc, *Dictionnaire raisonné du mobilier*, 4:40, "On commence à housser les chevaux de guerre vers 1220 . . . pour empêcher les traits de blesser les jambes, le cou et le poitrail du cheval."

1981   Williams corrects to *Qu'on Biaus Descouneüs apiele*.

2005   The lady's agreement provides that, if a suitor can successfully defend the causeway seven years, she will marry him. Malgiers has two years left. Hence he has been her suitor for five years.

2009-10   The syntax calls for *fiancié* (m.) to agree with *l(e)* (= that she will marry him if he defends the causeway for seven years). This is at odds with the rhyme required by *caucie*. A similar problem occurs in lines 1961-2 and 5585-6.

2032   Williams gives *ert* for a ligature that stands for *est* throughout the text.

2055-60   The term *paile* seems to refer to a wide variety of silk fabric that was used for cushions, coverlets, and the trappings of war-horses as well as for clothing. In this instance *paile* appears to be a generic word for silk, subsequently specified by the term *cendal* in line 2060. Viollet-le-Duc states that *paile* was a multicolored fabric or a brocade (*Dictionnaire raisonné du mobilier* 3:363). On samite, see the note to line 137. According to Verdelhan, p. 83, *cendal* was a light silk resembling taffeta, usually dyed red or blue and highly prized during the twelfth and thirteenth centuries.

2161   Perret suggests, (1991), p. 106, that there is material missing after this line and that the scribe's eye skipped from *metent* to *proumetent*. Her hypothesis rests on the abrupt and unannounced change in subject in 2162. This phenomenon is not infrequent in Old French texts and bespeaks what de Lage terms, p. 225, the "affective syntax" of an oral style that counts on tone and context for clarity. Note that it is possible to take 2161 with the following lines. (See T-L 4:255-7 for examples of *a genillons* to mean kneeling in prayer, among these *Erec* 2378 in Foerster's edition.) It seems, however, that when the adverb *souvent* is associated with the expression (1154, 2948) the context is rather that of combat.

2063   The gloves are an item of clothing given as token by the lady, in this case because it is her causeway that the knight is defending.

2094   Although there is no break in the text of the manuscript, there is no line to rhyme with line 2093, suggesting a lacuna. Platin's prose version reads as follows at this point: *"Le Descongneu luy a dit, 'Sire chevalier, laissiez nous passer par courtoisie et ne nous vueillez arrester, car nous avons bien hastivement a faire ailleurs.' Le chevalier de la chaussee luy a dit* **qu'il convenoit qu'il joustast ou qu'il demourast la dehors.** *Lors sont passez oultre la chaussee et sont venus aux lices pour jouster"* (n [i] v°, boldface added).

2172   Schulze-Busacker no. 764 is similar: *"Fortune torne en petit d'eure."*

2332   The manuscript has a mark of punctuation, two raised dots, after *ferons*.

2335   Williams reads *cese* and corrects to *cose*.

2359   Although there is no break in the manuscript text, the fact that there is no companion rhyme for *gesir* indicates that a line is missing. Platin's text suggests that this line might have contained the lady's wish to detain Helie: *"Et Helye est venue prendre congié d'elle, disant qu'elle alloit coucher elle et ses gens aval en la ville en l'hostellerie ou estoyent ses chevaulx.* **Helayne** *[= la dame]* **a prins grant peine a la retenir,** *mais elle n'a peu ains a prins congié et s'en est allee en la ville"* (n ii v°, boldface added).

2399-2400 *Ataces* were clasps attached to the cloak, one at each shoulder. Through these were passed ties or thongs (*tasiel*), which could be tied in order to hold the cloak in place. (See Goddard, p. 209, and Verdelhan, p. 101.)

2407   Williams reads *quis ciet*.

2424   *Se* is inserted above the line in a lighter ink and in another hand. I agree with Perret (1991), p. 106 that *fait* appears to be a mistake for *trait* although there is nothing in the adjacent lines to suggest a bourdon as the likely explanation. T-L 7:404-6 cites verbs of motion in connection with *le pas* used adverbially; among the examples listed I find *se traire tot le grand pas*.

2489   In the manuscript a word has been erased and *cacoit* written in in another ink.

2501   *Pluplee* for *puplee*. The same linguistic phenomenon is evident in *esclarbocle* for *escarbocle*, lines 1913 and 3140.

2517 ff   Compare the host in Pesme Aventure (*Yvain* 5159 ff.) and King Evrain in *Erec* 5432 ff.

2541   Line 2574 provides the correction: *lor pos de cendres*.

2552   The manuscript has punctuation, two raised dots, after *pas*.

2580   *Son* can have a collective sense and refer to a plural antecedent. (Ménard, p. 37)

2591   The meaning of *aligos* is problematic. T-L gives simply 'neck opening'. The description in Viollet-le-Duc, 3:400-403, is of a hooded cape worn over the tunic. Lampart's attire would thus suggest that he has made himself comfortable in order to relax. Woledge details possible meanings, 2:103-6: (1) without a tear, meaning in perfect condition; (2) bearing decorative cut-outs in the fabric, a practice considered to be fashionable as late as the thirteenth century. Woledge notes that, in an episode that echoes the Pesme Aventure in Chrétien de Troyes' *Yvain* (l. 5432), Lampart's garb may allude to Yvain's splendid *mantel sanz harigot*. In this case Lampart's attire is meant to impress one with its elegance and richness.

2613   The scribe has left the -*e* off the verb because it is lost in elision. Although he retains it six times before a noun beginning with a vowel (e.g., 564, 1676, etc.), I retain the form in the manuscript because it reflects the pronunciation and because an analogous form, *amain*, occurs at the rhyme in line 253.

2614   The great hall was the most important room of the *palais*. It was here that the feudal lord convoked his vassals to sit in judgment or to celebrate a feast; here the oath of homage was taken. It was a great vaulted space. The *grand'salle* of the archbishop of Sens could hold eight to nine hundred people, according to Viollet-le-Duc, *Dictionnaire de l'architecture*, 8:74 ff., and the one in the château de Montargis measured 55 yds. x 18 yds.

2618 ff.   Compare Erec arming himself on a rug with a leopard design (2589-2614).

2646   Picard *le* for *la* (*lance*). Cf. line 2664.

2713-4   *Trova* for *trovai*, *parla* for *parlai*; cf. also *cuida* in line 2716. See the note to line 242

2736   *mante* for *mainte*.

2739   Kibler suggests that a passage of some length describing Lampart's hospitality might be missing here. Platin's text reads as follows at this point: ". . . *ilz laverent les mains et se sont assis; ilz furent bien servis. Aprés soupper diviserent de plusieurs choses jusques il fut heure de coucher, qu'ilz sont allez reposer chascun en sa chambre, jusques au matin qu'il fut jour*" (n [iv] r°, boldface added). It is possible that Renaut's text did not detail the evening's festivities and that one missing line contained something like the portion in boldface. The verb *coucher* could have supplied the rhyme for line 2740.

2801-8   The description of the Gaste Cité owes something to *Perceval* 1749-61. Louveau, pp. 178-182, notes similarities between the Fair Unknown's adventure at Sinadon and that of Gauvain, his father, at Ygerne's castle (*Perceval* 7244 ff.).

2812   *venrés* for *verrés;* see the note to line 1855.

2816   I emend *grant* to *grans* for the sound of the liaison. The scribe gives *grans* in every case for the masculine, nominative, singular (e.g., 503, 705, 1247, etc.) except in line 4744 where he may have written *grant* because *tressor*, beginning with a *t*, follows.

2818   In twelfth-century castles, galleries ran along the sides of the great hall. These would have been set off by a series of archways fitted with shutters so that the gallery could be open or closed off from the great hall. See Viollet-le-Duc, *Dictionnaire de l'architecture*, 7:4. Fame's castle in Chaucer's poem presents a strikingly similar façade; see Whiting. Compare also Ygerne's palace in *Perceval* 7478-9.

2847-8   These lines assonance rather than rhyme.

2866   In his *Dictionnaire de l'architecture*, 2:260, Viollet-le-Duc describes twelfth-century mosaics that resemble what is being described in these lines. In imitation of late Roman mosaics, craftsmen fired intricately shaped bits of brick glazed in various colors—black, yellow, dark green and red characterize this period—which they then laid in patterns. In high-wear areas, these tiles alternated with marble and other hard stones.

2867   A *toise* measured roughly six feet.

2887-98 The musical terminology in these lines is difficult to translate because some terms fluctuate or overlap in meaning even within a certain period. Given the caveat that there is disagreement about the interpretation of some of these terms, we suggest the following descriptions of instruments not likely to be recognized by the general reader. Many of them are string instruments. The **harp** is a triangular shaped pillar-harp of a size to rest on one's lap. A **rota**, a triangular harp-zither held against the chest, was played with both hands since its strings are on both sides of the sound box. The **psaltery** is a box-zither, often trapezoidal in shape, and one plucked strings that were stretched across its top. The **citole** is a short lute with a body shaped like a holly leaf; one plucked its strings with a plectrum. **Vïele** and **gigle** overlap in meaning, both indicating bowed instruments. (See the note to line 22.) We translate *vïele* as 'hurdy-gurdy' in this instance so as not to repeat 'fiddle'. **Estive** and **muse** both designate bagpipes. The former may have had a softer, more delicate sound; if *estives de Cornouaille* are meant, then they are hornpipes, an instrument that comprised a small curved bell made out of horn and played with a bag or bladder. **Flageol** and **fretel** both indicate reed pipes; the former is a three-holed version. The **chalumel** or shawm is a small double-reed woodwind with a full, fresh tone. The **cor** is a curved horn, small or large, made of oxhorn or ivory, with or without fingerholes. The **buissine** or trumpet was probably used to play fanfares or simple melodies. The **moïnel** is a middle-sized horn. Two percussion instruments are evoked, the tambourine and the **tabor**, a small side drum that was slung from the wrist or shoulder and beaten with a stick.

2942   Although there is no break in the manuscript text, the lack of a rhyme for line 2941 indicates that a line is missing. Platin's text reads: "*Quant le Descongneu l'a veu, il voit bien qu'il fault combatre; il s'est eslongné a ung bout de la sale pour jouster et sont venus l'ung contre l'aultre par telle force que tous deux sont tombez a terre; incontinent ilz se sont relevez et ont tiré les espees et ont frappé l'ung sur l'autre . . .*" (o [i] r°, boldface added). As Adams remarks, p. 222, the missing line might perhaps have related the detail, albeit redundant, that the two knights fell to the ground.

2956 ff.   Compare *Lancelot* 1126-1134.

3057   For *coife*, see the note to line 267.

3060   Williams reads *molt* for *mort*.

3067   *claire* for *glaire*. For the use of *c* for *g* in spellings in the text, see the note to line 1534.

3075   Glass was not yet used in windows (Holmes, p. 97) and, in any case, would make no sense in this context, for how could the jongleurs make a racket by pounding on glass panes? *Fenestres* also indicates wooden shutters and passages in the *Roman de Rou* and the *Chevalier au cygne* describe warriors ripping *fenestres* from their hinges to use as makeshift shields (T-L 3:1715).

3076   *tresart* for *tresalt*, from *tresalir*, *tressallir* 'to shudder, shake violently.' (Note, however, that none of the examples in Godefroy and T-L show an inanimate subject.) As Perret (1991) observes, p. 107, the graphy *r* for *l* is not uncommon in texts showing a Picard influence; see *aligos* for *harigot*, line 2591, *arme* for *alme/ame*, line 2107. Platin's text reads as follows: ". . . *et ont fermé et ouvert les fenestres par si grand force **que tout le palais en trembloit** . . .*" (o [i] r°, boldface added).

3087   Williams reads *fus* for *fu*, *cius* for *ciel*.

3127   An *aumaire* or armoire was a shallow cupboard measuring perhaps 2 yds. high by 2.5 yds. wide and was used to store objects of value, according to Viollet-le-Duc, *Dictionnaire du mobilier*, 1:3.

3157   An intertextual echo exists in *Les Mervelles de Rigomer*, the romance that opens the manuscript containing *Li Biaus Descouneüs*. In this romance Gauvain must cross a bridge guarded by a great serpent. When it sees him approach, the creature bows its head humbly and refuses to fight: "*Quant li serpens venir le voit, Qui maint preudome ocis avoit, Ne li fist pas samblant de mal, Le tieste encline contreval Et s'ajenoille et s'umelie; Ce samble que merci li prie* " (13,847-52 in Foerster edition, p. 296 in Vesce translation).

3178   The manuscript text shows no break but there is no rhyme for line 3178, a lack explained perhaps by the fact that the previous couplet also rhymes in *-ie*. We must thus assume the possibility of a lacuna. Williams has not noted this in her edition. In order to retain her line numbering, the presumed line will be 3178.1.

3182   Although there is no break in the manuscript text, the lack of a rhyme for this line suggests a lacuna, unnoted by Williams. Here, too, the previous couplet has the same rhyme. In order to retain her line numbering, this presumed line will be 3182.1.

3238   *donnai* for *donna*; see the note to line 242, but observe that, in all other instances except line 2755, *-a* is given for *-ai* rather than *-ai* for *-a* as here. The *Pucele* echoes what she says here in lines 4973-4. If it was indeed the owner of the disembodied voice who equipped the hero, which would have been a relatively recent event, the hero would have identified the speaker immediately. Platin's text gives: ". . . *elle* [your mother] *te bailla cheval et harnoys et t'envoya a la court du roy Artus. . .*" (o ii v°) For Perret (1991), p. 232, the hesitation between the first and third person ("*Armes te donnai et espee* [3238]," "*Vostre mere vos adoba* [4973]") suggests an incestuous confusion between mother and mistress. For Harf-Lancner, p. 333, line 4973 simply clarifies that *donnai* in line 3238 is an instance of the frequent graphy *-ai* for *-a* and should be understood as a third person form. Guerin, p. 56, Guerreau, pp. 67-8, and Kölbing, p. 164, also conclude that the love of Guinglain and the *Pucele* is incestuous, basing themselves on the similarity of the two fairies' names, *la Pucele as Blances Mains* and *Blancemal*. (Perret gives the fairy mistress's name as *Blanchemain*.) Guerreau notes that Guinglain's affair with the *Pucele* is incestuous because her gift of armor confers upon her the status of godmother and the Church viewed "parenté baptismale" as equivalent to a relationship by blood in sexual matters. The similarity in the two names could be taken to underscore the fact that these two characters belong to the same fairy clan. (See R. Howard Bloch, *Etymologies and Genealogies*, p. 78.)

3249-52 An echo of *Erec* 23-26 and an articulation that recalls *Erec* 1808: *Ici fenist li premiers vers.*

3279   Purple was a rare and costly fabric, probably made out of silk imported from Tyre and Alexandria. It came in several colors and seems to have been worn chiefly by royalty. In this romance only Blonde Esmeree, a princess, wears *popre*. Verdelhan, pp. 88-9.

3327   Williams corrects to *Cascuns d'els cuidoit enragier* 'Each of
them went into a fury'.

3410   There is punctuation in the manuscript, two raised dots, after
feme.

3419   The sense of this line is garbled in the manuscript due to a
scribal bourdon: *len vit* occurs directly above *les vit* in the following
line. Four persons have come in (line 3423) but only three are
mentioned: Helie, Robert and the dwarf. The missing person must be
Lampart, who is present in line 3429. Platin's text bears out the
correction: "*Giglan remercya la pucelle de tout son pouvoir. Ainsi que
la royne parloit a luy vindrent Lampatris, la damoiselle Helye, l'escuyer
Robert et le beau nain.* (o iii r°)

3448   Both linings use the pelts of a species of squirrel whose coat
turns grey in the winter. *Gris* designates a lining composed solely of
the grey dorsal pelt. *Vair* indicates a checkered pattern achieved by
alternating the grey with the white pelt from the animal's belly.
Verdelhan, pp. 92-5. For *vair*, see the note to line 163.

3486   The procession of churchmen starts at the big church in the
faubourg commercial that would have developed around the walls of the
old *cité*. It then moves to the smaller church within the restricted space
of the *cité* and ends up at the seignorial *palais*, originally the *donjon* and
also located within the *cité*'s walls. (Pirenne, pp. 106-112.)

3563   We understand *marchoist* as the Pres. Subj. 3 of *marchier* 'to
border, be contiguous.' These lines echo *Erec* (3824-8): "*Et j'ai non
Guivrez li Petiz;/assez sui riches et puissanz,/qu'an ceste terre, de toz
sanz,/n'a baron, qui a moi marchisse,/qui de mon comandement isse.*"

3610   *Sa* for *sai.*; see the note to line 462. The manuscript has
punctuation, two raised dots, after *sa*.

3618   *Onnors* can mean 'fief' and Perret (1991) translates, p. 68, "que
la terre soit donc à lui."

3723   The manuscript has punctuation, two raised dots, after *pardoinst*.

3726   Williams leaves out the second *ne* in this line.

3759   As though she had overheard Guinglain's fervent exclamation here, the fairy mockingly repeats Guinglain's words in line 4457. In order to underscore this echo and because the aural dimension of the text is so clearly involved here, I prefer the emendation proposed by Bidder, p. 17, to the one given by Williams ("*Je ne gab pas*"). The presence of a mute *-e* at the cesura or before a pause is not unusual in octosyllabic texts of this period. See, for example, lines 214, 235 and 1320.

3784-5   The manuscript is garbled here. How does *se* (= *sé* for *ses*) *riches dras enperials* fit into the syntax? Furthermore, it is improbable, as Perret indicates in a line note, that war horses would be loaded up with baggage. This appears to be another *bourdon*, as *destriers* occurs directly above *deniers* in the manuscript text. Clearly *soumiers* or packhorses are meant and the next glimpse of the queen's retinue (3844) corroborates this.

3813-4   Schultze-Busacker cites these lines as a variant of proverb number 2026: *Qui ne fait quant il puet ne fait quand il veult.*

3815-6   Morawski and Schulze-Busacker proverb number 2192.

3817-8   Morawski and Schulze-Busacker proverb number 1101.

3824   Schulze-Busacker cites this line as a variant of proverb number 111: *Aprés grant joie grant corrous.*

3836   The sense of the text (specifically, line 3835) requires changing *quint* to *quart*. In her 1918 edition Williams makes this change; in her 1929 edition, she retains *quint*.

3843   The same hunting birds, including *gerfaus*, are grouped together in the marriage offer, lines 3575-6. Another possibility might be *tercels*, a male hawk, mentioned among the even greater variety of birds carried by the Pucele's hunting party, lines 3939-40.

3923   Williams construes "*I fuissent asiegé trente ans,*" which is a
misinterpretation. Guivret uses similar words to describe the imposing
castle of Brandigan (*Erec* 5346-9): "*Se France et la rëautez tote,/et tuit
cil qui sont jusqu'au Liege,/estoient anviron a siege,/nel panroient il an
lor vies. . . ,*" also noted by Perret (1991), p. 108.

3957   See the note to line 149 on saddle and harness.

3972-8 Exactly what kind of hat is the fay's *capiel*? It cannot be a
chaplet of flowers because this would not protect her face from the sun.
Quicherat, p. 188, describes hats, compact in shape, which were covered
with rich fabrics and decorated with pearls and gold braid, but would
such a hat have been wide enough to shade the face? Viollet-le-Duc,
3:120, mentions chaplets made of gold and jewels and Gay, 1: 324-326,
lists descriptions of elaborate chaplets on which were set flowers and
birds made of silk, gold and enamel, but these date from fourteenth and
fifteenth century inventories. (Is it possible that such hats were inspired
by models found in literature?) As regards the fay's *capiel*, it is not clear
whether the birds are appliqued, embroidered, woven into the fabric
design or sculpted in gold. At any rate, the curious impression conveyed
is one of studied déshabillé.

3982   For women's coiffure, see the note to line 1547.

4000   The manuscript has punctuation, two raised dots, after *vos*.

4053-4 For the rhyme *eüsse:fuisse*, see the note to lines 775-6.

4127   We take *le* to stand for *lé* or *les*, referring to both Guinglain
and Robert. Williams suggests this possibility in a note.

4129   See the note to line 4127.

4158   Williams changes *nos* to *vos*. Robert's active espousal of his
master's cause (as in lines 4159-60) justifies retaining the reading of the
manuscript.

4199-4203 Do these lines refer to the poet-narrator or to Guinglain? A hesitation between first- and third-person forms, including *vit* for *vic* in line 4200 and *son* for *mon* in line 4201, betrays the scribe's confusion; as we have remarked, *a trové* can be either one. The text here reflects the coincidence, one might say overlapping, of the hero's and the poet-narrator's subjectivity, (see Perret (1988b), p. 229.) Having noted this, I have chosen to attribute these lines to the narrator in light of the sustained first-person voice in the lines following.

4214   Perret (1991) points out, p. 108, that it would be more appropriate to attribute this line, and specifically *li*, to Guinglain than to Robert. The identical beginnings of lines 4212 and 4214 suggest a scribal lapse.

4283   The manuscript has punctuation, a raised dot, after *prist*.

4290   Compare the garden in the Joie de la Cour, *Erec* 5693 ff.

4309   This line is without a rhyme. It falls within a series of lines rhyming in *-iers*. Although it is possible that the scribe skipped a line, it seems more likely that he simply got tree names out of order. The occurrence of *paumiers* just above *pumiers* suggests a *bourdon*. The rhyme has been restored by exchanging *sapin* with *paumiers* in the following line.

4361   The manuscript has punctuation, two raised dots, after *prent*.

4369   *A soufert* for *ai soufert*; see the note to line 242.

4381-2 The sense of these lines is garbled in the manuscript. In her 1918 edition, Williams keeps the reading of the manuscript, in which she finds an analogous construction in lines 1329-30. In her 1929 edition, she emends the ligature *vre* to *vie* in line 4382: 'I would lose my life.' But this admission does not square with the statement in lines 4416 and 4418 that the Pucele wishes to hide her love from Guinglain. Platin's text suggests the correction to be made. In it the Pucele says to Guinglain: "'. . . *vos le faictes pour me decepvoir: car si je vous avoye donnee m'amour, je croy que quant vous auriez faict de moy a vostre voulunté que vous en yriés sans prendre congé comme vous fistes a l'autre foys qui fut grande vilennie a vous.*'" (p ii r°, boldface added)

4421   The syntax of line 4422, which contains the second part of a comparison between the suffering of Guinglain and the Pucele to that of Tristran and Isolde, justifies the change made by Williams.

4444   *Verra* for *venra*. In Picard **vinirat* became either *verra* or *venra* (Fouché, p. 397). This form occurs in the text alongside Central French forms (e.g., *venrés*, line 2349).

4451   I agree with Williams that the sense of the text requires *joians*, not *dolans*. (See line 4455.)

4515   I agree with Williams that the sense of the text clearly requires *regarde*. Lines 4508-10, 4516, 4520 and 4523 stress Guinglain's longing gaze.

4516   *venroit* for *verroit*; see the note to line 1855.

4553 ff.   There is humor in the clear reminiscence here of the ignominy suffered by Guinglain's father, Gauvain, when he fell off the Pont Evage or Water Bridge in the *Chevalier de la charrete* (ll. 5105-28 in Kibler's edition).

4557-8   *Retornier* is corrected to *retorner* because with two exceptions the text distinguishes rhymes in *-ier* from those in *-er*.

4677   Schulze-Busacker gives this as a variant for proverb number 1879: *Qui cuide bien faire ne doit pas estre blasmé.*

4683-4   *Reçoivre:croire* is an imperfect rhyme.

4736   Although there is no break in the text of the manuscript, the lack of a rhyme for line 4735 betrays a lacuna. Platin's prose version abridges the description of the garden and thus offers no hint as to what the missing line here or line 4752 below might have contained.

4752   The manuscript text has no break but the lack of a rhyme for line 4751 indicates that material is missing.

4768   For a description of twelfth-century mosaics, see the note to line 2866.

4770   *Ne vit* has been added at the end of this line in a different hand and ink.

4782   There is no break in the text of the manuscript but the lack of a rhyme for line 4781 signals missing material. In this case Platin's text suggests what is lacking: ". . . *la damoiselle qui l'avoit amené le tenoit tousjours par la main et dit a la damoiselle Helayne* [i.e., the *Pucele*], *'Madame, je vous ameyne ce pouvre prisonnier. Je vous prie que pour l'amour de moy il soit bien traicté.'. . .*" (p iii v°, boldface added.) As Adams notes, p. 223, *prison* could provide the missing rhyme.

4886   In Platin's text the hero says to the fairy, "*Il est vray que hyer au soir quant je fus couché, je ne pouvoie dormir ne reposer si fort pensoye en vous. . . .*"(p [iv] r°) Thus line 4886 might have read *si angoissés en vos pensoie.*

4905   The manuscript has a mark of punctuation, a raised dot, after *troverent.*

4908   The words *et dure* have been added in a different ink and what appears to be a more recent hand.

4909   *endura* for *endurai.* For the confusion of the graphies *-a* and *-ai* in the text, see the note to line 242.

4922   There is no break in the manuscript text but the lack of a rhyme for line 4921 indicates a lacuna. Platin's text, which abridges this exchange between the hero and his fairy mistress, gives no information about the missing material.

4925   The form *veilliés* is attested in line 2325.

4946   *are* for *aire*, 'floor, courtyard' (T-L 1:253-254) from which we extrapolate 'on the spot, right here'.

4952   There is no break in the text of the manuscript but the absence of a rhyme for line 4951 betrays a lacuna. As Adams notes, pp. 224-5, Platin's text suggests what is missing: "'. . . *je scavoie bien quant vous fustes ceans a l'aultre foys que nul ne vous scauroit tenir que vous n'allissiez avec la pucelle Helye; parquoy je ne vous donnay nul empeschement, et si l'eusse bien faict si j'eusse voulu. Je fuis celle qui vous fis ouyr la voix . . .*'" (p [iv] r°, boldface added.) The *mais* in line 4953 argues for this possibility: she could have prevented his leaving *but* did not because she knew the rescue of Blonde Esmeree would bring him honor.

4961   The form *so* is supplied from line 4979.

5007-8   For the rhyme *peüsse:fuisse*, see the note to lines 775-6.

5034   'marquis,' a fifteenth-century Italian title, is not really equivalent to *marcis* 'lord of a frontier fief or march'.

5149-50 *escramor*, an imaginary beast (Godefroy 3:436c cites only this instance); *espapemor*, an imaginary bird (FEW 7:583a cites only this instance).

5157   *pantine*, an imaginary sea animal (T-L 7:136 cites only this instance)

5183   In two other instances when vassals are enumerated (lines 3556 and 4060) dukes are mentioned as are *princes*, which would also fit the meter.

5263   Williams reads *me* and corrects to *ne*.

5303   *en* is a scribal slip for *et*. A tournament was usually held in the open countryside between two towns. (See Benson, pp. 8-9.)

5340   Guinglain's vulnerability to the lure of the tournament reminds one of Yvain.

5395-6 A proverb listed in both Morawski and Schulze-Busacker as number 1853.

5408 Schulze-Busacker cites this line as a variant of proverb number 562: *De tel fait tel retrait.*

5507 The manuscript gives the abbreviation *lan.*, which I spell out following the only other occurrence of this proper name in the text, in line 40.

5571 Brugger suggests the following emendation, p. 226, n. 58: "*Et Guenes, nés de Cirecestre'*," based on the possibility that the manuscript deforms two names from Wace, *Mauron, cuens de Guir[e]cestre (Brut* 1714) and *Jonatas de Dorcestre (Brut* 1718, 3824). I emend to *nés*, agreeing with Brugger that *niés de* 'nephew of', followed by a place name, makes little sense. (For the construction *né de* plus a geographical locale, see T-L 6:491. Perret (1991) suggests, p. 110, that *niés* may be a dialectal form.) However, I prefer to keep the form *Gunes* even though West and Flutre show it appearing only in *Le Bel Inconnu.* As for *Oïrecestre*, West cites only *Le Bel Inconnu* while Flutre equates this name with Worcester and cites occurrences in *Ipomedon* and *Yder.*

5574 The manuscript has punctuation, a raised dot, after *fu.*

5581-2 That *Careheuls* is a variant of *Caraés* (line 41), as West affirms, is underscored by the identity of lines 5582 and 42.

5585 Note that the syntax requires *fianchié* (m.) but the rhyme necessitates *fianchie* (f.). Similar rhymes occur in lines 1961-2 and 2009-10.

5591-2 I correct these lines according to the suggestion of Brugger, p. 226, n. 58, who found it suspicious that a knight named in no other romance, to our knowledge, be given an epithet applied to no other knight although many others could have qualified. Furthermore, the mention of *Libnus* occurs after the enumeration of the combatants and the description of their arming are completed.

5995-6 Compare *Erec* 2127-8: "*seles vuident, chevalier tument/li cheval süent et escument.*" The description of the tournament here echoes that of the great tournament at Tenebroc, where Erec displays his valor before Arthur's assembled barons, *Erec* 2097 ff.

5598   Although the manuscript text shows no break, the lack of a rhyme for line 5597 indicates a lacuna. Platin's text, which abridges the account of this tournament, provides no information about what might have been missing either here or in subsequent lacunae in this episode.

5699   Are *Gaudins* (5539, 5713), *Condrins* and *Baudins* (5702) the same knight? They appear to be for the following reasons. The title *roi d'Illande* identifies *Gaudins* (5539-40) with *Condrins*. The association with *Bruians* during the tournament, first in the pincer strategy (5697-5702) and then during *Guinglain*'s twin counterattacks (5713-15), identifies *Condrins* with *Baudrins* and *Baudrins* with *Gaudi[n]*. Both *Gaudins*, *roi d'Illande* and *rois Bruians* are among the knights on Arthur's team (5534 and following). In order to avoid confusion, I adopt *Gaudin* in each case to refer to this knight.

5713   I add -*n*, basing myself on the form contained in line 5539 and on the fact that the scribe quite frequently omits the bar indicating nasalization (see 246, 307, 319, 462, etc.).

5781   The rhyme *adrece:embrece* would have been pronounced *adrace:embrace* and is typical of Eastern dialects (Lorraine and Burgundy). See Pope, p. 495, ¶ xvii.

5830   The manuscript has a raised dot after *Guivrés*.

5938   There is no break in the manuscript text but the lack of a rhyme for line 5937 indicates a lacuna.

5969-70 *Recouvrier* is corrected to *recouvrer* because with two exceptions the text distinguishes rhymes in -*ier* from those in -*er*.

5993   There is clearly a scribal lapse in this line, which does not rhyme with line 5994 and which repeats the last two words of line 5991.

5997-8 These lines show assonance rather than rhyme.

6007 Although the text of the manuscript shows no break, the lack of a rhyme for line 6008 indicates that a line is missing.

6042 The term *vespres* here indicates the first day of tournament combat rather than a trial encounter the afternoon before the tournament proper began. Ménard (1988) discusses lines 6037-42, pp. 657-8.

6066-80 These lines are incomplete or missing because the lower corner of the folio has been torn off.

6103-4 These lines show assonance rather than rhyme.

6118-32 See the note to lines 6066-80.

6125 Preceding the *t* there is a minim.

6237-67 These lines have been added on a scrap of vellum that has been bound in between folios 153 v° and 154 r°. Only the recto bears the text. The hand appears to be the same. (Williams calls this folio 154 r°a.)

Index of Proper Nouns

Agolans a king from Escoce, brother of Margerie 1830

Aguissans RR 5917, 5971, 5975, 5981; Aguizans RR 5467; see Anguissans

Aguillars see Aguissans

Alixandre Alexandria in Egypt 3446

Amangons a king and knight of Arthur's 47, 5256, 5266, 5547, 5836, 5849, 6160

Amors the god of love 1731, 1733, 2464, 3125, 3677, 3752, 3760, 3769, 3772, 3776, 4013, 4016, 4131, 4137, 4176, 4179, 4185, 4188, 4197, 4211, 4215, Amor 4405, 4544, 4546, 4629, 4663, 4808, 4826, 4830

Anguisel see Anguissans

Anguissans a king of Escoce and ally of Arthur's; brother of Lot and Urien 5917, 5971, 5975, 5981, 6043; Anguizans 5467; Anguisel 6101; Aguillars 31

Aquins d'Orbrie knight of Arthur's 50

Arés a king, associate of Arthur's 42, Arels 5582

Artus Arthur, king of Britain 15, 176, 255, 412, 416, 481, 485, 1189, 1469, 1801, 2092, 2713, 2905, 3231, 3405, 4966, 4974, 4989, 5057, 5077, 5104, 5246, 5352, 5535, 5592, 5903, 5911, 5933, 5968, 6093, 6111, 6144, 6148, 6211, 6216; Artu 1183, 1187, 3313, 3359, 3611, 3887, 5567, 5965, 6238; Hartu 83

Baladingan(t), li Vallés de a knight of Arthurs' 46, 5503, 5644, 5651, 5657; see Baradigan

Ban, li rois de Gomoret King of Gomoret 5479, 5839

Baradigan, li rois de 5475; see Baladingan(t)

Baudins a king 5702; see Condrins, Gaudins

Becleus castle near which the sparrowhawk contest takes place 1502

Beduiers knight of the Round Table, Arthur's cup bearer; entitled to Normandy 37, 61, 105, 109, 119, 5575

Betee, Ille de la Mer the Dead Sea 3290

Biaus Coars knight of the Round Table 48

Biau Descouneü the Fair Unknown, name given hero by Arthur
131, 205, 381, 407, 441, 469, 975, 1041, 1985, 1106, 1227,
1481, 1742, 1780, 1867, 1981, 2087, 2387, 2922, 5084,
5199; Bials Descouneüs 1821, 3064; Bel Descouneü 571,
1085, 3232, 6267; Biel Descouneü 1478, 1871; Descouneü
281, 623, 685, 935, 1114, 1139, 1160, 1165, 1196, 1273,
1493, 1517, 1556, 1826, 2075, 2077, 2173, 2225, 2260,
2305, 2316, 2365, 2391, 2597, 2695, 2768, 2790, 2852,
2933, 2950, 3011, 3049, 3188

Blancemal fairy mistress of Gauvain, mother of Guinglain 3237,
5203

Blances Mains, la Pucele as fairy mistress of Guinglain, lady of
Ille d'Or 1942, 3681, 3949; la Biele as 3911; Demoissele as
3119; Celi/Cele as 3272, 3748

Bliblerieris RR 339; see Blioblïeris

Bliblis Byblis, who fell in love with her brother and, her love
unrequited, was transformed into a fountain (Ovid,
Metamorphoses IX) 4346

Blioblïeris defender of the Gué Perilleus 339, 437, 465, 523, 541,
835, 1213, 5122

Blonde Esmeree queen of Gales, daughter of king Guingras 3669,
3837, 3875, 5055, 5561, 5895, 6146, 6153, 6197, 6210

Braimant a Saracen king killed by Charlemagne (= Mainnet) 3039

Bralant see Brus

Bretaingne Britain, kingdom of Arthur 3513, 3600, 3663, 5130,
5534, 5837, 6215

Breton the inhabitants of Bretaingne 5200, 5751, 5796, 5864, 5869,
5959

Briés de Gonefort knight of Arthur's, lord of Gonefort 35

Bruians, li rois des Illes a knight, king of Illes 5549, 5697,
5701, 5715, 5750, 6091, 6161

Brus de Bralant knight, lord of Branlant 5658

Cadoalens king and ally of Arthur's 5753

Cadoc a king present at the tournament at Vale(n)don 5795, 5803,
5809

Cadoit RR 5795; see Cadoc

Canaan King of Baradigan 5476

Carados knight of the Round Table 44

Caraés knight of the Round Table 41, Careheuls 5581

Careheuls see Caraés

Carentins knight of Arthur's 44

Carlion seat of Arthur's court; Caerleon-on-Usk, Monmouthshire; < Welsh *kuer* + Latin *legionum*, 'city of legions' 2714, Charlion 11

Cartre see Gerins

Castiel as Puceles generally identified as Edinburgh Castle 5302, C. des P. 5336, 5455

Charlion see Carlion

Cité Gaste name given Blonde Esmeree's walled city, Senaudon, after it was laid waste by the sorcerers 1235, 2775; Gaste Cité 2491, 3390

Clarie sister of Saigremort, rescued from two giants 889, 1228

Condrins king of Illande 5699; see Baudins, Gaudins

Cornouaille Cornwall 1860, 3036, 5489, 5543, 5690

Costantinoble Constantinople 4754

Cote Mautaillie, Cil a la knight of Arthur's 49

Damesdius God 2434, 2908

Deon see Do

Descouneü see Biau Descouneü

Deu 1058, see Diu

Deu 5127, see Do

Dinaus knight of Arthur's 43

Do father of Giflet 1805, 1824; Deon 1811; Deu 5127; Due 6094

Due, see Do

Dunelie kingdom of Geldras; variant of Duvel(l)ine=Dublin? 5485

Duneline RR 5485, see Dunelie

Elanne Helen of Troy 4344

Elias duke present at tournament at Vale(n)don 5509

Elie see Helie

Elins li Blans, sires de Graies companion of Blioblieris, the Lord of Saies and Willaume de Salebrant 527, 971; Helin 1122; Heluins 1207, 1226

Enauder king at Arthur's court 38

Enee Eneas 4348

Erec son of King Lac, knight of Arthur's, King of Estregales 39, 5574, 5777, 5873

Eriaans knight of Arthur's 36

Escoce northeastern Scotland 1829, 1844, 5467, 5971
Espaingne Spain 3514, 5862
Estraus, d' title of Qes 50
Estregales Erec's kingdom 5574
Evrains li fiers sorcerer, brother of Mabon 3368
Fier Baissier name given the adventure in which Guinglain frees
        Blonde Esmeree from her serpent form by allowing her to kiss
        him 192, 3206, 4997
Fine Posterne title of Grahelens, identified with Finistère 5519
Floire see Flores
Flores, dus des Français a duke from France 5577, Floire, duc de
        France 5976
Floriens knight of Arthur's 34
France France, dukedom of Flores 5976
François the French 5577
Frisse a far-away country, possibly Phrygia in Asia Minor, or
        Friesland, or Dumfries in Scotland 5882
Gales Wales, kingdom of Guingras and Blonde Esmeree 3385, 3458,
        3846, 5056, 5215, 6219, 6223
Gales li Caus knight of the Round Table 41, 5256, 6164
Galigans castle of Lanpart's 2507
Galoain a count present at tournament of Vale(n)don 5877
Gandelus knight of the Round Table 5527
Gaste Cité see Cité Gaste
Gaudi RR 5713; see Gaudins
Gaudins King of Illande 5539, 5713; see Baudins, Condrins
Gavain Guinglain's father, Arthur's nephew 37, 93, 102, 265, 270,
        3216, 3226, 3235, 3361, 3512, 5102, 5202, 5231, 5234,
        5567, 5572, 6023, 6161
Geldras King of Dunelie 5485, 5826, 5851
Gerins de Cartre Count of Chartres 36
Giflet knight of the Round Table, son of Do, lover of Rose Espanie
        1804, 1805, 1811, 1824, 1836, 1840, 5127, 6025, 6094,
        6107
Goalens a king at Arthur's court 5253
Gohenet title of Hoel 5471
Gomet RR 5839; see Gomor(r)et
Gomor(r)et kingdom of Ban 5479, 5839
Gonefort title of Briés; deformation of Ocxenefort=Oxford ? 35

Gorhaut title of Gornemans 5529

Gormans knight of the Round Table 5529

Grahelens knight entitled to Fine Posterne, brother of Guingamuer 5519; given as Graislemier/Greslemuef in *Erec*, the only romance besides *Li Biaus Descouneüs* to name this knight

Graies title of Elins 527, 971, 1111, 1122, 1131, 1206, 1226

Gringras 177; see Guingras

Gué Perilleus ford defended by Blioblïeris 323, 539, 1009, 1214, 6026

Guingamier RR 5521; see Guingamuer

Guingamuer knight present at tournament at Vale(n)don, brother of Grahelens 5521

Guingras King of Gales, father of Blonde Esmeree 3309, 4033, 5197, 5287; Gringras 177

Guingla(i)n the real name of the Fair Unknown; son of Gavain and Blancemal, the fairy 3233, 3250, 3253, 3301, 3401, 3434, 3511, 3537, 3541, 3593, 3636, 3643, 3647, 3671, 3674, 3759, 825, 3833, 3860, 3863, 3868, 3880, 3909, 3929, 3934, 3995, 4079, 4107, 4124, 4130, 4161, 4189, 4211, 4219, 4247, 4261, 4285, 4333, 4341, 4356, 4384, 4412, 4445, 4478, 4483, 4488, 4505, 5421, 4556, 4582, 4589, 4600, 4651, 4698, 4701, 4719, 4778, 4821, 4826, 4862, 4867, 5027, 5053, 5101, 5210, 5218, 5242, 5244, 5260, 5319, 5338, 5353, 5371, 5377, 5386, 5388, 5397, 5411, 5413, 5435, 5444, 5458, 5666, 5711, 5717, 5730, 5771, 5781, 5792, 5800, 5810, 5816, 5825, 5832, 5861, 5874, 5927, 6017, 6032, 6044, 6048, 6084, 6097, 6102, 6107, 6113, 6147, 6155, 6157, 6192, 6202, 6211, 6235, 6241, 6256, 6260, 6264

Guinlains de Tintaguel knight of Arthur's, lord of Tintaguel 51

Guivrés King of the Irish, knight of Arthur's 5483, 5830

Gunes knight 5571

Hartu see Artus

Haute Montaingne, cil de la knight present at tournament at Vale(n)don 5513

Helie cousin of Margerie; lady-in-waiting of Blonde Esmeree 197, 725, 825, 841, 1012, 1015, 1043, 1231, 1843, 1868, 1945, 1991, 2306, 2314, 2487, 4987; Elie 2357, 2704, 3418, 3429

Helin see Elins

Raidurains knight who appears at the tournament at Vale(n)don 5523

Renals de Biauju Renaut de Bâgé; see Introduction, ix-x 6249

Riciers a count at Arthur's court 38

Robert Guinglain's squire 277, 511, 515, 611, 615, 618, 681, 695, 698, 703, 816, 860, 901, 917, 923, 930, 937, 959, 977, 997, 1232, 1494, 2339, 2363, 2481, 2581, 2663, 2769, 2848, 3421, 3431, 3436, 3538, 3741, 3756, 3763, 3811, 4113, 4117, 4128, 4213, 4221, 4223, 5384, 5404, 5413, 5420, 5423, 5430, 5793

Roge Cité, li rois de la a king who appears at the tournament at Vale(n)don 5481, 5952

Rollant nephew of Charlemagne, companion of Olivier 3038

Ronde Table see Table Reonde

Rose Espanie lady-love of Giflet 1724

Saies, li (bons) chevaliers de knight, companion of Blioblïeris, Elins de Graies and Willaume de Salebrant 528, 972, 1112, 1132, 1161, 1177, 1187, 1195, 1201, 1225, 5123, 6027

Saigremort knight of the Round Table, brother of Clarie 891, 6017, 6164

Salebrant title of Willaume

Segurés knight of Arthur's, brother of Mordrés 45

Sena(u)don walled city belonging to Blonde Esmeree; identified with ruins of a Roman town, Segontium, at the foot of Mount Snowdon in Wales 3388, 6119; Sinadon 3855, Sinaudon 6222; see Cité Gaste

Sors (de Montescler), li a king at the tournament at Vale(n)don 5495, 5506, 5613, Soir 5632, 5639, 5645; li rois de M. 5306

Table Reonde the Round Table 227, 249; Ronde Table 5591

Tesale Thessaly in Greece, renowned for its precious textiles 2280

Tidogolains dwarf, attendant of Helie 260

Tintaguel Tintagel in Cornwall, fief of Guinlains 51

Tors knight of the Round Table, son of Arés 42, 5582

Tristran nephew of King Marc, lover of Yseut; victor over giant Morholt 5614, 5617, 5616, 5637; Tristant 3037; Tristrans 35, 4422, 5254, 5304, 5583, 5624, 5627, 6162

Truerem, li quens de count, lord of l'Ille Noires 5515

Urïens knight at Arthur's court; brother of Anguisel and Lot 33

Valcolor unidentified place name 1004

Appendix

Renaut's Song

LEALS AMORS Q'EST DEDANZ FIN CUER MISE

I.   Leals amors q'est dedanz fin cuer mise
          Ne s'en doit mais partir ne removoir,
          Et la dolors qui destraint et justise
     4   Semble douçors cant on la puet avoir.
          Nus biens d'amors ne puet petit valoir
          Ainz sont tuit douz qant on les aime et prise:
          Ce doit chescuns bien entendre et savoir.

II.   8   Tels puet dire que la morz li est prise
          Per bien amer qu'il ne dit mie voir.
          Fals amant sont ke.l font per false guise:
          Malvais luier lor en doint Deus avoir!
     12   Qui en poroit morir en boen espoir
          Gariz seroit devant Deu al juïse:
          De ce me lo qant plus me fait doloir.

III.   "J'aim lealment senz trechier et senz faindre."
     16   Ceu dïent cil qui en vuelent parler.
          La lor merci, kant ce me font entendre
          Don fine amors puet adés enmeldrer.
          S'il savoient qu'il m'ont fait endurer,
     20   Lor falsetez en seroit espoir maindre.
          Non seroit, voir: trop me vuelent grever!

REJECTED READING 27 meuz sevent feindre [-*1*]

VARIANTS   Stanzas: C   I   II   III   IV   V   VI
                       O   I   II   III   IV   V
                       U   I   II   III   V   IV
                       GD   I:1-4 + II:12-14

I. 1. L. a. puis qu'en f. c. s'est mise -O, L. a. qui en f. c. s'est mise -GD
2. N'en doit jamés p. -OGD, d. jai p. -C 3. Maix l. d. ke -C, Car l. d. q. fin
amant j. -O, Que l. d. -GD 4. l'en la -GD 6. t. grant q. -CO 7. d. fins cuers et e.
-O

I.   Faithful love which is set in a true heart
              Should never leave it,
              And the pain that afflicts and mortifies
4   Seems sweet when one can have it.
              No benefit of love can be worth little;
              All are sweet when one loves and values them.
              Each person must clearly understand this.

II. 8   Someone may say that death took him
              For loving faithfully, but he is not speaking the truth.
              They are false lovers who do this falsely:
              May God cause them to reap a dire reward for it!
12   He who could die from love while hoping
              Would be vindicated before God on Judgment Day:
              I take comfort in this when I suffer the most.

III.   "I love truly, without trickery or deceit."
16   This is what those say who wish to speak about it.
              I am grateful to them since they make me understand
              How true love can continually improve one.
              If they knew what they have made me suffer,
20   Their falseness would perhaps be less.
              No, it would not: they wish to harm me grievously.

II. 9. De b. -C, Por b. a. qui -O 10. Maix f. a. ki per lor f. g. -C, Mais f. a. le font per f. g. -O 13. S'arme seroit sanz poinne et senz joyse -O 14. Por ce m'en lo quant p. me (m'i -O) -OGD; lo ke p. -C

III. 15.J'ain per amor s. -C; t. sanz confendre -O 16. Malgreit tous ceauls ki -C; v. trichier -O 17. La merci deu ce me font a aprendre -O; mercit ke lai me -C 18. En f. a. me p. muele amandeir -C; p. plus atendrier [-*1*] -O 19. S'il s. ke j'en ai endureit -C, f. empirier -O 20. en por s. [*with* por *expunctuated*] -O 21. v. qui droit voudroit jugier -O

IV.   Nus ne.s poroit de lor jangler destraindre;
           Tant les heit Deus, ne s'en vuelent oster.
    24   Ne plus c'on voit lo vant qant il est graindre
           Puet on savoir lor cuer ne lor panser.
           Nus ne se puet de traïson garder
           Fors que de tant que meuz [se] sevent feindre
    28   Que ne font cil qui muerent por amer.

V.   Dolce dame, qant ma mort vos vuet plaire,
           Ainz ne morut nus hom si dolcement.
           Or est bien droiz que la granz amors paire
    32   Dont je vos aim de cuer entierement.
           Et cil qui dit vos m'amez, il se mant.
           Ce poise moi; ire en ai et contraire.
           Pleüst a Deu qu'il fussent voir disant!

       IV. 22. De lor mentir ne lor puet nuls deffendre -C; N. ne p. de l. j.
desfendre -O 24. Nes con vairoit lou v. -C 25. on veoir l. c. -C 26. De traïtor
ne se p. nuls g. -C, p. de lor aguet g. -O 27. t. plux biaul se s. -C, m. se s.
plaindre -O 28. qui se m. d'amer -O

MS C presents a sixth stanza:

    36   Pris m'on sui oil dont ne me puis retraire,
           Se m'ont navreit el cors en regardant.
           Lais, k'en puix jeu? Il sont tant debonaire
           Ke j'en redous toute icelle autre gent.
    40   C'or li fuissent li mien ausi plaixant
           K'elle volsist de mensonge voir faire!
           Pues s'en deïst chascuns a son talent!

IV. No one could keep them from their lies;
God hates them so, yet they do not wish to withdraw.
24 One cannot know their heart or their thoughts
Any more than one can see the wind when it is at full
    force.
No one can detect betrayal
Except that false lovers are better at pretending
28 Than those who die because they love.

V. Sweet lady, since my death is intended to please you,
Never did any man die so sweetly.
Now it is right that the great love appear
32 That I bear you with all my heart.
And he who says that you love me is lying.
It troubles me; I am saddened and frustrated by it.
Please God such people told the truth!

V. 29. d. se m. -C 30. h. tant d. -C; bonement -O 33. ke dist -C, d. que
m'a. -O

[VI. 36 I am held prisoner by her eyes from which I cannot retreat.
They have wounded my body with long glances.
Alas, what can I do? They are so charming
That I fear these other people.
40 If only mine were as pleasing to her
And she wished to turn lies into truth!
Then everyone might say what he liked about it!]

RS 1635   L 217-1   MW 1304

Manuscripts:	C (Berne, Stadtbibliothek, 398) 124 r°-v°
	O (Paris, Bibl. Nationale, fr. 846) 78 r°-v°
	U (Paris, Bibl. Nationale, fr. 20050) 19 r°-v°
	GD (Vatican 1725: *Guillaume de Dole*) 76 r°
	Base: U
Attribution:	li aleus de chaslons (C)
	Renaut de Baujieu (GD)
Music:	O, U; empty staves in C
Versification:	10 a'ba'bba'b
	coblas doblas
Previous editions:	Brakelmann (1868) 369-70 (C)
	Chansonnier de St-Germain-des-Prés
	(= U facsimile)
	Beck (1927) v. 2: 182 (music O)
	v. 1: (facsimile)
	Williams (1915) 192-3 (O)
	Williams (1929) 192-3 (U), 199-204
	(music OU)

That this song was apparently well known is suggested by the fact that it is quoted in the *Roman de la Rose, ou de Guillaume de Dole*, ll. 1456-62, where it is attributed to "Renaut de Baujieu, De Rencien le bon chevalier" (ll. 1451-2). Gace Brulé addresses a Renaut in the envoys of three songs (RS 719, 1572 and 1779). In his edition of Gace's lyrics, Dyggve suggests that this may be Renaut de Beaujeu but cautions that it is impossible to be certain of this. Beck attributes the song to Alart de Chans or Cans in Artois (fl. 1233), who is thought to have composed RS 381, 513 and 1823. (Alix de Châlon married Ulrich II de Bâgé in 1185 and was thus Renaut de Bâgé's sister-in-law.)

MS C presents the most problematic version of the text. It shares certain aspects of its versification with the other MS versions: the mixing of rhymes in *-aindre/-eindre* with rhymes in *-endre/-andre* in stanzas III-IV (COU); identical rhyme in lines 4 and 11 (COU) and lines 15 and 27 (CU). Over and above this, the syntax of lines 10-11 is confused and the analogy with the wind in line 24 is garbled. Line 3 has *ke* for *ki* and line 19 contains an imperfect rhyme, *endureit*.

In MS O line 18 lacks a syllable unless *atendrier* is given four syllables. Line 15 contains a lexical problem in *confendre* (Williams misreads or corrects to *ofendre*), which does not appear in T-L or Godefroy. Only *confondre, confundre, cunfundre*, 'to destroy; to disappoint, revoke; to err, offend' is listed and this interpretation would not fit the rhyme. *Bonement* 'willingly' (line 30) is not as apt as *doucement* (CU), which continues the theme of the sweetness of love's suffering.

MS U presents the most satisfactory version. Stanzas IV and V are inverted. Line 27 is one syllable short, probably a case of the scribe leaving out the reflexive pronoun *se* that we find in CO. Line 10 reads *ke.l* where the syntax requires *ki.l*, a common error. The reading *douz* in line 6 is perhaps less apt than *grant* (CO), which contrasts with *ne puet petit valoir* in line 5, but as it does not distort the flow of the sense, it is retained.

GD's motley version is probably due to the confusion of the identical rhymes in lines 4 and 11. This is a common copying error; the scribe's eye skips from one word to an identical one further down in the text, thus omitting material. It is not inconceivable that it could be due to a mistaken memory of the song. (But see Tyssens 1935, p. 161.) The text of GD shares slightly more readings with MS O (see lines 1, 2 and 14) than with CU (lines 3, 13).

3-5	Note that there is internal rhyme at the cesura (*rime brisée*): *dolors, douçors, d'amors*.
4	*la* can refer either to *amors*, which is feminine, or *dolors*.
10	*ke.l = ki.l*
15-16	These lines are reminiscent of one of the narrator's interventions in *Li Biaus Descouneüs*, ll. 1243-1245.

18	*enmeldrer* is to be taken in an absolute sense, containing its own direct object. Godefroy, 3:204b, cites lines 15-18.
19	Understand *ce qu'il. . .*
23	Understand *que ne s'en vuelent . . .*
33	Understand *que vos m'amez . . .*
37	Ambiguity of *en regardant*, which refers to the lover's glances as well as to the lady's.
41-42	Note the *rimes brisées*: *volsist, deïst*.

A Note on the Melodies

This chanson provides a fascinating example of melodic *mouvance*, whether deliberate (someone improved on an old tune) or inherent in the process of oral transmission (elements that changed may be considered less essential in some way than elements that remained stable).

The melody in MS O and that in MS U are clearly the same tune in some sense, as shown especially by the endings of lines 2, 4 and 7. These are the crucial phrases that define the verse form as two *pedes* and a *cauda*. Line 5, which provides melodic contrast at the beginning of the *cauda*, is also similar though not identical in the two manuscript versions.

The individuality of the two tunes appears in the placement of melodic contrast. The melody in U remains within a very restricted range for the entire opening section. The two *pedes* are set off from each other by the opening gesture of f (or, more likely in performance, $f\#$) to g. G is the final, and central, pitch of the entire tune. The strongest contrast is reserved for the *cauda*: the melody rises higher than before, to d and e, and the first leaps also occur in line 5. Lines 6 and 7 provide a sense of return by referring to earlier phrases, but only the last half-line (phrase c on the diagram) is an exact repeat of the *pedes* ending, strengthening the sense of closure.

The tune in MS O, on the other hand, is laid out quite differently. The *pedes* portion is tightly organized: all four lines open with the identical phrase (phrase a), almost to the point of monotony. Contrast is provided by the varying cadence points at the ends of lines 1 and 3 (on the third scale-degree) as opposed to 2 and 4 (on the final pitch). By this means a clear open and closed ending is defined. In line 5, however, the melody really goes nowhere new: the high *d* has already been heard (in phrase b), and the cadence on the third scale-degree has been heard twice before. Furthermore, lines 6 and 7 are identical with the *pedes*. The literal repetition gives a somewhat square and rigid effect, whereas the tune in MS U is more fluid in shape, despite its more restricted opening melody.

No esthetic judgment is meant in comparing the two tunes. It is important to remember that the performer would probably have provided a good deal of expressive variety, certainly in interpreting the rhythm and quite possibly ornamenting the melody to some degree.

Comparison of O and U Melodies

Cadence points by scale-degree:

	Pes		*Pes*		*Cauda*		
line	1	2	3	4	5	6	7
O:	3	1	3	1	3	3	1
U:	1	1	1	1	3	3	1

(1 = the final, which is *G* in MS. U and in the transcription. I have transposed Tune 0 up a step to facilitate comparison. The consistent use of *Bb* in the manuscript makes the pitch patterns on *F* and *G* identical.)

Melodic structure:

Each line consists of two phrases divided at the caesura, which comes
very regularly after the fourth syllable.

line	*Pes*		*Pes*		*Cauda*		
	1	2	3	4	5	6	7
0 :	ab	ac	ab	ac	de	ab	ac
U :	fg	hc	fg	hc	d'e'	h'b'	h'c

   In Williams (1929), the music editor, Théodore Gérold, asserts
without any supporting argument that the rhythm is in the third mode.
I find nothing in either manuscript to support such an interpretation. I
have therefore chosen a rhythmically neutral transcription that reflects
the original notation as closely as possible. This should not preclude a
free rhythmic interpretation at the performer's choice.

The Melodies

Ms. O

Ms. U

Le - als a - mors q'est de - danz fin cuer mi -   se

Ne s'en doit mais   par - tir   ne   re - mo -   voir,

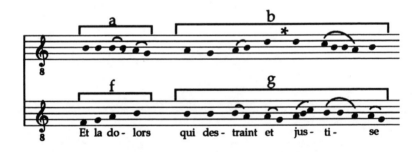

Et la do - lors   qui des - traint et   jus - ti -   se

Sem - ble dou - çors   cant on la   puet a -   voir.

Nus biens d'a - mors   ne puet pe - tit   va -   loir

Ainz sont tuit douz   qant on les aime et   pri -   se:

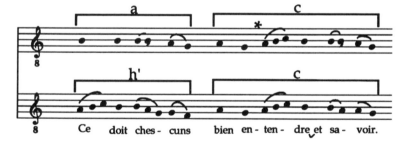

Ce   doit ches - cuns   bien en - ten - dre et sa - voir.

* The melody in O has been transposed up a step to facilitate comparison. The manuscript clearly has a Bb at each point marked with an asterisk, so the transposition to G (with C naturals) is justified.

** Possibly sung as F#

The Garland Library
of Medieval Literature